To Steve,
Lots
Joanne Hall

Spark

AND

Carousel

Joanne Hall

www.kristell-ink.com

Copyright © 2015 Joanne Hall

Joanne Hall asserts her moral right to be identified as the author of this book.

All characters appearing in this work are fictitious. Any resemblance to real persons, living or dead, is purely coincidental.

ISBN 978-1-909845-80-0 (Paperback)

ISBN 978-1-909845-82-4 (EPUB)

Cover art by Evelinn Enoksen
Cover design by Ken Dawson
Typesetting by Book Polishers

Kristell Ink

An Imprint of Grimbold Books
4 Woodhall Drive
Banbury
Oxon
OX16 9TY
United Kingdom

www.kristell-ink.com

Dedicated to the memory of Nathalie Cassiers,
my beautiful Luna.

For Jasmine, now she's old enough.

One

LIATHAN RAN, BARE feet skidding on damp earth. The russet grass slashed his ankles as he crested the last ridge and slowed, hands on his knees, sucking air. The egg-shaped stone weighed down his pocket, and he took it out for another look. He turned it round in his hands, admiring the mottled markings. It was the kind of object the Philosopher used to find interesting. Liathan hoped it might spark his curiosity.

Below his feet the hillside tumbled away, red grass fading to black, then to bare mud. Oily water lapped at the lake shore. They never drank from the lake. There were plenty of clear streams that fed into it, tumbling down from the mountains, made heavy with snow melt. It was Liathan's job to fetch water, now the Philosopher was too frail to carry the bucket.

The stone grew hot under his twisting hands, and he stuffed it back in his pocket. He took the slope down to the lake at a less breakneck pace, cold mud sucking the soles of his feet. The wind gusting down from the high peaks to the east carried the sting of rain. He watched the downpour sweep over the mountains towards the lake, shimmering bands of grey striping the overcast sky. He hoped the patch on the roof would hold.

The shack was the only home Liathan knew. Like the Philosopher, it was showing its age. The wooden boards had been replaced so many times there was nothing of the original cottage left. The shutters rattled, the door hung askew on its hinges, and water seeped up through the floor no matter how often Liathan chased it out with a broom. It was no place for an old man to die.

He forced the door open with a barge of his shoulder and the squeal of nails on slate, and dumped his satchel on the floor. He wrinkled his nose as the pungent stench of urine hit him. The old man had pissed the bed again. Liathan sighed, and moved in to strip the soaking furs.

The Philosopher had never been a large man, but now, lying on his back on bare boards, he looked like a crumpled piece of parchment. His grey skin hung in loose folds, and his liver-spotted scalp showed through a few remaining strands of hair. His eyelids fluttered. His hand, translucent skin stretched tightly over knots of bone, groped for Liathan.

"Liathan?" The old man's voice was petulant. "Where have you been? I haven't seen you for days."

"I went to fetch some water," Liathan lied smoothly. Sometimes he needed air, and space. "It's going to rain. Lucky I fixed the roof!"

The Philosopher shuffled into a sitting position, clutching the clean fur to his naked chest. He blinked slowly, like a night creature emerging into sunlight. "When does the boat arrive?"

Liathan bit his lip. This again. "Soon. I promise."

The old man chuckled, a wheeze that spluttered into a cough. "You wait 'til we get to Greenhaven! There'll be some sights there, young Luk!"

"Can't wait."

The Philosopher's rheumy eyes narrowed. "You are Luk, aren't you? I'm hungry . . ."

There was always a pot of stew simmering over the fire. Liathan spooned some broth into a bowl, ignoring the grumble in his own belly, and offered it to the old man. The Philosopher looked at him blankly, pushing the bowl away with a quavering hand.

"You said you were hungry."

"When do we get to Greenhaven? I like it there."

"A few days. Eat your stew."

This time the old man took an obedient mouthful, working the soft roots with empty gums. He swallowed, and sank back with a sigh. "It tires me out to eat, boy. Everything aches. I feel like I've been trampled by horses. Was I talking nonsense again?"

Liathan had to smile. "More nonsense than anything else, Master."

The old man passed a palsied hand across his face. "I feared so. Listen to me now, while my head is clear." He seized Liathan's wrist in a grip that surprised him with its strength. "I hate this, boy. I'm miserable. I've lived for two thousand years and I've always known who I was, what I was doing. This loss of control scares me witless. Do you understand?"

Liathan nodded, scared by the old man's sudden vigour.

"I don't want to go on fading like this, feeling pieces of my mind sloughing away. It hurts, all the time! Will you . . . help me?"

Liathan frowned. This wasn't fair. "I already do everything I can. What more can I do, on my own? If you let me get help –"

"We don't need anyone else!" The Philosopher's indignation exploded into a fit of coughing. "No one at all!" he wheezed, wiping the drool from his chin with the back of his hand in an angry, futile gesture.

"I didn't mean help me live," he went on in a hoarse undertone. "I meant help me . . . end it. Help me die."

"No." Liathan shook his head. "I can't . . . You can't ask me. It's wrong!"

"Just listen—"

"No!" Liathan pressed his hands to his ears. Childish, he

knew, but the old man wasn't beyond childish behaviour. "Stop talking about it! You're not going to die. Why would you even ask me that?"

"You're right." The old man sank back into the pillows with a rattling sigh. "I'm sorry, young one. I shouldn't have asked. It's not fair."

Liathan said nothing. The silence hung heavy and awkward between them. The Philosopher cleared his throat.

"Have you kept up with your studies?"

"I found an interesting pebble." Relieved to have something new to talk about, Liathan drew the warm stone from his pocket. The Philosopher clasped his hands around it and peered intently at the speckled surface. His green eyes flashed with their old spark.

"That is interesting, well done! But it's no pebble."

"What is it then?"

"It's an ancient bird's egg, turned to stone by time. Look closely." He ran shivering fingers over the surface of the stone. Liathan saw wings flutter as the mottling writhed into the shape of a bird, a raptor, hovering over an azure lake. Waves lapped the shore, talons flashed in the sunlight for a few heart-beats. Then the image was gone, and he stared once more into grey and black stone.

The Philosopher coughed. "I'm sorry, Liathan. I used to be able to do that for longer. Everything wears me out these days!" He patted the fossilized egg. "Why don't you have a go?"

Liathan squirmed. "I don't think I'm there yet . . ."

"Try it."

Liathan focussed on the egg, concentrating until his temples throbbed, feeling it warm to his touch. The markings blurred and fidgeted, but refused to form the vision the old man had cast. The more frustrated he grew, the hotter the stone became, until it scalded his palms. He threw it on the bed with a curse. "It's no good! I can't do it!"

The Philosopher stared at the tendrils of steam rising from

the stone. Deep creases furrowed his brow, but when he looked up his eyes were mild and blank. "Luk? I'm hungry. Is there any fish?"

Liathan sucked in a deep breath, fists clenching. "Outside. There's fish outside. I'll go and get some."

The old man chuckled. "Plenty of fish when we get to Greenhaven. You just wait!"

Outside, the rain swept down from the mountains in a fury. Liathan pressed his back to the wall of the hut, face upturned, letting the storm wash over him. Water streamed through his chin-length hair and dripped down his neck. Inside, the Philosopher's voice rose in a high grumble, and Liathan pulled his shirt up to cover his ears. The old man's brief moments of lucidity made his decline all the more horrific to witness. Two thousand summers of life reduced to an incoherent mess, wandering in his wits, rambling about fish and boats and bloody Greenhaven. Always Greenhaven! Greenhaven hadn't existed for centuries, if it had ever been real at all.

Liathan's tears were lost in the rain on his face. There was no dignity in his mentor's dying, and it wasn't fair. To either of them. The Philosopher had been in his life as long as he could remember. No father or mother, just the old man and Liathan living in the little shack by the soiled lake. The Philosopher said he had potential, that he should learn the ancient ways of his order. But Liathan didn't feel it. He liked hearing the old man's stories, though. Stories that would be lost, because Liathan couldn't remember them. Because he had no one to tell them to.

Feeling desperately lonely, he crouched on the lake shore. He watched the lightning dance between the high peaks. Maybe he should fetch help? The nearest village was three days walk. No man liked to live closer to Lydyce than that. There were too many ghosts here. That was why his mentor brought him up by the lake, in seclusion. Seclusion was fine for the young and fit, but now he needed a healer, or a wise woman.

By the time Liathan got back it might be too late.

He had just resolved to simply go, to abandon the old man and strike out for one of the anonymous hamlets between the lake and the Fairwater, the southern border of his world, when a wild cry rose from the cottage. He sprang to his feet, all thoughts of escape forgotten, and raced back to his master.

The Philosopher lay on his side, clutching his belly. Sweat gathered in the creases on his face as his groping hands twisted the bedfurs. Blood stained his lower lip and chin, and his eyes were wide and unfocussed.

"It hurts, Liathan! Make it stop!"

"I don't know how!"

To Liathan's horror, fat tears were gathering at the corners of the old man's eyes. He grasped the boy's shirt, and pulled him down until they were nose to nose. His breath was tainted with the rot destroying him from the inside.

Even so close, his fading voice barely reached Liathan's ears.

"Liathan, on the battlefield . . . When a man is dying . . . You remember what I told you, about mercy?"

Liathan tried to push him away. "I told you, you're not dying! You just ate your soup too fast."

"I haven't lived so long to be lied to by a snippet of a boy!" The tears fell fast now, mixing with Liathan's. The lie was broken. It lay shattered between them like a trampled eggshell. "I have the right to choose . . . my own exit. I'd do it myself if I had the strength."

A hard, round object pressed into Liathan's calf. The stone, forgotten where he had abandoned it in frustration. He dug it out from beneath his leg and felt it crackle and spark in his hands. The warmth was the smallest comfort.

"Will you help me, Liathan?"

He nodded. He couldn't speak. The stone grew hotter, responding to his frustration, his anger and grief. He slipped one arm around the Philosopher's shoulders, holding him close, and held the egg-shaped stone against the old man's chest, over his heart.

He pushed.

The hot stone slid into the Philosopher's chest like a blade carving a ham. Liathan's hand followed it. He felt the fluttering moth of his heartbeat, clenched his teeth, and kept pushing. All the while he held his mentor close, lips pressed against his forehead. He tasted the tears as they crept into his mouth.

The Philosopher cried out, and a long shudder ran through him. He jerked, eyes glazing as he slumped against Liathan's shoulder.

Liathan let him fall back on the bed. There was a neat smoking hole the size of his fist in the old man's breast, and he gagged on the smell of burning meat as the horror of what he had done overwhelmed him. He scrambled off the bed, retching into his palm, and fled before his master's accusing green gaze.

He had killed an Old One, a magic user. The others would come after him; hunt him down with their spells. Look inside his mind and rip out his spirit, leaving him a helpless, drooling child. Their vengeance would be terrible.

The wind shrieked across the lake, driving the greasy water before it, hurling the waves up the shore to crash against his ankles. He slumped to his knees on the shore, howling at the mountains.

"He asked me to do it! He wanted me to help him!"

The wind was pitiless, the mountains uncaring. Liathan felt utterly wretched, more alone than he had ever been. There was nothing here for him now. He had to get away, lose himself in a place where there were people, before the mages could find him.

But he couldn't move. The weight of his sorrow pressed him into the gravel shore and pinned him there, while the wind whispered his betrayal, breathed of horrors to come. The rain plastered him to the ground like wet parchment, leaching the colour out of the world.

He didn't know how long he lay there, staring across the restless water, feeling cold and damp seep through to his bones. Maybe he slept; a fitful, twitching sleep that brought no comfort. As the sky cleared, a warming shaft of late-afternoon sunlight fell across his tear-streaked face. Liathan stirred. There were things he must do before he left.

The old man lay where Liathan had left him; on his back, mouth and chest gaping open. Liathan half-expected him to stir, to berate him, to ask in a querulous voice how long it would take to get to Greenhaven. But his blackened and scalded heart was still.

"I hope you're in Greenhaven now, my master." He closed the Philosopher's eyes, and covered up the hideous scar he had wrought with the bedfur, trying to make him look comfortable. Even through his eyelids, Liathan still felt the old man's accusing gaze as he shoved his possessions into a satchel.

"You asked me to do it! Stop looking at me!"

The Philosopher said nothing. Liathan stood before the fire, brushing the tears from his eyes, battling the anxious crunch in his guts. His bag hung heavy against his hip. There was only one thing he could do for his master now.

He stoked the fire until the flames tightened the skin on his cheeks, and pulled a spluttering brand from the edge of it. Manoeuvring carefully, he ducked under the low doorway and stood on the shore for the last time. He took in the mountains, the black lake, the scarred earth, and told himself it was the light of the flame that made his eyes sting and water.

The wood was damp from the earlier storm. It smoked, refusing to ignite. Liathan kicked the walls and cursed and cried his frustration at this last indignity. The old man deserved better than this. His ending had been cruel and painful. His death rite should be glorious, and he was being robbed of it.

Liathan flung the useless damp torch aside. If the outside of the hut was too wet to burn, the inside, at least, was dry. He returned to the hut, and breathed fresh life into the hearth fire. The Philosopher lay as if sleeping, and Liathan checked again, just to make sure. His skin was cold and the pulse in his neck was still. In the stark light, the old man's thin features were all hollows and angles. He didn't look like a man any more, but a carved figure of marble.

Liathan bent to kiss his forehead for the last time. He wanted to say something, but the words died in his throat. All he could do was apply the torch to the wooden frame of the bed. It smouldered and flared up, gleefully devouring the bedfurs that covered his master's body, until the heat drove him back to the doorway, and then out to the lakeshore. The smoke was suffocating, forcing Liathan to retreat to the top of the nearest ridge. It poured into the sky in a column a mile high, a signal of his guilt visible for miles around. The green mages were sure to notice. They were probably on their way already. He didn't intend to be here when they arrived.

With a heavy sigh, Liathan hitched the satchel higher on his shoulder and turned his back on the burning cottage. Within a few strides, he started to run. Running from what he had done, running from those who would come after him. He knew he would be running for the rest of his life.

Two

KAYALL RAN, CHEST heaving, feet clattering on the cobbled streets. Running as if his life depended on his speed, which if he stopped to think about it, it probably did. The leap from the window had jarred his knees, and now every stride sent painful lances through his thighs. No time to massage the ache, even to catch his breath. Certainly no time to work an enchantment to evade his pursuers.

"Shit, shit, shit!" His cursing came in abrupt pants. His ankle turned on a loose stone and he stumbled. Why, by all the stars, had he worn heeled shoes this morning? He should have learned by now . . .

"There he is!"

Kayall risked a glance behind, in the pathetic hope that some other sap was being chased through the alleys of Lambury, but no such fortune. The three men pursuing him wore the tangerine sash that marked them as hirelings of the Fruit Master's Guild, and the grim-humoured expressions of men who broke people's arms for a living and enjoyed their work.

Kayall had no wish to increase their job satisfaction. He took off again, cursing his shoes, the pain in his legs, the charms of Thessa and the wealth of her father's guild. From now on, he swore, he would only dally with girls whose fathers couldn't afford hired thugs.

He burst out of the alley and twisted sharply to the right, hoping to throw the men at his heels into confusion. Ahead of him, up three shallow steps and behind a long colonnade, yawned the entrance to the Fruit Market.

Where better to hide from a patchcat than in his own den? Kayall took the steps in one leap, pushing through the bustling crowds. He stumbled into the cavernous hall. The noise and smell slapped him in the face, but he couldn't stop. He pounded along the lines of stalls, feet slipping on the mangled fruit littering the floor. He caught a stout middle aged woman by the shoulder, spun her round and shoved her in the direction of his pursuers. Her wheeling arm caught the end of a table, a precariously balanced plank laid across rickety legs. The far end of the table shot up in the air, catapulting fruit across the room. Over the chaos, Kayall couldn't hear the dull wet splats as it landed, but he heard the howls of indignation.

He ducked the punch of the irate stall holder, leapt a patch of evil-smelling sludge, and swung to the left to avoid the heav-ily-armed men pouring in through the opposite entrance. He scrambled onto a nearby table, and as the stall holder lunged, he planted a trampled-fruit footprint in the man's face and leapt to catch the trailing pepper-vines hanging down from the upper gallery.

He seized them, crushing gritty leaves to powder under his hands. The vine swung like a pendulum, smashed him into the wall and knocked the breath from his lungs. He rebounded off the wall, above the melee in the hall. His legs thrashed like a drowning man. One of his shoes, his stupid, highly-polished, expensive shoes, flew off and was lost amid the riot.

Kayall didn't have any breath left to curse. He scrambled hand over hand up the swaying, shivering vine, pushing past clusters of bright orange peppers that ripped free and tumbled to the stone floor to burst open in showers of seeds and pulp. If he slipped and fell, that would be his brains decorating the floor of the market hall.

More through luck and grim determination than any skill, he reached the balcony of the upper tier and hauled himself over, wheezing like an old man. The gallery was less crowded and the shoppers were more interested in the fight breaking out below than in chasing its instigator. Shoppers and stallholders brawled as a few enterprising souls took advantage of the distraction to stuff their pouches and pockets with free fruit. Through the chaos, the orange sashes of Boranth's thugs moved with quiet menace, heading for the stairs. From the opposite end of the hall, a detachment of the City Guard marched with the same purpose.

Leaning against the balustrade, Kayall groaned as he shook off his remaining shoe. He couldn't run with one foot an inch higher than the other. And he was rapidly running out of places to run. There only seemed one option, and he didn't fancy it much.

"You there!"

The shout came from the head of the stairs. Heavies barged through the crowds, weapons drawn. Kayall turned to the flight at the far end of the gallery, hope fading. He was pinned between Boranth's men and the forces of the law.

"Stop, in the name of the Guard!"

"Not likely!" The windows behind the row of stalls were half-circles, open to the elements, with a broad sill the height of Kayall's head. Vaulting the nearest stall, ignoring the protests of the owner, he leapt for the sill. He grabbed hold with both hands, swinging one leg out over the ledge. The drop to the ground was dizzying, and he clutched involuntarily at the stone beneath his fingers. Fall to his death or be skewered; it was a lousy choice.

He dangled, feet kicking in empty air as the city guards pounded up behind him. Presumably they would prefer to keep him alive. Boranth's men didn't care one way or the other, as long as his skull was smashed.

"Now there's no need—hey!"

The words receded as Kayall dropped, pushing to the left, his bare feet scraping stone. There was a ledge beneath the next window and his fingers caught it. He hauled himself up, muscles shrieking protest at this abuse, and lay gasping for a moment. He heard the clash of steel on stone, and shouting inside the Fruit Market, and he forced himself to his haunches, teetering on the narrow ledge. He did his best not to look down. If he shuffled sideways, it was only a short hop to the roof of a nearby house. He could lose himself in the slates and chimneys of the city, lie low for a spell while he worked out where to go.

"You!" A heavy hand grazed his shoulder, but Kayall was already gone. He hit the opposite roof with a grunt, scrambled over the top and down the other side, thanking the stars the houses were packed close together in the centre of town. It was an easy jump to the next roof, and the next. The pursuit had trailed off for the moment, and he crouched in the shadow of a chimney and considered his options. There was one person who might take him in, who had the authority to stand up to Boranth and the might of the fruit traders' guild. She wouldn't be happy to see him, but that couldn't be helped.

"I thought I told you never to come back here?"

Kayall stared at his bare feet, noting the hair sprouting from his toes, the dirt splashed around his ankles. His host's voice was crisp, but he detected a faint note of amused exasperation, and he clutched it like a man reaching for water in the desert.

"Come on, Tushkian. You wouldn't throw a man out in the street to be murdered, would you?"

"Not usually. For you, I might make an exception."

Tushkian Lambury pushed herself out of her chair and prowled the room. Her delicate feet were encased in brocade slippers, studded with tiny gems. Telesian, by the look of it.

"Those are nice shoes. Where did you get them?"

"Don't change the subject, Kayall." Definite amusement. Her smile tugged the corners of her eyes into crinkles. "Why are you here? Who have you pissed off this time?"

"The City Guard. The Fruit Market. Oh, and the Guild." He tried to make it sound casual.

"The *whole* Fruit Market?"

"There was . . . an incident . . ."

Tushkian sighed and sank back into her cushioned seat, gesturing for him to sit down. The strain was etched into her face. Looking at the widow's mark around her throat he remembered, guiltily and too late, that she had lost her husband just after Winterfest.

"I'm sorry, sweet. I'll go. I shouldn't have bothered you . . ."

"Stay." She flicked her hand again, more impatiently. "If you've caused trouble with the Guild, at least tell me what you did before I kick you out into the gutter."

"Thessa. That's . . . what I did."

"Boranth's daughter? Surely she's still a child!"

"Seventeen summers." Kayall shuffled in his chair. "At least, that's what she told me –"

"You didn't think to check? Kayall!"

He said nothing, but the heat travelled up his face. Tushkian snorted. "At least you have the grace to look embarrassed. You know how protective Boranth is of that girl!"

"I do now!"

She shook her head, stroking a hand over the neat grey bun at the nape of her neck. "I don't know if I can protect you, Kayall. The Guild is powerful. With Iver gone, Boranth is out to improve his position."

"I was sorry to hear about Iver."

"Ah well." She shrugged, but her eyes betrayed her grief.

"No point dwelling on the past. That might be why I haven't kicked you out yet!"

Kayall allowed himself a smile. "I'm a useful man to have around!"

"Or a dangerous one. It's not funny, Kayall." She rose, ringing a silver bell to summon a servant. "I'll have rooms made up for you. Let me talk to Boranth, see if I can calm him down without making too many concessions. You stay out of sight, and out of trouble!"

⚶

By the time his rooms were ready, evening had thrown a cloudy blanket across the city. Kayall stood at his window, moodily pushing the clouds around, darkening them to match his state of mind. He had known Tushkian since she was a gangly, awkward girl. He had watched her blossom into a woman, a mother, and a strong leader. He shouldn't have come here, shouldn't have brought politics into the bedchamber. But it was too late now. Bloody Guild. Bloody Thessa!

He tossed back a glass of wine, unleashed a short but savage downpour in the general direction of Boranth's mansion, and decided to go to bed.

When he lifted the latch to his bedchamber, the room beyond was dark, the shutters sealed against the night. He hesitated on the threshold, sensing menace in the darkness. A faint movement, a heartbeat that had no right to be there. Was that the slight scrape of a blade being drawn?

He groped for his belt knife, feeling pressure building in his head, a static tingle against the roof of his mouth. "Who's there? Show yourself!"

The lightning flashed, highlighting the room through the thickness of the shutters. Exposing the small, shadowed figure in front of the window. No more than a silhouette, but the light told him where to aim.

"Impressive." The woman's voice was wry. "I take it that was your doing, and not by chance?"

"Elvienne?" Kayall released the blade. "How did you know I was here?"

"How does anyone know anything?" She snapped her fingers, and the candles flared. Under the flickering light, her face was pale, more deeply lined than usual. Her green eyes were rimmed with angry red.

"Elvienne, have you been crying? What's happened?"

"Carlon died." As she spoke, she seemed to lose the power to hold herself upright. Her knees buckled. Kayall leapt forward and grabbed her as she slumped, guiding her into an armchair.

"When? How? Was he ill?" He sank to the floor at the old woman's feet, shaking his head. "Hells, no! What will we do without him?"

"We'll endure, as we always have." He was aware of her hand, reaching down to cradle his face, as a note of steel crept into her voice. "We have to take care of the boy."

It felt like Kayall's head was stuffed with wool. "What boy?"

"The starfall boy. Carlon's apprentice."

"Him. I forgot about him." He wondered why Elvienne suddenly sounded so cold. "Why does he need taking care of? Surely he's a grown man by now?"

Elvienne shook her head. "We have to find him. The boy is alone. He needs us."

There was a gaping hole in the world. His friend was gone, and he should have known, should have felt his passing. Should have done more. He had been making free with the women of Lambury while his friend died in a star-forsaken wilderness beside a dead lake. The world wasn't right.

"How did he die? Why? We don't age, we don't die . . ."

"I don't know. Everything's a blur. If we go to Lydyce, we might learn more."

"We?" Kayall backed away from her touch. "I'm not going anywhere near that hellish place, and nor should you. You know it's cursed."

"If Carlon could stand it, so can I. I need to know what happened. I hoped you'd come with me."

He stared at a spot just below her left knee, a small rip in her breeches, and did not reply.

"I leave tomorrow. I'll stay here tonight."

"Do as you please," he told her, "but there's only one bed, and I'm taking that."

&

Kayall was too tall for the couch. His feet kept slipping off the edge and taking the blanket with them, and he had to twist his neck around to approach a state of comfort. Not that he could have slept, even in his own bed. The hole in the world yawned wide, and if he stirred he would fall into it, be swallowed up as Carlon had been.

He heard Elvienne's soft, stifled sobs from the adjoining room. It sounded as if her heart was breaking.

Kicking the blanket to the floor once more, he rose, and wrapped it round his ribs like a rich maiden emerging from her bath. He padded across the room on bare feet and listened at the door. The bed creaked as Elvienne rolled over, and her crying was muffled. Kayall cracked the door open and slid into the room, moving with all the stealth he could muster. He climbed into the bed. Elvienne stiffened for a moment, then rolled towards him, an arm around his waist, one gnarled hand resting on his chest.

They lay together like that until morning.

&

Hammering on the outer chamber door woke Kayall from a fitful sleep. He was alone, and Elvienne's side of the bed was cold, her bedfurs left tangled.

The knocking came again. Urgent, angry knocking. The kind of knocking that would soon turn into kicking the door down. Where was the old lady? If people started breaking bits of Lambury Castle, Tushkian would be even more annoyed with him. He couldn't charm his way out of it, not with her. She knew him too well.

"All right, all right, I'm coming!" He swathed the blanket around him again, ran a hand over his hair, and cursed that he couldn't change his face to hide the lack of sleep. He flung open the outer door and glared. "What?"

The guard outside snapped off a crisp salute. "Lady Lambury requests your presence in her chambers." He tilted his head, as if waiting for a reply.

"What, now?"

"My Lady said you're to come at once."

"Can I get dressed first?"

"My Lady said right away." Behind him, the guard's larger companion rolled away from the wall he leaned on, brushing the handle of his dagger for emphasis.

"If you want to besmirch Lady Tushkian's reputation by leaving her alone with a naked man, be my guest." Kayall gestured extravagantly for the guard to lead the way, and made a play of dropping the blanket. "Oh dear, clumsy me!"

The skin on the guard's cheeks flushed scarlet. "Be quick then," he conceded.

"I've never dressed quickly in my life. I don't intend to start now. You wait here!" He swung the door closed before the guard could protest. Let Tushkian wait. If her need was urgent she could come to him.

When he made his hasty exit from Thessa's window he left his shirt behind, and the one he'd snatched from a line as he raced past was too baggy for his slender frame. He smoothed the creases and brushed the grime from it as best he could, pulled it down and fastened his belt over the top, leaving the laces at the neck rakishly undone. He located his earring, silver with a dangling drop of turquoise that matched his mage-given eyes, tangled and twisted in the hem of the blanket. No make-up, but the bags under his eyes gave a pleasing shadowed effect that made him look serious and mature, as if he had stayed up late solving the world's problems. A final run-through of his long fingers through his hair, and he was ready to face his Lady's displeasure. It was bound to be displeasure, after yesterday's events.

The smaller guard had vanished, leaving only his heavier companion lounging against the wall. He watched Kayall emerge with narrowed eyes. He nodded bluntly and turned away as if expecting Kayall to follow like an obedient puppy. There seemed to be no alternative.

The wooden floor of Tushkian's private audience chamber was smooth and sun-warmed against the bare soles of his feet, reminding him of his lost shoes. Tushkian stood by the window, looking out over the city. She held herself straight, but as he laid a hand on her shoulder he felt the tension and misery in her frame.

"Leave us." She didn't spare a look for the guard, but as he left Kayall felt her shoulders slump. The eyes she turned on him were dark-rimmed, like his own.

"You look tired, sweet. Why don't you sit down?"

"Because if I sit down I'll fall asleep, and then nothing will be achieved. Boranth is calling for your head on a spike. I don't know if I can hold him off."

He snorted. "Boranth is all talk."

"Not this time. He's threatening to call the fruitiers out on strike if I don't hand you over. And where the fruitiers go, every other guild will be forced to follow. I've already seen a representative from the Guild of Miners, saying Boranth's men are putting the pressure on." She shook her head. "I've let the Guilds get too powerful, and they know it. Now they're flexing their muscles. You've given them the perfect opportunity to see how far they can push me."

"If I apologise—"

"It's too late for apologies, Kayall!" She pushed away from him in exasperation. "Boranth wants you dead. If I protect you, he'll move for my position, and he might just take it. What will happen to my children then? No," she held up a hand. "The best, the safest thing for both of us would be for you to get out of town. I'll have to send men after you, of course, but that might buy me time to solve this mess."

He nodded, seeing her point. "I'll leave with Elvienne. Let me nip home and pack a bag—"

"Elvienne's already left. She said you didn't want to travel with her."

Kayall felt obscurely hurt by that. It was one thing to be invited and refuse to go, but she could at least have tried to persuade him to change his mind.

"Besides," Tushkian went on, "your house is being watched. You can't go back there."

"I can't travel without a change of clothes!" He extended his leg and ruefully regarded his feet. They had been particularly nice shoes.

"I still have Iver's clothes. He was about your size. You're welcome to take anything from his closet."

Iver might have been Kayall's size, but their styles were leagues apart. Tushkian's late husband had a few dress shirts for ceremonial occasions, but beyond that his taste belonged to an Estmarch farmer, all patched shirts and threadbare breeches. His hands lingered with longing over the dress shirts, the starched brocade, fur-trimmed collars and fringed epaulettes. With a sigh, he selected three of the least battered peasant shirts, a couple of pairs of breeches, and a stout cloak of forest green. Iver's feet had been bigger than his, but a thick pair of socks solved that problem.

As he regarded his reflection in the full-length glass, Tushkian padded up behind him and slipped her arms around his waist. "You'll never pass for a farmer. You're too much of a dandy!"

"It'll do." He swished the cloak to fall in dramatic folds about his hips. "I appreciate this, Tushkian. I'll take care of them."

"I know you will! I've arranged for a horse and provisions. It's waiting in the yard. Travel by the back streets and keep your head down, if you can." She kissed him lightly on the cheek, pricking his conscience like a bee sting. "Good luck!"

⚘

Trotting through the city streets, Kayall kept his hood pulled up over his head. Even sticking to the dingy back alleys, he couldn't shake off the feeling of being watched. He wished he could go home and gather his belongings, look around for a final time. Instead he turned his face southwards, joining the line of slow-moving traffic as it wound out of the city gate and spread out onto the plains to the east of the river.

As the crowds dispersed, he drew to a halt at the summit of a small hill and looked back at the granite city, nestled against its backdrop of hills and forests. It was a bright day in early summer, grey and white clouds tumbling across the sky. He slid from the back of the horse and sat cross-legged on the damp grass, stretching out with his mind. He pushed the clouds from one side of the sky to the other, building up the pressure in some until they were swollen and black as bruises, stretching others out until the sun streaked through in watery golden shafts. He directed the thinner cloud in the direction of the spires and turrets of Lambury castle. Hopefully Tushkian would realise this was his way of thanking her.

The fat rainclouds he sent to the north of the city, towards his own home. Let Boranth's spies feel the brunt of the weather. If they were going to keep a watch for him, he would make sure they had a miserable time.

With the clouds positioned to his satisfaction, he remounted. If he rode hard, he could catch up with Elvienne. The road that followed the left bank of the Lam was hard and well-travelled. He spurred his gelding into an easy canter, heading south, leaving the turbulent sky behind him.

Three

BASTIAN LOVED TO watch Allorise dance. She wore her blonde hair loose, curling down over her shoulders. She threw her head back and laughed as the Telesian merchant whispered in her ear. No simpering and giggling behind fans for Allorise. If she was entertained, or angry, everyone around her knew it. She let her passions show on her face, while Bastian held his close to his heart.

His mother appeared at his elbow, swirling a long-stemmed glass of Telesian blue in her elegant fingers. "You're not dancing, Bastian?"

"You know I never dance, mother." He sipped his wine, watching the light play through the azure depths.

"There are plenty of girls keen to dance with you. Why not pick one of them?" They both knew her efforts at matchmaking were for show. What did the youngest son of nine children have to offer, even one of a noble house? He didn't even have a holding of his own, as his older brothers had. A name, a pittance from his father . . . Maybe the peasant girls would go for it, but no Carey had ever married a peasant. He wasn't about to break that chain.

Besides, Bastian knew he was no catch, with his long nose

and sallow features. He was too thin, too tall, too awkward and graceless. Every woman in the room was out of his reach, and Allorise was the furthest of all.

Her laughter floated back to him. He set down the glass abruptly and turned away, seeking an escape route. His mother let him go with a gentle remonstration, lost under the shuffle of feet and the sprightly tunes of the minstrels playing in the gallery. Bastian sat below them, wondering how soon he could make an excuse to leave the room and head for his own chambers without attracting the wrath of his father.

His heart sank as he watched Allorise untangle herself from her partner, scan the room, and head in his direction. Too late to make a getaway now.

She stopped in front of him, hands on hips accentuating her waist. Her skirt fell in diaphanous folds to her ankles. He could see the shadows of her legs through the fabric when she stood with the light behind her, and she wore boots with buckles that hugged her calves.

"Dance with me, Bastian!"

"I don't like dancing, Allorise."

She extended her hand, and he caught a whiff of her perfume. "You have to dance with me, or I'll be forced into another round with that sweaty Telesian merchant. You wouldn't have me suffer that, would you?"

He let her take his hand and pull him to his feet. Her scent was stronger as he wrapped his arms around her waist. It made him dizzy. Her lips brushed his ear as she whispered catty remarks about the other guests at the feast; who was being cuckolded by his wife; who secretly preferred young men: who was wearing an unflattering dress to conceal an unwanted pregnancy. He laughed as they drifted to a halt, his hands on her full hips.

"You're a terrible gossip, Allo!"

"Every girl should have a hobby!" Her laugh held the silvery tinkling charm of a tiny bell. "Watch out, Mother's coming this way. I'll wager she's going to find me a more suitable partner!"

Lady Carey, omnipresent wine glass still clutched in her hand, lifted Allorise's hand from Bastian's sleeve. Her lips were narrow with irritation.

"Allorise," she said, "why are you wasting time dancing with your brother?"

"He smells better than that Telesian camel-dealer you partnered me with, for a start!"

"Marook is a well-respected trader, and I'm sure he smells perfectly acceptable. Go and dance with him! You're embarrassing him, leaving him without a partner, and that's not how we treat guests." She gave Allorise a gentle shove towards the Telesian as the music started up again. Allo stuck her tongue out at her mother and brother over her shoulder, before turning to the hapless, sweating man with a winning smile that Bastian knew was expertly faked.

Lady Carey scanned the room, one hand on her hip in a stance that mirrored her youngest daughter's. Picking out a partner for Bastian, a girl to further the interests of the Carey family. Someone so desperate to marry into money she wouldn't mind that it was only Bastian she was partnered with. He could see the calculation flicker across her face. She pointed.

"That one." She indicated a tall, dark-skinned girl with sparkling eyes and a ready smile. "Her father is related to Lady Caythen's first husband. They may have influence at court. Go talk to her. And don't distract your sister again!"

He nodded, the dutiful, diligent youngest son, and made his way through the crowd without seeing their faces. His lips were fixed in a humourless smile that made his cheeks ache. Allorise's laughter drifted towards him, and he paused, turned to seek her out. Even in the most crowded room, he always knew where she was, who she danced with, who she thought about taking to bed. They were fifteen moons apart in age, and they were closer than twins.

But her love alone was not enough, and it was slowly killing him.

&

The only sounds at the table were Lord Carey's lips smacking as he devoured his food, and the clink of the bottle against his wife's glass as the servant filled it a third time. Lady Carey waited until the maid moved away, then cleared her throat.

"I think the dance went well, don't you? Children?"

Bastian stared at his plate, prodding the swollen vegetables listlessly with his fork, trying to block out the mushing, squelching sounds coming from his father's mouth. Allorise shrugged.

"Well really!" Lady Carey set down her glass with a sharp click. "I arrange these events at considerable expense for your benefit, and you thank me with a shrug? Do you know how hard it is to find good partners for you?"

"You could let us find our own partners, mother." Allo's voice was sweet, but it held a sharp barb. Bastian laid down his fork and pushed his chair away from the table, ready to make a hasty exit before the powder keg exploded.

Their mother pursed her lips. "Don't be ridiculous, Allorise. I found husbands for your sisters, and they're perfectly happy. You could never make a match as good as Marook without my guidance."

Lord Carey smacked his lips, and nodded. "Marook!" The name erupted in a shower of spittle.

"The sweaty Telesian? Did you trouble to smell his armpits before you picked him out as a dancing partner? He reeked!"

"I don't pick husbands for you based on how they smell! You're twenty-seven, Allorise. Time is running out for you, if you want to have children."

Allorise folded her arms, elbows jutting forward aggressively. "Husbands? I thought we were talking about dancing partners?"

Lady Carey sighed. "Are you being deliberately obtuse, Allorise? Marook was very pleased with you. He offered to take you as his fourth wife, and your father and I accepted."

"Fourth wife?" Allorise's voice was cold. Bastian backed away another inch. He shook his head in warning at the approaching maid, who turned on her heel and slipped from the room.

"Fourth—wife!" Lord Carey punctuated his words by spitting seeds onto his plate.

"What happened to his first three wives?" Bastian asked. If Marook was a deranged wife-killer, he wouldn't be getting one clammy palm on Allorise.

"What are you talking about, Bastian?" his mother said. "Nothing happened to his first three wives. He's still married to them."

Lord Carey picked a gobbet from between his teeth, and groped for another piece of fruit, stuffing it into his mouth and spraying juice over the table. "Funny ways, these Telesians!" His voice was muffled with half-chewed food.

"I met his first wife," Lady Carey went on. "She seemed pleasant enough. I'm sure she'll be kind to Allorise. His second and third wives stay home and take care of their house. They don't travel much."

"Don't they have servants?" Bastian asked. Out of the corner of his eye, he saw his sister twitch with fury.

"Marook said his house is small enough to manage without them. His women do everything for him."

Allorise rose from the table. Her movements were slow, controlled. Bastian saw how tightly her reins were wound, even if his mother couldn't. She inhaled through her nose, nostrils curling.

"His women do everything for him? Do you expect me to be a spare cartwheel to a man who already sounds very much married? A serf?"

"You won't be a serf, Allorise –" but her mother's interruption was ignored.

"I won't be any man's fourth choice! How dare you expect me to settle for that?" She slammed her palms down on the table, rattling the plates.

"Allorise!" The voice was a rumble, strengthening to a roar. Lord Carey heaved to his feet, bloated paunch straining against his stained shirt. His fists ground into the remains of his meal. "You will do as we say, or you're no longer part of this family. Do you hear me?"

The command burst from his lips, spraying food across the table, into his daughters face. She stood silent, white with fury, juice dripping from her hair and down her chin. Her father collapsed back into his seat, dragged down by his own bulk.

Allorise turned smartly, and headed for the door with long, confident strides, shoulders set. Bastian wondered if she was leaving the room, or her family. He didn't dare follow with his mother's cold, wary eyes on him. She extended a trembling hand and poured more wine, as Lord Carey resumed his noisy chewing.

The room smelled of sweat and old man, a musty, cloying scent. Allorise closed the door behind her, holding her breath as it clicked shut. She could see nothing in the darkness, but the bubbling snores of her father rose from the bed, pushed up against the wall beneath the shutters. Her mother hadn't made it upstairs. Allorise had left her passed out on a guest couch, head lolling as the drug in her wine took hold. She had a different potion for her father.

As she approached the bed he snorted, sitting half-upright and muttering something unintelligible. Allorise set the tankard on the bedside table and lit a candle. Her father's huge, round eyes blinked at her.

"Who—?"

"It's me, father. You asked for a hot drink?"

"Did I?" He scratched his head, where his thinning hair brushed his ears. "I suppose I must have . . ."

"Here." Allorise slipped into bed beside him, pulling the fur cover up to her knees. She wrapped an arm around his shoulders and brought the steaming flagon up to his lips, helping him drink as if he was the child and she the concerned parent. He managed half the cup, dribbling a little, and settled back against the pillows she propped up for him.

He patted her hand. "You're a good girl, Allorise. My little star."

That had been his pet name for her, when she was a young girl. She hugged him tighter.

"How are you feeling, Dada?"

"Weary. My bones ache. Where's your mother?"

"Downstairs. She'll be up soon."

He closed his eyes, forcing them open again with difficulty. "Don't you go fighting with her, Allo. I know she can be difficult, but she wants the best for you. We both do."

"I know you do." She watched his eyelids come down again, and his head dropped on to her shoulder. She listened to his breath falter and catch in his chest, and then still. No mist formed on the little mirror she held up before his lips, and no pulse beat in his throat.

"I'm sorry, Dada," Allorise whispered. She laid him flat and rolled the cover down to his waist, exposing his flabby chest and the distended curve of his belly. She had to work quickly, before his spirit fled. She cursed herself for not checking all the windows were closed before she started. It was too late now.

She ripped a thick hank of hair from her scalp. It was hard to separate the blonde strands under the candlelight, and harder to tie them around her father's pudgy fingers. She took two long needles of bone from her purse, and bound the loose ends of the hair to them. She splayed her father's hands out on either side of his head, like a marionette held up by strings. All the while she watched his lips, hoping his spirit wouldn't escape before she was done.

Wisps of smoke gathered like wraiths at the corners of her father's mouth as she pulled back the sleeve on her left arm. From her belt, she drew a blade. Not a pocket knife like the peasant girls carried, but a smooth jet handle fixed onto a savage shard of serrated glass. The candle flames licked along the blade as she held it up to the light, delaying. This was the hardest part.

Two practice cuts on her upper forearm. They didn't hurt as much as she'd anticipated, and that gave her courage. Tightening her grip on the blade, she forced herself to watch as she pressed the edge deep into her skin, and drew it across her pale flesh.

The slashed flesh was white, dotted with red spots that expanded and merged as the wound filled with blood. She twisted it under the light, steering the dripping blood in patterns down her arm, and exulted. This was something she could do, something she could control. The need for control had brought her here tonight, set her on the unspeakable course she was committed to.

Allorise laughed softly as she held her arm above her father's mouth, watched the scarlet drops splash on his parted lips. The smoke of his gathering spirit roiled thicker, taking on a crimson hue as her life seeped into it. It squirmed, as if trying to evade her touch. She snatched for it, but her fingers passed through the mist as it drifted up, an insubstantial shape brushing against the shutters, seeking a way out.

Allorise sat back on her heels, arms extended in a gesture of embrace, and sucked in a long breath. The swirling spirit struggled, spectral fingers clawing at the drapes. But blood called to blood, and would not be denied. Slowly her father's spirit was drawn towards her, until she reached out and caught it between her palms, crushing it into a bright ruby spark.

She swallowed the spark, feeling the heat travel down her throat and spread through her core. She laughed again, smearing the blood across her arm as a tattoo of honour. Lifting the needles from the pillow, she felt fresh energy surge through her hands, through the strands of her own hair that clasped her father's fingers. As she raised them he sat up in bed, shaking his head in confusion.

"Allo? What's going on?"

"Nothing to worry about, Dada." She kissed him on the forehead, twisting the needles to snap the strands of hair, the last piece of the spell. Now her blood caged his spirit, and as she learned to perfect the spell he would dance to her will. This was only the beginning. "You got a bit tangled up, that's all."

"I feel strange," he grumbled, as she settled him back in bed.

"Probably something you ate. Shall I take this cup away and send up fresh?"

"No, I'm not thirsty. It feels like I've lost something . . ."

"Go to sleep." She slipped the needles into her purse. "Whatever it is, we can look for it in the morning."

He nodded, eyes closing. "You're a good girl, Allorise. Where would I be without you?"

&

"Allo? When did you take up knitting?"

Allorise smiled sweetly at her brother, bone needles clicking in constant motion. "It keeps my hands busy."

"I never thought I'd see you with such a mundane hobby. Here's mother now, better hide it!"

Allorise slipped her hands under the table, still clicking faintly as Lady Carey joined her children for breakfast. "No sign of your father this morning?" she asked, rubbing the dark circles under her eyes. "I must have been ill last night. I don't think I made it to bed!"

Allorise felt a nudge against her ankle as her younger brother kicked her under the table, making her drop a stitch. She didn't dare look up and catch his eye, his inevitable grin. Their mother was often ill at the end of the day, the empty wine glasses indicating the path of her sickness.

"Father will be here," she said.

Lady Carey took the lid off the nearest dish and regarded the contents with displeasure. "Scrambled eggs. Didn't we have them yesterday? And what is that infernal clicking sound?"

Bastian nudged her ankle again, and she shook her head, an almost imperceptible movement that only he would notice.

"I think the servants are up to something," he said. "I'll ask them."

Pathetic. She'd taught her brother to lie better than that. Lady Carey arched her eyebrows, but was distracted from further interrogation by the shuffling step of her husband making his way into the hall, supported by a cane and the arm of a servant. He looked pale, and his gait was jerky, but otherwise he appeared normal.

He took his seat, and Allorise's needles fell still. She watched him under lowered lids, and wondered if Bastian could hear her heart thumping.

"Will you eat, dear?" Lady Carey offered the metal dish that held the eggs.

Her husband snorted. "Not hungry. Tastes like ash in my mouth."

"Not hungry?"

"Is that strange?"

It was very strange; his tremendous appetite never slacked; but Lady Carey was too polite to say so. Allorise felt her lips twitch.

There was an awkward silence at the table, small talk, long pauses, the scrape of cutlery pushing uneaten food around plates. Allorise rested one hand on the needles on her lap, stroking her fingers down their length.

Her mother pushed away her eggs, nibbled at the edges. She sighed. "I must write to Marook, letting him know we accept his offer for Allorise's hand."

In the hush that followed her announcement, the only sound was furious clicking from beneath the table.

Lord Carey's mouth dropped open. "I don't think so," he said.

"What do you mean, Aldo? We discussed the proposal . . ."

Allorise smirked at the sight of her father trying to squint at his own lips, which were suddenly outside his control. She would get better at this with practice.

"I will not allow my youngest daughter to be married off to a sweaty foreigner!" Allorise's fingers flashed faster than she thought possible. Her head ached with the effort of concentration.

"I see." Lady Carey clasped her hands on the table in front of her, very still. "When did you decide this?"

"Last night. Allorise came to me. My darling daughter –" his jaw worked furiously, fighting the words that spilled from his throat, "- she begged me to spare her from that fate. How could I refuse?"

"How indeed?" Allorise muttered. Bastian glared at her, but she ignored him.

"Then what will we do with her?" Lady Carey snapped. "It would have been a profitable match. It would have enhanced our influence in Behenna—"

"I don't care about bloody Behenna! I want her here, looking after me!"

"I'll take good care of him, mother," Allorise cut in. Her father spluttered, a flush of crimson on his weathered cheeks.

"Then I suppose I should write and turn him down. He won't be happy . . ." Lady Carey rose, and drifted from the room with a vague, preoccupied air that Allorise knew well.

"Bastian, follow her and get a drink down her throat. That'll make her feel better."

She waited until his footsteps died away before moving to the seat next to her father, and stroking his hand. "How are you feeling, Dada?"

His eyes narrowed. He retained that fraction of control. "You've done something to me, haven't you? You horrid child, undo what you've done!"

"So you can sell me off to the highest bidder? I don't think so, Father." She twitched her needles, making his arms jerk up and down like a puppet. "I control my own destiny. And now it seems I control yours too!"

"What demon trickery is this? Let me go!" He squirmed and writhed, held firm in his chair. The needles thrummed with magic.

"I can't let you go, dear Dada." Allorise put on her sweetest voice. "Your body hasn't realised yet that you're dead. I snap these needles, I break the strings, and your heart will stop in an instant. Really, I'm doing you a favour."

"A favour? I - "

"Hush now!" The weaving of her spell stilled his furious lips. "You will only talk when I command it, only say what I want you to say. The rest of the time you will be silent and still as a corpse. Which, don't forget, is what you are. I can return you to the realm of the dead any time I choose, if you try to fight me. Will you resist?"

She allowed him the freedom to shake his head.

"You're lucky, you know," she went on brightly. "No one can kill a dead man. I've made you immortal!"

She watched him fight to speak, to raise a hand to her, with dispassionate calm.

"You're not well, are you, Dada? I fear the rule of Cape Carey has become too much for you in your declining years. Let me help you. Let me lift the burden from your shoulders."

She rang the bell for a servant, a frail tinkling. "My father needs some documents drawn up and witnessed, don't you, Father?"

Lord Carey could only nod, dumb and furious, ensnared in his daughters web.

Four

LIATHAN HAD NEVER travelled as far as the banks of the Ferrybane, four days hard walk to the west of the lake, and he had never seen a barge, or so many people gathered in one place. Burleigh was a small walled town that straddled the banks of the river, a resting point for the barges travelling to and from Lambury. He stood on the wharf and gaped at the lumbering horses that pulled the boats, at the gaudy painted vessels, every one unique and brighter than the last, and at the bargees, who had seen more of the world than he even knew existed. They were mostly short, with muscular arms, and they shouted at each other in an incomprehensible dialect.

"Out of the way, gawper!" A sharp elbow nudged him in the back, and a heavy hand cuffed him round the skull before he could dodge. Shaking his head to clear the ringing in his ears, Liathan stumbled for the calm of a nearby alley. From there he could spy on the wharf without getting in the way. He kept to the shadows, watching with fascination as the bargees loaded and unloaded their wares on the riverbank. Some of the crates were nailed shut and banded with iron bars. They looked heavy; the men carrying them sweated and strained. Others were open, and they were the ones that made Liathan's nose twitch and his mouth water. There was fruit in the crates, and he hadn't eaten for two days. He watched the weak sunlight splash off the wet stone of the quayside, the golden whorls painted on the hulls of the boats, and the red and green fruits and vegetables stacked in their boxes.

Hunger gnawed his guts, made him light-headed and reckless. These busy merchants wouldn't miss a handful of fruit. He could dart out, grab some, and be away before anyone noticed him.

As soon as he committed to his action, he realised it was a mistake. Fatigue made him slow, and clumsy, and the wharf was wider than it looked from the alley. As his hand fell on the box of smooth green fruits, their waxy skins tempting beneath his fingertips, a much larger hand clamped down on his shoulder.

"I told you to get out of the way, you little snitcher!"

Liathan let go of the fruit as if it had burst into flame. "I wasn't stealing, honest!"

"My arse you weren't!" His captor spun him round to face him. He was a weathered man with dark, curly hair, greying at the temples. He wore a jerkin of tanned hide, clumsily dyed in green and red, and his feet were bare, with dark hairs sprouting from the toes. He looked Liathan up and down with narrowed, gleaming eyes. "You look pinched, mushtie. Are you grumbling?"

"Grumbling?" Liathan's belly gave a loud gurgle, and the man laughed.

"Your gut tells me you are! These are cookers you're trying to snitch. They won't do you any good without a fire to roast them over. I guess you don't have any burnings?"

"Burnings? Fire? No, I—" Liathan stumbled over his words. He was so tired he couldn't think. He sagged, and would have fallen if the bargee hadn't caught him by the elbow.

"You sit here," he said, indicating one of the iron-bound crates. "My woman might have food in the galley she can spare.

No running off, mark!"

Liathan sat, arms wrapped around his calves, chin resting on his knees. He watched the bargees hustle back and forth, loading and unloading, making loud, boisterous deals with the men of the town that involved a lot of head shaking and, at their eventual conclusion, back-slapping. More boats arrived as others left, adding to the good-natured chaos.

"Here you go, little mush." In the hubbub, Liathan hadn't noticed the curly-haired man returning until he held out a pasty towards him. "Careful, it's hot!"

Liathan spat the hot filling back into his hand. "Thanks!" he mumbled though a mouthful of pastry, swallowing hard. The hot lumps sliding down his throat made his eyes water.

"Welcome. What brings you here snitching my wares? I should take you home to your da for a hiding."

"No Da." Liathan took another bite, more cautious this time. "No home either."

"Who looks after you then?"

He shrugged. "Me, I suppose."

"You're doing a pretty poor job of it, by the looks of you!"

Liathan bristled. He might be hungry, and muddy from the road, but he had got here alive.

The bargee sat down beside him, and took another pasty from inside his jacket. "I'm Ram," he said, cheerfully. "You got a name, mush?"

"Leyon." If the Old Ones were after him, they might be able to hear his name uttered across time and space. He didn't want to make it easier for them to track him down.

"Where you hailing from, Leyon?"

A moment of panic. He didn't know the names of many towns. What if this kindly stranger knew people, and went asking after him? He waved his pasty vaguely at the building behind him. "Back east, you know . . ."

"If you don't want to say, my nose won't take a skinning for it. I don't care if you're on the run. Just don't go snitching from me again!"

"I won't." Liathan felt the heat rising in his face. "I'm sorry—"

"What's past is past. What are you going to do now? Cross onto the plains, or head back east?"

"I hadn't thought . . ." All he had thought about was reaching a town, trying to lose himself in a crowd. But Burleigh was too small, too close to Lydyce. The Old Ones would find him easily here. It would be the first place they would look. "Not back east. Where are you going? If you don't mind me asking . . ."

"We're heading south. We join the Fairwater at Tashk Mill, then on to Riversmeet and down the Lam to Cape Carey. From there, who knows? Plenty of opportunities in Cape Carey for a travelling man. They say it's the biggest city in the world."

"Is it?" Liathan asked.

Ram shrugged. "Beats me. When I've been to every city in the world, ask me again and I might tell you!" He glanced sideways at Liathan. "You might be a strapping lad with a meal in your belly. Want to come along for the ride?"

"Come with you? On your boat?"

"Unless you want to swim along behind." Ram rose abruptly, brushing the crumbs from his lap, his movements awkward and embarrassed. "If you want to, that is. You're not obliged. We leave sharp when we're loaded, mind, so make sure you stick around!"

"Your wife won't mind?"

"You hang about—hey!" This last was directed at the crew loading the barge, as they staggered with a heavy bolt of cloth. "You watch what you're doing there, or feel my boot on your arse!" He hurried to deal with the clumsy porters, leaving Liathan to swallow the last of his pasty and consider the offer. There seemed no alternative. Maybe he could make himself so useful that Ram would keep him on. Barge life seemed an easy way to stay on the move, to keep running as long as he could.

He caught the final few crumbs in his palm, licked it clean

and wiped it down his thigh, before scrambling after the barge master.

⚜

The living quarters of the barge were narrow, with a low roof and a lintel above the door that caught Liathan hard on the forehead, raising a painful ridge above his temple. He swore.

"We don't have language like that on this boat, young man!" At first he hadn't spotted the slender woman, dressed in brown and gold, at the far end of the galley. The room was dim, the light coming down in neat squares from the open hatches on the deck, making the shadows thicker.

As she approached he realised she was tiny. Her head didn't reach his shoulder. She wore breeches and a man's shirt, knotted at the waist to gather up the spare material, and her hair was pulled back into a gold lace chignon. In her hand she carried a wooden spoon, and she thwacked him across the upper arm with it as a greeting. "Are you the boy Ram told me about? I'm Arabie."

"I'm Leyon." The false name sounded more natural on his tongue now he had said it a few times. "Thank you for letting me come on board."

"You'll have to earn your passage, mark. There's no room for wastrels on a barge. Can you cook?"

"I cooked for my da when he was sick. I'm not scared of work, Mistress Arabie."

"Just Arabie." The second blow with the spoon was softer, more affectionate. "I think you'll do. If not, I'll feed you to the fish! Get up and help my man cast off now. He'll show you what needs doing."

A shudder ran down the length of the barge, and Liathan gripped the door frame, unsure on his feet. Arabie chuckled. "That's something you'll have to get used to. Now scoot!"

‡

It didn't take long for Liathan to grow accustomed to the gentle motion of the barge. The countryside slipped by, growing wilder and more rocky as they drifted downstream towards the trading port at Riversmeet. The routine never varied. Up at first light, it was Liathan's job to tend to the horse before he could eat breakfast, then a day's travel, broken only for lunch and to rest the mare who plodded along beside them, tethered by a long rope to the prow. When they moved upstream, Ram explained, the mare would tow the barge, but with the flow in their favour this was an easy journey for her. Sometimes Ram taught him how to steer the barge, and Arabie told Liathan about the country they travelled through. At night he slept beside the couple on their triangular mattress wedged into the bow end of the barge, breathing in their scents of wood and water.

Occasionally he even stopped looking for signs of pursuit. But when dark clouds gathered to the North, he steeled himself for the blow he knew was coming.

"You look edgy, boy. Anything wrong?"

Ram steered the barge over the last section into Riversmeet, and the waters grew rough. Liathan sat beside him, ready to throw ropes or do whatever was asked of him. He ducked as a large black crow flapped overhead.

"I don't like birds. I don't trust them."

"Birds can't hurt you, Leyon. You got a reason to distrust them?"

"Where I used to live, the crows would come down and snatch food out of your hand if you didn't watch out."

Ram nodded, as if chewing over this fact. "Never heard of that," he admitted. "Eagles you should watch out for. I've heard of them taking babies from the deck if they were left unguarded. But a crow . . . The only thing I've seen them snatch is the eyes of the dead, and I wouldn't want to see the like again." He shuddered.

"When did you see that?" Liathan asked.

"In the war. I was a young man then." Ram snapped his mouth shut as if biting off the words, cast a wary glance at the hovering crow, and changed the subject. "We put into Riversmeet tomorrow. You'll have to start earning your keep, boy!"

The crow squawked and flew off. Liathan let himself relax. "What do you want me to do?"

Riversmeet sat at the junction of three rivers, sprawling across the banks and the grassy island that lay at the heart of the confluence. The waters were turbulent; the currents pushing the boat in every direction. If it wasn't carefully handled, it could spin out of control and smash into the banks, but Ram knew his vessel and these waters well and he handled her confidently through the swells, while Liathan hung onto the side and tried not to reveal how sick he was feeling. Arabie freed the horse and led her along the bank, and as Liathan raised his head she gave him a grin of encouragement.

"We'll make a bargee of you yet, Leyon!"

He could only groan in reply. Even the welcome sight of the wharves rolling into view didn't comfort him. Towns meant people, people who might remember him. Especially if he was the hapless boy who stumbled off a barge and threw up in the street.

"Here." As the barge emerged into calmer waters, Ram tossed a mooring rope out to his wife, and drew Liathan towards the rear hatch. "I've got a gift for you."

Liathan stuck his hands behind his back. "I don't want any more from you. You've given me so much already . . ."

"Shut up and take it, will you?" Ram thrust a bundle of cloth at Liathan, and he had no choice but to seize it or let it fall. He shook it out.

It was a cloak, dark brown, trimmed with the gold braid Arabie was so fond of. Ram watched anxiously as Liathan swung it over his shoulders.

"Do you like it? She had to guess the size . . ."

"Arabie made this?" It was better quality than anything he had previously owned.

"Try the hood," Ram urged.

The sweeping hood came down to his nose. He could barely see out from under it, and it shadowed his whole face. "It's a bit big," he mumbled, not wanting to seem ungrateful.

"That's how she made it. It'll hide your face from them you don't want to see it, if you know what I mean . . ."

Liathan felt a warm rush in his chest at the words. His throat was tight and he couldn't speak, but Ram seemed to understand, as he clapped him awkwardly on the shoulder and spat into the river. "You're a good kid," he muttered. "Whatever you're running from . . . We just want you to be safe. Now," he raised his voice to carry to the shore, "get across and help your mother with the horse, son!"

By the time the work was done it was too late for the barge to depart. Ram made good coin from the day's trading. He declared that Arabie should have the night off, and they would eat in one of the many taverns on the island. Liathan had never been in an inn, and the noise, the smells of malt and sweat and sawdust, the jostling at the bar, almost sent him running back into the street. The bargee found them a table in a dark corner, acquired by leaning on a nearby pillar and glaring until the occupants swallowed their drinks and moved off, muttering about the atmosphere.

He pressed Liathan into a chair. "Hold the table," he said. "I think you can take your hood down now. Dressing like a mage will only attract attention!"

He elbowed his way to the bar, returning with three brimming flagons of ale. "Get that down you, my boy!"

Liathan had other things on his mind. "What did you mean about dressing like a mage?" he asked.

"You know, big hood, grumpy face, hiding in dark corners."

Arabie chuckled at her husband's description. "A lot of people don't trust mages," she explained.

"*I* don't trust mages," Ram butted in, with a sour expression as he gulped his drink. "Bloody mages lost us the war, interfering like that . . ."

"Keep your voice down!" Arabie said. "Folks are still touchy about it."

"It's been years," growled Ram, but in a lower voice.

Liathan sipped his ale. It was flat, and slightly warm. "I thought mages did good things," he said, keeping his voice measured. "Like healing people."

Ram snorted, spraying beery foam across the table. "They do what suits them and no more, Leyon! Yes, they'll heal your sickness, for a price. And stars help you if you cross them. They can hold a grudge for generations. They're long-lived, and they *never* forget."

Liathan though sadly of his mentor. Seeing him lose his memory, become a stranger, had been the hardest thing to witness. He had no doubt the other Old Ones would never forgive or forget his crime. How could they, when he couldn't forgive himself?

He shuffled deeper into the shadows, clutching his flagon as if it could protect him from the green-eyed spirit of vengeance that was hunting him down.

⚗

Riversmeet was compact, hemmed in by the rocky lands around. But Cape Carey, a moon of travel south of Burleigh, sprawled out on both sides of the river, throwing out long arms in an embrace. Liathan could smell the city long before he saw it. The fringes of the town, outside the protection of the walls, were a vast slum. Wooden shacks thrown together in haphazard fashion bloomed like fungus from a sea of stinking mud. Stinging flies rose in buzzing clouds and swarmed around the barge. Liathan scrambled below decks with his hand pressed to his nose, choking on the fetid stench. Arabie tied a scarf soaked in perfumed oils across his face so he could keep working.

"How can people live like that?" he asked, gasping.

"What choice do you think they have?" Arabie's face darkened. "You could have ended up in a place like this, if we hadn't taken you on."

His cheeks flushed at her disapproval. "I know that. I appreciate everything you've done for me. You don't know how much . . ."

She threw her arms around his waist impulsively. "Oh Leyon! How could we have left you in Burleigh when we had room for you on board? You're family to us now. You'll never end up in a slum, I promise you that."

The hair at the crown of her head tickled his nose and made his eyes water. He screwed them closed, feeling dizzy as the barge rocked beneath his feet.

"Do you feel sick?" Arabie pushed away from him with a concerned expression. "Is it the smell of the slums?"

"No, I'm fine." Liathan managed a feeble grin under the mask.

"Then you can help me peel some roots for dinner, can't you?"

The river was sluggish, and the slums dragged on for mile after stinking mile. The only good Liathan could see in the situation was that he wasn't walking through them. He stayed below decks as much as he could. He was becoming immune to the smell, but the sight of the filth and poverty sickened his heart, and he couldn't look on it for too long, or listen to the pleading of the beggars at the water's edge as the barge slipped past. It was a relief when the solid grey walls of the city loomed ahead.

"Do you want to come to the Watergate with me, Leyon?" Ram asked, steering the laden barge closer to the bank, brandishing a pole at a few scroungers who braved the wrath of the guards patrolling the riverbank. "We have to get a docket to pass through."

"What's a docket?"

"Like a permit." Ram hopped over the side on to dry land and gave the mare an affectionate rub on the nose as he passed. She cropped the strands of grass that pushed up through the cracks in the flagstone pavement running alongside the river. On the far side of the pavement was a high wall, and beyond that, the slums. Even if he could no longer see them, Liathan could still smell them. He pulled his cloak further over his face and his scarf up over his nostrils, tasting the bitter tang of perfume.

Ram laughed. "You look like a bandit, my boy!" He reached out and twitched Liathan's hood up, so it swept his eyebrows. "Hide in plain sight, son. If you walk around looking like a criminal, folks will only notice you more."

"Thanks!" Liathan's voice was muffled, and the perfume stung his lips and tongue. He wanted to spit. He followed Ram up the path, keeping a wary eye on the pacing guards.

The Watergate was a fortified arch over the river. The water flowed through a steel grille that was raised to let a steady flow of barges through, if they had the correct documentation. Barges queued up to pass, and Ram and Liathan joined a line of people waiting outside a hut by the gate to receive their dockets, passed through the window by a bored man in uniform. He barely looked at them as they arrived in front of him.

"Cargo?"

"Mainly cloth from Riversmeet," Ram told him. Liathan's ears pricked up. He knew that wasn't all they were carrying. He had shifted so many boxes in the hold, he knew what each one contained, that concealed under the slowly ripening fruit were smaller boxes, crammed with shining stones.

"Anything else?"

"Just some fruit." Ram shrugged, dismissing the interest. "Not too much, all the money's in cloth at the moment."

"Cloth and fruit." The official flourished his writing stick. "Here you go." He pushed the parchment through the window at the bargee. "Next!"

"Why didn't you tell him about the starstones?" Liathan asked in a low voice, as they returned to the barge.

"What starstones?" Ram's face was a portrait of innocence.

"You know what I'm talking about."

"Listen," Ram helped him back on board, keeping a firm grip on his upper arm. Liathan tried not to wince at the pinch against his bicep. "You never saw any starstones. You don't know anything about it. Startide has the stone trade in Cape Carey sewn up tighter than a Telesian's arse, and I can't afford to pay them off."

"What's Startide?"

"Best you don't know, mush. The less you know the better."

"Is Leyon asking about Startide?" Arabie asked, as they descended the ladder into the galley. "Was there trouble at the gate?"

"Not a drop." Ram handed his wife the docket. "You go up top and see us through. The boy and I will start shifting this cargo."

As soon as Arabie's heels disappeared out through the hatch, Ram took a seat on a crate in the hold and unwrapped a wad of spyme. He offered a hank of the pungent chewing herb to Liathan.

"Go on, son. It'll calm your nerves."

Liathan took a thin strip, rolled it up, and stuffed it in his mouth.

"The wifey doesn't like me chewing, so don't let on I shared!"

Ram stretched his legs out. He seemed in no hurry to arrange the cargo. "We'll be in Cape Carey a few days. Do you plan to stay here, or come with us when we leave?"

Liathan chewed slowly, enjoying the mild buzz the herb gave him. "Would you be happy to have me along?"

Ram grinned. "More than happy. But there's good opportunities for a bright boy in the city. I don't want you to dismiss them before you've considered them. You could apprentice to a trade, for a start." He grew serious. "That'd give you Guild protection from whatever you're running from. Better protection than Arabie and I could provide. Think on it."

"I will." Liathan had already made up his mind, but there was no harm in seeing what the city offered, so he would know what he was turning down.

"Good for you!" Ram gurned as he shifted the spyme from one side of his mouth to the other, and stood up. "Let's get these boxes shifted, boy. They won't move themselves!"

The barge was only half unloaded by sunset, when Ram vanished into the murky alleys of the city with a small box clutched tight under his cloak. He didn't say where he was going, and Arabie didn't ask. Liathan guessed Ram had done this enough times that his wife did not question it.

"Will Ram be all right?" he asked, as she hauled a bucket of water over the side and dropped a pair of soapstones in it to work up a lather.

"Do you want to help me scrub the hold?"

He frowned. "Not really, but if you want me to . . ."

"Get out of here." He could see her anxiety in the set of her shoulders, the way she ground the soapstones together with fierce concentration. She cleaned like a demon when she was worried. "I can do without you under my feet this evening!"

Liathan took this as his invitation to depart. He had one

foot on dry land when Arabie called him back, and stuffed a small purse into his hand. "Don't get too drunk," she told him. "We've a busy day tomorrow. And—be careful. City taverns can be rough."

"I'll watch out," he promised, strapping the purse on to his belt, as Arabie bent her head over the bucket once more.

Dusk had given way to night, and the first few stars gleamed above the rooftops. Liathan kept one hand on his coin, the other on his dagger. The streets of Cape Carey at night were only a little less crowded than they were in daylight, but the people who came out after dark had different trades, and different natures. During his wandering Liathan was offered ale, a pinch of dark powder he declined to sniff, a punch on the nose, and met a number of young women and a few men who wanted to show him what they promised would be "a good time." It was all rather overwhelming, and he ducked down a side street and into a quiet tavern for a relaxing drink.

As he pushed open the door the tavern went from quiet to silent, a hollow in the thrum of sound as every eye assessed the newcomer, then bubbled up again as they dismissed him as a nobody and returned to their conversations. Perturbed, Liathan headed for the bar. He counted the coin Arabie had given him, and ordered a pint.

"Hello sailor." The light, trailing touch on the back of his neck made him jump, splashing ale down the front of his shirt. "Are you going to offer me a drink?"

"Is there any reason why—oh!" The girl who slithered on to the bar stool next to him was so beautiful she stole his breath. She had blonde hair, festooned with clips and ribbons, that tumbled halfway down her back. Her eyes, slanted like a cat's, were so deep blue they were almost violet. She pouted, and ran her delicate tongue across scarlet lips.

"Would you like a drink? I don't buy drinks for girls if I don't know their names . . ."

"That seems a wise policy." She smiled, and Liathan felt himself melt. "My name's Chalice. I think you spilled your beer."

Her eyes flicked down disdainfully, and Liathan realised the drink he had slopped down his front was spreading out into a large, damp stain. He dabbed at it, forgetting in his confusion that he was still holding his flagon, and splashed more ale over his thigh. He bit back a curse, and floundered around for something intelligent to say.

"Chalice? Like a bucket?"

She giggled prettily, one hand over her mouth. "You're so funny, sailor!"

"Why do you call me 'sailor'?" Liathan hailed the barmaid to bring a drink for his companion.

"You came in on a boat, didn't you? You were unloading at the wharf this morning . . ."

Liathan was certain Chalice hadn't been on the wharf while the barge was being unloaded. He would have noticed her.

She sipped her ale and dabbed her lips. "You're very quiet. You bought me a drink, I should know your name. It's only fair!"

"I'm Leyon." He blushed under her appraisal, and took a gulp of his drink to hide his embarrassment.

She leaned forward. The lace of her low-cut blouse fluttered with every breath as she laid a hand on his arm. "Living on a boat must be exciting! Where have you come from?"

"Riversmeet. Before that we were . . . somewhere else." Somehow his flagon was empty, and another one had appeared in front of him. He didn't remember paying for it.

"You must see some sights from the barge?"

Chalice was easy to talk to, especially after the second pint. Her fingers drummed on his skin, her eyes fixed on his face as he rambled on about the country he had seen, and life on the river. She nodded and smiled and made interested noises. Her cherry lips were slightly parted, and when she smiled he could see her upper teeth. She was enchanting. He wanted nothing more than to lean forward and kiss her.

Her mouth was as soft as he'd imagined. He felt her stiffen in surprise, then relax. All at once she was kissing him back, one hand twisted around the back of his neck to press him close to her, the other resting intoxicatingly on his thigh. Her tongue brushed his earlobe as she whispered an invitation to go somewhere more private.

Liathan was walking on clouds as he slipped off the bar stool. Chalice caught his hand and led him across the room and out of the front door. The gusts racing down the alley carried the whiff of horse manure and approaching rain.

Chalice pulled him into a doorway, lips against his throat, hands fumbling at his belt. "I thought—you wanted somewhere—more private!" He squirmed under her touch, heart thumping.

"What are you talking about? This is more private!"

"Than the bar!" He caught her roving hands, raised them to his mouth and kissed her perfumed wrists. "Don't you have a room we can go to?"

"What about your boat?" Chalice giggled at his expression. "I've always wanted to do it on a boat! Why not?"

"Because the people I live with are there!"

"Your parents?" She raised her eyebrows. "We'll have to be extra quiet then, won't we? Come on!"

She ran out into the alley, pulling him after her. She was a force of nature, and he was swept along with her, with the excitement of the moment. If this was what the city was like, he never wanted to leave.

A shadow fell across the end of the lane, blocking out the light from the busy road that intersected it. Chalice's step faltered, and she dropped a pace behind Liathan. "Maybe we shouldn't go that way . . ."

"Maybe you're right." Liathan turned, to find the other end of the alley blocked by two heavy-set men wielding stout wooden clubs. Chalice uttered a little squeal of fear.

"You might well squeak, my girl!" The voice came from behind them. "Is this what I told you to do?"

"We were going to the barge, Shadow! I was going to find the stones for you –"

"The stones will be long gone, you little dimwit! You were going to fuck him, weren't you?"

She bristled. "So what if I was? You're not the only man in Cape Carey –"

"I'm the only one to give you a roof over your head, you little tart! Get out of here before I lay into you as well!"

Chalice ducked under Shadow's outstretched hand and scampered down the alley, leaving Liathan alone, backed against the wall. It had all happened so quickly, but the happy alcohol fuzz had drained away, leaving him cold and exposed.

"Listen," he held up his hands to ward off Shadow's advance. "I didn't know she was with you, or I would never –"

His breath exploded from his lungs as Shadow smashed the club into his stomach. He doubled up, clutching his belly, too shocked to cry out as a second blow fell across his shoulders. It pitched him forward, face down in the grime of the alley. His teeth clicked as they met in the flesh of his bottom lip and his mouth filled with blood.

Hot rage at his humiliation flooded through him. His skin burned. The cobbles beneath his palms grew hot with furious energy. He groaned, tried to rise, and a boot slammed into his jaw, rattling his teeth in their sockets.

On hands and knees, he spat, blood and saliva fizzing and steaming as it hit the ground between his bunched fists. The heat rushed through him, pushing out the pain, replacing it with a core of burning fury. He barely felt a club crack across his spine.

"Leave me alone!" He clutched the wall as he staggered to

his feet. It felt like liquid under his hands.

"Haven't you learned yet?" Shadow's face pushed close to his, sneering, ugly. Liathan could see every pore of his skin, the grease around his hairline, the sweat gathered in the lines at the corners of his eyes. He had never seen anything as clearly as he saw Shadow's face for those brief seconds, his fist swinging round to smash Liathan's face into the wall.

It connected. Liathan's skull crunched against the wall, which dissolved under the impact of his shoulder, pitching him into the tavern. His fall was caught by the sharp edge of a table in his kidney. He retched, dizzy and bewildered. The room was full of light and sound, and his head whirled. What the hell had just happened?

Shadow grabbed his collar, spun him around, and punched him in the face, sending him flying over the table to hit the floor on the far side. Fleeing feet kicked him in the ribs as he struggled to stand.

He couldn't even see Shadow. The room was a blur of red and black. A woman cried out in alarm. "Did you see what he did to the wall?"

"Fucking wizard!" Shadow lunged at him with a roar, grappled him round the waist and slammed him into the wreckage of upturned tables and spilled pints. Liathan snatched up a broken chair leg to defend himself, driving it into Shadow's face as it burst into flame. The older man howled, clawing at his eyes as his skin blistered and popped. He sprang to his feet and fled, hands over his face, hair smouldering. Liathan ran after him a few steps, casting aside the scorched wood, then slowed as he became aware of a hideous sucking silence behind him.

Everyone not smart enough to have fled the ruined tavern was staring at him in horror. He caught the whisper on their lips.

Magic! Magic used to maim and blind. He must have done it, but he didn't know how. The other mages would find out;

they could be flapping towards him right now, in the guise of storm crows, ready to snatch out his eyes.

The barkeep approached him, nervous, nodding to the other men in the tavern to surround him.

"Stay back!" Liathan waved his hands in vague threat. He knew it would do nothing, but the nearest man jumped back, clearing a path for him through the vanished wall. Liathan hurdled the debris and fled into the night. He didn't know, didn't care, where he went. His only thought was to hide until dawn, make his way back to the river, and leave town with Ram and Arabie as soon as possible.

&

The doorway where Liathan spent the night was uncomfortable and reeked of urine, but he was too exhausted to run any further. He slumped to the ground, pulled his cloak over his head, and lay trembling. He was scared to close his eyes. When he did, the fire came again, the stink of burning flesh, Shadow's animal howl. Had he really caused that?

He had scarred Shadow, and he had pushed a burning stone into his guardian's chest until his heart stopped. He needed to keep away from people until he understood what was happening and how to control it. Getting out of the city would be a start. As the sky lightened to a drizzly grey, he sat up, wincing. His torso was a mass of bruises, his bottom lip swollen. He had lost a tooth at the back of his mouth, and the one next to it was bleeding, and wobbled when he pushed his tongue against it. He was smeared with mud and blood, and when he took a leak, his piss was stained scarlet.

He knew if he headed south, he would eventually come to the river where it bisected the city. With the sun lost behind a thick blanket of grey it was hard to tell which way south was, but he set off, hoping he could find someone to direct him.

There were few people about at this early morning witching

hour. The night people had faded away with the light, and the daylight people were only beginning to stir. Liathan was glad there was no one around to witness his humiliation. He dreaded to think what Arabie would say when she saw him.

As he limped at last into a street he recognised as leading to the wharf, Liathan scented smoke. Fat flakes of wet ash drifted in the air like lazy bluebottles, sticking to his skin. Ahead, the wharf was quieter than usual. Loading and unloading continued, but the banter between the dock workers and the bargees was muted. No one paid him any attention as he made his way along the bank to where Ram's barge was tied up.

A stout length of rope sealed off that section of the wharf, but no one was guarding it, and it was a simple matter for Liathan to swing his legs over it. He looked around eagerly for the barge. "Ram! Arabie!"

The smell of smoke was stronger here, the drifting ash thicker. There was no sign of barge or horse. They wouldn't have left without him, would they?

"Arabie!"

"Hey you!" A grey-haired man with a stoop clattered out of a building on the far side of the rope. "You're not supposed to be over there!"

"I'm looking for my barge," Liathan explained. "My friends. Did they leave?"

"Your friends? Oh!" The man took his arm and helped him back over. He kept a firm grip on him as he steered him into the office, and nodded at his companion. "Antono, get the boy some wine. He was with the barge."

Antono scuttled off to do his bidding.

"Did my friends leave?" Liathan asked again, baffled.

"Not as such. I'm sorry, lad - "

"What do you mean, 'not as such'? Either they left or they didn't!"

The old man sighed. "There's no easy way to say this, so I might as well show you. Through here." He kept a controlling hand on Liathan's elbow as he ushered him into an inner room. The shutters were closed, dim grey light streaking through the louvres, falling in narrow bands across the sheets that covered the floor. Covered that which had once been human.

"There was a fire. It caught hold very quick. By the time we realised . . . I'm sorry, boy."

Liathan stared at the shapes of Ram and Arabie.

"Were you very close?"

He turned and walked from the office, not seeing, not hearing, dimly aware that the old man was talking to him. He could make little sense of the words. Something about waiting for the guard . . .

He leaned against the wall of the hut, resting his aching head on cold damp stone. His eyes stung, and he rubbed them, leaving damp smears in the dirt on the back of his hand. The river was blurry, but he heard the steady tramp of feet approaching. He straightened as an officer of the city watch paused in front of him and looked him up and down.

"You been in the wars, lad?"

"No." Liathan sniffed, staring at the floor, refusing to make eye contact.

"There was some trouble here last night. You know anything about that?"

"No."

The guard leaned forward, and sniffed. "Your clothes smell of smoke. Fancy explaining that?"

Liathan said nothing.

"I think you should come along with me while I look into all this—oi!" As the guard lunged for him, Liathan ducked under his arm and hared off down the quayside. "Stop him!"

Liathan bolted down an alley, scrambled over a low wall, through a private garden. Another alley, across a square, round a stall selling bread, and he stumbled to a halt at a dead end. There was no sound of pursuit yet, but there would be soon. He ached, from the crown of his head to the soles of his feet, and he wanted nothing more than to lie in the gutter and give in to his sorrow. One day he would be able to rest, but now, there was nothing he could do but run.

Five

LORD CAREY HAD taken to his bed. The effort it took to control him was exhausting, so Allorise had invented an illness for him and confined him, twitching and cursing, to his quarters. She told the servants that only she was allowed to see him. She didn't want them to fall ill, and it wasn't a burden to her to bring her beloved father his meals and make sure he was turned in bed. She was such a dutiful daughter, giving up her hopes of marriage to care for an ungrateful man who mumbled curses and spat every time she came near.

"Won't you eat, Dada?" The flesh of his cheeks was beginning to sag. She hadn't anticipated that as the processes of his body stopped, he would be unable to digest food. She was lucky he had always been such a fat man. He pressed his lips together and turned his face away as she hovered the spoon in front of his mouth. "I could force you to eat, but I don't want to do that . . ."

"I'd rather choke!" She seized the opportunity his words offered to wedge the spoon into his mouth and tip it sharply upwards, so he was forced to swallow. "Doesn't do me any damn good. Look what you've done to me!"

He pushed against her arm with weak, palsied hands, cold

and pale as the belly of a dead fish. A chunk of flesh was missing from the base of his thumb, and the bloodless wound gaped.

"I can't taste, I don't bleed, I don't heal!"

"Oh nonsense, Father! Hush now." She pressed him back against his pillows. "I have business to attend to. I'll be back soon. If you could sign these papers, it would be most helpful." She laid them on his lap and picked up her needles.

"I'm not signing them! What are they?" His right hand twitched towards the stylus on the bedside table, and he wrestled it into submission with his left. "Stop it! Tell me what you're up to!"

"I need to free some capital. The pittance you give me isn't enough to live on any more." Allorise pouted. "This signs over some of our assets in the city to me, to do with as I please. Don't look so worried!" She laughed. "I'll make sure you and Mama are left comfortable!"

"Why do you need money? I gave you everything, and you repay me like this!"

"I don't want to rely on you, or any man, to take care of me. I can make my own way in the world." Allorise smiled, twisting her needles, forcing her father's hand to make a scratchy mark across the bottom of the parchment. She took it from him and sealed it with wax, bending his finger to press his sovereign ring into the soft putty. She patted his hand affectionately, and something writhed beneath the cold flesh. She dropped it quickly.

"I'll let you sleep now, Dada. Don't worry. I'll take care of everything for you."

Tucking the needles into her belt, she left him lying limp and helpless on the bed. She closed the door quietly behind her, and nodded at the guard on duty. "My father is sleeping. See no one disturbs him."

"Your mother asked to see him again this morning, my Lady."

Allorise stroked his arm and flashed a smile. "I'd hate for

my mother to get sick too. Tell her I've spoken to a healer, and he advises her to stay away. I think she should go and stay with my brother, outside the city. I may suggest that to her. How are you feeling, Boran?"

"Quite well, my Lady."

"See you stay that way. I trust no one more than you, to protect my family while I find a cure for this sickness!"

The guard blushed. "Thank you, my Lady. I hope you find it soon."

"I have meetings with healers this afternoon, in my chambers. Between us we'll find a way."

She trotted down the stairs, hands clasped with worry, to find a maid waiting for her at the bottom. Her eyes were wide and scared. "My Lady! The plague doctor is here to see you."

"You didn't get too close, did you, Vio?"

The girl shook her head.

"Thank the stars for that. I don't want you to get sick. Make sure no one comes in while I'm talking to him, won't you?"

Vio clicked her heels together. "Absolutely, my Lady."

"Good girl!"

The plague doctor sat on a high-backed chair in Allorise's outer reception chamber, the former domain of her father. He was still wearing his cloak, hood pulled up tight over the top of his close-fitting mask, which curved forward like the beak of a crow. He stared through sealed circles of glass as she closed the door and barred it.

"Come into my inner chamber, doctor."

He followed her with shuffling step, into the inner room which was sparsely furnished with a bare table, two tapestry-backed chairs, and a bureau. He groped for the back of the chair. "I don't see well with the mask on, Lady," he apologised in a muffled voice.

"Well, take it off then. It's a good disguise, but it's not as if either of us actually has the plague."

"Not the plague, no, but . . ."

"Then take it off. I can hardly hear you with that leather over your mouth."

The plague doctor pushed his hood back, and raised his hands to the strap at the back of his head. He released the clasp, and let the beaked mask drop to his lap. Allorise hissed. "What happened to you?"

"I'll come to that, because it'll be of interest to you, Lady." Shadow brushed his fingers across his swollen, blistered face, and winced. "What news of your father?"

"The stupid servants believe our story. They're terrified to go near him." She drew the document from her breast, and tapped him with it, teasing. "He's sick, but not too sick to sign the paper!"

"What does that mean for Startide?"

"I now control a number of properties in the city. We can use them as we please. Some of them might have sitting tenants. Find out about them for me, maybe we can make use of them. How did the Gilded Lily respond to our offer?"

"As you'd expect." Shadow scratched the raw skin on his cheek. "Turned it down flat. I'm trying to get a girl on the inside. Chalice, you know her?"

Allorise shook her head.

"She's smart, and suited to that line of work. She'll tell us how we can break them down."

"Can she be trusted?"

"She knows how to keep quiet." He scowled, puckered skin stretching around his mouth. "We might have another problem. There's this boy . . . Magic user. It was him did for my face, in front of a roomful of people at the Black Rat two nights ago."

"Magic user?" Allorise straightened in her chair. "What do you know about him?"

"Not as much as we should. Calls himself Leyon, came in on a barge. The bargee was smuggling starstones into the city."

He drew a small bag from beneath his cloak and pushed

it across the table towards her. Allorise upended it and picked through the handful of stones. They were mostly of inferior quality, worth only a few gold coins, but there were a couple of sparklers. These she picked out, the rest she returned to the bag and handed back to Shadow.

"You can sell these on the open market," she said. "Take a couple for yourself, and bring me the coin. What happened to our smuggler?"

"One of my associates stabbed him, and fired the barge, but the boy wasn't aboard. He was seen on the wharf the next morning, but no-one's spotted him since."

"Is he still in the city?"

"My men are searching every barge that leaves, looking for our little arsonist. If he's found he's to be brought here, not to the Watch."

"Well done." Allorise loosened the purse at her belt. "The treatment for that wound must be pricey. Take something towards it."

"Thank you, Lady. Should I do anything more about the boy? Do you want him taken care of?"

"Taken care of in a permanent way? Not at all!" Allorise licked her lips, mulling over her options. "How old is this brat?"

"About fifteen summers."

She smiled, nodding to herself. "A very pliable age. Unpredictable. We can't have a young magic user running round the city causing trouble. Find him and bring him to me. Without hurting him, if you can restrain yourself."

Shadow stared at the table with a dour expression, and did not reply.

"I mean it, Shadow. He could be a powerful tool if we can control him. Find him and bring him to me, before anyone else gets hold of him."

Six

THERE WAS A line in the earth surrounding the obliterated village of Lydyce. Outside the border, the grass had the russet tint so common in the Estmarch. It swished around Kayall's ankles as he walked. Inside the line, the grass was scrubby and grey, struggling through the earth and wilting in the sun. Even the air seemed tainted; an unpleasant sensation on his lips and tongue that made him shudder as he trekked in Elvienne's footsteps down the last hill towards the murky lake. He caught up with her on the shore, the icy wind from the mountains blowing her grey curls into disarray.

"This place is a wasteland," he declared in disgust. "I can't believe Carlon and the boy lived here so long. Was it like this last time you came?"

"Lydyce is stagnant. Nothing grows here, nothing changes."

She refused to elaborate, walking away down the lake shore with her head bowed. Kayall sensed she didn't want to be bothered with questions. He trailed behind her, feet slipping on the rounded pebbles that were even harder to walk over than cobbled city streets. He missed the city; the crowding, the taverns, even the smells. Elvienne declared Lydyce a wasteland, but to Kayall's eyes the rest of the countryside wasn't much better. There was nowhere to buy replacement shoes, for a start.

The old woman was muttering to herself, and he scrambled to catch up and hear what she was saying.

"A boy drowned building the jetty, and we lit his bone-fire on the shore. The flames turned the moons to blood, and the dragons howled in the mountains, but we kept building. How can that be gone forever?"

"Elvienne, what are you talking about?"

She sighed. "I lived here once, for a while. Long before you were born. We built that jetty, or one that came before it . . . I forget . . ." She wiped her eyes with one finger. "Standing around crying won't get anything done. The cottage was over here."

The roof had collapsed on the cottage, but the gable end and most of the back wall still stood, scorched and rain-lashed. It was clear to Kayall that they would find nothing there. He hung back while Elvienne probed the ruins, sifting through the ash with a long stick, wrinkling her nose and uttering enchantments under her breath. He sat on a rock and watched the wind whip flurries across the lake. It was a barren place, with no cover. Nowhere to hide, and that made his skin itch.

He twisted round sharply as stones clicked behind him, but it was only Elvienne, frowning over an object in her hand. "What have you got there?" he asked.

"I found it in the rubble. It sang to me. It needed to be found."

Kayall shuffled up and let her sit down beside him. She showed him what she had found. A smooth grey pebble, shaped like an egg, smudged with ash from the burned cottage. Elvienne blew the loose ash off, and wiped the stone on her skirt. To Kayall, it looked very ordinary, but when he laid a hand on it he felt it thrumming with power.

"Can you talk to it?" he asked.

Elvienne frowned, poring over the stone, twisting it in her hands. Blurred images flashed across the surface, too fast for

Kayall to take in.

"I can feel his potential." Elvienne's voice was distant, her will focussed on the stone. "He's strong, but untamed. Carlon didn't train him well . . ."

"Why was that? He must have realised –" Elvienne cut him off with a sharp gesture.

"Something's happening," she said. Her hands shook, and tears crept down her cheeks, lodging in the lines on her face. "He was so sick . . ."

"The boy?" Kayall craned to see what was happening, but the parade of images was too tiny, and too swift.

"Carlon. He lost his wits, and . . . no! Oh no!" The pebble tumbled from her hands as she covered her face and sobbed.

"What happened?" Kayall hugged her against his chest, dreading the answer. She must have seen their friend's death, and it was too much for her to bear. He felt a prickle at the back of his own eyes, and blinked furiously as his vision blurred.

"The boy. The boy killed him. Killed him with that stone."

"How? No," he amended. "Don't tell me. I don't want to know."

He sprang to his feet and kicked the stone away, into the waters of the lake. How could Carlon have been murdered? And by the boy he was meant to be training! He clenched his fists, nausea rising at the depth of the betrayal. "I'll hunt him down. He'll suffer for what he did. Carlon deserved better than that."

"You can't say that. He was dying, he was in pain. Who knows what drove Liathan—?"

"He had no right!"

Elvienne rose, pulling her dignity around her like the shreds of a tattered cloak. "I can see there's no talking to you about this. You don't want to find the boy –"

"Oh, I want to find him all right." Kayall's knuckles were white, clenched around the hilt of his dagger.

"Not for the right reasons! Go back to Lambury, Kayall.

Your anger won't help our cause." She turned her back, dismissing him utterly with a simple gesture.

"I can't go back to Lambury!" Her stride did not falter. "Elvienne? Shit!" Kayall booted another pebble into the water and sank down onto the stone once more, head in hands, palms strangely damp. He wiped his eyes angrily. He could not stay here, in this wilderness, and Tushkian had made it clear he should keep away from Lambury. Where could he go?

He looked up. Elvienne had vanished over the brow of the nearest hill. He wiped his face, pushed the quivering anger deep into the pit of his belly. It could wait. It could wait until he found Liathan. Found him and punished him. Elvienne's misplaced compassion for the brat wouldn't protect him from Kayall's fury. He would tag along with her until she found Carlon's apprentice, and then the stars help him.

He pushed the clouds around moodily, like a child building blocks and then knocking them down in a fit of temper, until he judged enough time had passed that he would be able to catch up with Elvienne without looking as if he was chasing after her. He threw one last ill-tempered cloud towards the mountains, and froze as he felt the cold kiss of steel against the nape of his neck.

"Get up." The unseen holder of the blade was calm. Experienced. "Keep your hands where I can see them. No wizard tricks."

"I don't do 'wizard tricks'." Kayall tried to keep his voice as calm as the stranger's. "You have no idea who you're dealing with, do you?"

"I know enough." The cloth he slapped across Kayall's face reeked of sweat, rather than sleep-inducing herbs, but it still made him choke in surprise and disgust. Caught off guard, he barely had the chance to struggle as his assailant bound his hands behind him, jerking them into position.

"No talking, no hand waving. I'd like to see you magic your way out of this one!"

So would I, though Kayall, as the prod of a sword in his kidneys forced him back up the shore, past the cremated ruins of the hut where his friend had died. He wondered if Elvienne would sense his predicament. There must be a way to call to her.

His captor shoved him in the small of the back and he stumbled, heels snagging on the rocks. The right one ripped clear and he stumbled, thrown off balance by the jolt.

"Fucking dandy! Take them off!"

The blade scratched his spine as Kayall crouched to release the buckles and kicked both shoes and socks free, feeling cold earth and stone beneath his soles. He tried to pick the shoes up with bound hands, and his captor snatched them and flung them towards the lake. "No time for that, pretty boy! Get moving!"

Kayall still hadn't seen his assailant's face, but he had the impression of a large man. The voice was deep and rich. There was no tremor in the tip of the blade, and Kayall guessed he wouldn't hesitate to use it. His bare toes stubbed on the rocks as he stumbled up the shore towards a trio of horses, held by a big, placid-featured man who scanned him with little interest.

"You took your time, Cavan," he grumbled. "The others will be wondering where we got to. This him?"

"You see anyone else in this shithole?"

"I thought he left with a woman . . ." The moon-faced man shrugged. Kayall wriggled his toes against the cool earth, sending tendrils of energy down his legs into the ground, spreading out like a web. He hoped Elvienne would heed his call, wherever she had gone. He didn't have much time to send his signal; a sharp jab in the ribs distracted him and severed the connection.

"You going to get on this horse?" Cavan demanded. "Or don't wizards ride?"

"I told you, I'm not a bloody wizard. How do you expect me to mount with my hands tied—!"

The air erupted from his lungs as his assailant lifted him and flung him over the back of the horse, head and feet dangling, pommel digging into his abdomen. His nose was full of the warm scent of horse, and it was strangely comforting. If these men wanted to kill him, he would be dead already. Cavan mounted in front of him, replacing the equine smell with one that was more musky and cloying.

Kayall couldn't hear his abductor's conversation over the sound of hooves, the harness jangling and the wind rustling the grasses, but he guessed they were taking him back towards the river. Back to Lambury. The horses wore no livery, but the fingerprints of the Fruitmasters Guild were all over this. Where in all hells was Elvienne?

The horse pulled up with a jolt. If Kayall hadn't been crammed between the stinking man and the high-backed saddle, he would have fallen to the ground. He twisted his head, trying to see what was going on. They couldn't have reached the river already.

"You! Get down!"

The blow around the mage's head set his ears ringing. He slithered from the saddle and slumped on the ground, dizzy and confused. Cavan hauled him up by the shoulder, shaking him until his teeth rattled. "Is this your doing? Some stinking wizard's trick?"

Blocking the route ahead was a sheer wall of rock, higher than a horse could jump. Weathered and patterned with moss and lichen, it seemed to have grown out of the landscape. It had been there for centuries.

It had not been there this morning.

"Can we go though it?" Moon-face kicked the wall, and swore. There was nothing spectral about it. Kayall's lips twitched in a suppressed smirk. "Or round it, Cavan?"

"We'll have to go round. This is going to hold us up far too long. Fucking wizards!" Cavan vented his frustration with a boot to Kayall's gut that left him doubled-up and wheezing.

Before he could regain his breath, Cavan had lashed his hands to the pommel of his saddle.

"You walk from here," he said. "That way I can keep an eye on you!"

Kayall grinned. "It's not me you have to look out for!"

"What are you—Mother of stars!"

The ground in front of them split open like an over-ripe fruit. With the dull scrape of a blade emerging from a sheath, a second rock wall burst through the gap, stretching high above their heads and out to either side, throwing out grey arms to form a circle around the trio and their plunging, terrified horses. Moon-face fell on his knees, clutching at his chest, lips working a silent charm against evil magic. Cavan, more practical, rounded on his prisoner.

"You're doing this! Make it stop!"

Kayall shrugged. "How can it be me? Do you see me waving my hands about and muttering incantations? No? Because that's what wizards do!" He ducked, but couldn't dodge the swinging fist that connected with his jaw and threw him on his back in the dirt. He glared up at Cavan, and spat. "You decided to take on *mages*. How did you think it would end?"

Cavan dragged him up, fist bunched in the fabric of his shirt. His eyes rolled in fear. "I said make it stop!"

There was a slow crunching, like a body dragged on gravel. The stone walls shook, thin trickles of loose dirt streaming off their flanks. Kayall felt the energy pulsing up through his bare feet into his calves, as the ground trembled, and the ring of stone began to tighten

"The walls!" On his belly, Moon-face gibbered in fear. "The walls are closing in!"

"Shut up, Arne!" Cavan gave Kayall a furious shake. "Who's doing this, if not you? The woman? Tell her to stop, before she kills all of us!"

"Not the woman, no. I don't know who's doing this!"

"Liar!" Cavan shoved the mage away from him. He fell

against the wall, felt it pushing against his back with steady, unstoppable force. He laid his cheek to the cold earth.

Elvienne? Elvienne, are you trying to kill me?

He felt the hesitation, the pressure ease, just for a moment, before it resumed as if his words had gone unheard. He kicked at the wall, trying to force it away with his shoulder, but it pressed in on him. Solid, implacable. The horses bucked and snorted in fear, and a hoof caught him under the ribs, steel shoe ripping open shirt and skin. He rolled on his back, looking up at the diminishing circle of sky, feeling the stone push him beneath those trampling hooves, and he drummed his heels against the ground and howled in helpless frustration.

"Elvienne, you bitch! Let me out!"

He didn't know if he spoke aloud, couldn't hear his own voice over the cries of his captors, the grinding of stone, the relentless pressure in his chest. And then he was sliding, sliding through stone. Or rather, the rock was sliding over him, scraping his skin to rags with sharp, clawing fingers. He breathed in dust, choked, couldn't move with the weight that bore down on him, crushing his lungs. He could hear cracking, and wondered if it was his bones shattering, one by one . . .

All at once the sky was clear, and beautiful blue, so bright and startling he had to turn his face away. He felt the jab of a knee in his back, capable hands slicing through the rope that bound his wrists, lifting his shirt to inspect his injuries. He groaned. "If you ever do something like that to me again—"

"You'll know to expect it, won't you?" Elvienne's voice was prim. "Where are your shoes?"

"Bastard threw them in the lake—what does that matter?" He struggled to sit up, wheezing and indignant. Now the threat of death was lifted, he could feel the burning line of pain along his ribs. "You almost killed me! What were you thinking?"

"Listen." She unrolled a bandage from her pack and wrapped it tightly round his ribs. He winced at the pressure on his torso. "We need to find Liathan. This is bigger than us. Bigger than the Kingdom. I won't have anyone prevent me from finding that boy. Certainly not the hired thugs of a Guildmaster. Why didn't you tell me there was a chance they were following you?"

"I didn't think they were!" Kayall rubbed the blood back into his hands while Elvienne fixed the dressing. "Boranth needs to be less protective of his daughter. He's lucky I'm such a gentleman."

"You can tell him that if he ever catches up with you." Elvienne helped him to his feet, her grip surprisingly strong for an elderly woman. "The stones tell me Liathan went west from here. I assume he was heading towards the Ferrybane. We might find news there. Now we have two fresh horses . . ."

The horses that had formerly belonged to Boranth's men were cropping the grass. They seemed to have recovered from their ordeal in the ring of stone remarkably well. They certainly looked less disturbed than Kayall felt, but they kept their distance from the pillar of stone that rose from the earth like a limbless tree. Its surface was rough, and small plants clung to crevices in the rock as if it had stood there for many years.

"What happened to them?" As soon as Kayall asked the question, he wasn't sure he wanted to know. "Are they dead?"

"No." Elvienne's lips were thin as she headed towards the horses.

The base of the pillar was as wide as two men, standing close together. Kayall shuddered. "Elvienne! That's barbaric!"

She said nothing, but her shoulders lifted in a slight shrug.

"You can't leave them like that!"

"I can't have them follow us either." At his disgust, she relented. "When we find the boy, I'll let them out."

"*If* we find him, you mean?"

She shook her head. "Failing to find him is not an option. The more time we waste, the more danger he's in. Him and everyone around him. Including us, even the ground we walk on. So let's find him, shall we?"

Seven

THE RAIN TRICKLED from the overhanging eaves and dripped down Liathan's spine. He shivered, trying to back deeper into the corner where he had wedged himself to rest. He hadn't slept for three nights. His eyes were raw and gritty, and the streaks of rain on the wall opposite swirled in his vision, taunting him with elusive images. If he closed his eyes for just a moment, they would go away . . .

He jerked his head upright with a curse. It was too dangerous to sleep. The mages would find him, or the Guard, or . . . He clutched his temples, trying to remember who else he was running from. His flight from the wharf was a blur. The only thing that stood clear and terrible in his mind were those two broken shapes, sleeping under white cloth. The thought stung his eyes, making his nose dribble. He wiped it with the back of his hand. It was bleeding again. He stared down at the smear of blood in blank confusion, watching the stain swirl to form a snake between the base of his thumb and his wrist. It hissed, tongue flickering, head weaving from side to side.

"Why are snakes coming out of my nose?"

"You're bleeding." He hadn't heard the footsteps approaching down the alley, but now he stared at a pair of small boots, no bigger than a child's. They were cracked and stained, the soles held on with tattered string, and an inch of bare ankle protruded from the tops to meet the ragged hem of a wide, thick skirt, splattered with mud. "You need help. Come with me."

She wasn't a guard, and her almond eyes, sparkling blue in a deep tan face, told him she wasn't an Old One. The old man had always told him the eyes were the windows to the spirit. You could tell an Old One by their eyes. "Taking the green," he called it.

The girl extended a hand to him. She had a narrow face, with a pointed chin. Her hair was bundled on top of her head, held back with a bright strip of cloth, festooned with ribbons and trinkets. A copper-dipped leaf hung from one earlobe, a tiny bell from the other. When she moved her head, it made a faint tinkling sound.

Liathan gaped at her outstretched hand without comprehension. "Who are you?"

"No one uses their real name in this city. Do you want my help or not? I've been watching you for two days. You're lucky you've survived this long!"

Lucky. A smoking hole in an old man's sunken chest. Bodies huddled together under a white sheet. He didn't feel lucky, but he had escaped the worst fate, so far. He tried to rise and swayed, clutching the wall for support. "Will there be food?"

"You need a bed to lie on more than you need food. Come on, let's get out of the rain." The girl tucked her arm though his. He tried not to lean on her as they walked, but it was hard to stand upright.

"If I can't use your name, what can I call you?" Liathan asked. He hoped talking would help to keep him awake. The process of forcing one numb foot in front of the other felt like too much effort.

"You can call me Carousel."

"What does that mean?"

Her laugh set the bells in her hair jingling. "Have you seen travelling players? Sometimes they have a game. You sit in a chair hanging from a chain joined to a pole. They spin the pole around ever so fast, and the chairs spin out." She sniffed in derision. "That's a carousel. It's a babies' game. You've never seen one?"

"I grew up in the country," he offered.

"Really?" Her eyebrows, plucked to two thin lines, arched. "What's that like? It must be strange, coming here."

"Have you always lived here?" Liathan wanted to know more about this mysterious, confident girl, who walked through the rain with her head held high. He wondered fleetingly if he should trust her. He had trusted Chalice, and she led him to disaster. But the promise of food, and a bed, was a powerful lure, strong enough to override his dulled instincts.

"As far as I can remember. Quick, this way!" Her grip tightened on his arm as she steered him down a side street, away from the tramp of guard's boots. "It starts getting busy soon. It's easier to hide in a crowd."

Liathan was too tired to think. It was easier to let her lead him, on heavy, dragging feet, past the traders setting up their stalls for the day and brushing the detritus of the night before into the gutters. Carousel dropped to her haunches and snatched up a handful of berries, wiping the dirt from them on her richly-patterned skirt. She burst one between her lips, and made a face.

"You can have these, stray boy. They're going off, and you need them more than I do!"

The mauve berries tasted of dust and were flecked with green mould, but Liathan wolfed them down as if they were nectar. He couldn't remember the last time he ate.

Carousel watched him with approval. "Feeling better?"

"A bit. Thank you."

"When we get to where we're going you can have a proper meal. And a sleep." She took his arm and dragged him on again.

"Where *are* we going?" Liathan, the edge taken off his hunger, found the energy to be curious again.

She grinned. "You'll see!"

A stall holder on the far side of the street beckoned them over. He was piling cheap ceramics too high on his stand, teetering piles of crockery that looked as if they would overbalance at the slightest breath of air. They were gaudily painted, and many of the bowls and plates were already cracked, as if they had tumbled to the ground too many times already. Liathan leaned against the wall, reluctant to prop himself up on such a fragile edifice. The trader regarded him with narrowed eyes.

"Friend of yours, young Caro?"

"He's all right," she confirmed. "I'll vouch for him. What do you want?"

"Can you tell Noble I'll be late with the payment this moon? My wife's sick, and we've fallen behind with our wares . . ."

She shrugged. "I might tell him. I might forget. What's it worth to you to make sure I remember?"

The stall holder scowled. "You're all the bloody same, you lot."

"Would you rather deal with us, or Startide? I've heard the Silver Lady is a lot less patient than Noble . . ." Carousel held out her hand and wiggled her fingers expectantly. "Be smart."

The older man blew out his cheeks. "It's blackmail, that's what it is, Caro. And from a girl young enough to be my daughter. He's bringing you up all wrong!"

She smiled as he pressed a bright copper into her palm with poor grace. "I expect I'll turn out all right. Any other news?"

The stall holder sulked. "It'll cost you a copper to hear it, missy!"

She laughed. "Don't be daft! You wouldn't want me to get into trouble, would you?"

"I'd like to preserve your hide, if possible. There are a lot of patrols about today, make sure you don't run afoul of them."

She tilted her head, alert to the warning. "City Watch, or

Lord Carey's men?"

"Both. Just watch out."

"I'll be careful." She flashed a smile that didn't reach her eyes and moved away. Liathan had been grateful for the rest. His feet dragged as he stumbled in her wake. "If anyone asks," she said in a hushed voice, "tell them you're my brother."

They looked nothing alike, but he was too exhausted to argue, struggling to keep up with her long strides, through streets that grew more crowded as the rain eased and the sun punched patches of blue in the clouds above the city.

Carousel was right. It was easier to hide in a crowd, to duck away from the guards who seemed to be on every street corner as they made their way across the city to the southern districts, where the faces grew darker and the scent of spice thicker in the air. The houses were crammed close together here, and dark-skinned children played freely in the gutters. The girl seemed to relax as the overhanging upper storeys closed in above their heads to form a tunnel, with only a thin strip of patchy blue-grey sky between them.

"The City Watch won't follow us here," she said, twitching her skirts away from the muddy, grasping hand of a small boy who was trying to haul himself up by them. "Carey's men might, but they don't usually bother with people like us."

"People like us? What do you mean, people like us? And where are you leading me?" Liathan looked around in distaste. "It smells funny here."

"It's the spices the Telesians use in their food. This is the Telesian Quarter. It's not far now."

"Telesians?" Liathan looked with curiosity at the men and women passing them in the street, the women long-limbed, arms and legs covered, the men free-striding, rough-chinned and tall. They had an air of elegance which would have made him feel shabby even if he hadn't been sleeping in the gutter for three nights.

"Don't stare!" Carousel slapped him on the arm. It stung.

"My grandmother was a Telesian. Haven't you ever seen them before?"

"I told you, I grew up in the country! I thought we were at war with them!"

"Not for about twenty years. Did you grow up in a hole?"

"In a way." He shrugged, and she asked no further questions, taking a sharp right at the end of the street. The houses fell away, and Liathan blinked in the unexpected brightness. The smell of spice was driven from his nostrils, replaced with the pungent aroma of sluggish, dirty water. A tributary of the river snaked around the corner of the street and blocked his path. Directly ahead of them was a rough wooden footbridge, and, on the opposite bank, a high stone wall, breached with a rusty iron gate which squealed a protest as Carousel swung it open.

Beyond, the ground was boggy. Liathan pulled his foot free with a sucking sound, and watched the brackish water flood into his footprint. The grass was green and brown, and brambles sprawled across his path, catching the hems of his breeches. He followed in Carousel's wake, stepping high as they slopped across the swamp to a raised flagstone pavement, clipped clear of the pervasive brambles.

It was like walking down a street of miniature houses, if the street was silent and all the dwellings sealed with stone. Every tiny house was subtly different; some had pointed roofs, some curved, some had columns on either side of the doors decorated with carven trails of ivy or images of voluptuous women, others were modest and plain. Liathan brushed his hand across the rough stone as they passed. "People don't live here, do they?"

"Not while they're alive!" Carousel laughed at his sharp intake of breath. "The Telesians don't burn their dead," she explained. "Usually they bury them, but the ground's too soft here." She stepped off the path and dug the toe of her boot into the yielding mud to illustrate. "The water stands in any hole you dig. So they lay the bodies in these tombs."

Liathan looked around with fresh interest. "It must go on for miles! How many tombs are there?"

Carousel shrugged. "I don't think anyone's ever counted."

He followed her through a labyrinth of paths. She moved like she had travelled this way many times, and he was too exhausted to do more than trudge in her footsteps. If she ran off and left him now, he would never find his way out again.

She stopped at last. They were in an older part of the cemetery. The brambles were sharper here, the bindweed that scrambled over the ancient tombs thicker, more determined to cling to the stone. The carvings had been obliterated by weather and time, and many of the tombs were cracked and crumbling. Carousel stepped off the path, and the undergrowth parted before her as if accustomed to being bent back. It sprang back into shape as her body passed through it. The brambles were not so gentle with Liathan. They clawed his arms and legs, ripping fine lines in the fabric of his clothes, and painting a tattoo of blood across his bare skin. He was panting as he caught up with the girl. She stood flat against the wall of a tomb. Her skin was unmarked.

"Sorry about that." She thumbed a few spots of blood off his cheek. "I'm used to going this way. You learn where to tread." She laid her hands flat against the wall, stepped sideways, and vanished.

Liathan blinked. A second ago there had been a girl, now there was only empty wall before him. Panic gripped him.

"Carousel? Where have you gone?"

"Right here!" Her voice was muffled. "Step forward, and then sideways. Trust me!"

Liathan sucked in a deep breath, and stepped forward until his cheek pressed against the gritty stone. Turning his head to look in the direction Carousel had vanished, he saw a fissure in the stone where the wall had dropped away from the roof, leaving a crack just wide enough to squeeze through. The pressure of stone hemming him in was uncomfortable, but it only lasted a few seconds.

"Mind your head." In the dark, Carousel sounded amused, and her warning came a fraction too late as Liathan straightened and smacked his skull on the low roof. "Hang on, there's a light around here somewhere."

He heard the scrape of candlestones close by, and a light flickered into life. The space they stood in was narrow, stone caskets piled up to the ceiling on both sides of the room, looming over them. At the far end of the passage a black hole yawned in the floor, and Carousel's candle revealed a rough flight of steps leading down.

She held the light high and he followed her, scraping his heels on the narrow stair. Another room, below the first, but identical. The stench of ancient bones and dust was cloying. Liathan covered his mouth with his hand as Carousel swung to the right and vanished between two stacks of caskets. He wished she would stop doing that.

Her candle bobbed and weaved in the wider passage ahead, a bright spot of comfort in a decaying place of death. The passages twisted and turned, as bewildering as the path through the cemetery. The damp, musty walls gave way to dry stone, tunnels barred by locked doors, which Carousel opened with a key that hung around her neck. Liathan guessed they were moving further away from the river, but he couldn't tell in which direction.

After an age of underground wandering, they came to a shallow flight of five steps, leading up to an iron-studded door that had no keyhole. Carousel knocked, and a slit in the door opened to release a beam of light. Liathan couldn't see the face beyond it, nor could he catch the muttered exchange between the door-guardian and the girl, but the hatch slammed shut and the door swung silently inward, spilling a friendly glow into the dark corridor.

If the light was welcoming, the smell of roasting meat in the room beyond almost drove Liathan to his knees. His belly ached, and he wrapped his arms tight around it to try and control the cramps as he followed Carousel up the steps.

There were two long tables down either side of the chamber, and everyone sat at them appeared to be eating. Carousel beckoned to a man with a helmet of tight grey curls, but her words were muted by the sound of chewing, the scrape of forks against plates, the gentle slop of gravy on bread. Liathan drifted towards the table, helpless in the grip of his hunger, the smell of food bursting in his nostrils and mouth.

"Here!" Carousel pushed a roll into his hand; pork and dripping gravy, wrapped in crusty bread. "Eat and walk. Noble wants to see you now, before you fall over in a faint!"

His mouth stuffed too full to reply, Liathan swallowed hard, wincing as he forced lumps of bread down his throat. He licked the warm gravy from his fingers, and sucked it from where it had splashed down his shirt. He could feel the warmth travelling down his gullet, and he belched, feeling a little sick.

"Don't spew it all back up again," Carousel chided. "You want to make a good impression on Noble, don't you?"

Liathan gulped, eyes watering, and wiped the worst of the gravy from his mouth with the back of his hand. There was nothing he could do about the state of his shirt, or his hair. Carousel grinned, tweaking an errant tuft behind his ear. "You'll do. I don't think he cares what you look like."

She pushed him through the door ahead of her into a small audience chamber, bright with the light of torch and candle. Liathan stepped forward into the glare, feeling naked and exposed. He could see nothing but brightness, and he screwed his eyes shut, after-images dancing on his closed lids. He swayed.

"For Calarian's sake, fetch the boy a chair before he falls over!"

Liathan felt someone press him down by the shoulders, and hard wood at the back of his knees. He slumped, grateful but bewildered.

"Shuffle it over here, kid. Let's get a look at you."

His vision was starting to clear now. He rubbed his eyes.

"Carousel love, snuff some of those candles. And then go and make sure there's a bed made up for the boy."

With the blazing light dimmed, and Carousel dismissed, Liathan huddled in the chair, biting his nails. All thoughts of making a good impression drained from his head.

"Are you scared? You don't need to be scared. We'll look after you here."

The man Carousel had called Noble leaned forward, elbows on his desk, a smile tugging the corners of his generous mouth. His skin was dark, not tan like Carousel's, but like the dark between the stars, and his close-cropped hair clung to his head like moss on a stone. He steepled his hands under his chin and regarded Liathan with amusement.

"You're not what I expected, Leyon of the Estmarch."

Liathan bit his tongue. Noble might know the name he travelled under, but he didn't know his real name.

"If that is your real name, which I doubt. No," he held up a hand, "I'm not going to ask you. Once you tell someone your true name, you give them power over you. True names are for those that walk in daylight."

He extended a large hand, long-fingered, heavy with rings. A Telesian gesture of friendship. Liathan shook it.

"You can call me Noble. I've been watching you since you caused that little scene in the Black Rat. I'm sorry about your friends."

"Thank you." Liathan's voice cracked with thirst. Noble poured him a mug of ale from the decanter on the table, and pushed it across to him.

"That'll wet your throat, kid. Suppose you tell me what happened at the Rat?"

The ale was strong, and it made his head spin. Liathan said nothing.

"I know you used some kind of magic. That's the only

explanation for it. Can you control it?"

Liathan stared at his knees, shook his head.

"Would you like to learn how?"

The question, framed gently, caught him off guard. "You can teach me that?"

Noble laughed. "Not me! I don't have a magical rib in my chest. But my friend here, he can find out what you're made of, and how you can put it to use. Would you like him to try?"

"Your friend—?" Focussed on Noble, Liathan hadn't noticed anyone else in the room. Now the shadows gathered in the corner rippled, like a man throwing off a cloak, and a stocky figure stepped forward. He had a wide, flat head, his bulging eyes rimmed around with jet. His skin, chalk-white, was patterned with black lines, twisting and curling over the contours of his face. Designs of leaves, of the constellations, of strange twisted geometry. The spirals looped down his neck and vanished beneath the loose black shirt he wore. Liathan wondered if the markings went all the way down, and he giggled. The ale was definitely going to his head.

"Dweller, see what you make of him," Noble ordered, leaning back and taking a sip of ale. "Is he what we think?"

The patterned man crouched before Liathan, and took his chin in his hand, twisting his face around to study it under the light. His eyes were bulbous and watery, like the blistered whites of two fried eggs. Liathan's own eyes watered in sympathy under the scrutiny. It felt as if his brain was being sucked towards the front of his skull, tendrils like ivy wrapping around it and dragging it forward. The swirls on Dweller's face shifted and shimmered, reaching out to strangle him.

Liathan felt the heat building in his chest, fury at the invasion by this stranger, whose hoary nails gripped the front of his shirt. Dweller's eyes bulged and stared, swirling white in his field of vision, sending creepers into his mind . . .

"Get off me!"

There was a crack, the sharp scent of smoke, and Dweller

was hurled across the room to crash upside-down into the opposite wall. He hit the floor in a crumpled heap and lay still, steam rising from his skin. Noble half-rose from his seat.

"Dweller?" No reply. "Have you killed him, Leyon?"

Liathan stared down at his hands. They shook like leaves in a gale, and tendrils of smoke rose from his fingertips. "I didn't mean to hurt him!" The exclamation came out in a rush, words tumbling over each other. "I only wanted to stop him poking in my brain. I didn't know that was going to happen!"

Dweller groaned, raising his head, and Noble relaxed back into his chair and took a long drink, watching with keen interest as the little decorated man forced himself to his knees, clutching the edge of the desk to aid him to his feet.

"Well?"

Dweller rubbed his temples and grinned, revealing teeth filed to sharp points. "I'd say there's a spark there. It's untamed, and I can't pin down the nature of it, but it's strong."

"Not green magic then?" Noble asked, topping up Liathan's drink.

"Not by his eyes."

"Good," Noble declared. "Then we can use it. That's if you're willing to join us, young Leyon?"

"Join you?" He yawned, suddenly sleepy.

"Join the Nobility. We can protect you, hone your talents. All I ask in return is your loyalty. Can you promise me that?"

It seemed little to offer in return for protection, and training. And Liathan was too exhausted to question the pact. He nodded.

"That's settled then. All you need now is your name."

"My . . . name?"

"To disguise your true name, which will be held between you and I, and the Dweller who knows all. What do you think, Dweller?

The little man was drawing his cloak of shadows back around him, fading into the wall. With his aching eyes, Liathan could barely see him. Even his voice was fading. "He has a spark . . ."

"Spark, yes. A spark of power, a spark of life. From now on, Leyon of the Estmarch, your name will be Spark."

Liathan felt he should say something, offer his thanks, but his limbs were leaden and his head was dropping down onto his chest. He barely felt the ale flagon fall from his numb fingers, but he heard Noble chuckle.

"Stars bless the child. Look at him. Little Spark, completely sparked out."

Eight

THE TRAVEL CASES were piled beside the door to the hall. Coming down the stairs, Bastian disturbed an empty wine bottle with his foot. It bounced away in front of him, coming to rest against the largest chest. He sighed. "Mother!"

"She's already in the carriage." Allo's voice was ragged. "I had the servants put her there when she passed out. We'll stack the bags around her. Are you packed?"

This was the conversation he had dreaded. "I'm not going."

"What do you mean, you're not going? She threw a small bag out of the front door and turned on him, hands on hips, with an irresistible pout. "You have to go! What about the plague?"

He caught her round the waist. "I can't leave you on your own with Father, can I? It would be wrong." He would die if he was forced to walk out of the door and leave her behind in this house of sickness.

She pulled away, frowning. "What about Mama? Someone needs to look after her . . ."

"Jago will take care of her." Their oldest brother had a holding a few days ride out of the city to the east. His wife was a sturdy, capable woman; Sharna would be able to handle their volatile mother well.

Allorise shook her head. "I won't hear of it, Bastian. It's too dangerous."

"If it's too dangerous for me to stay, it's much too dangerous for you to be here alone!"

She faltered. "Dada asked me to stay. He needs me, I can't leave him!"

"Allorise, my Allo," he gripped her shoulders, gazing down into her upturned face. "You don't have to cope with this alone. I'm staying with you, and that's final."

"I'd rather you—" Bastian pressed a finger to her lips to silence her, and nodded to a scurrying servant. "Load up the coach. I won't be joining you."

Allorise smiled, and leaned her head against his shoulder. "I hope you won't find me boring company. I have to spend so much time taking care of Father. He won't trust anyone else to look after his affairs!"

"Maybe I could help. I want to help, Allo."

"Maybe." Bastian wrapped his arms around his sister's waist and they watched in silence as the few remaining servants carried the last of the luggage from the hall, leaving the two youngest children of House Carey alone in an echoing mansion with only their dying father for company.

🔥

It was remarkable how quickly the streets cleared before the passage of the plague doctor, as though a flapping cloak of contamination billowed around him as he walked. The plague doctor and the Silver Lady walked side by side along the banks of the river, careful not to touch. If not for his garb, they could have been two friends out for an evening stroll along the avenue, beneath the whispering poplars that concealed their words.

The Silver Lady dressed to match her name; robes the colour of moonlight, and a sweeping hood to conceal her face. She walked briskly, a clipped stride that revealed her irritation.

"Trust my brother to finally grow a spine, just when I need him out of my life!"

Shadow's voice was muted by leather. "Will he interfere?"

"With the business? I won't let him. You don't need to worry about that. But his presence makes things . . . *awkward.*"

"Do you want me to take care of him?"

Allorise was shocked at the suggestion. "Of course not! He's my brother!"

Shadow waved placating hands. "It was just a thought, my Lady."

"Put it from your head. My family are not to be threatened." Her lips snapped shut, and they walked the next twenty yards in angry silence, before Shadow cleared his throat.

"Starstone prices are up, my Lady. The scarcity is beginning to pinch."

"Don't let it pinch too much," she told him. "Let's not price ourselves out of the market. What about the bawdy houses? Is the Lily still holding out?"

He nodded. "I fear so. I think Noble has something over them, or maybe the Dame is just loyal . . . Perhaps we should let the Lily go?"

"And show weakness?" Allorise shook her head. "I've worked too hard and for too long to risk throwing it all away. Not when it's all coming together at last. I hate to say it, but we need a razor man down there. Show the Dame that Noble can't protect her, and hopefully she'll turn to Startide."

"And if she doesn't?"

"We've tried persuasion. Now let's apply force. She'll come round when she starts losing money and customers."

Behind the mask, Shadow's face was unreadable. "As my Lady wishes. Talking of the Nobility . . ."

"Must we?" Allorise flounced, seating herself on a bench

overlooking the river and taking out a soft cloth to buff her long nails. "The Nobility irritate me. Maybe I can set dear Bastian to sort them out?" She giggled at the thought of Bastian taking control of anything. Her brother was a study in weakness.

"They'll irritate you more when you hear this." Shadow sat beside her, and eased his fingers under the edge of the long-nosed mask to scratch the peeling skin beneath. "The Nobility have the boy."

"The mage-born brat? Damn!" Allorise flicked the cloth at the tiny flies that swarmed under the trees. "I didn't expect Noble to move so fast. We'll have to get him back. That wretched man inspires too much loyalty."

"Not from me." Flakes of skin drifted from beneath Shadow's mask to land in Allorise's lap. She looked at them in disgust.

"How fortunate I am to have your loyalty, my faithful Shadow. Believe me, it will be rewarded. Just get me the boy."

᳞

The house felt much bigger with everyone gone. Allorise had left for the evening, Bastian watching from an upper window as she climbed into her private carriage. She'd checked her reflection in a small hand mirror before drawing up the hood of her moonlight cloak. She was so beautiful; her perfection left a gnawing in his guts that strong drink couldn't quench. He leaned his head against the window and watched her drive away from him, down the path and out through the heavy iron gates that defended the Carey stronghold from the city his family were sworn to protect.

He was still sitting there, frozen in place, awaiting her return, when a tentative knock came at the door. It was a struggle to lift his head from the cool glass.

"Enter!"

A maid, one of the few who had stayed behind. She

curtseyed, while he tried to remember her name.

"It's Vio, isn't it? Is something wrong?"

Her skin had a greenish tinge. "I think you should see this, Lord Bastian."

"What is it?" He pushed down off the window ledge, grateful for the distraction.

"There's a smell . . ."

"Just a smell?"

She grimaced. "You need to come with me, sir. I've never smelled anything like it!"

Vio led him down the stairs to the first floor, and along the wide, carpeted landing to his mother's private reception chamber. This was the room where she drank small, elegant glasses of wine with the society ladies of Cape Carey, while their husbands talked business in the hall. In the evenings, the glasses were larger, and she handled them in a less elegant fashion.

The room hadn't been used since Lord Carey fell sick, but that was no reason for the rotten stench that billowed forth as he opened the door. He choked, pulling his shirt across his nose and swallowing bile. Vio hung back, refusing to set a foot across the threshold.

"Has a rat died in here?" he asked her, gasping. A dozen putrid rats, by the stink. "Run and get some scented candles. We'll drive the smell out, or mask it, before Allo finds out."

Vio was only too keen to run off at his bidding, and Bastian pressed on into the room alone, trying not to inhale the rancid air too deeply. The room was gloomy, and he fumbled with the window catch and threw back the shutters, hoping the fresh air would drive out the smell and relieve his nausea. He sucked in a lungful of city air, tainted with horse-dung, smoke and ale, and turned back to the room. He was determined to find the source of the smell and get rid of it.

There was a faint scratching at the edge of his hearing, almost lost under the noise drifting in from the city. It sounded like mice crawling in the space between this floor and the next, tiny claws skittering over the woodwork. There was a darker patch on the ceiling, and he wondered if it was damp coming through. As he stood staring at it, he saw something small and wriggling drop from the ceiling and vanish behind the sideboard.

Not a mouse. Bastian dragged a chair below the patch of damp, and climbed up onto the sideboard. Straining on tiptoe with the tip of his dagger extended, he could reach the ceiling. He made an experimental prod at the dark stain on the plaster, expecting to make a small hole and scare whatever was scratching. Instead there was a rustle, like silk sheets sliding over each other, and the plaster sloughed away. The hole gaped, not black, but white and wriggling, pouring forth a stream of bloated, squirming maggots that cascaded over him, in his hair, in his eyes, down his shirt. Bastian yelled, stepping back from the stream. The room lurched as he fell, He crashed against the chair and brought it down on top of him on the carpet. He lay, winded and stunned, feeling tiny bodies wriggling all over his skin. Then he was sick.

"Lord Bastian? Lord Bastian, should I fetch water?"

Vio's voice came from far away, but as Bastian realised when he raised his head, that was because she stood outside the door, still refusing to enter the room. He spat out a few last chunks of vomit and a couple of wriggling bodies that had crept into his mouth, and swallowed, trying not to be sick again.

"Wine," he croaked, rolling onto his hands and knees. "And get this mess cleaned up!"

"There's wine in the sideboard, sir."

"Don't be such a bloody coward, Vio! Maggots won't hurt you." She didn't move, and he wrenched open the cupboard himself. He grabbed a glass and poured himself a generous measure of Telesian blue, knocking it back in two large mouthfuls.

The second glass steadied his nerves, and by the third he

was beginning to see the funny side of the affair, especially now most of the maggots had burrowed under the edge of the carpet and only a few were still dripping from the hole in the ceiling. He extended the bottle towards Vio. "Come and have a drink with me!"

She took a few tentative steps into the room, looking up as if she feared another onslaught from above. "Shouldn't you find out where they're coming from, Lord Bastian?"

"Yes, I probably should." He clambered to his feet, clinging on to the sideboard for support and shaking the last few maggots from his hair. "I'll check my father's room, to make sure they're not coming from there. You stay here and clean up."

There was a guard on his father's door, at Allorise's insistence. She was paranoid about the sickness spreading, but Bastian had not expected to be opposed. He looked down in surprise at the short spear blocking his entry. "What's going on here?"

"Lady Allorise said no one was to go in, sir."

"Yes, but she didn't mean me . . ."

The spear didn't waver. "She said no one was to go in," the literal-minded fool repeated, a fraction louder.

"Are you defying me? I remind you that with my mother sick and my father incapacitated, I'm the head of this household. Allorise is out, and I need to speak to my father. If you don't let me in, you can start looking for new employment!"

The spear tip wobbled, then dropped. Bastian patted the guard on the arm as he passed. "Don't worry," he assured him. "I won't tell my sister. It can be our secret!"

Lord Carey's room was dark and airless. The shutters were closed, smothered by heavy velvet drapes. All the furniture was stained black and old, hulking shapes in the gloom. Bastian gestured to the guard. "You there, bring me a candle."

He could dimly make out the figure of his father, a pale white shape in the great dark bed. There was an evil stench, like that in his mother's reception chamber, magnified by the close atmosphere of the room.

"Father? Father, can you hear me?"

The guard handed him the lit candle, and Bastian held it high over the bed. The yellow light washed over his father's face, the sunken cheeks, the empty folds of skin hanging loose around his jowls. His eyes were open, staring sightless at the ceiling, and from the bed came the same silken rustle and faint scratching Bastian had heard in the room below, just before the ceiling collapsed.

Father!

The cry died in his throat as he fell to his knees and buried his head in his father's sunken chest.

Nine

TIME TO PUT you to work, young Spark!"

Spark looked up as he heard his name echo down the long hall where the Nobility gathered to eat. He had mooched around underground for several days, trying to stay out of the way and learn the ropes at the same time. Carousel seemed to have taken a shine to him. Wherever he went she'd crop up, with her ready smile, keen to tease and help him out in equal measure. Noble's smile widened to include her. "You too, my fine lady. Time to strap on your dancing shoes!"

Carousel skipped to her feet, clapping her hands in delight. "Where to, Noble?"

"Round the back of the Woodsman's Rest. The customers like something young and pretty to look at, and you're both."

She beamed. Spark felt an unreasonable stab of envy at being excluded from the compliments.

"Spark, go with Mule and Auster," Noble told him. "They'll look after you, and show you what to do. Carousel, you're with the troupe. I know you'll do me proud, and when you do," he smiled, "we need to start talking about your future. Go get changed now."

She ran to do his bidding. Mule, a long-faced, dour man,

tapped Noble lightly on the elbow. Spark was close enough to overhear his words.

"Are you sure you want to hit the Woodsman? The Silver Lady won't like you working her patch."

"Then make sure she doesn't find out! She's trying to sew up all the territory on this side of the river, but I won't be muscled out, I promise you. She'll soon learn to keep to her own streets. If she doesn't, we'll have to teach her. Spark!" Noble beckoned the boy closer. "Go with Mule. Do exactly as he says. If he tells you to run, you run, got me?"

Spark nodded, and followed the doleful Mule out of the room and through the warren of passages leading back up to the cemetery. It was only as they emerged through the narrow gap in the walls of the tomb concealing the entrance that he realised Mule hadn't spoken, and he had no idea what was going to happen.

"Mule? What's going on? Who's the Silver Lady?"

"Listen," Mule rounded on him and grabbed him by the arm, squeezing his flesh until he bit back a squeal. "You don't talk about her, not outside of walls. You just watch out for her and her friends. Do as I tell you and we'll all get home safe. You follow me?"

"Absolutely."

"Good." Mule's lips snapped shut with a finality that brooked no argument. Spark sighed, and followed him through the trampled, boggy paths in the nettles and ivy, along the flagged pavements and out of a different gate to the one Carousel had brought him through.

It was a bright blue autumn day. The sunlight hurt his eyes after so long underground. Spark shivered in the chill air as he hurried after his companion through the maze of streets, the scents and colours of the Telesian Quarter falling behind them as they headed towards the centre of the city, which seemed drab in comparison.

The Woodsman's Rest was tucked down a narrow side

street, its overhanging upper storey almost propped up by the house opposite. To Spark, all these narrow alleys looked the same, but he assumed Mule knew where he was going, right up to the point where he led him straight past the front door of the tavern without giving it a glance. He headed towards the end of the alley and turned sharp left, into a street so narrow two men would have struggled to pass each other. Another left turn, and Spark was surprised when the buildings fell away to leave an open space, longer than it was wide, as if an entire row of houses had been wiped from the face of the city. The space was paved. Tired-looking grass struggled up between the slabs. There were benches outside the back door of the Huntsman, and a couple of taverns opposite. It would have been a convivial space in summer, and even with autumn closing in it was warm enough for men to sit outside, chew spyme, and murmur amongst themselves as they played dice.

There was little dice-playing going on this afternoon. A theatrical troupe had set up in the square, and drawn up a thick wire between two posts, twice as high as a man's head. The circus master kept up a constant stream of banter, and he drew a curious crowd.

Mule slipped into an empty seat, and indicted for a serving maid to bring him two drinks. He sat with his back to the spectacle, paying it no heed, and took a pair of dice from his belt pouch. In a low, casual voice, he said, "Do you see Auster? Look, but don't look like you're looking."

Spark rattled the dice, watching over Mule's shoulder. "I see him."

"Move when he moves. He'll meet you."

Spark kept one eye on the dice game, the other on the tall, freckled southerner lurking in the shadows of the building opposite. The ringmaster was hitting his stride now. He had a fire eater going through his routine, but Spark felt that the crowd were restless, hoping for something more.

Auster pushed himself off the wall, moving as if bored. He

didn't even look their way.

"Should I go now?" Spark asked.

Mule nodded. "If it all goes arse up, we meet by the Horse Fair Bridge. You know where that is?"

It seemed pointless for Spark to tell him he had no idea. "I'll find it."

The dice rolled across the table. Two fours.

"Get moving. Don't go straight to him, lurk at the edge of the crowd. He'll come to you."

A four and a three.

"Be careful, kid."

He sounded almost affectionate. Spark downed his drink, and wandered over to the fringes of the crowd, which thickened as people emptied out of the nearby taverns to watch the fun. The fire eater, on an elevated platform, blew a plume of flame over the heads of the watchers. There were gasps and a smattering of applause. Caught up in the moment, Spark clapped along with the rest, until he felt a light touch against his elbow.

"Hey kid, you're new. Enjoying the show?"

Auster was tall and thin, with large white teeth that overlapped his lower lip, like a coney. His skin, as white as his teeth, was dusted with freckles. He winked, and beckoned Spark back a few steps.

"When she does her stuff," he said, in a low voice, "we get in, do what we must, and get out. Watch me, and do as I do. If you think you can't hack it, fall back. If you fuck up, yell and run. I'll meet you by the bridge. If you get caught, someone will come for you. Noble never leaves a man behind. Have you got all that?"

Spark nodded. "I think so."

"Don't look so sick. You'll be fine! Here she comes now. Follow my lead."

A ripple ran through the crowd, a collective sigh at anticipation rewarded at last. Auster drifted back to the fringes, slipping the knife from his belt. Spark drew his own blade, but his hand shook, and he had to clamp his fingers around the hilt to steady his grip. Were they going to stab someone?

The circus-master was making an introduction, in jubilant tones, but Spark couldn't hear the words over the blood buzz in his ears. The crowd roared and stamped impatiently, and Auster seized the moment to dart in.

Spark saw the flash of his blade. It was over in a heartbeat, the slash, the victim's purse slipping from belt to hand to bag in one silky movement, and Auster moved on as if nothing had happened. His target didn't even twitch.

Auster winked as he passed. *Your turn*, he mouthed.

The tremble in his hand was back. Spark bit his lip, forcing his will down his arm, stilling that treacherous quiver. The crowd, almost a single entity, had its back to him, hooting and cheering at something he couldn't see.

Auster nudged him, and pointed at a heavy man, with rolls of fat spilling over his belt. On the belt, bouncing with every movement, his money-purse was loose, carelessly tied. It was a moment's work to lift it, slash the strings, and press it back into Auster's outstretched hand. Spark felt sure the rapid thumping of his heart would raise the alert, but all the fat man did was stretch up on his tiptoes to see over the heads of the crowd.

They moved away, Auster offering Spark a toothy grin. He flicked the blade of his dagger to indicate another victim. Motioning Spark to stay back, he moved in. The target pushed forward into the crowd, and Auster pushed with him.

Left alone, Spark scrambled up onto a nearby bench. He wanted to keep an eye on Auster, and he was bursting to get a good look at what the crowd was watching. He wasn't short, but wherever he stood a taller man seemed to be right in front of him.

He balanced on the bench and watched the girl climbing the pole. She wore a costume of iridescent feathers and lace. As she stood on the tiny plinth at the top of the pole, arms stretched to the sky, one long, bare leg stretched elegantly behind her, the crowd sighed as one.

She straightened, and Spark's breath caught. This vision, this glittering bird with the long, shapely legs and the tiny waist, balancing high above the crowd like a feather poised on the breeze, was Carousel.

He wanted to call to her, but his heart was in his throat, choking off his words. She stepped out onto the wire with a light, springing step, blowing kisses to the crowd. Far above their heads, Carousel danced on air, feathers fluttering in the breeze, making it look easy. While below . . .

"Hsst!" At the hiss from the level of his knees, Spark remembered why he was here. Auster glared at him. "Get down!" he whispered furiously. "Do you want everyone to notice you?"

Shamed, Spark scrambled down from the bench. Auster gave him a light shove. "Come on kid, do your job and we can get out of here."

"Sorry, yes." Spark rubbed his eyes, trying not to look up.

"A couple more and we'll have a good haul. Over there." Auster pointed and stood back. It was clear he wanted Spark to work alone.

He tried to focus on his target, a thin man in an embroidered, long-sleeved surcoat that screamed money. His purse was as fat as a kindling woman's belly, and it hung over his hip beside his dagger. A tricky lift, but Auster must think it worth the risk. The mark stared skywards, open mouthed at Carousel dancing on the wire overhead.

Spark wriggled through the crowd until he came up against the merchant's side. The man smelled of musky Telesian perfume, and his oiled hair was slicked back from his forehead towards his collar. His hands hung limp, his fingers heavy with gold and gems. The coins in his purse clinked faintly as Spark brushed against it, and he held his breath, wondering if the merchant would notice.

The music—Spark had not heard the music before, but Carousel must have been dancing to it the whole time—the drums and lyre reached a thrumming crescendo. The crowd surged forward. Something was happening on the wire above. Distracted, Spark made a clumsy lunge for his target's purse, severed it with his blade as Carousel cartwheeled impossibly, high above his head, across the square. A glittering pinwheel of girl and feathers.

"Hey! You little shit!"

The purse was in his hand. Spark stared at it dumbly, and at the shallow, bleeding slash in his victim's leg. A hand clamped down on the back of his neck and he stared cross-eyed at the blade pressed below his nose. The merchant scowled at him. "What the fuck are you doing? Give back my coin, you little bastard!"

"Let go of me!" Spark felt the heat, the panic, rising through his chest. Quicker this time, heightened by fear and adrenaline. "Get off! You don't know what's going to happen!"

The merchant shook him until his teeth rattled. "Oh, I know what's going to happen. You're going to give back my coin, and then I'm going to hand you over to the City Watch!" He seized Spark's arm above his knife hand and twisted it savagely.

"That hurts!" An eruption of fire, rushing along his arm, thrust the merchant away from him. The man cursed, stumbling back, clutching at his hand as the blade clattered to the ground.

"Here!"

"Don't push!"

"What's wrong with you?"

The merchant regained his balance. "That little thief tried to magic me!" He pointed a smouldering hand at Spark. "Get him!"

At the mention of magic, there was a sinister stir through the crowd. No one was watching Carousel any more. Spark looked around desperately for Auster and Mule, but they had vanished. He was on his own.

There seemed only one thing to do, and that was brazen it out.

He made a few vaguely mystic passes, aided by the sparks trailing from his fingertips. "Yes, stay back! I am the last of the ancient order of Flame Wielders, and I can burn you all with a gesture!"

The nearest men backed off. "He doesn't look all that," someone muttered.

"He hasn't even got green eyes!" the enraged merchant insisted. "He's no bloody mage! Let's get him!"

"Get back!" He waved his hands again. No sparks. Nothing. "I'm warning you . . ."

"Get the thief!"

"Smash his head in!"

"Come on!" Spark felt a fierce yank at his collar. "Run!"

In her skimpy costume, Carousel was all legs. They were all Spark could see as she dragged him by the hand through the crowded streets, hurdling the pavements and scrambling over low walls. "Where did Auster say to meet?" she panted over her shoulder as they fled.

"Horse Fair Bridge. Do you know where that is?"

"It's not far, come on!"

Another alley, another wall, higher than before. Carousel scrambled up to sit astride it, long, bare leg hanging down, knees grazed by the rough stone. She hitched her costume up to better cover her breasts, and extended her hand down to Spark. "We're near the Horse Fair now. I don't think anyone's chasing us. Though stars know what the Trader district will make of these stupid clothes!"

"I think your clothes are fine," muttered Spark, as Carousel dropped down the far side of the wall. If she heard him, she didn't respond.

Carousel needn't have worried. Everything was for sale in the Trader district. She could have been bought and sold five times over before they reached a stall selling cloaks. She elbowed Spark in the ribs. "I'll distract him." She nodded at the stall holder, an angular Telesian with a drooping moustache.

"You steal a cloak. Meet you at the end of the street!"

"Carousel, I think I've done enough stealing—" but she wasn't listening as she made subtle adjustments to her costume, her stance. All at once her shape was more revealed, yet somehow she had exposed no additional flesh. She strolled towards the stall holder and struck up a conversation, asking him about fabrics, running long fingers along the hems and stitching, drawing him towards the far side of the stall. Spark waited until his back was turned. He grabbed a cloak and stuffed it under his arm, scooping up the trailing fabric and ducking out of sight before the Telesian could turn and catch him in the act. Moving like a crab, he scuttled away from the stall, heart racing, limbs tingling with adrenaline. It was as good as cutting purses; the risk, the thrill. He could see why Auster wore such a broad grin. He felt his own mouth stretching as he scampered towards the spot Carousel had indicated.

She joined him there, ambling through the crowds as if unaware of her semi-naked state, or the admiring glances it drew. She took Spark's arm and nudged him into the mouth of a nearby alley.

"Did you get it?"

Spark slipped the cloak from beneath his arm and bundled it into Carousel's outstretched hands. She grinned. "Feels good, doesn't it?"

"Little bit!"

"I'll miss it when I move on." Carousel swung the forest-green cloak around her shoulders. It fell to her knees, covering the scanty costume. A few lonely feathers drifted to the ground at her feet.

"Move on—?"

"Let's go to the bridge." She didn't elaborate on her comment. "It's this way."

The Horse Fair was busy, and no one spared them a second glance now that Carousel was covered up. They picked their way through the piles of dung that gathered flies on the cobbles, and finally arrived at the bridge, a wide, single-span arch that swept high over the tumbling waters of the River Lam. No one was there waiting for them.

"What do we do?" Spark asked.

Carousel shrugged. "Hang about, I suppose." She hugged her cloak tighter around her. The wind was cold, pushing a squall of rain before it, and she glowered at the darkening sky. "It's going to piss down. Let's hide under the bridge."

There was a narrow tow path under the bridge, damp, slippery and green. Spark clung with his fingertips to the brickwork, uncertain of his footing while Carousel forged ahead. His nails brushed soft fabric, and he yelped in alarm as a hand snaked out of the shadows and seized his wrist.

Carousel spun around, balancing on one leg, elegant as a dancer. "Who's there?" Her clouded expression cleared. "Oh, it's you. I thought we were in trouble!"

Spark glared at Dweller, his heart hammering in his ears as the patterned man oozed from the darkness against the wall. "What do you think you're doing, lurking about and scaring people? You could have had me in the water!" He felt an idiot, squawking like a girl in front of Carousel. She laughed.

"That's what Dweller does! He likes the dark, don't you?"

"I prefer it, yes. Our business is more successful when it's shielded by shadow. I didn't mean to scare you, Spark."

"You didn't." His face was hot. "Not really. I just . . . didn't notice you there."

"Of course you didn't." Dweller smiled. His teeth were tiny spear-tips. "Noble sent me to bring you home. He's pleased with your work, but he thinks you two out alone might cause trouble and attract attention. He has new work for you, Carousel."

"For me?" A slow smile of delight lit up her whole face.

"Come back with me now, I'll keep an eye on you."

Dweller shrunk back against the wall, becoming one with the bricks and mortar, the light and shade. Spark struggled to try and pick him out of the shadows, but he knew Dweller was watching them with his bulbous fried-egg eyes as they clambered back up the bank and crossed the bridge.

"I'm not sure I trust him," he whispered to Carousel, out in the middle of the bridge, away from the shadows.

"Dweller's a good man," Carousel said, firmly.

"Is he though? A man, I mean? He doesn't look like any man I've met, and the way he fades in and out . . . It's not natural!"

"He's a good man to have on your side," she reiterated. "Don't try and make an enemy of him, Spark. You don't need any more enemies."

He stared after her in concern as she strode away over the bridge. He knew he had plenty of enemies, but how did *she* know that?

✦

Dweller shadowed them back to the secret tunnels under the cemetery. Spark caught the occasional glimpse of him, flitting between patches of shade and darkness. No one else seemed to notice. Even looking directly at the little man their eyes skimmed over him, like mayflies dancing on the surface of the water. Spark envied the talent. It must be easy to hide from people if they couldn't see you in plain sight on a crowded street. He resolved to ask Dweller how he did it, but when he had the chance to talk to the patterned man alone the following evening, Dweller would not be drawn.

"It's a talent I have. It comes from my mother," he said. "Noble is looking for you. He has an appointment, and he wants you to go with him."

"Me?" Spark was flattered, but surprised. Noble had shown an avuncular interest in him since he arrived, but he had never asked Spark to accompany him anywhere. "Why me?"

"Because he asked for you. He's waiting, so hurry before he

changes his mind!"

Spark scampered to do Dweller's bidding. Noble was waiting in his office, a cloak as black as his skin draped around his shoulders, dropping down to reveal the handle of the sword slung across his back. Spark's step faltered. He had never seen Noble armed with anything more than a dagger.

"It's all right, Spark." Noble grinned, white teeth flashing. "If I'm going above ground, I like people to see I'm armed. There won't be any trouble. Want to come along?"

"Where are we going?"

"Somewhere fun!"

Noble's stride was long, and fast. Spark had to walk briskly to keep up. Noble led him through unfamiliar tunnels, and out onto the streets in a narrow space between two high walls. Boxes were stacked to form a makeshift set of steps, and Noble loped up them easily, swung his leg over the wall, and dropped down into the alley below.

Spark followed, landing on the balls of his feet. Cape Carey had so many alleys. Even on the finest streets, you could round a corner and find yourself thrust into a grimy underworld, while the upper crust of the city passed by oblivious only a few yards away. There were two cities, the visible and the hidden, and he was a citizen of the dark.

He had never seen Noble above ground before, but the older man moved through the lanes like he owned them, supremely confident, purposeful. Everyone they passed seemed to know him. Some touched their foreheads in a Telesian gesture of respect, others simply stared. And Noble knew them all. He had a kind word for the woman sitting in the corner selling puppies from her skirt, a bag of sweetmeats which he flicked towards the cluster of children that trailed after him with wide eyes and pleading, outstretched hands. One old man, wall-eyed and frail, bowed as Noble pressed a coin into his hand. He mumbled his thanks through toothless gums, and Noble nodded gracefully as he moved on.

"They treat you like a king," Spark observed.

"That's because I look after them. Better than their so-called lord and master!" Noble jerked his head contemptuously in the vague direction of the Carey mansion, halfway across the city from here. "They're grateful, just like the ladies we're going to meet tonight. Try and keep your wits about you, though. A man can lose more than his head on Squeezetitty Lane."

There were plenty of young women plying their trade on Squeezetitty Lane, squashed into tiny bustiers, leaning forward so Spark could view the goods on offer. They swarmed around Noble like gaudy butterflies, stroking his face, whispering in his ear. He shook them off with an apologetic bow. "Not tonight, my fine ladies! I have business at the Lily."

There was fluttering at this, consternation. "Yennica hoped you'd stop by," one of the girls said. "There's been trouble . . ."

"What kind of trouble?" But she closed her mouth and shook her head. "Not for you to say? Fine. I'll talk to Yennica, see if I can sort it out."

The Gilded Lily stood at the end of the alley, on the corner of a more upmarket street. The face it presented to the city was a respectable tavern and boarding-house, but the back entrance on Squeezetitty Lane led to a far less reputable establishment. The hidden city, hiding in plain sight.

The door was on the first floor, reached by a set of wooden steps. Noble bounded up them two at a time, and rapped with his knuckles. Spark hung back, nervous. The women on the street made him blush and squirm with their pawing. He didn't think he could handle a house full of them.

"Don't look so worried!" Noble grinned at him as the little hatch in the door slid back. "I've come to see Yennica." He addressed the unseen figure behind the door. "Are you going to let me in? It's chilly out here!"

The fat, soft man behind the door bowed low as he ushered Noble in, and moved to close it firmly in Spark's face. Noble laid a hand on his arm. "He's with me."

"Forgive me." The high-voiced man looked down the length of his long nose at Spark, as if he didn't believe the boy belonged in such exalted company. "Mistress Yennica is in her office. Would you like me to show you the way?"

"I know the way."

Noble's feet made no sound in the richly carpeted hallway, the pile as thick as a winter coat. Spark trailed along behind him, wondering at the way the carpet extended up the walls, textured like moss. The many doors leading off the corridor seemed organic; it was hard to see where the walls ended and the doors began. He wondered what lay behind them. Was Noble taking him to a whore?

The corridor ended in a more elaborately decorated door than the ones they had passed before, overlaid with a bright tapestry depicting erotic scenes. Spark's face grew hot as he looked at it. "Is that even possible?" he wondered aloud.

"Oh yes," Noble flashed him a grin. "All of them are, except that one, top left." He knocked before Spark could get a good look at the offending pose, and opened the door without waiting for an invitation.

The woman in the shimmering blue dress spun around at the sudden intrusion, then relaxed. Her face broke into a smile. "Noble! You got my message? I'm glad you came so quickly."

Noble frowned. "What message? What's going on, Yennica?" Her movement towards him, the twitch of her wide skirts, revealed a thin girl in a blood-spattered shift, sitting in a high-backed chair. Her wrists were lashed to the armrests with wide swathes of ribbon. She was as pale as her smock, but the razor slash stood out harsh on her cheek. The wound was half stitched with black silk, the upper half hanging open. The abandoned needle dangled against her cheek. Spark pressed his hand to his mouth as he gagged.

Yennica surveyed him without interest. "Who's the boy? One of yours?"

"I found him in the gutter. He's useful to have around."

Noble shrugged. Yennica dismissed Spark from her attention and turned back to her sewing. The girl flinched as she swabbed the cut with wine and forced the needle through her skin, drawing the edges of the wound closed. Noble hiked himself up on the edge of her high desk, toes brushing the floor, and watched her work.

"Is this what the message was about?" he asked. "There's nothing remarkable about a whore getting slashed."

"But three in four days? That's personal, Noble. I don't care what you say." The girl squirmed, and Yennica tapped her hand. "Keep still, Trinity. I don't want to make a mess of this."

"Three razored in four days?" Noble straightened. "All on the face? You're right, that is personal. Someone's trying to put us out of business."

"You're done," Yennica said to Trinity. "You can go. You can stay here a week, until you find a better place. Maybe Noble has a tavern job going?" The madam looked at him hopefully.

Noble stretched across the desk and grabbed a parchment and writing stick. He scratched out a note in his elegant hand, folded it around a silver coin from his pocket, and pressed it into Trinity's palm. "Take this to the Queen's Revenge," he said. "I've told them they're looking for a tavern maid. They're good people, they'll take care of you. If they don't, come find me and tell me. I look after my girls."

She bobbed a curtsey. "Thank you, Noble. Thank you, Dame Yennica."

Yennica sighed. "I wish I could keep you on. But you un-derstand . . ." She spread her hands in a gesture of helplessness as she showed the scarred girl out of her office. She really had been quite pretty.

Yennica shut the door behind her and glanced at Spark. "Can we talk in front of the boy?"

"I trust him. He's given me no reason not to."

Yennica shrugged. "If you say so."

"Who's slicing up your girls, Yennica?"

"I couldn't say, but that scarred-up chap from Startide was round here again last moon, badgering me to let them in on our action. I told him to go -" an anxious glance at Spark, "- go jump in the river. But you!" The colour rose in her cheeks. "I give you a cut to protect us! What are you going to do about it?"

"I'll put a stop to it. We already have too many tavern wenches, and not enough whores." Noble hopped down off the table. Spark saw his anger in the set of his shoulders, the way his fingers twitched over his dagger. If he had been Spark, someone would be on fire by now.

"How?" Yennica demanded. "We don't know it's Startide."

"I can find out. Our burned friend Shadow will meet a dark fate one of these nights, and the Silver Lady with him."

"Shadow—?" The name squeaked out of Spark's mouth before he could swallow it. Noble rounded on him.

"You know Shadow, Spark?"

Yennica scowled. "I thought you said we could trust him!"

"Knowing someone and working for them aren't the same thing." But a crease appeared between Noble's brows, and his voice was deceptively gentle. "How do you know him, lad? You weren't in Cape Carey long before we picked you up."

"We met in the Black Rat. There was a girl . . ." Spark stared down at his hands. "You know I blew up the wall . . ."

"I know that."

Yennica's snort indicated she hadn't known. It was hard to tell whether she was impressed, or disdainful.

"Shadow was there," Spark went on. "His scarred face—that was me. I did that to him." His own face burned with shame.

Yennica looked at him with a touch more respect. Noble laughed. "I knew it! There's more to you than you let on, kid! Shall I let you go after him?"

Spark's eyes widened, and he shook his head.

"No, you're not ready yet. But it's time we turned your talent to our advantage. Speaking of talent," he turned back to

Yennica, "I came to talk to you about a girl. I thought she'd be an asset for you. Now I see you might really need her!"

"I certainly can't afford to lose girls at this rate. What's she like?"

"Young. Hot-headed. Great legs, good dancer."

Yennica smiled. "It's not her dancing skills that interest me, Noble. How young is she?"

"Seventeen summers. Old enough." Noble grinned. "You want her?"

"I need as many girls as I can. Send her over." She nudged him out of the way and grabbed a parchment. "She can have Trinity's room. What's her name?"

"Carousel."

Ten

KAYALL VAULTED THE side of the barge and landed on the wharf. He wrinkled his nose, breathing in the shit-and-sweat stink of the city. It felt like coming home. They said Cape Carey was the biggest city in the world. Plenty of fun to be had here, if he could duck off searching for that wretched brat and give Elvienne the slip.

She followed more sedately, smoothing her skirts. The smells he inhaled had her reaching for a cloth to smother her nose. "Well," she said, emerald eyes searching around her, "here we are."

"Looking for one boy, when we don't even know what he looks like, in the biggest city in the Kingdom. Just because the bargees said he might be here doesn't mean he is. If he's not, what then?"

"We keep looking."

Hells, she was infuriating! Stubborn as an old mule when she had an idea in her head. She marched off down the wharf, not bothering to see if he was following. She seemed to know exactly where she was going.

Kayall caught up with her. "You've been here before. Where are we going to stay?"

"The Mouse on the Table. Nomi's a good sort. It's safe for us."

The Mouse on The Table was a military tavern, filled with men off duty from the nearby garrison, aspiring members of the City Watch, and a few private guards in livery. The bar was ruled by an immensely tall, broad woman. Her hair was as pale as wisps of lamb's wool, and she had chalky skin and tiny, watery pink eyes. She bore down on them like the tide.

"Elvienne! It's been too long! You've changed your face again!" The white woman squashed the mage in a generous bear hug. "How long has it been? Who's your friend?"

"It must be twenty years. Maybe twenty-five, I lose track. I was here with the Queen's Alliance during the war. You remember her, Nomi?"

"Of course. She was a good girl. Handy in a bar fight too." Her voice lowered a fraction. "I hear there's war in the northeast. Some trouble with Atrathenes. You know about that?"

"It's the first I've heard of it." Elvienne shrugged. "I doubt it will affect us down here. Kayall and I have our own work to get on with."

Kayall leaned on one of the many wooden pillars that supported the roof as they chatted. He scanned the bar in leisurely fashion, wondering if the pale woman had any intention of offering him a drink. It appeared not, as Elvienne and Nomi reminisced about their shared past. He would have to make his own entertainment.

There was a dice game going on at a nearby table. It didn't seem to be loaded, but he watched for a while to make sure, until eventually a young soldier shuffled his chair up to make a space. "Join us if you're interested!"

Kayall snapped his fingers at a passing wench for a drink, told her Elvienne would pick up the bill, and settled in with a pint for an evening of gaming and idle chat. Maybe he could uncover some clues to Liathan's whereabouts, but if not, at least he could have a good time.

It was some furred creature. A mouse, which would be appropriate. It must have crawled into Kayall's mouth and died during the night. That was the only explanation for the taste and texture of his tongue.

He groaned. If he moved his head, it might drop off and roll away across the floor. All things considered, that might help him feel better. He couldn't feel any worse, with hot, sweaty legs tangled around his and the bedfur rucked up uncomfortably beneath his hip. He tried to shift the legs, but they were a dead weight.

From what he could dimly recall, there had been beer, and gaming, and suggestive whispers in his ear. Then there was nothing but a horrible black gap yawning in his memory.

The only thing worse than drunken sex with a stranger was drunken sex you couldn't remember enjoying. Kayall struggled out from beneath those sprawled legs and rolled the young soldier onto his back, hoping a clear view of his sleeping face would help him remember his name. No such luck. The best he could hope for was to sneak out before the boy woke up and started asking awkward questions. He was practised at dressing swiftly and silently, and he gathered his discarded clothes and jewellery, swiped a slash of powder across each eyelid, and combed his hair with his fingers rather than risk disturbing his bedmate by looking for a brush. It wasn't the best look, but it would do for now.

He let himself out on the landing, closing the door behind him with a soft click. He wondered whether Elvienne had stayed up drinking and chatting with Nomi all night. The smell of frying bacon drifting up the stairs made his mouth water.

Elvienne, are you downstairs? Save me some bacon?

He grinned as he called out to her. He knew she would regard a request for breakfast as a trivial, wasteful use of magic, but it was sometimes fun to goad her.

His foot was on the top step when her voice in his head called to him. *Get your own breakfast. Have fun last night? Did you?*

Her giggle was positively girlish, and it wasn't in his mind. It came from the room across the landing. He pushed the door open and saw Elvienne sitting up in bed, her modesty protected by a draped bedfur. A dark head nestled on the pillow beside her. She raised her finger to her lips and winked.

Elvienne! He's young enough to be your grandson!

Several-times-great grandson, if you're being blunt. Brynmar's an old friend. We get together when our paths cross. She slipped out of bed, clutching the fur to her torso. *I'll have cheese with my bacon, if you're offering.*

Kayall made a hasty exit before she decided to drop the fur. His bladder was nagging him. The privy was a simple wooden stall across a square yard at the back of the inn. The morning air was cold, tightening the skin of his face. He shivered as he hurried across the cobbles, mud splashing up the flapping legs of his trousers. He had noticed last night, between ales, that trousers were worn tight in the city this autumn. He would have to get them altered.

There was no door on the privy, which was just a hole in the ground that let onto a fast-flowing stream of water, sweeping the waste from the tavern's patrons towards the river. He sniffed in disdain as he unlaced his trousers.

There was a faint click, a sound at the edge of hearing, and the whirr of an insect. Instinct or magic made him duck, without knowing why. He heard a dull thud. In front of him, driven deep into the wood at the back of the stall, an arrow trembled. A single lonely feather tumbled into the waste stream.

"Shit!"

He stumbled back, splashing a stream of piss down his leg, and spun around. There was no archer in sight, but that didn't mean he wasn't hiding, already reloading, ready to plunge a barb straight through Kayall's heart.

There wasn't time for magic. Kayall threw his arms above his head and raced for the door of the inn, expecting any moment to feel the piercing stab through his breast, his back, his eye. He stumbled through the door and into the narrow corridor beside the kitchen, colliding with Nomi, who carried a large covered platter. It was like running into a wall.

"Hey!" She swung the tray skilfully over his head, keeping everything balanced. "Where are you off to in such a hurry?"

"There's someone—" he gibbered, flailing his arm back towards the yard, "there's someone out there *shooting* at me!"

Nomi kicked the door closed, and dropped the bar with her free hand. "Come and get some breakfast," she said, as calm as if he had strolled in from the yard and told her it was raining.

"Didn't you hear me? Someone was trying to kill me!"

"People are always trying to kill people. Aren't you green mages immortal?"

"Not if someone sticks an arrow through our chest! Then we die like anyone else!"

Nomi shrugged. "Didn't know that. You keep that dark!"

"Wouldn't you?" His trousers were wet, and reeking. He had pissed down his leg.

"Come and have some breakfast." Nomi waved the tray at him.

"I'll have to get changed first."

The soldier had gone when he returned to his room, and the bed looked large and empty, furs kicked down and rumpled. Kayall removed his trousers, sniffed them in disgust, and lobbed them out of the window. They were out of fashion anyway. Let the street rats steal them if they wanted them.

He only had one spare pair, in delicate fabric and pale cream that would get filthy as soon as he wore them on the city streets. They were wide in the leg too. And clean trousers meant a clean shirt to match. Changing his clothes, toying with his hair and makeup, calmed him down. He wasn't afraid any more, but he was perturbed. Why would anyone in Cape

Carey want him dead?

By the time he got down to breakfast the slab of white fish topped with melting cheese and bacon was cold, and the mug of warm wine was tepid. The soldier chased the last of his food round his plate with a thick slab of bread. He looked up as Kayall entered the room, and pushed his hair off his face, offering him a dazzling smile. Shit, what was his name?

Elvienne?

I'm not going to help you, she admonished. *You shouldn't be such a slut.* She sat next to the man she had bedded. By the creases around his eyes and the grey wings above his ears, Kayall guessed he was around his fortieth summer. They shared a two-handled wine cup with the familiarity of lovers. The only seat at the table was next to the soldier, and as he slipped into the chair he felt the unnerving brush of a hand against his thigh. He managed what he hoped was a winning smile.

Nomi pushed her empty plate away. "Kayall tells me someone tried to kill him in the yard. Is there anything you two think you should tell me?"

"Really?" Elvienne stiffened. "Did you get a look at him?"

"All I saw was an arrow whizzing past my ear. I couldn't even tell you where it came from." No need to mention in front of everyone how he had pissed down his leg.

Her eyebrows drew together. "It could be coincidence. Can you think of anyone in the city who might want to kill you?"

"I can always think of people who want to kill me, but most of them are at the other end of the Kingdom. It could be coincidence. Mistaken identity."

"Let's hope so."

He hoped she would drop the subject as she turned to her companion, chatting casually about the breakfast and his plans for the day. Nomi cleared the plates, and Kayall was left with no one to talk to but the boy from last night.

Calbrath. His name is Calbrath. Try and remember it this time.

He smiled at her, but she wasn't looking at him, all her attention on Brynmar. Calbrath's hand was on his leg, his mouth pulled into a concerned pout. "I don't like the idea of people trying to kill you."

"It's an occupational hazard." The room was hot, the boy's mouth too close. Kayall rose, downing the last of his wine with a grimace. "Talking of occupations, Elvienne, isn't it time we set about doing what we came here for?"

"If you insist." It wasn't like Elvienne to be lazy. She must have had a more tiring night than she was letting on.

"Or we could tour the markets. I need new trousers, and a pair of winter boots . . ."

That got her to her feet. Once he started shopping, she would lose him for the day.

"Will I see you later?" Calbrath asked Kayall.

Elvienne answered on his behalf. "We're staying here for the foreseeable future. Why not come back tonight?"

"Why did you tell him that?" Kayall hissed, the moment they were out of the front door. "Now he'll turn up again this evening, and I'll have to be pleasant to him!"

"Would that be so awful? Besides," she shrugged, "maybe he won't. Maybe you're not the catch you think you are?"

He stared after her for a moment as she bustled away down the road. "Elvienne? How can you *possibly* say that, when you know me?"

Her laugh drifted back to him, mocking.

"What about you?" He easily caught up with her, with his long stride. "What face did you wear, to get your man into bed?"

"This one."

It was his turn to laugh. Her face was like an apple left too long on the tree, and her hair was spun cobweb. "Come on! Really?"

"Brynmar always says he likes my eyes."

Of course. The one thing Elvienne never changed about

her appearance was her eyes. Sharp and bright as starstones, they sparkled with mischief as brightly as they did with rage. They were mischievous now, challenging him to make further comment. Kayall shrugged and changed the subject. "Are we going to hit the markets?"

"You wish. We're here to do a job. I want to get a look at this tavern Nomi told me about, where the wall collapsed. That smells like magic to me."

If the markets weren't an option, a tavern was the next best thing. He could do with a drink to calm his nerves. The shooting incident had shaken him more than he cared to admit.

The streets were bustling, and it was a long carriage ride to the Black Rat, only a few streets away from the river. The carriage was cheap, and Kayall felt the springs digging through the thin leather of the seat into his buttocks. He watched the city roll past the window, the taverns, the shops. The wealthy women in their floor-length cloaks clopped past like prancing horses in their high shoes, arm-in-arm with men in flounced shirts and thigh-hugging breeches in a range of bright hues. Shirts were ornate and trousers were snug this season. He felt like a northern bumpkin before this parade of fashionable southerners.

"Elvienne, if we don't get some decent garb we're going to stand out like scarecrows in the city."

The answer was a faint snore. Lulled by the rocking of the carriage, the old woman had fallen into a doze. For a moment, Kayall debated ducking out and leaving her to her investigations, but the rollicking he would get for it wasn't worth the trouble. She really couldn't have slept much the previous night.

The carriage drew up on the wharf where they had arrived the day before. The river ran high and fast, and the bargees threw sandbags out to defend their hulls from the harbour walls. Kayall gave Elvienne a sharp nudge. She snorted and blinked awake. "We're at the wharf," he said. "Did you want to start asking questions here, or at the tavern?"

"Might as well start here." Typical, when he was gasping for a drink. She clambered out of the carriage, leaning heavily on his arm, and looked around. "Let's ask in that hut over there. Give me a moment."

He had seen it a thousand times, but Kayall could never get used to watching Elvienne change her face. Her features blurred, shifted, in a way that made his eyes water. Her nose grew longer, her cheeks puffed out, pushing out the lines until the planes in her face resembled the smooth, soft carapace of a much younger woman. Her hair straightened and darkened, tumbling around her shoulders, and her bent back straightened. The years dropped away, but her eyes were still Elvienne's, gleaming with the wisdom of ages.

Kayall tried not to imagine what was going on beneath her dress.

"Come on then."

Another woman stood before him. Her accent had the flat vowels of a Cape Carey native. He shook his head. "Lose the voice. It sounds like you're a local, so why would you be asking directions?"

"Good point. Is this any better?" She slipped with no apparent difficulty into the melodic, distinctive tones of Northpoint.

"Not bad. Where are you from, anyway?"

"Originally?" Elvienne shrugged. "I can't remember. Somewhere in the Estmarch, I think. I've always liked the place, and the people. Our lost boy is an Estmarcher, too. Let's find him and bring him home."

No one on the wharf had noticed her transformation. According to Elvienne, people who saw her change thought she had always looked that way. Something in their minds blocked them from seeing the magic. With an appealing swish of her hips, she led Kayall towards a long, single-storey building that fronted the wharf. There was an office tacked on the end of it, a lean-to with a dusty counter and a hand bell. Elvienne rang it, and leaned on the counter, twitching the front of her dress an inch lower than it needed to be.

"Behave yourself, woman! You're old enough to know better."

"I've been through knowing better and now I'm out the other side," she retaliated, as the door leading to the warehouse swung open.

The man who answered the bell wore his greying hair in two long plaits down his back, like an Atrathene. It was a pity, Kayall reflected, that he had so much at the back of his head, and none at all at the front, otherwise he would have been rather attractive.

Elvienne simpered. It was embarrassing to watch.

"Can you help us? We're looking for our friend's little boy. He's run away from home, and you know how rough the streets can be. Have you seen him?"

She described Liathan as they had seen him, reflected in the memory of the stone, and the wharfman nodded slowly.

"Run away, you say? Where from?"

"Riversmeet," Kayall told him. It was close enough to the truth. "We think he might have got a lift on a barge, or stowed away . . ."

"There was a kid, a while ago now." The wharfman stroked his chin with a thick forefinger. "The Watch was looking for him. I'm not sure how much I should say . . ."

"The Watch? Is he in trouble?" Elvienne asked.

"There was a fire. The barge he came in on caught light, and the couple who lived on it were killed. No one's seen the kid since, but he's got a few questions to answer!"

"Oh, the poor boy!" Kayall did not share Elvienne's shock. Liathan was responsible for three deaths now, and their pursuit of him suddenly felt less like a game. "You've no idea where he might have gone? Never mind. Thank you anyway, for your time. Maybe you could direct me to a tavern, so that I can ask questions there? I hear there's an inn called the Black Rat not far from here?"

The wharfman's directions to the Black Rat proved only that he couldn't tell left from right, and eventually Elvienne was forced to stop and ask the way. When they found it, the front door was barred.

"There may be a side entrance." Elvienne trailed her hand across the stonework, and frowned. "It's not a happy building. Strong magic was worked on these walls, and they don't like it."

"Our boy?"

"I'm afraid so. He's getting more powerful, Kayall."

"Well," he shrugged, "at least we're on the right track. Let's catch up with him before he does any more damage!"

She vanished round the side of the building, and he heard her exclamation of surprise. Following her, he saw why the front door was barred. There was no need to have it open, when the wall at the side of the building had crumbled to reveal the inside of the tavern. Chairs and tables spilled out on to the cobbles, and despite the damage, the Rat seemed to be doing a brisk trade.

Kayall brightened. This was more like it. By unspoken consensus, he parted from Elvienne and drifted towards the nearest card game, playing out under the sloping eaves. "Mind if I join?"

He snapped his fingers at a passing tavern maid to bring a drink, and pulled up a chair. A woman with tight-cropped hair gave him a loaded glance, but her two older male companions shuffled their chairs up willingly. They were playing a local variant of Three-Eyed Dog he had last played back in Lambury. He hoped he could remember the rules through the post-drinking fuzz in his mind.

A few hands passed in idle chit-chat before he felt it was the right time to bring up the subject of the gaping hole in the side of the inn that no one seemed to be worried about. A sudden gust sent two cards fluttering off the table, and the woman, who had introduced herself as Wenna, dived to retrieve them.

"Windy out here," Kayall shrugged, "but I'll bet it's no less windy inside! Why the huge hole in the wall?"

"Some magic bastard did it—ow!" The balding man, Erron, had obviously been on the end of a hefty kick from his Telesian companion. "All respect to you green folk, of course. Not that you would . . ."

"Of course not," Kayall replied smoothly. He was annoyed they had the measure of him so quickly. That must be why they had been so careful to lose. "Not all magic is green magic. What—"

Wenna straightened, smacking her head on the table as she rose. "I'm not hurt," she assured him, slapping the cards back down on the table with vim. "Are we still playing?"

Elvienne was still flirting by the bar, chatting to a lanky merchant who was waving a bandaged hand around to illustrate his point. He wondered if she'd found out anything. She showed no sign of wanting to leave.

"I'm in for another hand." Kayall hoped Erron would say more about the magical damage to the side of the Rat, but he didn't want to push it. "Farish? How about you?"

"I'm in," the Telesian confirmed, shuffling the deck.

Kayall drew a lousy hand. Even with his companions trying to lose, he had little chance. It was almost a relief to see Elvienne break free of her suitor and head towards him.

Any news?

When you're ready. Those are terrible cards, don't you want to finish the game?

Not especially. He could hear her grinning as she took a seat at a nearby table.

Wenna regarded him over the top of her fanned cards. "You look distracted, mage. Concentrate on the game. Unless there's somewhere you'd rather be?"

"I'd like to be wherever you are, sweet." He expected her to giggle, or at least blush. She did neither, only scowled. Maybe he had read her signals wrong, in thinking she was interested.

His cards weren't improved by the second pass, and by the third he was doomed. "I've got nothing!" He slapped his dismal hand down on the table, and watched Wenna pocket her winnings with a wry smile. He rose. "Gentlemen, mistress, this has been fun. We'll have to do it again."

Erron muttered something dark about playing with mages. He had had a losing afternoon. Farish shuffled the deck again with a questioning glance at Wenna, but she shook her head. "Better quit while I'm ahead," she said. "But I'll play the mage again, he's bought my dinner tonight. Where are you based, mage?"

"The Mouse, in Splinter Alley. Do you know it?"

"I've been past there." She grinned. "If you're going to be around, I might drop in for a pint!"

"I might see you then." He knew he had read her right. He strutted as he left the table and rounded the corner into the more upmarket thoroughfare.

Elvienne caught up with him by a rank of carriages. She had reverted to her usual face. "Find out anything useful?" she asked.

"That it's not smart to play Three Eyed Dog with a cheating bastard Telesian? I don't know if that counts as useful . . ."

She cuffed him lightly round the head. "You're lucky you've got me to watch your back!"

"Why, what did you find out?"

"It seems Liathan has embarked on a new career as a cutpurse. I was talking to a merchant at the bar who had an encounter with him that left him with a badly burned hand, behind a tavern called the Woodsman's Rest. We're going there now. We can walk, it's not far."

"We seem to be lurching from inn to inn. I'm sure I should be more drunk at this point!"

"You should keep your wits about you. You don't know when someone's going to take another shot at you, do you?"

"I'm sure it was a coincidence." But the prickle at the back of his neck told him it wasn't. The same prickle now, which set him looking over his shoulder, checking the reflections in shop windows as they passed.

"You're edgy," Elvienne observed. "What's wrong?"

"You know that feeling, when you think you're being followed?"

"I only ever have that when I'm being followed."

"Do you have it now?"

Elvienne quickened her stride. "Yes."

"I thought so." Kayall stretched his mind into the sky, reaching for cloud, pulling long strands down around them, building up a wall of fog so thick and sudden that in a moment he could barely see his hand before his face. That should conceal them, muffle their footsteps, give them a chance to get away. Elvienne shivered and clutched her cloak tighter as the moisture clung in tiny droplets to her hair.

"That's fine, you don't have to thank me." Kayall's breath steamed in the chill.

"I won't. It's not me with an assassin on my tail."

There seemed no answer to that. Kayall swallowed a curse and followed her, dragging the cloud with him. Elvienne seemed to know unerringly where she was going. It wasn't long before the swinging inn sign for the Woodsman's Rest loomed out of the mist in front of them, and the yellow glow of fresh candles invited them in. Kayall lunged towards the door, but Elvienne pulled him back.

"This way." Her nose twitched, and she set off down the street and into a narrow alley between two tapering houses, down a steep flight of steps, and out into an open, paved square behind the tavern. "We should be able to see if anyone comes close now," she said. "Let the mist go."

Kayall released his hold, watching the cloud break up into strands, swirling away from them to let the weak autumn sunlight gleam through. No one in sight, but that didn't mean someone wasn't watching from an upper floor, tracking him with their bow. He shuddered. "Let's get on with it."

The coppery taste of magic was just a faint hint in the air, but it was enough to tell him they had found the right place, if the scorch marks on the ground hadn't given it away. Deep black lines scored across the cracked pavement. Elvienne prodded them with her toe, and her face paled.

"We have a bigger problem than I thought," she said.

"What?" Kayall had to get down on his knees to see what she was looking at. The crack was wider than his arm, and even reaching into it he couldn't feel the bottom, stretching away beyond his fingertips into the darkness. "It goes a long way down . . ."

"Too far down, and who knows what might crawl out of it?" Elvienne winced, clutching her ears at a sound only she could hear. "The stone is crying, Kayall. Soon it will start to scream. I fear young Liathan has unleashed something terrible on the city."

Eleven

I DON'T UNDERSTAND. HE WAS *dead.* Dead and rotting, Allo! I saw it myself!" Bastian watched his father moving jerkily around the garden, like a puppet with too-short strings, mouth working in what looked like soundless curses.

"How much wine had you drunk that night?" Allorise sat next to him on the carved stone bench, hands busy at her constant knitting, needles dancing up and down in the light from the brazier. "I asked Vio, she said you were steaming. Then I fired her for gossiping."

"Leaving us with no servants. Very bright, Allo."

Lord Carey sat down on an identical bench at the far end of the garden, head dropping onto his chest. Allorise laid aside her handcraft and massaged soothing ointment into her calloused fingers.

"I wasn't steaming. Vio saw it too, the maggots coming through the ceiling." He shuddered at the memory of their tiny, writhing bodies falling on his skin.

"I expect a rat had died."

"A rat? You didn't see it, Allorise! They were all over me!"

"There we are then." She pressed her lips together in a tight little smile, and picked up the needles once more. "You'd had a bottle or two of wine, a nasty encounter with a dead rat, and hit your head. The rest is clearly hallucination."

Bastian longed for another bottle or two of blue. He knew what he had seen. What he had thought he had seen. His father, rotting away in bed, holes opening in his decaying flesh. But his father was walking towards him now, between the raised beds and delicate little fountains, lips pulled back across his teeth in an approximation of a smile. He wasn't healthy, but he certainly wasn't dead. He even managed a nod at his children as he lurched past, eyes rolling, lips twitching.

"See? He's fine. If he had been dead, you can stake your life Jago would have been here before he was even cold."

His father didn't look anything close to fine, but he was up and walking about, and that was a relief. Bastian allowed himself a wry chuckle. "He would have ridden the fastest horse in from the country. He wouldn't even have stopped for a piss!"

Allorise pursed her lips. "Don't be crude, Bastian. It's a worry. The best we can expect from our dear brother is a grace-and-favour cottage in the slums!

"If he doesn't marry you off to a horse trader!" She stiffened, and he realised, too late, that he had stung a nerve. "Jago wouldn't do that to his baby sister. He'd want you to stick around, if there's room for you once he's moved all his babies in."

"How many has he got now?" she asked. "Six? I can see myself playing nursemaid for the rest of my life. Thank the stars Dada seems to have rallied." Her eyes followed their father's unsteady passage around the garden. "It's such a shame he's lost the power of speech now. Poor Dada. I'm afraid it won't be long until your vision comes true, Bastian! What will we do without him? What if Jago casts us out?"

Bastian had no answers. Allorises's bottom lip quivered as her wide blue eyes silvered with tears. He slipped an arm around her shoulders and drew her close, trying not to tremble as her hair brushed his mouth. For a moment she rested her head against his chest and clutched his hand, before she abruptly broke the connection.

"I should go with Dada. He might fall. I'll look into hiring new staff. We can't take care of him on our own."

"If you think that's wise. I wish you hadn't got rid of Vio."

Their father vanished into the mansion. Allorise sheathed her knitting needles like twin daggers, and stuffed the wool into the pouch at her belt. She scowled. "She talked too much. It got on my nerves."

Bastian watched her walk away, hips swishing under the long silver skirt that embraced her curvaceous thighs. He waited until she disappeared into the house before stretching out on the bench, still warm from the heat of her body. He pressed his cheek to the stone, and groaned.

⚜

Allorise found her father slumped on the black-and-white tiles in the hall, where he had fallen when she cut his wires. His mouth hung open, a dry, dusty cave, the severed root of his tongue twitching like the docked tail of a carriage hound.

"Come on, Dada." She jerked him to his feet, marvelling at how light he was, bones housed in a patchwork shell of skin. "At least I can talk to you, now you won't sell my secrets! Poor Bastian," she glanced back towards the garden door, making sure he wasn't following, "he's crazy with love for me, you know?"

Lord Carey made a hacking sound, deep in his throat. Disapproval, or disgust.

"I think I've convinced him he didn't see what he saw. Time to get him a new playmate. Something to distract him, now dear Vio is no longer with us."

Her father's head lolled against her shoulder as she guided him up the stairs to his room and laid him flat on the bed.

"Let's see how the repairs are holding up. You should be

proud of me, Dada. Running a business and a household, knitting, and now sewing!" She pushed up his shirt. The fresh skin, the smooth, young, feminine skin, covering the holes gnawed by maggots, sat well against the wrinkles and curling white hairs that had always belonged to her father. The stitching around the patches was neat, almost invisible. Allorise was pleased with her handiwork. At least seeing her father walking about had made Bastian shut up about maggots.

She patted the patches of smooth skin with affection. "Dear Vio. She was always useful to have around. Shall I get a Telesian girl next time you need patching up?"

The hacking again, deeper.

"You're right, it would look odd. I'll take some money from the Startide coffers to hire a new maid. Jennica at the Lily is beginning to crumble. I should have the deeds for you to sign within the moon. Would you like me to bring you a whore, to celebrate?"

His eyes closed as she pulled his shirt down to cover the patchwork of scars, and she stroked his hand. "Dear Dada. Sleep now. You need to conserve your strength . . ."

⚶

Allorise had arranged to meet Shadow in a private upstairs room of the Queen's Revenge, just off the Horse Fair. It was a Nobility tavern, but the risk was worth it to be able to flaunt her wealth before the children of the gutter. From where she sat waiting for him in the window seat, she could see the crudely-painted sign swinging back and forth in the breeze. Allorise had met the late Queen once, long ago when she was a girl, and she doubted the veracity of the sign. The woman she met had been too small, too wrapped up in her babies, to have taken revenge on anyone. It was most likely a lie, but if it made her gentle sex look stronger, Allorise was happy to go along with it.

There was a rap at the door. Shadow. Allorise twitched her

skirts to expose her shapely calves, and let him hang for a long moment before she invited him in and bade him sit.

He let the plague doctor mask fall to the table with a grateful sigh, and scratched the shiny, puckered skin across his cheeks. He had been repellent even before the mage brat made such a mess of his face. Ugly, but useful, and he would do anything she asked, now no other woman would have him.

"Any luck with the Lily?" she asked.

He shrugged. "Not a chance. Chalice tells me Noble's just getting new girls in to replace the ones we slashed. And we can't meet here again; one of them's working behind the bar downstairs. I had my mask on, but I swear she gave me a suspicious look."

"We'll have to meet at my house from now on." That was annoying. The wine was fine in the Queen's Revenge, and the chef made especially delicate crab puffs. They'd only hire a scarred whore because Noble had his hands so tightly round the owner's coin purse that they couldn't be pried free.

Shadow pulled his lips back from his teeth. "I'd like that."

I'll wager you would, you scalded alley cat. She kept her smile fixed in place. "Noble's obstinacy is infuriating. I think it's time to escalate our campaign against him. I want the rat driven out of his hole and exterminated."

"You want war with the Nobility?"

She nodded. "If that's what it takes. That's why we need the mage boy. Any luck finding him?"

"Noble visited the Lily with a boy. It's my guess our dark friend is keeping him close."

"If I had a pet mage I wouldn't let him out of my sight either. What?" as Shadow straightened in his chair.

"There are a couple of Old Ones in town, if the rumours are true. Green magic. Might we not turn one of them to our hand?"

"If they're persuadable. Do you think they are?"

He chuckled. "The woman, perhaps not. But the man looks

like he could be talked into anything."

"Find him, and find out. A green wizard would be a handy weapon."

"Indeed it would. Talking of weapons . . ." He pushed back his seat, and groped for his crotch.

Allorise sighed inwardly. There was always a price. Shadow was pathetically predictable when it came to asking for his reward. She hitched up her skirts around her dimpled thighs, while outside the portrait of the Queen squeaked a rhythm, to remind her that she wasn't yet as strong as she'd like to be.

"Do me one favour?" Allorise laid one hand on Shadow's chest to halt his eager advance.

"Anything, my Silver Lady." Lustful sweat lent a sheen to his burn scars as he groped for her, calloused fingers digging into her buttocks.

"Put the mask back on first."

Twelve

"SPARK, SPARK, YOU won't believe what Noble just told me!"

Carousel raced across the dinner cavern, the ends of her headscarf unravelled, flying like flags behind her. The bells in her hair chimed her excitement. "Wake up, you lazy sod! It's the best news!"

Spark tried to feign sleep, but it was impossible as she shook his arm and cuffed him about the head. "Wake *up*!"

"What's going on? I could hear you shouting all the way across the room!"

Her eyes were bright, chest heaving with exertion. "Noble wants me to go up to the Lily! Isn't that wonderful?"

He sat up, careful not to bang his head on the overhanging rock, and swung his legs over the side of the bed. He had felt sick about breaking the news to her, hoped to put it off until morning, but Noble had beaten him too it, and for some reason she was happy? Maybe she didn't understand the nature of business conducted at the Lily. It was up to Spark to let her know.

"Carousel—" but she was climbing into the bunk beside him, nudging him over and slipping her cold, smooth legs beneath his blankets.

"Budge up." She elbowed him in the ribs. "I'm cold. You don't seem very happy."

He budged up. She was all elbows and knees. "Carousel, about the Lily . . ."

"What about the Lily?"

"You know it's a—" he felt himself blushing, "a *whorehouse*?"

She threw her head back and laughed, one of her braids striking him gently across the cheek. "Oh Spark, you're so funny! Of course I know it's a whorehouse! What else would it be?"

He squirmed. "Why do you want to work in a whorehouse? You do know what goes on there?"

"I'm not completely naive, Spark!" She chuckled. "It's good work, indoors—"

"Lying down," Spark chipped in.

"Lying down," she agreed, with a grin. "It's a chance to earn some copper of my own, and it gets me off the streets. What's wrong with that?"

"Aren't you worried about getting hurt? Some of the girls there," Spark winced at the memory, "some of them had their faces slashed." He groped under the blanket for her hand. "I'd hate that to happen to you."

"It won't," she declared. "Noble won't let anything happen to me."

"Are you sure?" Noble had provided for Trinity, but what happened to the other girls who'd fallen to Startide's razor man? Spark hadn't thought to ask, and now he didn't know how to broach the subject.

"Can I tell you something?" Carousel lowered her head until her lips almost brushed Spark's ear. "Promise you won't tell?"

"I promise." He tingled at the unexpected touch.

"Noble looks after all the girls he sends on. Looks after them personally, if you know what I mean . . ." Her eyes were bright.

"Personally? Oh . . ." Understanding dawned. "You like him."

Carousel shrugged. "Everybody likes Noble."

"Not the way you like him." The bitter stab of jealousy in his gut. Noble would take Carousel to bed, and then she would move on to the Lily, where men would pay for the honour. At least until she got her face cut open, or worse. "I don't want to talk about him. I don't want you to go to the Lily. It's dangerous."

"I know." She squeezed his hand. "Thanks for the concern. But staying with the Nobility is dangerous, especially for a girl. Don't you ever wonder why there are no girls down here?" She shuddered. "If Startide, or the Watch, get their hands on you . . . Let's just say it's worse for girls. Noble wants us to be safe."

"Safe, and making money for him while they're on their backs!"

She moved away from him, frowning. "We all owe Noble, Spark. You too. Did you honestly think you'd never have to pay him back?"

⚶

Noble's office was the heart of the underground complex. He controlled the Nobility from there, a spider in a web, and the door was always open. People streamed in and out, dropping off stolen goods, collecting money, begging and returning favours, and Noble greeted them all as friends and equals. But his private rooms, the ones no one was invited into, were down a long corridor and through three sets of double-barred doors, each with their own set of guards.

"It's like a fortress down here!" Spark observed. Despite his earlier misgivings, he was glad he had come this far with Carousel. She was quivering, and her face was pale. She kept fussing with her hair, pausing to adjust her clothes.

"Do I look all right?" she asked for the fourteenth time, licking the back of her hand and smelling her breath.

"You look . . ." Beautiful. Terrified. Like she shouldn't be here. "You look fine. Caro, are you sure you want to go through with this?"

A long pause. "Yes," she said. "Yes, I do. I've wanted to for a long time. And I get to go up to the Lily! I wouldn't want to go there without, you know . . . I don't want to give my innocence to a stranger."

Spark caught her hand as she fussed with her braids once more. "I'm not a stranger."

She chuckled. "You?"

"Why not me?"

"You're not a stranger, but you're not Noble either." She grinned. "You're like my little brother. It would be weird!"

"You've only got two summers on me, Caro. I'm not a child."

"Nor yet a man." She tapped his cheek with a light forefinger. "It's sweet of you to offer, but it has to be Noble. I owe him."

"You don't owe him that much." Spark scowled.

"I owe him my life." She turned away. "You have no idea."

Carousel refused to be drawn on the subject, but as they reached the final set of barred doors she reached for Spark's hand, and squeezed it. "I'm glad you're here," she said.

The guard on duty ushered her past, but stopped Spark with a firm hand to his chest. "Just Carousel," he said. "You can wait outside."

"Do you want me to wait. Caro?"

She nodded, with an anxious glance over her shoulder.

"Then I'll wait." He wanted to say more. Telling her to have fun seemed crass. "Just . . . be safe?"

"I'll be fine."

The doors swung shut behind her and Spark slumped into the seat the guard offered, trying not to think, unable to think of anything but what was going on beyond those iron doors. He would wait as long as it took. He would be here for Carousel when she came out.

＊

The doors clanged together at her back, cutting off the air and sounds of the corridor. Ahead, there were stairs leading up, carpeted with velvet and gold brocade. At the top was a curtain hung with bells. It chimed as she pushed it aside, heralding her passage. Beyond the curtain were more stairs, twisting and backtracking on themselves until she didn't know whether she faced north or west, and more curtains of shimmering bells. By the time she reached a square landing, and another door, she was breathless. At least here there were long, narrow windows, but she had to stand on tiptoes to look out.

She was higher than she had expected, above the level of the city walls, which stretched away north and east below her. She could see the winter sun gleaming off the helms of the guards on patrol, and the gently rolling country beyond. That was where Spark said he came from. Carousel wondered what it was like. She had never set foot outside the city. She would go there, once she had copper of her own. Take a basket, like the real nobility did in summer, and sit on the banks of the river to lunch and lounge in the sunshine.

"Enjoying the view?" The whisper behind her made her jump. She hadn't heard the door open, and when she spun around, startled, it was still firmly closed. There was no one in sight.

She sighed. "That's not funny, Dweller. What are you doing here? Come out so I can see you!"

The shadows shifted as the little man stepped forward, bulbous eyes scanning her up and down. "I was waiting for you."

"Why?"

He extended a hand, pointed nails tapping her wrist. The marks on his skin reached the very tips of his fingers. "I'm Noble's personal guard, his most intimate friend. How could I be anywhere else? Come." He opened the door and bowed, ushering her ahead of him into Noble's private chambers.

Noble's reception chamber was sparse, a low table, two couches, a long sideboard and a shelf full of precious books. Carousel glanced over them. She was aware of their value, but the marks on the spines meant nothing to her untutored eyes. Large glazed windows looked out, one over the city, the other to the stubbled fields beyond the river.

He was waiting for her, lounging against the sideboard, glass of wine in hand. Casual, as if they had encountered each other in this way a hundred times in the past. Carousel's heart fluttered, and her face was hot. She felt stupid and awkward. If he laughed at her she would turn and run.

He showed no sign of laughter. He poured her a glass of wine, and pressed it into her shaking hand. He didn't even frown as a few drops slopped onto the woodwork at his feet, merely dabbed the spillage with the toe of his boot. "Don't worry about that," he said. "I'm always spilling things. That's why I don't have carpet in here!"

He was trying to put her at ease. She was grateful, but she wished he would just get on with it, do what he had summoned her here to do. Every inch of her skin tingled as he took her hand and led her, not to the bedroom, but to the sofa.

"Why don't you take your boots off?" he suggested.

"Aren't we - ?" Noble raised a finger to her lips.

"Patience, Carousel. Drink your wine. We have plenty of time."

The wine looked like a potion, pale blue, fizzing with bubbles. Wine was for the wealthy. She drank it too fast, and it made her head spin. Noble sipped from his own glass, watching her with kindly eyes, exchanging pleasantries about the weather, the way she had her hair. She was wondering if he was going to make a move when he abruptly changed tack.

"You get on well with young Spark, don't you?"

She nodded. "He's not so young. Sometimes he acts it, but I think it's because he came from the country . . ." Her glass was empty, and Noble topped it up without waiting for her to ask for more.

"Does he ever talk to you about his past?" She shook her head, took a large gulp. "About his magic?"

"He told me he can do things that scare him. He doesn't like talking about it." Carousel felt a tug of disappointment. Maybe Noble didn't want her at all, if he had only brought her here to talk about Spark.

"He'll have to get over that if he's to be useful to me." Her glass was almost empty again, and Noble drained the last dregs of the bottle into it, and set his own down on the table. The wine had slipped down her throat as easily as fruit juice. "But you know I didn't bring you here to chat about Spark."

His hand moved up to her hair, catching the trailing end of the bow that held the mess of braids off her face, letting them tumble around her cheeks. "That's better." He rolled the end of one of her braids between his fingers, and Carousel heard, as if at a distance, the click of shells and the tinny chime of bells. "You should wear it loose when you go to the Lily."

"I will." She would have agreed to anything with his lithe fingers brushing her cheek, curling round the back of her neck to bring her mouth closer to his. He tasted of wine, and he kissed better than the boys in the back alleys, who were all tongue and spit and clumsy groping. The muscles of his chest were solid under her hands as he moved above her, slipping a hand up her skirt to caress her bare thigh.

Was it going to happen here, on the sofa? Her leg slipped off the narrow couch as she moved, kicking the table, sending the empty wine bottle clattering to the floor. She startled. "Oh! I'm so sorry!"

Noble sat up, shaking his head. "Nothing broken. Do you

want to move into the bedroom? It might be more comfortable for you."

If she said yes, there was no going back. If she said no, she wasn't ready, Noble would take it that she didn't want to go to the Lily. And working at the Lily was the best chance she had to make something of her life, to be more than a street rat.

"I need to pee. Do you have a privy?"

"I can do better than that. Through that door." He pointed as he bent to retrieve the fallen bottle. "Take as long as you need."

Carousel scrambled to her feet, swaying, clutching the arm of the sofa for support. The wine had gone straight to her head. How much had she drunk?

"Do you need a hand?" Noble was openly grinning now. "You look a little wobbly . . ."

"I'm fine." She managed to make it across the floor to the door he had indicated, pawing for the handle, trying to pull together a shred of dignity. She had expected to find a simple stone privy beyond the door, a bench with a hole in it. What she found was a bathroom, with a red and black mosaic floor, an iron tub on clawed feet, a sink, a mirror, and wonder of wonders, a pump for running water. It splashed over her hands, ice-cold, and she threw some up into her face to cool the wine-heat in her skin. She looked at herself in the dusty mirror as she groped for a towel, water dripping from her chin. Her hair looked good, unleashed from the band that held it back, but her eyes were wide, her face narrow. She looked like a frightened little girl.

Carousel drew in a deep breath. She could do this. This was what she had wanted, hoped for, dreamed about. Noble was a decent man. It would be fine.

She dried her face, controlled her breathing, teased her hair into something more mature. Time for the show.

Noble wasn't on the couch when she returned to his reception chamber, but the door opposite stood ajar. She approached nervously, bare feet padding across bare wood, and hesitated in the doorway. The room beyond was in shadow, shutters drawn, no candle lit.

"Can I come in?" she asked.

"Of course."

"I can't see where I'm going . . ."

"Hold on a moment." Carousel heard the scratch of candlestones, saw them spark. The flaring light was too bright for her eyes. She blinked hard, and Noble's bedchamber swam into focus.

The bed was the biggest she had ever seen, wide enough for two people to lie comfortably side-by-side, with long bolsters propped against the headboard. Noble lounged against them. He still wore his breeches but he had taken his shirt off, his dark skin a striking contrast to the milk-white sheets. There was a glow deep in the pit of her stomach at the sight of him lying there waiting. Waiting for her.

"Should I shut the door?" she asked.

"Leave it open a crack. It gets stuffy in here." He patted the space beside him. "Join me."

He had opened another bottle of wine, and poured her a fresh glass. She shook her head. "I don't normally drink wine. I've probably had too much already . . ."

"It's to help you relax." He pressed the glass into her hand. "I want you to drink it. I want this to be fun for you." He grinned as he spoke, as if it was already fun for him.

Carousel knocked back the wine in three massive gulps, and handed back the glass. Noble chuckled. "I like a girl who's not scared to swallow!"

He didn't elaborate on what he meant by that, as he caught her round the waist and pulled her across the bed towards him. His mouth sought hers as he pressed her close and slipped her skirt down over her hips and thighs. She kicked her legs free of the constricting cloth, and Noble slipped a hand between her legs. His other hand flicked open the buttons of her blouse and pushed it back off her shoulders.

"Relax," he whispered. "Tell me what you like. What do you want me to do?"

"I like what you're doing now." His massaging fingers found a spot that made her gasp, sending sparks racing up her spine to burst like fireworks in her skull. Her hips moved in instinctive response.

"I can tell." His mouth dropped to her breast, nibbling and teasing, but it was the rhythmic movement of his hand that made her press against him, yearning for deeper contact.

"Not yet, Caro," he muttered, in reply to the question her body was asking. "You won't get this consideration at the Lily."

She barely had time to wonder what he meant. He withdrew his hand, ignoring her little moan of disappointment, of craving, and pressed her gently onto her back. Her head was lost for a moment between the bolsters before he shifted them to prop her up. Her fingers brushed the closed-cropped curls of his skull as his mouth and tongue moved down, over the curve of her belly, seeking the spot that had whipped her breath away with just a touch.

This time she cried out, arching her back, heels drumming on the mattress. She felt him laugh. "You can make as much noise as you like, Caro. There's no one around to hear!"

She gave in to the sensation. The other girls, the ones who told her men put things inside you to hurt you, they must have never been with Noble. Never experienced anything like this. Her body pulsed to his touch, and she was panting as he sat up, wiping his mouth on his upper arm in a casual movement.

"Don't stop!"

"I'm not going to stop," Noble assured her. But he had stopped, moving up to kiss her. She tasted herself on his lips, the sharp tang of a metal drinking cup, as he pulled her off the bolsters and flat, pinning her arms above her head. She felt pressure between her legs, and she tensed at the sudden, sharp pain.

"It's fine, it's fine. Don't fight it . . ." Noble pushed again, something tore, and he was deep inside her. It was uncomfortable. She preferred what he had done with his mouth, but he seemed to be enjoying it, a look of fierce exultation on his face.

"Try not to tense up, Carousel. You're a bit tight. It might hurt."

It already hurt, but she couldn't tell him that. She should be having a good time. If she pretended to enjoy it, maybe she would. She let out an experimental moan.

"That's my girl!"

He thrust harder. It wasn't so bad, now she was getting used to it. She moaned again, spurring him to greater efforts as she clasped her thighs around his waist, letting him in deeper. This was better.

She felt a tingle as a flicker of movement caught her eye. The candle had burned low. She turned her head to the side, and this time her gasp was not of arousal, but shock. Dweller knelt by the bed, his face only inches from her own, bulbous eyes wide and staring. He grinned, raised a whorled finger to his lips, and faded into the darkness.

"Did you—?"

"Like that, do you?" If Noble had seen the watcher in the dark, he made no sign of it. He groaned, slumping across her, chest heaving. She felt wetness trickling between her legs as he rolled off her. She lay there, heart thumping, trying to work out what had happened.

Noble propped himself up on one elbow and stroked Carousel's hair out of her eyes. "Did you come?" he asked.

"Did I what?"

A frown shadowed his face. "If you have to ask, I guess you didn't. That's a shame. Tonight was all about you, Caro. When you go up to the Lily . . . Well, the men there won't always be considerate to your needs. I wanted to make sure your first time was good. Don't look so worried!" He smiled. "Not every girl makes it the first time, even under my expert tuition!" He flopped onto his back, tongue working over his teeth. "Can you fetch me some spyme, love? It's in the top drawer, far end of the sideboard."

He lit a fresh candle from the stump of the dying one and handed it to her. The shifting shadows made her skin crawl. She wondered if Dweller was still there, lurking in the darkness, staring at her as she walked naked across the room and rummaged in the drawer. Her thighs were sticky with blood and fluid, and her skin itched where Noble's sweat dried on it. She wanted a wash. Would it be rude to ask?

She ripped off two chunks of spyme, popped one in her own mouth, and took the other back to Noble. He had draped the sheets over his body. She felt exposed, standing on display beside the bed, feeling the herb heighten her senses as she chewed it, coursing through her limbs.

Noble took the drug she offered, and lifted up the sheets so she could slip underneath them. Carousel frowned. "Don't you want me to go back to my bunk?"

"Stay with me tonight. In the morning, I'll have Dweller send out for a maid to draw you a bath. I'm sure you'd like that."

"A hot bath?" His skin was warm against hers, the smell of spyme like spice on his breath. Now the pressure was off, the deed done, she felt good. She wanted him to touch her again.

"Hot as you like." He gathered her to his chest, and blew out the candle, plunging them into darkness. Carousel looked around for the whites of Dweller's eyes. She couldn't see them, but that didn't mean he wasn't there, watching over her as she lay in Noble's sleeping embrace, only a thin sheet to conceal what the patterned man had already seen. She was exhausted, but she didn't get much sleep that night.

Noble woke her with the dawn, shutters open to reveal the light spilling over the rooftops of the city. She watched the sunlight shift patterns of gold and black on his skin as he moved above her, inside her. She knew what to expect this time, and it hurt less. She felt a ripple run through her, but she didn't think it was that elusive peak Noble had referred to.

He left her sprawled on the bed, sheets tangled around her legs. She heard him talking in the adjoining room, his voice muffled, and a male reply. It must be Dweller he was talking to. Noble laughed, and Carousel wondered if they were comparing notes on her performance. She felt herself blush, and pulled the sheets up over her head, looking for a safe place to hide.

The door clicked. "Caro?" A tender touch on her shoulder, through the sheet. "Carousel, are you awake? I sent down for breakfast, but if you're not hungry . . ."

She had hardly eaten yesterday, through excitement and nerves, and it was only now she realised how famished she was. She could lie here and feign sleep, but that would mean missing breakfast. She sat up. "Can I bathe first?"

"The girls are bringing up buckets for your bath. Hot ones, just like I promised!" He rummaged in the clothes chest at the end of the bed and came up with an oversized shirt. It couldn't be his, it would swamp his lithe frame. "Fling this on," he said. "Can't have you walking around naked, can we?"

Carousel struggled into the shirt. It came down to her knees. It seemed pointless for the short walk from bedroom to bathroom, but as she emerged into the reception chamber she realised Dweller was still there, wide eyes flicking up and down as they drank her in. She blushed.

"Noble said I could have a bath." She didn't need to feel so defensive. She had as much right to be here as Dweller did.

He looked as if he was going to make some scathing comment, but he settled for jerking his head towards the bathroom. "The girls are filling the tub."

She lowered her voice. "You won't come in, will you? I'll scream if you do. Does Noble know how you like to watch?"

"Who said," he sneered, "that it was *you* I was watching?" He turned away with a snort of derision, and picked up the book he had been reading as if she was no more than a buzzing fly that had mildly annoyed him.

Shaken, Caro went into the bathroom. There were two girls in there, girls she didn't know, who looked at her and giggled behind their hands. She shooed them out and sat on the edge of the tub, trailing her hand in the steaming water, trying not to think about what Dweller had said. At least the room was bright white, with no shadows for him to hide in. She made sure the door was locked.

Once she was sure she was alone, she let the shirt pool on the tiled floor and swung one leg over the side of the bath, wincing at the scalding heat. It took a moment to become accustomed to the warmth. She couldn't remember ever having a hot bath before, and she had never been in a tub big enough to lie down in. The water came up to her chin, and only her feet bumping against the far end of the bath prevented her from slipping completely under the water.

Her thighs ached, she was exhausted, and the hot water lapping around her shoulders was as comforting as a hug. Unconsciously, her hand slipped down to where Noble had been, trying to replicate the feeling of his fingers sliding back and forth. It was easy, and it felt good.

She stayed in the bath until the water grew tepid, soaking away her aches, exploring with her fingers and thinking of Noble, of the men who would come to the Lily. It was the smell of warm bacon that finally dragged her from the water. She dried off, pulled on the shirt and wrapped a smaller towel round her damp hair, leaving the wet one draped over the end of the bath.

The smell of bacon wafted stronger as she opened the door. She was relieved to see Dweller had vanished, from sight if not from the room. On the table in front of the couch were dishes of scrambled eggs and bacon, of stewed apple with raisins, and hot fruitrolls, soft and steaming. As she sat down Noble poured her a cup of milk.

"Nice bath?" he asked. "You were in there a long time. Were

you daydreaming in the tub?"

"I might have dozed off," she lied, blushing. "I was quite tired . . ." She crammed a spoonful of scrambled egg into her mouth so she wouldn't have to answer any more questions.

"We'll go when you've eaten. I had Dweller bring you some clothes, and he's taken the rest of your things to the Lily. Yennica's looking forward to meeting you."

Carousel swallowed hard. The egg burned her throat. "I'm going now?"

"No sense hanging about when you could be making money!"

She couldn't argue with Noble's logic, but the meal was suddenly tasteless on her tongue. She forced down the remainder of her egg and bacon, trying not to think about how much her life had changed in less than a day. She pushed the bowl away from her and drained her glass.

"I'm ready."

"You're a good girl. You'll be fine. Hurry and get dressed." Noble narrowed his eyes. "Leave your hair down."

When she returned he was waiting by the window, looking out over the city. He turned, and offered her a dazzling smile. "Come on, Caro," he said. "I'll walk you there."

He took her arm and steered her out into the corridor, nodding to the guard on duty, an older man than the previous night. "Any problems?" Noble asked.

"Only the boy, and he's been no trouble."

"The boy?" Noble raised an eyebrow.

The guard pointed. Spark was curled up in an alcove, blanketed with the older man's cloak, snuffed out like a candle. "He was awake until nearly dawn," the guard said. "Then he sparked out, so I covered him up. Nice kid."

He had waited for Carousel, as he promised he would. "Can I wake him up to say goodbye?" she asked Noble. "He waited up all night . . ."

Noble shook his head. "We haven't got time for long

goodbyes, Carousel. Besides, I expect he's exhausted. Let him sleep."

"But—"

"I said come on."

There was no mistaking the command in his tone. Carousel sighed, but trailed down the corridor behind him obediently, through the halls where she had spent the childhood that she was now leaving behind. She was aware of curious glances directed her way, and she kept her head up, meeting every eye with a proud glare. They were still street rats, some of them had been that way fifty years or more, but not her. She was moving on to a better life.

Noble had spared no expense. A closed carriage waited outside the cemetery gate to whisk her away to her new life. She just wished Spark was there to wave goodbye to her.

$$\text{\scriptsize ♨}$$

Spark stirred at the nudge of a boot against his ribs. He opened his eyes to see the broad, decorated face of Dweller leaning over him, so close he caught a whiff of the older man's spicy breath. His neck and back were stiff from lying on cold stone. He groaned. "Help me up?"

Dweller obligingly extended a hand and hauled him to his feet.

Spark glanced at the door. "What bell is it? Is Carousel still in there?"

"Your little friend has gone, Spark."

"Gone? What do you mean, she's gone?" Spark took a step towards the door, and Dweller held him back.

"She left for the Lily, not long after dawn. Why, did she forget to say goodbye?"

Spark shook his head, confused. "But—I waited for her! She must have walked right past me, and she didn't think to wake me up?"

"You can't trust a whore, Spark."

"She's not a whore!" But she was now, he remembered belatedly. That was exactly what she was. It was all she would ever be.

"Probably thinks she's better than all of us now she's bedded down at the Lily." Dweller snorted in derision. "Come on, you and I have work to do."

"Are we picking pockets?"

"Not today." Dweller set off down the corridor. Spark had no option but to follow if he wanted to keep him in sight. "Noble thinks it's time you started earning your keep."

"Don't I earn my keep already? I bring in good coin . . ."

"He says," Dweller unlocked a small door off the corridor, and showed Spark inside, "that it's time you start doing what we picked you up for. You're wasted as a cut-purse. You could be much more than that."

Spark baulked on the threshold of the empty room. "I won't whore for Noble, if that's what he means."

Dweller laughed. "Of course not! Who would want your skinny arse? We have pretty boys for that!"

"And does Noble take care of them, the way he does with the girls?"

Dweller gave him a shove, forcing him up against the wall, muscled arm hard across his throat. The sudden move caught Spark by surprise, and he barely had time to struggle. Dweller's eyes were huge, whirling whites all he could see as he choked.

"Listen." The little man pressed harder. Spark gagged. "Noble loves all his people. Loves them all equally, and wants them to be safe. There's nothing obscene in what he does, and I'll kill you if you say there is!"

He let go all at once. Spark dropped to his knees, spluttering for air. Dweller kicked him lightly onto his back and stood over him, one foot on his chest.

"The only reason you're alive right now," he said, speaking slowly and clearly, as if Spark was too dense to understand, "is because Noble plucked you from the gutter. He could send you back with a snap of his fingers. He saved you because he thought your skills would be useful, so damned well start using them!"

"You mean my magic, don't you?" Dweller allowed him to sit up. Spark scowled. "I don't know how. I can't control it."

Dweller dropped into a crouch in front of him, eyes bright. "How did you come by it in the first place?" he asked.

Spark shrugged. "I've always had it. The old man –"

"Your father?"

"He wasn't my father," Spark explained. "He was like a guardian. He looked after me when my mother died. I don't remember her. He was teaching me about my magic, but he said we had plenty of time. Only then he got sick . . ."

He trailed off. He didn't want to think about that awful time, when he had watched the old man who had been father and mother to him slip further and further away, until they didn't know each other any more. Carlon had been dead long before the last breath left his lips.

"I don't want to talk about it."

"What colour were his eyes?" Dweller demanded.

"I said I don't want to talk about it!" Heat flared along his arms, and he grabbed his right wrist and held it to the floor. Dweller bared his teeth.

"It breaks free when you're angry, is that it?"

Spark nodded. "Mainly. Or upset. I haven't ever tried to summon it. I want it to go away."

"If you've had it all your life, it's not going to go away," Dweller said. "So let's try and get it under control. That's why I brought you here. To train you." He caught Spark's hand and pressed it between his own. "It's gone now, hasn't it?"

"It flares up, and then it goes away," Spark admitted. "It never lasts more than a few moments."

"How does it feel when it flares up?"

"Like flames travelling along my arms and legs. Arms

mainly."

Dweller pushed up Spark's sleeve. "It doesn't burn your skin?"

Spark shivered at the memories. "Not mine, no. Other peoples."

"Let's see it." Dweller hauled him to his feet. Spark stood in the middle of the bare room, feeling miserable and useless, empty hands dangling at his sides. "Hit me with it."

"I can't."

"Yes you can." Dweller slapped him on the chest. "Think about how you feel when you're angry. What sets it off?"

"I don't know. It just happens."

Dweller prowled around him, fading in and out of sight in a way that made Spark's head ache. "Useless boy," he muttered. "What's the point in having a skill if you're too scared to use it?"

"I'm not too scared to use it," Spark insisted. "I know what you're trying to do, and it won't work. I can't make it come on demand."

"You know who can come on demand? Your friend Carousel . . ."

Spark stiffened. "What are you talking about?"

Dweller was behind him, but when Spark twisted round he had faded into the shadows once more. His disembodied voice hissed in Spark's ear. "I saw her!"

"Saw her doing what?" If the aim had been to confuse Spark rather than make him angry, Dweller would be doing a fine job.

"I saw her spread her legs for Noble. I was right there in the room. She loved that—"

"Shut up!" Spark clamped his hands to his ears, but he couldn't shut out Dweller's insidious voice.

"She wasn't thinking about you. All those men will take her at the Lily, and not once will she think about you that way. Only about Noble, and how he made her squeal. I could see her little tits wobbling as he fucked her, and that's something you'll never see—"

"Shut up, I said!" Furious power surged through him, wild, out of control, lashing out to blast a scorched hole in the wall in front of him.

"Come on, Spark, see if you can find me!" Dweller slithered in and out of sight. "Maybe I'll pop down to the Lily and have a go on her myself. How does that sound to you? Of course," there was a flicker of movement in the corner of Spark's eye, and he spun around to face it, "you'll never be able to afford her, but I'll tell you all about it when—"

"Fucking shut up!" Spark staggered backwards, thrown by the force of the bolt erupting from his palms. Dweller screamed, a hideous sound, more animal than human, doubled up and clutching his stomach as the flames took hold of his cloak. He writhed on the floor, screaming, beating at the flames as they devoured his body.

"Help me, damn you!"

Terror held Spark prisoner for a moment, then released him. He fled, the screams of the dying man echoing in his ears. He didn't stop running until he reached the cemetery gate, and only then because his lungs were bursting and he was crippled with a stitch.

He had killed Dweller. He sagged at the realisation, knees hitting cold stone. The painted man had only been trying to help, and he had killed him. Worse, he had left him to die screaming on the floor.

"It was an accident!"

The city didn't care that he howled his grief, his innocence. Noble wouldn't care. He would cast him out, if he didn't slit his throat. Maybe that was no more than Spark deserved. Everything he touched, he destroyed.

He dragged himself to his feet, clinging on to the gate for support. He could go back, beg forgiveness. Maybe Noble would only cast him out. Or he could run. He felt like he'd been running forever. He was so tired. It would almost be a relief if Noble or the Old Ones caught up with him, cut off his trail of destruction.

He couldn't go back, couldn't face Noble's condemnation. The city lay before him, and every man's hand would be raised against him now. Noble, Shadow and his cronies, and the Watch. In the biggest city in the world, he had only one friend. One person he could trust. He needed to see her once more before he died.

It was a long walk across the city to the Gilded Lily. Wiping the tears from his eyes, Spark set off to find Carousel.

By the time he reached the Lily it was dark. Cold flakes of sleet dropped from the sky to splatter against his hood. Winter was closing in fast. The caverns below the cemetery had been cosy, lively with preparations for Winterfest, only a moon away. If Spark was still alive by Winterfest he would be spending it on the streets. He tried not to think about what would happen to him when it snowed, as he climbed the wooden steps and hammered on the customer entrance of the Lily.

The hatch in the door slid back, and the eunuch's wary eyes glared at him. "You're Noble's kid, aren't you? Have you got coin?"

Spark hadn't even considered that he might need money. "I'm not a customer," he explained. "I'm here to see Carousel."

"The new girl? Sorry kid." From what he could see, the eunuch shrugged. "No one sees any of the girls without money. That's the rules."

"But—" he thought quickly. "I've got a message for her. From Noble. He said it was urgent."

"A message from Noble? That's different, then. Give me the password and I'll let you in."

"Password?" Spark's heart sank. "He didn't tell me any password . . ."

"Then you can't come in without coin." The eunuch moved to close the hatch, almost trapping Spark's fingers in the snapping wood.

"You let me in before!" he protested.

"You were with Noble then. Come back with Noble, the password, or some coin, and I'll let you in. Otherwise stand out here all night."

A blade appeared, pressed against Spark's fingers. "Move them," the eunuch added, "or I chop them off. Your choice."

Spark withdrew his hand and the hatch snapped shut. He rested his forehead against the wood for a moment, struggling not to give in to despair. Maybe if he found Carousel's window he could throw a stone up, attract her attention. All he wanted was to talk to her.

He debated knocking on the door again, but decided against it. That eunuch was too quick to draw blade. Instead he retreated to the far side of the street and sat in a doorway, knees pulled up to his chin, feeling gut-sick and miserable.

But the city didn't stop for Spark's misery. He could see the lantern lights in the windows of the brothel opposite. He glared at the men who tramped with depressing regularity up the steps, under the light of the red-shrouded lantern swinging above the door. Sometimes they came in laughing groups, egging each other on. More often they were alone; merchants in their sleeveless coats, hard-faced soldiers from the garrison, plump old men who moved with furtive, crablike steps, trying to keep to the shadows. Spark saw every face, imagined every bulging purse. His Carousel was in there, dancing to the whim of these men, and there was nothing he could do. His clenched fists scraped impotently on the stone, and at a rowdy burst of laughter he sprang up, clutching his dagger, before sinking back down again to helplessly watch the parade.

His dagger . . . He toyed with it, listening to the jingle of coin exchanging hands at the top of the steps, the door opening and closing to let men in and out. He didn't have coin, but he knew how to get it. All it would take was a little skill. And the idea of robbing a man on his way to pay Carousel for her favours was a grimly satisfying one.

He drew the blade, moving silently, sticking to the shadows until he came to a waste alley. It was no more than a narrow slip off the main alley, so tight a fat man couldn't have squeezed down it. This was where the waste from the windows above piled up, or was swept from the highway. It stank, and he heard rats rustling, but it would do for cover.

He lurked in the darkness. Three men passed by, soldiers by their bearing, and he shrank back. They didn't see him, or if they did, he wasn't worth a second glance. The next set of boots, pacing briskly on the stone, walked alone. Apart from them the alley was deserted.

Spark swallowed his fear. He had cut plenty of purses, but holding a man up was different. He hoped he would hand the purse over without a struggle. He hoped he wasn't too big.

Spark stepped out of the darkness, brandishing the knife. "Hand over your purse!"

"The hells with you, kid!" His victim wasn't tall, but he was bulky, and his hands flashed to his own blade. "Get out of my way or I'll cut you open!"

Spark lashed out wildly at his victim's face. "Give me your purse!" His hand was wet, slippery, and the knife fell from his grip. The man stood there, staring at him, eyes wide and blank. His shirt was black. Spark was sure a moment ago it had been white.

The merchant made a gurgling sound and crumpled, knees collapsing under his weight. He pitched forward and Spark caught him as the door at the top of the stairs burst open, and the light swayed.

"Hey!" the eunuch called. "What's going on down there?"

Spark kept his voice low and his face turned away, hoping the doorman wouldn't recognise him. "He's too drunk for a whore, I think!"

"Carry him home then. Don't scare off our customers!" The door slammed. Spark was alone in the alley with a dead man in his arms.

"Shit! Shit, I'm sorry! Why didn't you just give me your purse?"

His lashing blade must have caught the stranger's life vein and ripped it open. This wasn't what he wanted. All he wanted was to see Carousel. Why did there have to be so much death?

They staggered together for a moment, caught in a morbid embrace, Spark teetering on the edge of panic. There was blood on his hands, on his clothes. The eunuch would know he had killed. He would tell the Watch, and Spark would dance on the end of a rope. He felt sick. Everything he did was wrong, and ended in disaster.

I'll say goodbye to her, and then I'll run. He didn't know where he would run, only that it had to be far from the city, far from people, so he couldn't hurt anyone. The border wasn't far; maybe he could lose himself in the vast deserts of Telesia. Better to die of thirst alone than to take another life. But he had to see Carousel one last time.

He stuffed the body of his victim as far down the waste alley as he could stand to go before the stench overwhelmed him. If he was lucky, no one would find it for a few days. The rats would feast tonight, and he shuddered at the thought of their swarming grey bodies. He cut the man's purse free of his belt and withdrew.

"I'm sorry," he repeated. The alley rustled into life.

Spark had no time to check for bloodstains on his skin. The best he could do was draw his black cloak tightly around him, and hope the blood splashed on it didn't show up under the lantern. Swallowing his sickness, he made his way up the steps and knocked on the door once more.

The hatch rattled back. The eunuch sniffed his disdain. "You again? I thought I told you—"

Spark held up the purse. "Can I see her now?"

JOANNE HALL

"Of course." His tone changed at once, unctuous and oily, as the bolts on the door rattled back to admit Spark into the carpeted corridors of the Gilded Lily.

The fat man held out his hand. "Five silvers," he said.

"Five?" Spark had no idea how much whores cost, but it seemed excessive.

"This is a classy place. If you want to argue, I can make it six?"

"I don't want to argue. I just want to see Carousel." He counted out the coins into the eunuch's chubby paw. The purse seemed a lot lighter when he was done.

"She's with a customer. You can see another girl, or you can wait."

"I'll wait."

"Downstairs, in the bar."

Spark shook his head, lips pressed tight. "I'll wait here."

"It'll cost you extra."

This time he handed over the coin without protest. If he went down to the bar, he was likely to be arrested or stabbed before he got to see her.

The eunuch shrugged. "You're a decent kid. Wait in my office. I'll show you to her room when she's free."

The office was as padded and soft as the man who held it. It stank of an excess of perfume and an undertone of sweat. Spark sank into an armchair and risked a glance at the deep red stains on his shirt. It didn't matter how hot the room was, with its blazing fire, he wasn't going to take his cloak off and reveal his crime. He was itchy and perspiring by the time the doorman returned.

"She's free now," he said, bluntly. "Though the poor girl could use a rest. Are you sure you don't want another whore?"

"I don't want to bed her," Spark insisted. "I just want to talk."

The eunuch had no eyebrows to raise, but his brow twitched. "One of them, are you? You be careful with her."

"What are you talking about?" Spark padded behind him, along the corridor and up a flight of stairs to the next floor.

"We get a lot of your sort in here. The ones who say they want to talk are always the ones . . . Well, let's just say their tastes would be better catered for at the Drover's Wheel, if you know what I mean." He winked.

Spark had no idea what he meant, but he would have felt stupid asking, so he just nodded.

"Here you go." The eunuch knocked on the door and withdrew. "Have fun!"

"Come in!" Carousel's voice was muffled. Spark waited until the eunuch had vanished back down the stairs before he opened the door.

She was standing by the window, with her back to him, gripping the sill as if she was steeling herself to jump. She did not look round as she spoke.

"Just lie down on the bed. I'll be with you in a moment."

"Carousel?"

"Spark?" She whirled around. Her hair was loose, tumbling around her face, and she wore a low-cut dress, hiked up at the front, chest and thighs on prominent display as she ran into his embrace. "Spark, I'm so sorry! You were asleep, and Noble said we had to hurry, and I didn't want to wake you—how did you get in here? And why are you covered in blood? Are you hurt?"

"Long story." He shot the bolt on the door and sank down on the bed, exhausted. "A purse lift that went wrong. It's not my blood. I—I had to come and see you, to say goodbye. I'm leaving the city."

"Leaving the city? Why?"

"I killed Dweller." The words were heavy on his tongue. It was a relief to set them free.

Carousel sank down beside him, one hand clasped to her mouth. "Dweller—you didn't? What happened?"

"It was an accident." That didn't make it any better.

"Shit, Spark! Noble's going to *gut* you!"

"You think I don't know that? Why do you think I'm leaving Cape Carey?"

She shook her head, stunned into silence for a moment. Then, "So why did you come and see me? You paid, I'll do what you want . . ."

"Not for that! I told you, I wanted to come and say goodbye. Now I've seen you, I'll go."

"Wait." She caught his wrist. "Don't go yet. Stay a while."

"I thought you were busy. With customers."

Carousel sighed. "Hells, Spark, I need a break! Will you stay, before Armagin sends anyone else?"

"The fat man on the door?"

She nodded.

"How many have you had today? Three?"

"Five." She lay back on the bed, crumpling the sheets in her fists. "I'm tired, Spark! And I'm sore. They—they don't like to take their time . . . ."

Spark wasn't sure what she meant by that, but she looked miserable, her tears streaking the make-up round her eyes. It wouldn't hurt to stay. After all, he had already paid for the time.

He stroked her hair back from her face. "Why don't you sleep?" he suggested. "I can wait until you wake up."

"Would you?" She reached out, squeezed his hand. "You're a sweet kid, Spark. I'd like that." Her eyelids were drooping even as she spoke, and she rolled away from him on to her side. Still clutching her hand, Spark curled around her back, breathing in her perfume. Absently, she drew his arm down over her shoulder, and patted his hand. He wanted to kiss her bare throat, but he thought she'd had enough of kissing today.

Spark woke abruptly, wondering if the hammering was in his head. It took a bleary moment to realise that it wasn't, that Carousel's bedroom door was rattling under a barrage of knocking. He scrambled to his feet, blinking sleep from his eyes. "What's going on?"

"You've stayed over your time." Carousel's eyes were wide, her face white with fear. "I've got another customer. You have to leave!"

"I don't want to leave you here, Caro. You're miserable."

She shrugged, sadly. "I expect I'll get used to it."

The hammering came again, and a voice from the far side of the door chilled Spark's blood.

"Spark, if you don't open this door right now your entrails are going to be decorating the cemetery gates!"

"Shit!" Of course Noble would know exactly where he had gone. Spark was only surprised he hadn't got here sooner.

He grabbed Carousel and pushed her away from him, feeling the growing tingle in his hands. She landed on the bed hard as he raised his arms in front of him. "Spark! What are you doing?"

"Getting us both out of here!"

The fire burst forth, the first time he had ever wanted it. The window blew out, scattering glass and splinters over the street below. People ran for cover as the heat from his hands ripped the stones from the walls of the building and sent them flying across the road. Carousel screamed, burying her head in her hands, but Spark laughed. It was working. Finally he felt he had some control over his power, and it sent a thrill through him.

The door broke free of its hinges. Noble tumbled into the room, choking on the smoke and dust. Spark caught a glimpse of white eyes and bared teeth as he snatched Carousel up from the bed and held her to him with a strength that seemed to go beyond mere human. The stones of the wall were red-hot, melting around him, and the winter wind howled sleet through the ripped-out gap in the front of the Gilded Lily.

Noble lunged for him, and Spark, with Carousel limp in his arms, leapt through the smoking hole and ran for his life.

Thirteen

D ID YOU HEAR about the trouble on Squeezetitty Lane last night?"

Kayall looked up from his lunch, his attention caught more by the street name than by the prospect of hearing yet another anecdote about how someone somebody knew had had their arse kicked. The citizens of Cape Carey seemed to like nothing better than a good story about a bloody fight.

The raconteur at the bar had an appreciative audience, and he held up his empty flagon for a refill before carrying on with his tale. "You all know the Gilded Lily?"

"We all know you do!" someone retorted. There was sniggering at this wit. Kayall edged his chair a fraction closer.

The old man supped his pint. "Yes I do," he said. "There's no shame in it. I get lonely since my wife died."

Kayall felt a touch of sympathy for him, and there were kindly mutters from the men at the bar. The wit in the audience cleared his throat. "What was the trouble, Connell?" he asked.

"Fire, and some kind of explosion." Connell lowered his voice. "Magical happenings, if you ask me . . ."

Kayall pushed his plate away and ambled to the bar to order a flagon, keeping his turquoise eyes downcast.

None of the men spared him a glance. They were too busy scoffing at the old man's tale.

"I'm telling you, it was magic! I heard it from a fellow who heard it from a girl . . . Don't laugh! You go down and take a look. The whole side of the building's ripped out! Only magic could do that!"

"Seen it with your eyes, have you?"

"No, but this girl told my friend . . . No, listen . . . One of the whores had a client in, and he fired the building and kidnapped her. Young kiddie, by all accounts. Noble's spitting for his blood. I think the boy was one of his before he went rogue."

Who in hells was Noble? And had Liathan added kidnapping to his list of crimes? He needed to be reined in, or put down. The talk at the bar moved on to other things, the results of last night's dog fights, the shortage of starstones for Winterfest gifts, whether the Carey family would open their halls to commoners during the festival. Kayall, his curiosity piqued, resolved to find Elvienne and take a look at the destruction of the Gilded Lily for himself. Maybe they could pick up Liathan's trail from there.

Nomi came to clear his plates, and he caught her burly forearm. "Who's Noble?" he asked.

She frowned. "You haven't got tangled with the Nobility, have you? That's the kind of trouble I can do without."

"Who are the Nobility?"

Nomi shook her head. "Stay away from Noble's lot, Kayall. And from Startide. This is my place. I won't have it turned into a street rat battleground." She moved away before he could ask any more questions, and he was left to wonder what additional trouble Carlon's lost apprentice had got himself into.

⚘

The answer was a considerable amount, judging by the gaping hole in the upper floor of the Gilded Lily. Kayall saw it as the carriage rumbled over the cobbles of Greenhaven Street, past upmarket haberdasheries and jewellers. The shops should have been doing a brisk trade this time of year, but they were mostly deserted. The city watchman on duty made them get out and walk a long way short of the building, and as Kayall emerged he felt the low-level hum of discharged magic in the air. It made his head throb. Elvienne winced. "Powerful," she said.

"You're not wrong." The idea of so much power in the hands of an untrained child was frightening. The watch had thrown a rope across the street to keep onlookers back from what remained of the Gilded Lily, but they were close enough to see the havoc Liathan had wrought. The window, and the wall around it, had blown out with such force that glass and stone were embedded deep in the plaster of the building opposite. Scorch marks like the smears of blackened fingerprints stained the outside of the Lily, and rubble was strewn across the street. Kayall picked up a lump of stone, melted into twisted fantasy. "Elvienne, look at this!"

She paid him no attention. She knelt in the road, ignoring the tutting and barbed remarks of the Winterfest shoppers as they tried to get by her. "Come and see this," she said.

Kayall shrugged. "More cracks in the pavement, like we saw before. So what?"

"These are wider." She looked up at him, fluffy white eyebrows drawn together in irritation. "You still don't see it, do you?"

Kayall didn't know what he was supposed to be seeing, but he dropped down beside her. The magical resonance was stronger here. It felt like his eyes were vibrating in their sockets. The stone trembled under his hands, the crack drawing apart. The movement was so slow he couldn't see it, but he could feel it, and the stones were hot under his fingers.

He sat back on his heels. "This isn't just left over from our little maniac?"

Elvienne shook her head. "I told you he'd unleashed

something. Now it's finding its way out, crawling towards the surface . . ."

"A demon?"

"More than one, I think. Liathan has cracked the world. He's opened a doorway into hell, and now the beasts that live down there are forcing their way through." She was pale as she rose, clinging on to his arm for support.

Kayall looked around, at the bustle of shoppers, the teaming city. "How many people live in Cape Carey?" he asked, in a hushed voice.

"Too many."

Too many people crammed together, in winter, and a horde of demons clawing up through stone and earth. Fighting to emerge, to take back the world of light they had been banished from. He sucked in a long breath, and released it slowly.

"Oh fuck."

"We should tell someone," Elvienne said. "The Careys?"

"Never mind the bloody Careys, we should find that wretched child and make him fix the damage he's caused! Unless you think you can do it?" Kayall had no illusions about his own inability to deal with the crisis. His realm was air and sky, Elvienne's was earth and stone. If anyone could seal the gaping, expanding cracks that rucked up the cobbles, it was her. But she shook her head.

"This is more power than I've ever felt. Carlon always said Liathan was special, as he was born in Lydyce. The boy has power from the stars. That's why he took him on!"

"And the stupid old man didn't think to train him properly?"

"He thought he had time!" Kayall's words stung more sharply than he intended. The tears swam in Elvienne's eyes, and she dashed them away angrily. "We think we have forever. I know you do, anyway."

Kayall thought of the arrow that had so narrowly missed him at the Mouse. He nodded. "Sometimes I forget we don't. We certainly don't now. If what you say is true, the forces of hell are going to be joining us for Winterfest."

"So we're back to our main problem," Elvienne said. "How do we find the boy?"

"I have a hunch," Kayall said. "I heard he was involved with some kind of criminal gang, the Nobility. Do you know anything about them?"

Elvienne shook her head. "Nothing at all. When did you find this out?"

"Lunchtime. I think Nomi knows something about it, but she clammed up when I tried to get her to talk."

"Try again. I'm going to speak to Lord Carey, to tell him his city sits on quicksand."

They were walking back towards the carriage rank, Elvienne stopping every few paces to prod the cracks in the pavement with her stick, when a cloaked figure moved to intercept them, walking purposefully but blocking their way. Kayall nudged Elvienne in the ribs, and she looked up and scowled.

"We have no need of plague cures, my friend," she said.

The plague doctor nodded his beaked head, his eyes two blank, shining circles of glass. Kayall never trusted men who hid their eyes. The eyes were the windows of the spirit.

"I don't bring plague cures," he said, voice muffled by the thick leather. "I don't think you mages need them. You don't get sick, do you?"

"Never." Elvienne liked to keep up the illusion of immortality. It was what most people believed, and it was unbecoming to their Order to show weakness.

"I thought I'd run into you here."

Kayall shrugged, trying to make light of it. Something in the hidden man's demeanour made his skin crawl. "That's us," he said. "Never far from chaos and destruction!"

"My Lady would like to see you. Are you free?"

Kayall exchanged a glance with Elvienne. "That depends on who your Lady is," she said. "We don't answer the beck and call of the noble houses unless we choose to. Certainly not those that hide behind masks and send servants to summon us."

"Forgive me." The plague doctor bowed, beak sweeping the ground. "My Lady Allorise Carey is worried about," he waved his hand at the ruin of the Lily, "things like this. Wild magic loose in her city. She would be reassured if you would meet with her."

"We'd fix the problem quicker if people would let us get on and do our job—" Kayall began, but Elvienne laid a hand on his arm to cut him off.

"I thought Lord Carey ruled the city? Allorise is his wife?"

"His daughter. Lord Carey is . . . incapacitated. Hence," he gestured to his garb. "Most of the family have fled to the country, but Lady Allorise and her brother stayed to care for their father."

"Such devotion," Kayall muttered sarcastically.

"Will you come?" The plague doctor sounded eager. "She sent me with a carriage."

"Into a plague house?"

"Why would that matter to you? You're a mage. You don't get sick."

He had him by the balls there, Kayall reflected. "Elvienne?"

"I'll go," she said.

"Alone?"

"Why not? Afternoon tea in a noble house and a chat with a devoted daughter sounds like a good way to spend the afternoon. You," she fixed him with a sharp glare, "find out what the White Giantess knows. I'll meet you back at the tavern."

Kayall knew a dismissal when he heard it. He nodded. "Just . . . be careful." *Don't breathe in too deeply. This stinks of more than plague.*

She gave no sign that she heard his silent warning. With a terse nod, the plague doctor linked his arm through hers to help her over the ruptured cobbles towards the liveried carriage that stood waiting. Left alone, free of her disapproval, Kayall stood in the middle of Cape Carey's most celebrated shopping streets. The shop windows beckoned him in. It would be rude to decline their invitation.

⚜

Elvienne watched her travelling companion dive into the nearest tailors with a small sigh of affectionate exasperation. Kayall's worst vice was clothes, but there were far more terrible vices. Let him have his fun, as she would have hers. There was nothing wrong in enjoying a touch of luxury where she could get it, and the Carey carriage was luxurious, with deep, blood-red upholstery. The city cabs had skin-thin seats, and you could feel the springs digging in every time they went over a bump. You couldn't feel the springs in this carriage at all. It even had windows that rolled up and down, and delicate, fussy frilled curtains that could be closed for privacy.

The plague doctor sat opposite. With his concealed eyes, he was more like a sculpture than a man, sitting bolt-upright with his hands clenched in his lap. He looked out of place among the opulence, and the more she studied him, the less like a healer he looked. His forearms were meaty, and she could see the bulk of muscle under the cloak. He sat like a fighter about to go into the arena, tense, one foot constantly tapping. He didn't speak, even to make polite conversation.

Elvienne had run out of polite remarks about the weather three centuries ago, and it was a change to be able to sit and quietly observe. But she was jolted out of her silence as the carriage rolled past the castle gate without slowing down.

"I thought you were taking me to see Lady Allorise?"

The plague doctor looked out of the window at the grey wall as they rumbled by.

"She's not at the castle," he explained. "They haven't lived in the castle for a while. Too drafty and uncomfortable. I'm taking you to the mansion."

Elvienne thinned her lips, but held back a comment about this breach of security. If the war in the north-east came south, if the demons rose, the Careys would dive back behind their curtain walls soon enough. She hoped they weren't too neglected to hold against assault. Something else to ask Allorise.

The coach rattled across a bridge, wide and smooth, painted gold balustrades dusted with the light snow that had fallen the night before. The first of the season, but the heavy sky promised more to come. She hoped Liathan had found shelter, wherever he was. Once she had dealt with this Carey woman, she resolved to go back to the Lily and see if she could pick up his trail. Magic that powerful, if he kept using it, would leave a trace she could follow.

The carriage swept through a high, imposing pair of gates and slowed to a halt. The plague doctor hopped out, tipped the coachman, and held out a hand to assist Elvienne to the ground. She was impressed at his display of manners, but had misgivings as she looked at the house. There was no footman waiting at the door to greet them. Half the windows were shuttered, the defensive ramparts were too small to hide behind, and there were big windows on the ground floor. Even for a manor house, the Carey mansion was poorly fortified.

Not just poorly defended. As Elvienne scanned the house, she felt a cold sensation, like insects with myriad icy feet racing up and down her spine. There was something wrong in the Carey mansion. She couldn't pin it down to specifics, but it made her skin crawl. Dark magic had been worked within these walls. The resonance of Liathan's anger had hummed through the streets outside the Lily, but this was something far older, far darker. As they approached the door, she trailed her fingers in casual fashion along the whitewashed stone, and clamped down the urge to snatch her hand away. The stones of the Lily had grumbled, but the stones of the Carey mansion screamed their torment. They had witnessed evil, and they writhed in pain.

It's a wonder the whole place hasn't collapsed. Allorise Carey must be made aware. Someone in her house diced with the most fell powers, and they had to be stopped.

The plague doctor held the door open for her and ushered her into the expansive, marbled hall, which echoed to the sound of their footsteps. Dust gathered in the corners of the stairs, and the brasswork was dull. Where were all the servants? A place this size should be bustling with life. The feeling of discomfort, of wrongness, grew by the moment.

"How many staff does Lady Allorise employ?" she asked. The plague doctor shrugged, but before he could reply, a male voice hailed them from the galleried landing above.

"Shadow! I've told you before, you don't let yourself into my hall, and you certainly don't bring strangers here. What's going on?"

The frowning young man approaching down the stairs was tall and cadaverous, with arms and legs that seemed too long for his body. He moved with an easy, loping stride. Beside her, Elvienne sensed the plague doctor bristle. She stepped forward.

"You are one of the Carey family?"

His scowl deepened. "I'm Lord Bastian Carey, yes. Who in all hells are you? A friend of Shadow?"

"Shadow brought me to see Lady Allorise. Is she free?"

Bastian jerked his thumb at the plague doctor. "You've done as my sister asked. Now get out."

"I think I'll get something to eat," Shadow said. "Is the cook around?"

"Get out, I said!"

Shadow shrugged, and headed towards the kitchen with deliberately insolent slowness. Bastian watched him leave, but as the door slammed behind him he turned back to Elvienne. His smile was polite, but brittle. "You didn't tell me your name," he said.

"My name is Elvienne. Your sister asked to see me, and it's vital that I speak with her."

Bastian sniffed disdainfully. "More Startide affairs? No," he held his hands up, "I don't want to know. I don't get involved in my sister's business. She's with my father, but I'll show you to her chambers and let her know you're here."

Elvienne filed away the reference to Startide in her memory. Nomi might know what Bastian was referring to, but if he assumed she was part of this Startide, she wasn't about to disabuse him. The evil she felt didn't come from Bastian. There was discomfort there, unfulfilled desire, but nothing malign. Maybe it came from one of the servants.

She ran her hand along the banisters as she followed him upstairs, and made a show of looking at the dust darkening her fingertips. "Are you having trouble with your staff, Bastian?"

His eyes narrowed. He didn't like her familiar manner, obviously, but Elvienne bowed her head to no one. "Most of our staff left with my mother," he said. "It's just me and my sister, her personal guard and the cook now."

"And Shadow?"

"Shadow doesn't work here." He turned from her abruptly and strode away down the hall. She had to walk fast to keep up with his long stride, walking stick clicking a rhythm on the wooden floor.

Bastian showed her into a neat reception chamber, all pastel colours and soft frills. "Take a seat," he said. "I'm sure my sister won't be long."

Elvienne prodded the sofa with her stick. "I prefer to stand," she said. "If I sink into that, I might never get out again!"

Bastian shrugged. "Please yourself." The door thumped shut behind him. Elvienne waited until his footsteps retreated down the hall before she moved.

First she changed her face. Bastian, if he came back, wouldn't remember her original face, and she was certain Allorise wouldn't treat an elderly woman with the respect the situation demanded. She blurred her features, let her hair darken and grow long, gave herself an aquiline nose and high cheekbones, added a good five inches to her height. She would be a Midlander, familiar with Court, accustomed to respect. One who would not humiliate Allorise by telling her what to do. From the furnishings of the room, she looked soft, as if she needed help. She must be struggling, with her father so sick and the servants fled.

She checked her appearance in her pocket mirror, pinned up her hair, dusted some powder on her nose and cheeks. That would do. There was still no sound in the corridor, Allorise was taking her time, so Elvienne decided to see if she could learn anything more from the house.

She leaned her palms flat against the wall and pressed her forehead to the plaster, feeling the tiny movements of the old building, contracting in the cold air. She stretched out with all her senses. The lives, the emotions, of the Carey family and the servants who lived with them had seeped into the fabric of the building. She could feel them through plaster and stone.

The wash of frustration and inadequacy—that had to be Bastian. She felt the touch of another spirit, laced with confusion, fear, and a desperate desire to escape. She wondered if it was Allorise, but the thoughts were those of someone older, already beaten down by life. The cook, maybe.

Elvienne probed deeper, with a growing sense of unease. Nothing good happened in the Carey mansion that she could uncover. Only fear, and pain, and, behind that . . .

She recoiled with a gasp, breaking the fragile contact. The shadow that lay over the manor was deepest black, revelling in evil and chaos. And it was watching her. Twisted and triumphant, it knew she was here, and it was coming for her. Coming fast.

Allorise?

Elvienne hurried to the window and swung it open. It was a long drop from the first floor to the ground, but the rear wall of the mansion was overgrown with sturdy vines that held firm as she tugged them. She swung a leg out of the window, searching for a toehold, as the clipped footsteps in the corridor hesitated outside the door. By the time Allorise reached the window, all she would see was a long-legged, elegant woman striding across the faded winter lawn towards the back gate of the mansion.

◊

Arms laden with his purchases, Kayall arrived back at the Mouse as dusk gathered, feet blistered and aching, with a niggling pain in the small of his back that only ale would cure. He dumped the cloth-wrapped bundles into the arms of the tavern maid with a wink, a flicked copper and a request for her to take them to his room, and retired to the bar. He had the vague feeling he should start looking into Noble's activities, that Elvienne would be sitting at their usual table with a half of ale and a reproachful glare. He was relieved she was nowhere to be seen, in any guise.

Calbrath leaned on the bar. He waved, and patted the stool beside him. Kayall debated whether or not to pretend he hadn't noticed. It was fun to roll around in bed, but he wasn't looking for anything more serious, or permanent. But Calbrath was generous with getting the drinks in. He took a few steps in his direction when he felt a light touch on his elbow.

"Hello stranger. I hoped I'd find you here. Fancy a game?"

It took a moment for Kayall to recognise Wenna from the card game at the Black Rat. She fluttered her eyelashes and held up a deck of cards. He couldn't refuse an invitation like that. He offered Calbrath a rueful shrug, and was rewarded with a nod of understanding. The soldier would be happy on the edge of the fire for now.

"Three Eyed Dog? Carey Variant? Pint to go with it?"

She smiled. "Yes to all three. Though I might be the one buying drinks when I've cleaned out your pockets!"

"No chance. I had a bastard's luck last time. Won't happen again!"

JOANNE HALL

"We'll see." She let him buy her an ale, and he watched the curve of her hips in their snug breeches as she headed for a nearby table. *Not bad,* he thought to himself. He hoped Elvienne wouldn't turn up and ruin his fun.

Wenna shuffled the cards with expert hands, and fanned them before her on the table. "You draw," she said. "Dealer calls, stars are high, queens are wild."

"How did a nice girl like you end up so sharp with the cards?" Kayall watched her deal with admiration.

"Experience." He waited for her to say more, but her cool blue eyes were focussed on the cards in her hand. Her fair hair was boyishly short, tousled. If she let it grow it would have a curl to it. She wore a man's shirt, with a tightly-laced jerkin over the top to ward off the cold, and he found himself wondering what lay beneath it. Distracted by the thought, he lost the first three hands by a humiliating margin.

"You're right," she said. "You do have a bastard's luck. Either that or you're really bad at cards. I recommend a new career, mage!"

"I'm not usually *this* bad!" He sighed as she lay another triumphant hand across the table, and noticed her flagon was empty. "Another pint?"

Wenna scraped his coppers into her purse. "I think this round is on me, don't you?"

She returned from the bar with two brimming flagons.

"You haven't told me what brings you to Cape Carey," she said, sipping her pint. "Secret mage business?"

He shrugged. "Not really secret. I'm looking for someone."

"Someone from the city?" Her eyes narrowed. "I meet a lot of people on the gaming tables. Maybe I can help you?"

"Maybe you can." Liathan was too young to be found at the gaming tables, but Noble wasn't. "You know a man called Noble? I think he heads up a gang of some sort."

She nodded, and spoke in a low voice. "I don't know him, but I know where you can find him. Want me to take you there?"

"Tonight?" People coming through the door were shaking the rain off their cloaks. The Mouse was warm, and there was ale here, and good company. Without Elvienne here to nag him, Kayall was reluctant to move.

Her fingers brushed his wrist, and her eyes sparkled. "I wasn't planning to leave the Mouse tonight. Another hand?"

‡

Wenna was an early riser. By the time Kayall struggled free of the blankets she was already up and dressed, running her hands through her hair in front of the mirror and frowning. "I sent down for breakfast," she said. "It's not raining at the moment, but it's cold. It might come on to snow, so let's get it over with."

Elvienne? There was no reply to Kayall's query. Maybe his comrade was asleep. It would be a coup for him if he could pick up Liathan and bring him back before she was even out of bed.

"I'll follow you down," he said.

She nodded, terse, unaffectionate, as she laced her boots. "Don't be long. Some of us have to work for our coin."

He wondered what was eating at her as she let the door bang shut behind her. She'd had no complaints last night, joking that it was a pity his skill with his hands didn't extend to the card table. The ways of women were unfathomable. Men were much easier to deal with.

The frost had scrawled patterns on the tiny window, and Kayall dressed for snow. He sized up his purchases from Greenhaven Street, selecting the thickest breeches of bright blue, so tight he had to lie down to fasten them. He chose a cream shirt, navy jerkin and a striking red cloak with a lacy black overlay that he had fallen in love with, even though it meant rejecting a few other items so that he could afford it. He twirled it in front of the mirror before draping it casually over his shoulders, dusting his eyes and cheeks with powder, and slipping mismatched earrings through the holes in his earlobes. He looked the perfect city gentleman.

By the time he arrived downstairs, the porridge Wenna had ordered was cold. She lurked impatiently by the door, glaring at the sky. He only had time to gulp down a few mouthfuls, and chase them with a mug of warm wine, before she insisted he follow her out into the cold grasp of the morning air. Despite the chill the streets were busy. In the Telesian quarter braziers on every corner sold hot, spicy snacks. Wenna would not be drawn on where they were going, but she led him over a narrow bridge and through a high iron gate, into the Telesian cemetery.

A thin sheet of ice coated the ground. It broke under Kayall's tread and the mud sucked at his boots. The path was slippery, but he stuck to it as he followed Wenna between the frost-rimed mausoleums. She walked with a confidence Kayall didn't share. He was unnerved by the quiet, and the tiny, magnified sounds that pierced it; the snap of a twig, the harsh cry of a bird. There was no sign of Noble.

"Wenna, there's no one here. I think we should go back."

"It's not much further." Without warning she dived off the path, feet slurping through the mud, pushing aside the trailing brambles. "The Nobility live in caves under the cemetery. Just through there."

She pointed at the tomb directly ahead of them. The brass door on the short end stood ajar, a narrow band of darkness within. Wenna hung back. "Go on," she said. "You wanted to come here. You go first."

The metal was cold. It stuck to Kayall's bare fingers as he swung the door open to reveal the yawning entrance to the tomb. Had something scuttled, in the blackness of the grave? "Wenna, I don't think—"

His thought was lost beneath the explosion of pain in his head, and he pitched forward into darkness.

Fourteen

HOWEVER BITTER THE winds were that whistled down the streets of Cape Carey, at least there were plenty of high walls to provide shelter. Out in the slums, the single storey shacks fashioned from metal sheets and waste wood did nothing to ward off the weather. Carousel clasped the tattered blanket tighter around her thin shoulders, and shivered, pressing her back into a corner between the two huts. It offered meagre shelter. "This is ridiculous," she muttered again.

Spark's lips were too numb to form a reply, and he worked them soundlessly. He was pressed close against her side, but he could feel little warmth from her body. He dug through his pockets with useless fingers, knowing the gesture was futile. The last of the coin was long gone.

"I think we should go back to the city."

He shook his head. "They'll kill us, Caro. You know that."

"You'd rather stay here and let the weather do Noble's job for him?" She scowled. "He might have calmed down by now. He wouldn't let us die on the streets. We can make too much money for him. Speaking of money . . ."

"No." Spark's voice was flat. "I won't let you whore yourself.

There must be another way. What about your friend in the city? I thought we would have heard from her by now?"

"Maybe she's scared of Noble." Carousel fidgeted, trying to get comfortable on the frozen ground. "If you won't let me sell myself, then how about you?"

Spark shook his head, tight lipped. "I'd rather die," he said.

"You'd rather die? That's what's going to happen, Spark! We're going to freeze to death because of your pride!" She scrambled to her feet, moving with difficulty on stiff limbs.

He caught her wrist. "Where are you going?"

"We have to keep moving. If we don't, we'll freeze where we sit. I'm going back to the gate to see if I can scrounge some food off the guard. Are you coming?"

She was right, it was better to keep moving. Spark tried to stamp some life back into his feet, and was rewarded with the tingling pain of pins and needles driving up though the thin soles of his boots. He winced as he tramped along behind Carousel, back through the wind-battered slums towards the doubtful sanctuary of the city gate.

The snow scudded over the frozen ground, pushed into swirling patterns by the intermittent gusts of wind. It wasn't snowing at the moment, but the sky promised it would be soon. Ahead, Carousel let out a little whimper and stopped in her tracks.

"What's wrong?" Spark asked.

She pointed. Sprawled across the street in front of them was a dead man, one arm flung out before him as if stretching for the shelter he had never reached. His face was turned towards them. His lips were black, and the snow had settled on his eyelids and the inside of his upturned ear. Spark nudged him with his boot, checking if he was really dead. His torso was as stiff and unyielding as a lump of wood.

Carousel edged past the body, holding her skirts away from it as if she feared the touch. Spark rubbed his moist eyes with the back of his hand. "Shouldn't we burn him?" he said.

"With what? If you can magic up a fire, why didn't you do it before?"

Spark stared at his palms ruefully. "I wish I could."

Carousel snorted. "Fat lot of good you are. You can magic us into trouble, but you can't magic us out of it!"

"It isn't like I haven't tried!" The magic had fizzled and died like a damp firework. He wasn't frightened, or angry, just cold and miserable, with a burning tickle at the back of his throat that was the only heat he could find. Carousel turned away with a muttered curse and strode off, leaving him with no choice but to plod along behind her, or stay here with the corpse. He kept walking.

Most of the people in the slums who had the option of shelter had tucked themselves away, wrapped in tired blankets, like animals sleeping out the winter moons. Gathered in a miserable, shoving throng around the gate were the men and women without shelter, the poorest of the poor, scratching with broken fingernails to try and get back into the city that had cast them out. Pinch-faced and ragged, they muttered their displeasure, but not one of them had the strength for a fight. Carousel brushed them aside and strode up to the gate. How long, Spark wondered, before she became like the women who were old before their time, clasping their swollen-bellied babies under their ragged shawls and staring blankly at the wall before them, too defeated to protest the unfairness that kept them out? He didn't want to see her like that. She might be thin, cold and hungry, but the fire that burned within her still fluttered with life, as she strolled casually towards the nearest guard. He lowered his pike to block her way, but a smile tugged his lips.

"Hello Carousel! Back again?"

"Afraid so! Got anything to eat?"

He pressed a small bag into her hand. Spark took an involuntary step forward, mouth watering at the prospect of eating for the first time in two days. "Don't shout about it," the guard warned her, tapping his lips for a kiss.

It wasn't whoring. Not really. Spark swallowed his envy as Carousel passed the bag back into his hand. It was all he could do not to rip it open and gorge on the nuts he could feel through the thin paper.

"Any messages for me?" Carousel asked the guard, lithe fingers dancing across his breastplate. Still not whoring. "I know I keep asking . . ."

The guard grinned. "You're in luck. I might have a message for you in the guard house." He winked, the gesture taking in Spark, silently fuming. "That's if your guardian will let you out of his sight!"

"He will if he wants to eat!" With a swish of her hips, Carousel followed the guard into the gatehouse, and the door slammed shut behind her.

To the hells with her. Spark didn't want to think about what she was doing in there. He tore the paper from the bag and crammed a handful of the sharp little nuts into his mouth without even peeling off the shells, hoarding the bag close to his chest to keep it from the prying eyes and grasping hands of the people around him. He forced himself to save the bottom half of the bag for Carousel, hoping she would return.

The sky darkened, and the snow fell in flurries. Still Spark waited, shifting his weight from foot to foot to try and ward off the cold, crumpled bag clutched tightly in his hand. It seemed an age before the door swung open, spilling lantern light across the frozen ground.

Carousel emerged, walking unsteadily, clutching a cloth bag. She gave Spark a nod. "We can go through now. My friend's waiting for us at the Woodsman's. It's not a Nobility tavern, so we can go there safely. Keep your head covered, just in case."

He followed her through the postern gate, not daring to ask what she had done to obtain permission to pass. There was muted grumbling from the milling horde, but no vocal protest, and the door closing behind them cut off the tired voices.

As it shut, Carousel shook open the bag, and the scent of warm fruitrolls rose from within. "Want one?" she asked, with a grin.

Sparks hand twitched towards the bag, but he resisted the urge. "You promised me you wouldn't whore yourself," he said.

"Who says I did?" She flicked the bag out of his reach with a sour expression. "If you don't want to eat . . ."

"I didn't say that." She relented, and allowed him to dip his hand into the bag. The fruitrolls were crumbly under his fingers, and the spiced apple burned his tongue. He rubbed his thumb across his lips, making sure he consumed every last flake.

"Feel better?" Carousel asked. Spark nodded. "Come on then, let's get to the Woodsman's before the snow gets so thick we can't see our way. I'll buy you a half."

"With what?" She tapped the purse at her belt. Spark scowled. "No thanks."

"Remind me not to help you out in future." She stamped away through the snow, a bright shape hunched against the cold. Spark had to follow her. He had done a poor job of protecting her so far, and it was his fault she was here.

She offered him another fruitroll, and he shook his head.

"Oh come on, Spark! Truce?"

He scowled.

"I know you're wild at me, but what else could I do? I got us back into the city, didn't I? Do you think I enjoyed doing that?"

"Then why do it?" he protested. "I can look after you. I *want* to look after you, but you won't let me!"

"You're sweet." She cuffed him lightly round the head. "Eat your roll and shut up."

By the time they reached the Woodsman's Rest Spark was almost warm, and his thighs ached from ploughing through the fresh, powdery snow. The tavern was quiet. Caro pushed him towards a small table in a dark corner and made her way to the bar to buy drinks. He watched her chat to the barmaid as the older girl dipped the leather flagons in a huge barrel and brought them up, brimming and dripping.

"Hello, stranger!" The unexpected touch on the back of his neck startled him. He had not seen or heard anyone approach. Chalice slid into the seat opposite and winked at him. He bristled.

"That seat's taken."

"By your lady friend at the bar?" Chalice raised her voice. "I hope she's got enough coin to buy me one!"

"Listen, Chalice, we're meant to be meeting someone, so if you could—"

She leaned on her elbow and fluttered her lashes as Carousel hooked a nearby stool over with her foot and slopped the ales down on the table. "Have you two met already?" she asked.

"I met the sailor boy before you did, Caro." Chalice bared her teeth. If it was a smile, it was devoid of both humour and warmth. "What name do you go under now, sailor?"

"Sailor?" Carousel raised an eyebrow. Spark silenced her with a shake of his head. "He's Spark now, whatever his name was before."

Spark scowled. "I didn't know you two knew each other."

Carousel laughed. "I've known Chalice since I first landed on the streets. You can help us out, can't you, Chalice?"

"I can try." Chalice snapped her fingers for a drink to be brought to their table. "You're a pair of bloody fools, though. Noble's scouring the gutters looking for you. Carousel, he says when he catches up with you he's going to send you to the Drover's Wheel. You don't want to go there, do you?"

"What happens at the Drover's Wheel?" Spark asked. Both girls ignored him.

"Is there anywhere we can hide in the city?" Carousel asked.

"Not with me," Chalice said at once. "I don't want to go to the Drovers any more than you do. I heard a rumour there might be a job up at the Carey mansion. My friend said they were looking for a new maid."

Carousel sipped her pint, looking thoughtful. "I heard Old Man Carey was sick. Plague or something."

Chalice shrugged. "That's all I've got," she said. "Take it or leave it. They're in a hurry to find someone, since Vio ran off to the country. Coin might be good."

"What about the boy?" Carousel jerked her head towards Spark. "Is there work for him too?"

Chalice set down her empty flagon. "They might have something in the kitchen. Tell them you come on Shadow's recommendation. That might get you in with Lady Allorise." She stood up. "I have to go now. I've risked a lot coming here to talk to you. Good luck!"

"Thanks, Chalice. We won't forget it. Will we, Spark?" Carousel kicked him under the table as he failed to respond. "What's the matter with you?" she demanded, as the door banged shut behind Chalice, cutting off the icy winter draft. "You've got a face like spit. Don't you think it was good of her to help us?"

"I don't know. I don't trust her, Caro. Why was she being so nice?"

"How can you say that? She's my friend. You don't even know her!"

"She got me beaten up, the night I arrived in town . . . Her friend Shadow—I burned him. There's no reason he would help me."

"You don't know that was her fault. Shadow probably doesn't even know she's helping us." Carousel pressed her lips in a firm, stubborn line, and he knew it was pointless arguing with her about Chalice's trustworthiness.

"I suppose we could check the Carey mansion out," he said reluctantly. It wouldn't do any harm to look.

"In the morning." Carousel nodded at his half-drunk flagon. "Better make that last until kicking-out time. I can't afford to buy you another one!"

The front stoop of the Woodsman's Rest was cold, and narrow, but at least the overhanging lintel provided minimal shelter from the wind and the flurries of sleet. Spark wrapped his arms around Carousel's waist for warmth, her teeth rattling next to his ear. Even with her body pressed up against him, it was impossible to think of anything but the cold. In the distance, the warning bells of the watch jangled incessantly. He wondered vaguely if they were looking for him. At least if he spent the night in a cell it would be out of the wind.

The door creaked open, and there was a muted exclamation. "What are you two doing out here?"

"We'll move along." Carousel let go of him, and the chill wind sliced through his bones. Spark gasped, tottering to his feet, trying to rub the life back into his numb limbs. The landlord frowned.

"Do you kids have anywhere to go?"

Spark shook his head.

The wire-haired man glanced up and down the street. The bells sounded closer, and a whiff of smoke gusted towards them. "Come in quick, before anyone sees you. You can bed down in the bar tonight, as long as you're gone with the dawn. Don't tell anyone, mind!" He ushered them back through the door, brushing the snow from Carousel's damp cloak. "I could lose my ale licence if Lady Carey found out I was taking non-paying lodgers."

"We could sweep the floor," Spark suggested. "Then we'd be working for our keep." He hoped Caro wouldn't suggest selling herself again. The landlord was married. He might take offence and chuck them back out into the winter night.

Carousel didn't seem in the mood to suggest anything. She stood and shivered, lips blue, snowflakes melting in her matted hair, until the landlord lifted her sodden cloak from her shoulders and replaced it with a dry blanket. He guided her gently towards the low fire burning in the hearth. Two sofas were pulled up on either side of it, and she sank into one, a sigh escaping her lips.

Spark pulled his own blanket up to his chin as the landlord barred the door. "Why are the watch bells going off?" he asked. If they were looking for him, he didn't want to get this kind man in trouble.

The landlord shook his head, face dour. "Trouble in the city, these past three nights. I'm surprised you haven't heard."

Spark coloured. "We haven't been inside the city . . ."

"A few demons have broken through. We haven't had an incursion since I was a lad. Hopefully the watch can stamp it out before it spreads."

"Demons?" Spark sat up. "Where have they come from?"

"From the hells. Where else?" The landlord snorted. "Bad for business all round just before Winterfest. Not that you need worry about it. The watch know what they're doing. Get your head down now, lad. You'll need to be up with the sun."

Even the thought of demons rampaging through the streets of Cape Carey couldn't keep Spark awake, lying on a worn leather sofa with the firelight burnishing his face. Carousel was already asleep, dreaming, if the fluttering of her lashes against her cheeks was any indication. He tucked the blanket tighter around his shoulders, and let his head fall onto the arm of the couch.

♦

Spark woke to the sound of the landlord unbarring the door. His throat burned, and his nose dripped mucus. The landlord pressed a warm bread roll into each of their hands as he showed them out into snow two inches deep, stained crimson with the blood-hued sunrise. His teeth tore into it as he trudged along, sniffing. He looked around for signs of demons, but the streets were quiet.

"Have you ever seen a demon, Caro?"

She laughed, but did not reply.

"The landlord said there were demons in the city . . ."

"We'll be warm and dry under the Carey roof before long." She grinned. "I won't let a demon eat you, my little friend!"

His boots crunched rhythmically through the snow. "What if the Careys don't need any staff?"

"Then we're no worse off than we are now!" Caro's perkiness was irritating to his sore head.

"I don't trust Chalice."

"I don't care." She rounded on him, temper flaring. "Would you rather try for a job with Lady Allorise, or die in the gutter? Noble will find you if you don't freeze, and then maybe you'll wish you had frozen!"

Common sense told him she was right. Instinct whispered that she was wrong.

"Carousel, I've got a really bad feeling . . ."

"Lace it, Spark. I don't want to hear it."

They passed the castle, shuttered and grim. Spark trailed his forefinger along a broad crack in the breastwork, which mirrored the crack in the pavement at his feet. His head burned. Maybe he was getting a fever.

The bridge was deserted, a sheet of ice so treacherous no carriage could cross. Spark clung to the balustrade as he slipped and skidded his way across, and the icy metal ripped the skin from the tips of his fingers. He swore.

"What's wrong now?"

Carousel had a dancer's poise. She didn't even have to hang on, and she didn't look the slightest bit ruffled.

"My fingers are bleeding."

She huffed in frustration. "Stop making excuses, Spark! Don't you want to get out of the cold?"

"Of course I do."

"Come on then." She took his arm, half-dragging, half-propelling him across the ice. He could hear the breath rattling in her chest, and he sniffed back the mucus dribbling from his nose. She was right. She had to be right.

The gates to the Carey manor house were tall, wrought of black iron, rimed with frost. Spark peered through them at the sprawling house. It made the Gilded Lily look like a humble cottage, and it stared back at him with blank black eyes. He drew back with a shudder.

"I don't like it, Carousel. It's unnerving."

"Unnerving? It's got walls and a roof, and probably a fire and blankets. What's wrong with it?"

"I don't—"

But she was in full spate now. "And what's wrong with *you*, while we're at it? Bad feelings? To the hells with your bad feelings! What's the alternative? Now come on!"

He raised a hand to the gate. The house glared at him. There was an unaccountable sense of wrongness about it. Something toxic, writhing in the dark, yawning, waiting from him to walk like a dumb sheep into its open maw. The darkness was so powerful he took an involuntary step back.

"Carousel, I don't want to go in there, and I don't think you should, either. I think we should leave. It feels really bad . . . ."

"Oh, that's it!" He barely felt her slap across his face, but it left a burning mark across his cold skin. He staggered, ankle twisting on the frozen ground, and fell, striking his hip so hard it brought tears to his eyes. Carousel stood over him, her shadow blocking out the light. "Screw you, Spark! I'm going in to find work. You can freeze out here for all I care!"

He could only watch through watering eyes, as she turned away from him. The frost-patterned gate swung open silently at her touch, and the walls of the Carey mansion swallowed her up.

Fifteen

IT WAS SO dark Kayall wasn't sure whether his eyes were open or closed, not that it made any difference. The back of his skull pounded in synchronicity with his heartbeat, and when he raised his hand to investigate the lump swelling under his skin, he felt the blood clotting in his hair. He hoped, irrationally, that the blow wouldn't lead to the start of a balding patch.

A balding patch? That was what his mind had decided to worry about? He shook his head, and instantly regretted the movement as it set off a wave of nausea. His eyes were growing accustomed to the darkness now. When they were open, his surroundings were a slightly less dense black.

Not trusting his legs, he crawled across the floor until he found a wall, and used it to haul himself upright, fingertips scraping against cold, damp stone. There must be a crack in the stonework; he felt a cold breeze against his face, but no light penetrated the dark of the tomb.

He stumbled towards what he hoped was the entrance, barking his thighs painfully on the raised sarcophagus in the middle of the room, cursing Wenna, the treacherous bitch. What had he done to her to deserve this? Lost hand after hand of cards, given her all his consideration in bed, and she rewarded him by knocking him out and leaving him in the dark? When he got out of here he would hunt her down and demand an explanation. Right before he wrung her neck.

His probing hands landed on cold metal. It felt like a door. He pushed against it. It didn't budge. Even heaving with his shoulder didn't move it a fraction. Kayall hammered with his fists, his blows ringing hollow in the chamber.

"Hey, Wenna! This isn't funny any more!"

No reply.

"Whatever I did to you, I'm sorry! You can let me out now! Wenna?"

The silence told him all he needed to know. Not the quiet of someone waiting to reveal themselves, but an absence. Wenna had gone. She had left him here, sealed in.

"Wenna! Shit! Let me out!"

It was useless and he knew it, even as he pounded his fists bloody on unyielding steel. She was not coming back.

With a final curse he spun around and slumped, his back to the door, aching head resting against the metal. If he only had a candle, or ale in his hip flask, it wouldn't feel so bad. For the first time, it dawned on him that there was a real possibility he could die here, his bones on the floor of a long-dead Telesian's crypt. How often did they open these doors? Was there a Telesian ceremony where the descendants of the dead visited the one who had passed on, with food and gifts? Or had he read that in a lurid fiction, or heard it in a tavern? His headache made it hard to think.

No, he would not die here. Steeling himself to move, he crawled around the edge of the room, feeling for any cracks between the stone floor and the walls, any patch of earth that might allow him to dig his way out of his prison. He found nothing, the floor smooth, no gaps between the flags that he could slip more than a fingernail into. Even that frustrating draft, when he located the source, came from a tiny hole no wider than his finger, high up in the wall. When he put his eye to it he could see daylight, when he put his mouth to it he could shout, but he had the crushing feeling it was pointless. The cemetery was vast, deserted, and the enclosing stone muffled his voice. Besides, who would come to the rescue of a spirit shouting from inside the tomb? Any sane man would run, rather than investigate.

Elvienne, Elvienne, where in all hells are you?

No reply. Why couldn't he reach her? Had something happened to the old woman? Or was it his own ability failing him? Either way, he was on his own, and he was trapped. He could think of only one way out . . .

He shook his head as the prospect flitted across his mind. It had been too long since he used that power, the one he had sworn never to use again. It was more likely to bring the walls crashing down on top of him than to get him out.

You'd be dead either way.

Him, and a lot of other people. Liathan had cracked the world once already. Kayall could only make it worse. There had to be another way.

He curled up, back against the door, watching the finger-thick sliver of light track across the floor. When it vanished behind a cloud, he wept. He should have had a thousand years. This wasn't how he would have chosen to die, starving to death in the darkness, cursing the thread of air that would keep him alive for too long.

He wept and slept and woke and yelled and hammered on the door and wept again, over and over, until his throat was sore and his dry tongue stuck to the roof of his mouth. No one was coming to help him. Elvienne had abandoned him. Wenna had turned on him for no reason he could fathom, and he couldn't even reach the sky to vent his frustration and grief on the weather, or send a signal to let anyone know he was here. He had never felt so impotent, so helpless. Was this how Carlon felt, at the end? And the boy, the boy had killed him without mercy when the old man became too much of a burden . . .

We're not supposed to die like this.

To fall gloriously in battle, saving the world, was one thing. To die humiliated and weak, smelling of piss, that was a different matter. It made him furious. Kayall hammered his fist against the door, beat out a tattoo of frustration and despair at his death.

Only this time there was a reply.

At first he thought he was hearing things. The terrible thirst played tricks on his exhausted mind. He hit the door twice more, and was rewarded with two answering thumps from outside, and a high, childish voice, muffled by the door.

"Is somebody in there? Are you a phantom?"

Kayall's mouth worked, but his lips and throat were too dry and sore to form any words louder than a whisper. He beat the door again, renewed hope lending strength to his limbs.

"I'm going to get you out. Don't go anywhere!"

Don't go anywhere . . . As if he could! Kayall would have laughed if he could, but he sank to his knees on the stone in front of the door and offered silent thanks for his deliverance.

He didn't know how long he waited for his rescuers to return. There was no way to judge the passage of time in the crypt. He had passed into a half-doze, forehead pressed against the door, when he was disturbed by the reverberations of their return, the ring of fists against steel.

"You in there?" A man's voice, anxious. "Can you speak?"

Kayall hit the door in reply. They would have ale. Even water would do. The prospect of cool liquid wetting his parched lips almost sent him into a delirium.

"We'll have you out soon." There was noise outside, shouted instructions, the squeal of metal against metal. The top of the door bowed inwards under pressure, spilling welcome daylight across the floor, and Kayall screwed his eyes up against the brightness. He blinked away tears, and for the first time he saw the interior of his prison, a small, rectangular room, bare save for the stone coffin on a plinth in the centre. The plinth was carved with Telesian characters, presumably the names of the dead. He counted himself lucky his own name wasn't scratched into the rock.

Now the door was bent inwards, the noises from outside were magnified. There was a dull thump as some forward-thinking spirit pushed a half-full water skin through the gap to land on the floor beside him. Kayall pounced on it, trembling fingers fumbling with the stopper in his urgency, letting the cool ale splash over his chin and his shirt as he drained it dry.

"Don't drink it too fast!"

The warning came too late. He doubled up and vomited, but at least he could speak now, had washed the prickly dryness from his tongue. He stepped away from the puddle of vomit as the door bent in a few more inches, and a groping hand appeared in the gap.

"Grab on," the man's voice said. "We'll haul you out."

The corner of the twisted door scraped painfully against Kayall's stomach as he gripped the willing hands and let them help him scramble out into the sunlight. He slumped on the pavement outside the tomb, gasping his thanks.

Four men surrounded him, and one offered another skin of ale. Kayall managed to sip it this time, hoping he could keep it down and take the edge off his raging thirst. He could hear an excited, high voice, declaring pride that its owner had been the one to rescue the stranger.

One of the men, balding, with prominent ears, bent down and studied him. "Are you a mage?"

"I'm afraid so."

"You couldn't have magicked yourself out? How did you end up in there in the first place?"

"I was tricked." Kayall's face was hot. "It's complicated . . ."

The man straightened and turned to his nearest companion, lanky and buck-toothed. "Auster, we'll have to take him to

Noble," he said. "You and Mule bind his hands. That way he can't get up to any wizard tricks."

"I'm not a wizard," Kayall protested, as his arms were dragged behind his back.

The balding man shrugged. "Whatever you say. I'm not taking any chances."

"I came here to see Noble. There's no need—ow!" as the ropes bit into his flesh. "Not so tight!"

"Shall we bind his eyes and mouth too, Hamfist?" Auster asked.

"Better had. I don't want him muttering incantations and suchlike."

"Come on! I'm here to—" Kayall's words were smothered as a black bag descended over his head, cutting off the precious daylight and his words with one swoop. He gagged on the sacking as the drawstrings tightened about his throat.

It was worse than the tomb, in some ways. At least in there he had the freedom to move about, to watch that tantalising sliver of light. Trapped in the wrong end of a bag, he could see nothing. He felt a knife jab into the small of his back. If he wasn't so dehydrated, he would be sweating. His steps were unsteady as his captors forced him down the path. He wondered if Wenna was hiding somewhere nearby, watching, and he mentally cursed her.

Several times he stumbled off the path into freezing mud that snatched at his ankles, and every time the men who had taken him prisoner guided him back onto the pavement. Not roughly; they didn't seem keen to hurt him, beyond the suffo-cating bag and the cold tickle of steel against his spine. Perhaps they feared magical wrath should he get free. Right now Kayall was saving his vengeance for Wenna.

He heard the scrape of another metal door, and he baulked, feeling the naked blade dig in a little harder. Why rescue him, only to bring him to another tomb? He felt a nudge with an elbow, and Hamfist's reassuring voice. "It's all right, mage.

We're not going to lock you in. Watch out, there are steps down here . . ."

Stone scraped at his feet. The steps were narrow, leading downwards in a tight spiral, and with his bound hands he couldn't cling to the wall for support. They moved at crawling pace, one man ahead to steady him, the other behind with the knife. Maybe he could kick their feet out from beneath them and make a getaway, but if they were taking him to see Noble, rather than to his death, he could bear the humiliation of being bound and hooded. Several times he slipped, and the sudden jolt set his heart pounding. He was relieved when they reached a flat floor again.

There were more steps down, none as precipitous as the first, and the sound of doors opening, and closing behind him. Many doors. By now Kayall had lost all sense of direction and time. He judged by the way his captors voices echoed that they were in a large cavern, and he could hear activity, muffled through the sacking that covered his ears. At least it was warm down here, and when Hamfist relented and lifted the hood from his head, Kayall's eyes watered with the unexpected firelight.

"Noble says he'll see you soon," Hamfist said. "I can't untie your hands, but do you want something to eat?"

Now the savage edge had been taken off his thirst, Kayall realised he was famished. He nodded, trying not to appear too eager. "I don't know how long I was trapped for," he admitted, "but it seems a long time since breakfast. I'd be grateful for anything you can spare."

Auster and Mule had vanished. Hamfist helped him sit down on a long bench at a nearby table. "I'll see what I can rustle up," he said. "Don't try and make a run for it, you won't get far!"

Even if Kayall had considered running, the smell of stew bubbling over the fire was enough to keep him pinned to his seat. The cavern he was in was vast, its high, craggy roof reinforced with wooden beams. Sleeping nooks were carved into the walls like combs in a beehive. Some of them were occupied, and he watched a girl of around fifteen summers climb up the wall hand over hand, from one gap to the next, until she vanished into her own nest. Nearby, a trio of hard-faced men played cards, and someone was tuning a lute. The discordant ring of strings pierced the low hum of conversation. No one shouted, no one ran. It felt like a family kitchen, if the family was a hundred strong and lived inside a mountain.

Hamfist returned, carrying a rough wooden bowl half-filled with stew. "We can't spare much for strangers," he apologised as he sat down, "but we try to be hospitable."

"Does your hospitality extend to untying my hands?" Kayall asked.

Hamfist chuckled. "Not that far, sorry! Not until the boss has seen you. Won't be long now. Either I feed you, or you don't eat."

The smell of food was making Kayall dizzy with hunger. If the choice was to submit to being fed, or not to eat at all, it wasn't really a choice. Hamfist grinned as he spooned the hot stew into Kayall's mouth. There wasn't much meat in it, but the roots were chunky and soft, and it carried a hint of Telesian spice that lifted it into the realms of the delicious.

Kayall wouldn't have cared if it tasted like old boots, he was so hungry. He swallowed and licked his lips. "What are you grinning about?"

"I haven't fed anyone like this since my youngest son was old enough to hold his own fork." Hamfist looked up, and signalled to someone behind Kayall's back. "Get this down, then Noble will see what he makes of you."

"What's he like?" Kayall asked, between eager mouthfuls.

"Noble? He's a good man. Looks after us." Hamfist swept his arm around the cavern in an expansive gesture. "I'd think twice before you decided to cross him, though. He doesn't let go of grudges easily."

"I'll bear that in mind." The spoon scraped on the bottom of the bowl. "Any more where that came from?"

"Maybe later," Hamfist said. "Come on. Let's not keep Noble waiting. I'm going to have to hood you again." He raised the bag with an apologetic shrug.

"One question?" Kayall's voice was muffled as the sack descended, enclosing him once more in musty darkness. "Why are you called Hamfist?"

The man laughed. "I'm clumsy. Ham-fisted, they say. Sometimes I kill people by mistake."

He drew the strings tight, choking off any reply, and steered Kayall across the room. Even though he couldn't see, he was conscious of eyes on him, watching his progress. Hamfist spun him round, one hand on his shoulder, until he was reeling and didn't know what direction he faced. They walked a few dozen more lurching paces, until a heavy hand on his shoulder forced him to stop.

"I'll take it from here, Hamfist."

The voice was male, well-spoken with a southern accent. He was pressed into a chair by the hand, and felt the ropes that bound his wrists being sliced free. His fingers tingled and stung as the blood returned to them, and he swallowed a curse.

"I'm freeing your hands," the voice went on, "because I like to think I can trust you. If you prove me wrong with any magical tricks, you won't leave this room alive. Nod if you understand me."

Kayall nodded. He felt fingers at his throat, loosening the hood and tugging it free. He blinked at the blaze of candle-light, trying to focus. Behind it, a figure moved to sit at a desk, and Kayall heard the clink of glasses.

"Ale?"

"Always." His vision was clearing now. "Are you Noble?"

"That's what my men call me. What do I call you, mage?"

"Kayall." His hand twitched towards the goblet.

Noble arched his eyebrows. He was dark skinned, even

more so than a Telesian, black as fine velvet, with straight, gleaming teeth and a ready smile. But there was a hard glint in his coal-dark eyes, and his sword-arm was muscled beneath a flowing chiffon sleeve. He would be a powerful enemy.

Well, Kayall was powerful too. At least, he would be after a wash and a decent night's sleep. A kingpin of the underworld shouldn't make him feel this nervous. He was tired, that was all.

"You're very free with your true name, mage." Noble pushed the goblet across the table, and Kayall caught it.

"That's because I have nothing to hide," he said, watching those black eyes for a hint of anger.

None came. "I like an honest man. What were you doing in the tomb? I hear you were coming to see me before misfortune tripped you up."

Kayall sipped his ale, warming to Noble with his easy manner, his generosity when it came to drink. The ale was an expensive one.

"It wasn't misfortune," he said, "but treachery. When I find Wenna . . . ."

"You won't find her," Noble said. "She'll be halfway back to Lambury by now, to tell her paymasters at the Fruitier's Guild that she left you suffocating in the dark, and that you won't cause them any more trouble. The hounds are off your scent, my friend."

It took a long moment for the impact of his words to sink in. "Wenna was—she was working for Larmegan? He sent her to kill me?"

Noble shrugged. "I don't know names. Only transactions."

"How did you know they were after me?"

He laughed out loud at this. "There's very little that escapes my notice, my magical friend. But you, and the woman you travel with, your purpose here eludes me, and I don't like that. If mages are taking an interest in my city, I want to know why."

As the conversation had progressed, Kayall became

increasingly aware of a prickle at the nape of his neck, the presence of someone else in the room, standing close behind him, breathing softly. When he glanced over his shoulder there was no one there.

"I'm looking for a boy," he said. "One of ours. He killed his mentor and ran away. I heard there was—" was that a shuffling in the shadows? Kayall groped for his blade, remembering belatedly that Hamfist had lifted it from his belt. "There was a fire, at one of the whorehouses you run? We think our lost boy was behind it. I came to see if you'd had contact with him. If he was here now, or you knew where he'd gone. Not to interfere in your affairs. We just want the kid back so we can train him."

Noble nodded. "I know the boy. We called him Spark. Nice kid." He sighed, and topped up the ale flagons.

"Do you know where he is now?" Kayall asked.

"I wish I did. There was this girl, pretty, smart, willing . . . I'd been training her up for years. She was going to bring in really good coin." Noble's face darkened. "The first night I had her working on her back, young Spark bursts in and runs off with her. Blew out the whole side of the building. It's going to cost more than Carousel would have earned in her lifetime to pay for the damage. Believe me," he leaned forward on his elbows, "I want to find the boy as much as you do. Because when I find him, I'm going to hold him down and rip his guts out, really slowly . . ."

"I'm tempted to join you in that!" Kayall's chuckle died away as he realised there was no trace of humour in Noble's face. "We should work together to find him," he said. "He poses a greater danger to the city than you know."

Noble nodded. "You're talking about the cracks."

Hells, was there anything the man didn't know? Kayall squirmed inwardly as he thought of some of his own past misdeeds. Elvienne would be massively affronted. She had the old-fashioned belief that some knowledge should be reserved for mages alone, to dish out when magical wisdom was needed.

"How do you know about the cracks?"

"You're not the only one with arcane knowledge, Kayall." Noble beckoned to the empty room behind Kayall, to the fluttering shadows. "I think you should talk to the mage, my friend."

The shadows coalesced to form a small, human shape that thrust its misshapen head forward defiantly, arms folded across its chest. Kayall recoiled, knocking his half-full flagon across the desk and onto the floor as he made the sign against evil. "Stay back from me! I know what you are!"

"Then you know that signs and curses are useless superstition." The patterned figure bent with an audible grunt and retrieved the cup, wiping up the spill with the trailing folds of his cloak. He placed it on the table, taking care not to touch Kayall. Now that his heart had returned to its usual position and stopped racing, he had time to study the creature. Noble refreshed his drink, and he lifted it with shaking hands.

"Forgive me," he said. "Coming out of the dark like that . . . You're not quite what you appear, are you? Are you man, or demon?"

Dweller leaned against the desk, and helped himself to the ale pitcher. "Both," he said, "and neither."

"How is that possible?" Daring, Kayall prodded Dweller's arm. Solid flesh under the cloak, well muscled.

"My mother was a demon." Dweller spoke in a flat tone, bulging eyes focused on the far wall. "She found her way to the surface. She was attacked in an alley by seven human men. She was strong, my mother, but not strong enough, not against seven. One of them put me in her belly."

Kayall shuddered. "Is that why you're here? To find your father? Or to get revenge?"

"Demons have a longer life span than humans. Not as long as mages, but he would still have died long before I was grown."

Noble scowled. "While all this is very touching, it doesn't solve our twin problems. Finding the boy, and fixing the damage he's done. Dweller, show the mage what Spark did to you."

The halfbreed pushed aside his cloak and lifted his black shirt to reveal the livid burn scars, fanning out from the base of his breastbone across his dark-sworled skin. "You can see his strength," he said, letting the cloth fall.

"I know his strength. He pushed a hot stone into his mentor's chest, right into his heart. My companion said it was mercy, but I don't see how it could have been . . ."

"There's no doubt he's dangerous, and needs to be checked," Noble said. "I take it only Spark can seal the cracks he's made in the city?"

He directed the question at Kayall, but it was Dweller who answered. "It is, and he has to do it soon, or they'll be pushed wide open. I've already—" He broke off at a furious knocking on the door, and looked enquiringly at Noble. "Should I fade?"

The dark man shook his head. "You're fine where you are." He raised his voice. "Come in!"

Auster was at the door, limbs flapping, copper hair flopping in his eyes. He looked startled to see Kayall, obviously relaxed, sharing a drink with the lord and his devoted minion. "Is it safe to talk, Noble?" he asked, breathless.

"I think so. The mage isn't going anywhere."

Was that a threat? It was couched in such a mild voice Kayall wasn't sure. He decided he would live longer if he read every word from Noble's lips as a veiled warning.

Auster wiped the sweat from his brow with his sleeve. "There's trouble at the Woodsman's Rest. Demon trouble." He glanced at Dweller. "I don't know if I should say . . ."

Noble's frown deepened. "You can talk in front of Dweller. I trust him. So should you."

"Forgive me, but you trusted Spark . . ." Auster trailed off as Noble's fingers twitched towards the blade at his belt.

"We're not talking about Spark. What happened at the Woodsman's?"

"You know the square out the back, the one we work for purses?" Noble nodded. "Seems there was a demon breakthrough there. Tore the cobbles wide open, and the earth beneath. About ten of them burst through, ripped up the back of the bar. Luckily it was mid-afternoon, so they only killed six people, but the landlord was one of them, and his wife's not likely to recover from her wounds. Then they scattered. Fuck only knows where they are now, but where they found a way in . . ."

"More will follow." Noble finished the thought for him. "Thank you, Auster. The Woodsman's belongs to the Silver Lady. Find out if she's going to pay to heal the wounded. If she doesn't, we will, for the usual pledge. Get a few men down there, try and prevent the tavern from re-opening for as long as you can. Nothing hurts Silver more than a wound to her purse, and her pride!"

"Yes, boss. Anything else?" Auster ripped off a sloppy salute.

"Not at the moment. Thank you for bringing this to my attention." Noble kept his expression a careful blank until the door clicked shut behind Auster. Then he scowled deeply, and muttered a curse.

"This is happening sooner than I expected. Shit! We need to find that boy before it costs us any more, in lives or money!" His eyes fixed on Kayall. "It seems we need to join forces, mage. If we find him, can you help him to repair the harm he's done?"

"I can try. I can't promise he'll listen to me," Kayall admitted.

"Make him listen. We'll find him, you help him with the demons, and then—" he paused to take a long drink.

"And then what?" Kayall asked.

"And then we kill him."

Sixteen

THE GATE TO the Carey mansion swung shut behind Carousel with a soft creak. If she looked back, she would see Spark peering between the bars, so she kept her gaze focused directly ahead of her. There would be an entrance to the servants' quarters at the back of the building, but it was cold, and she was in too much of a hurry to seek it out. She strode up to the front door, gripped the knocker, and brought it down on the wood before her courage could fail her.

There was no reply. She felt like a fool standing there, ears stinging in the wind. Maybe Spark was right after all. She knocked once more, loudly, and as she was about to turn away she heard a soft tread.

The door swung open silently. "Can I help you?"

The hall beyond was bare, but a few candles burned, and it was warmer than the streets. She would have done and said anything to be inside, even if only for the duration of an interview. She bobbed a curtsey. "Forgive me, sir. Is the lady or gentleman of the house in?"

The thin, gangling man who had opened the door snorted. "I suppose you'd say I was the gentleman of the house, though I'm reduced to opening my own front door to beggars! What do you want, girl?"

"Sir, my Lord . . ." Shit, she couldn't remember what she was meant to call him! "Sir, I was told you were looking for a maid. I've come to offer myself for the position."

"You heard wrong, girl. We don't need a maid." He moved to shut the door, and she wedged her knee in the gap.

"Sir, if you'll give me a chance . . . I can cook and clean. I'm hard working. All I need is lodging. Not even food!"

"I told you once—" but he was interrupted by a golden voice, tumbling down from above like birdsong.

"Bastian? What's going on?"

Carousel seized on his distraction to inch more of her body inside the door. Bastian glared at her.

"Nothing, Allo. Just getting rid of a waif. I've told her there's no work, but she doesn't seem to understand what I'm saying."

"You could at least let her in. It's freezing outside!"

Bastian let go of the door with considerable reluctance, and held it open for Carousel to pass into the hall, slamming it behind her to cut off the draft. She stood in the Carey hall, ice crystals in her hair, looking up at the smiling woman who leaned over the banisters.

"You want to be a maid?" she asked.

"I heard there was work here, my Lady."

"We could use a new maid. It's been difficult since the last girl left—Bastian, she's cold! Do we have any hot food in the kitchen?"

"I doubt it," he said.

"Could you go and see?" The woman, Allo, picked her way down the sweeping curve of the stairs, carrying a candle that made her hair look like spun gold.

Bastian didn't move. "We don't need another maid," he insisted. "We're fine as we are. When mother comes back we'll have all the staff we need."

"That might not be for moons! It's so cold outside. Would you cast this mite onto the streets?" Her lips narrowed. "I told you to find her something to eat."

Overcome with daring, Carousel begged a favour. "My friend is outside. He's looking for work too. Can he come in?"

"By all means." Allo nodded to Bastian, who opened the door and glanced out.

"No one there, Allorise," he said.

"Really? Then he misses out, doesn't he? I wouldn't worry about him. I expect he's found somewhere warm." Allorise extended her hand to brush Carousel's cold cheek. "Your hair could be pretty," she said. "What's your name, my dear?"

"Carousel, my lady."

"Carousel? Oh!" Allorise raised her hand to smother a charming giggle. "Like the fairground ride? Do you like to ride the carousel, Bastian?"

"Not since I was a baby," he snapped, glowering.

"My brother's no fun!" Her smile widened to include Carousel in the teasing. "Get her something to eat, Bastian. We'll be in mother's reception room."

Carousel glanced out of the window as Allorise steered her past with a hand on her elbow. There was no sign of Spark. He had probably run off and was sulking somewhere nearby. She would look for him later. Right now it was more important to secure her position with the Careys.

Allorise directed her into a room with deep couches around the walls and a high cabinet with glass doors in the corner. Carousel saw the light glinting off the bottles of wine as Allorise unlocked the door and poured her a small measure.

"Sit down," she said, pressing the glass into Carousel's hand. "Who told you we needed a maid?"

"My friend Chalice, my Lady."

Allorise shrugged. The name obviously meant nothing to her. "Did she say why the last girl left?"

"No, my Lady. Only that you were looking for someone." The wine was palest blue, translucent. It made the heat rise in her face.

"I see." Allorise sipped from her own glass, looking thoughtful. "Have you worked as a maid before? What did you do before you came here? You look like you haven't eaten for days!"

"I've been a maid," Carousel lied, hoping it was just the wine making her blush. "I lived in the country. I came here on a barge."

"Really?" Allorise arched her neatly plucked eyebrows. "You must tell me all about that some time."

The door thumped open. Bastian entered backwards, carrying a platter of cold meats and cheeses and the thinnest savoury biscuits Carousel had ever seen. "I couldn't find anything hot," he said. "Will this do?"

"Meat? For the help?" Allorise shook her head and turned to Carousel. "You may have cheese and biscuit, dear." She took her own generous helping of meat and cheese, piled high on the biscuit, and nodded approval. "Go ahead. You look like you need it."

Fighting down the urge to snatch up the plate and devour everything on it, even the meat, Carousel took a biscuit and a slice of cheese and nibbled at it, trying to make it last as long as she could, savouring the flavour. The biscuit was tasteless, but the cheese was strong and crumbly, with veins of blue running through the white.

"She eats like a mouse, doesn't she, Bastian?" Allorise observed. She was smiling, though, and that made Carousel feel better about the teasing. Without knowing why, she desperately wanted the approval of this beautiful, vivacious woman who lived in a different world to her, where wine and meat were freely available. Even more than that, she wanted to stay in the warm.

Bastian took a seat on the couch opposite his sister, long legs crossed at the ankle. He looked hungry, but he didn't touch the plate. She glared at him. "I'm sure Carousel would prefer a private interview, Bastian."

He held up his hands. "I won't say a word. If you want to hire a street rat—"

"She's not a street rat. She says she came on a barge."

"That makes a huge difference, does it? Fine . . ." he lapsed back into silence, grey eyes watching Allorise eat with strange intensity.

She licked her lips, catching the last crumbs, and dabbed her mouth delicately with a manicured hand. "The last girl left because she was afraid of sickness," she explained to Carousel. "My father is very ill. That's why our mother and the rest of the servants fled to the country—"

"She doesn't need to know our entire family history, Allo," Bastian interrupted. "Is she a hard worker?"

The question wasn't directed at her, but Carousel answered it anyway.

"I am. I'm quick to learn, and I'll do anything you ask me to."

"Anything?" Allorise giggled, a delightful, infectious sound. Carousel didn't know why it was funny, but she couldn't help smiling. "I can tell we're going to be friends, Carousel! When can you start?"

※

For a long time Spark leaned against the gate post, hugging himself to keep warm and wishing he could swallow his senseless terror of the Carey mansion, walk up to the front door, and beg for work. But fear held him back. Of the unknown, of the darkness.

Carousel wasn't coming back. If he stayed here, unmoving, he would freeze. It was time to leave the city. It would be warmer if he headed south. Telesia was meant to be a land of deserts and humid jungles. But first he had to get out of Cape Carey, before he killed anyone else, or before they killed him. Stamping life back into his feet, he followed his nose north, heading for the nearest city gate.

The flow of pedestrians increased as he approached the gate. He guessed it was always busy, even in winter. Everyone was dressed more warmly than him, and a few of the women threw him sympathetic glances as they passed. He would be glad to escape the scrutiny. But as he neared the walls his heart sank. The guard on duty was deep in conversation with Hamfist, one of Noble's men.

Spark shrank back into the crowd. The only reason Hamfist would be talking to the guard was to warn him to look out for someone trying to escape the city. Noble was closing the net around him, and he was trapped. If his former master had a watch on this gate, it was likely he had one on all four gates. He turned, trying not to make it too obvious, and pushed against the tide, back towards the heart of the city.

A middle-aged woman caught his arm, and his heart sank. Of course it wouldn't be that easy to get away. "Where are you going, kid?" she asked, flapping at him with the end of her shawl. "You don't want to go back towards the river!"

"I don't?"

"Not if you've got any smarts. You should get out now before it all goes to hell!"

Spark glanced over his shoulder at the gate. Hamfist lounged against the wall, idly picking his teeth and staring with open contempt at everyone who passed through. He couldn't go that way.

"Come with me now." The woman hauled his arm. "You look half froze. Where are your parents? We'll get you set up and find—ow!" Spark wrenched free with a shove that sent her sprawling into the arms of her companion. He fled, hearing her shouts behind him.

"They'll find you and eat your liver, and serves you right, you little bastard!"

It wasn't until he stopped running, three streets away, that Spark started to wonder why Noble would want to eat his liver.

Maybe it was a local phrase, but he hadn't heard it before. He shrugged it off; it didn't matter. What mattered was finding a place to keep his head down until the Nobility took their watch off the gates and he was free to leave. He dug his toe in the dirty snow in the gutter, and wondered about Carousel. He hoped she was all right. He didn't understand the darkness that hung over the Carey mansion, but it made every inch of his skin crawl.

I'll talk to her tomorrow, he promised himself. It was probably his imagination. Carousel would be fine, working indoors. Anything was better than the Lily, or the streets.

The wind cut through him like a blade as he stood indecisive on the street corner. It was hard to think with the ache in his head, and his lungs. He shivered. He should find a tavern, scrounge a drink from a sympathetic barmaid, and huddle in the corner until the landlord threw him out. And what then?

The noise and warmth emanating from the tavern down the street made up his mind for him. He would go back to the Woodsman's Rest, to the kindly barkeep who had let them thaw out by his fire. Perhaps Spark could persuade him to let him work in the kitchen in exchange for lodging and a little food.

Feeling more cheerful, he set off, sticking to the shadows. Once he found shelter, everything would be all right.

⚶

The streets around the Woodsman's Rest were deserted. There was a faint hum in the air that made the throbbing in Spark's head increase in tempo. It tasted metallic, and his steps slowed. He fumbled for his dagger, taking a little comfort from the familiar frayed leather wrapped around the hilt.

Someone had kicked in the door of every house and shop on the street. Most were hanging off their hinges and some lay in splinters on the frozen ground. There were broad smears and splashes of crimson on the scuffed snow, broken furniture and abandoned weapons.

Heart racing, Spark forced himself to go on. It was too quiet, no signs of life. The snow was drifting down from the sky once more, fat flakes mixing with grey clumps of ash. It was hard to tell where the snow ended and the ash began. He couldn't smell burning, with his nose clogged with snot, but he quickened his pace.

Around the next corner he stumbled across a rope strung across the street at knee height. The road was cordoned off at both ends. Spark heard voices coming from inside the burned-out shell that, only the night before, had been the Woodsman's Rest. A pall of smoke hung over the gutted building, and shrouded bodies were lined up in the street opposite the front entrance.

Spark backed up a step, bile rising at the sight, at the memory of Ram and Arabie, who had been so kind to him. Who had met the same fate. Was he cursed, that everyone he met died by fire?

Carousel!

She needed to be warned. He turned to run, and snatched a choking breath as a long, slender arm closed around his throat.

"Little Spark. Fancy finding you here!"

The southern drawl, the freckles on the exposed wrist emerging from a frayed cuff . . . Spark held himself as still as he could. The blade rested in his hand, and his fingers twitched of their own accord as he tried to make his voice sound casual.

"Auster. I wasn't expecting to see you here."

"Obviously." Spark felt Auster's arm loosen a fraction. "Nor I you. How lucky for both of us."

"Look, I've got coin . . ." Spark fought down the temptation to dig in his pockets. "How much will it take for you to forget you've seen me, if Noble asks?"

"More coin than you can afford, kid."

Spark's guts squirmed. "That's what I thought you'd say.

What happened here?"

Auster's hand shifted to his upper arm, keeping a tight grip. "Demons. There are a lot of them roaming the city in the last few days. They've broken through from somewhere. A smart kid," he gave Spark a little shove, "wouldn't be sleeping on the streets. Come back with me now. Noble only wants to talk to you."

"We both know that's not true!" With a wrench, Spark twisted in Auster's grip, and jabbed the stout knife into his upper thigh. Auster let go with a curse so loud it brought the watchmen running from the wreckage of the inn, but Spark wasn't about to hang around and explain himself. He took off, haring through the deserted back alleys, scrambling over low walls, heart racing, chest heaving, until the sounds of pursuit died away.

Exhaustion forced him to stop running.. His limbs felt heavy and torpid, and he clung to the nearest wall, doubled up, gasping and inhaling nothing but powdery snow. He could barely see his hand in front of his eyes. He should have been cold, but his face was burning. He wanted nothing more than to lie down and sleep. The snow looked so soft, inviting as a luxurious bedfur. But to sleep was to die. There was nothing he could do but keep walking, putting one foot in front of the other, with no idea where he was going or even where he was. Just to keep moving, to stay alive . . .

Carousel stared out of the window of her attic room. It had been snowing heavily, on and off, for the whole of the four days she had been in the Carey manor. It was freezing standing in front of the open shutters, and it was pointless. Even if Spark walked past the gate, she wouldn't be able to see him in the blizzard. All she could do was hope he was all right, that he had found shelter and stayed out of Noble's clutches.

The bell above her door tinkled imperiously, summoning her to Allorise's reception chamber. Carousel was getting used to the bells now, and she hurried to do her lady's bidding. She flung open her door, and almost barrelled into the Plague Doctor, who was lurking outside.

She glared at him. "What are you doing here?"

She was sure he was grinning beneath the hook-beaked mask, but his eyes were blank grey circles of glass. "I go where I please," he said.

She shuddered. "Stay away from me. Lord Bastian told you once already." She moved to push past him, and the Plague Doctor grabbed her arm.

"Lord Bastian doesn't command me any more than you do!"

"Get off me!" She pushed him away, running down the stairs on light feet, hearing his muffled laughter echo from the square galleried landing above.

She hesitated at the foot of the stairs, to smooth her skirts and catch her breath, shuddering at his touch on her arm. The masked man had been sniffing after her ever since she arrived, but he was a favourite of Allorise, so Carousel could say nothing. She hoped he would get bored soon, move on to easier prey.

She tucked her hair behind her ears, and knocked politely on the door to Lady Allorise's reception room, awaiting her summons before she let herself in. Allorise sprawled on the day bed, a luxurious white fur pulled up to her hips, idly leafing through a book. She let it slide to the floor as she saw Carousel, and smiled.

"I'm glad you're here," she said. "I'm stiflingly bored. There's a party at my friend's house this evening. Do you want to go?"

Carousel was puzzled. "Are you inviting me as your maid, my Lady? It's my job to go where you go . . ."

Allorise giggled, swinging her legs round and patting the couch beside her, inviting Carousel to take a seat. "Of course not, silly little Caro! I'm inviting you as my friend. Only," her elegant fingers flicked one of the bells in Carousel's hair, "we'll have to do something about this."

"My hair?"

"And your dress. And those hideous boots! Oh, I can dress you up!" She clapped her hands in delight. "It's going to be such fun!"

Carousel had a different idea of fun, but Allorise's smile was so bright and eager that she was happy to go along with it without protest. An afternoon of playing dress-up doll to her lady would help take her mind off Spark, and off the masked stranger lurking outside her room.

༄

"What do you think?" Allorise beamed. Carousel struggled for the breath to reply. Her corset was laced so tightly it was cutting her in half. Allorise had let down her hair, raked through the tangles, taken out the ribbons and bells and consigned them to the waste bin. The face in the mirror belonged to a stranger. Her hair was longer than she'd realised, falling past her shoulders in awkward kinks and stray curls. Allorise had darkened her eyelashes and brushed a strip of pink powder across each cheek. It wasn't as gaudy as her performer's make up, but she didn't look like herself.

"Try walking in the shoes, Caro."

They dangled from her hand, strappy and delicate. The heels tapered to an impossible point, like walking on twin daggers. Allorise clasped Carousel's ankle, as if she was the servant, and strapped them on, pulling the buckles tight. Caro's toes were crammed together, poking out of the top. How could she walk through the snow in these? Getting up was hard enough, with the stays of the corset digging into her flesh. Carousel teetered, clinging on to the back of the chair for support. She took a few tentative steps, and her left ankle turned beneath her, depositing her on the carpet. She swore, a most unladylike expletive.

"You'll never fit in if you curse like that!" Allorise raised one hand to cover her laughter, and extended the other to help Carousel back to her feet. "Keep practising. We have a bell until we need to leave. I'll make sure the carriage picks us up from the door!"

By the time a bell had passed, Carousel could make her way the length of the corridor and back without falling on her backside. Allorise was delighted with her progress. She let Caro lean on her arm as they made their way downstairs to the hall with the chequered floor, to await their carriage.

"Is Lord Bastian coming with us?" Carousel asked. Despite her reservations, she had been surprised to find herself warming to Bastian. He had a dry sense of humour and shared her dislike for the Plague Doctor who haunted his halls.

Allorise laughed. She laughed a lot at the things Carousel said.

"Bastian? Of course not! Bastian doesn't go to parties!" She leaned closer, her lips brushing Carousel's ear, and whispered.

"He likes you though!"

"Me?" Carousel had seen Bastian looking their way, when she served Allorise her breakfast or sat sewing with her in her chamber, but she hadn't thought anything of it. He was a noble, a true lord, as high above her socially as the clouds above her head. "Do you think so?"

"I know he does. He's my brother, I know everything about him." Allorise squeezed her hand as the carriage wheels rumbled across the frozen gravel outside. "Do you want me to arrange for you two . . . ?"

Carousel felt her face burn, but she was saved from replying by the arrival of Shadow, acting as coach driver, opening the door on an icy blast of wind. He pinched the flesh of her upper arm as he helped her into the carriage, and she bit back a yelp. She refused to let him know he'd hurt her.

"Lady Allorise—"

"You don't need to address me as your Lady," Allorise said.

"We're friends now! Play a good hand with Bastian and we could be sisters!"

Carousel doubted that would ever happen. "Allorise, why is the Plague Doctor driving the coach?"

"Shadow does all kinds of jobs for me, as well as treating Daddy. Poor Daddy!" She looked despondent. "He doesn't seem to be getting any better. I don't know what more we can do for him . . ."

Carousel didn't know what to say. She was barred, as Bastian was, from the corridor on the third floor that led to Lord Carey's room. Only Shadow and Allorise ventured back and forth to treat the sick old man. That was why the other servants had left, Allorise told her, as she sniffed and dabbed her eyes. Said how grateful she was that Carousel was with her, so she didn't feel so alone. Even now, her eyes were filling with tears. Caro tried to change the subject.

"Who's hosting the party?"

"No one you know," Allorise said. "How would you? These are people you need to get to know to get anywhere in the city, little Caro. People you need to keep on your side."

"Will there be dancing?" Carousel wasn't sure her feet, enclosed in the crippling shoes, would be able to withstand even a sedate trip around the dance floor.

Allorise chuckled. "There's always dancing! And food, more food than you can imagine. Last summer we took our houseboat downriver for three days, and the party . . ."

She rambled on about the soirees of the previous summer. Carousel drank it all in, fascinated by the idea of a house on a barge. The bargees lived that way, of course, but Allorise made it sound so glamorous, being able to travel where you pleased and have day-long parties on the river. By the time the coach pulled up at their destination Carousel was eager to join in the fun, stupid shoes or no stupid shoes.

The carriage stopped opposite a pair of high iron and brass gates, topped with a coat of arms. The gates stood open, and beyond them she could see a single-storey villa, set out on three sides of a rectangle looking out onto a frozen pond. A few people were sliding on the ice, shrieking and clinging to each other as they skidded about. Carousel hung back. It didn't look the way she had imagined a high society party to be. Braziers glowed at the edge of the pond, and the smell of spicy toasted nuts drifted towards them, making her mouth water.

"Come on!" Allorise gestured for Shadow to hand them down into the street. Carousel glared at him before he could make a move, and he kept his nipping fingers to himself. She stood in the road, feeling the ice gnaw her bare, crushed toes. It seemed a long walk across the street to the gate. Allorise surged on ahead, gaily calling greetings to her friends, leaving Carousel stranded.

She felt Shadow grinning at her. "Aren't you going to the party, little Carousel?"

"Bugger off." She took a few unsteady steps, felt her feet skid out from under her, and groped for the side of the carriage. Her hand fell on empty air, her leg twisted, and she landed with a thump in the gutter.

Shadow laughed as he whipped the carriage away, abandoning her to the ice. "Good luck!" he called. She bit back a curse and dragged herself to her feet, wavering like the skaters on the pond, with nothing to cling on to.

There was more laughter, a lot of it, and when she looked up from her unsteady feet she saw Allorise and her friends clustered around the gate, some of them openly pointing and grinning. Allorise had her hand over her mouth, in shock or amusement, but she was making no effort to give Carousel a hand. Well, she could walk to the bloody gate herself!

Carousel took three determined steps. This time she pitched forward onto her face, with a jolt that knocked the breath out of her.

The gale of laughter was louder this time. Carousel lay where she had fallen, hot tears melting the snow that clung to her eyelashes, face burning with embarrassment. She wished she could go home.

"I think she's really hurt!" A man's voice sounded a note of concern amid the hilarity, and Caro heard boots crunching towards her. She squeezed her eyes shut, blinking away the tears as a knee draped in red velvet landed in the snow in front of her face. A hand clasped her shoulder. "Are you hurt, miss?"

"I'm fine." She sat up, rubbing the snow off her face while her rescuer brushed down the fur Allorise had lent her. Her knee was bleeding, a striking red trickle against the white. He withdrew a cloth from his sleeve with a flourish, licked it, and applied it to the wound.

"You must be Carousel," he said, with a grin. "Allo has written us all letters about you. You know how to make an entrance!"

She had no answer to that, but the fact that Allorise had already introduced her to society, even by letter, made her feel a little better.

"I'm Korl." The man helped her up. "Do you want to lean on my arm? You'll never get there on your own, not in those shoes!"

"They are stupid shoes, aren't they?" She clung to him, grateful for the support. He was very tall, all legs and arms, with a shock of blond hair poking out from beneath the brim of his hat, and a black fur jacket that came down to his knees.

"Very fashionable, I'm told," he said. She snorted her derision.

"Come on," he added. "Let's find you a seat, and some food. She's all right, everybody!" He raised his voice to carry to the crowd at the gate, adding in an undertone for Caro's ears alone, "show's over, you bastards!"

The audience dispersed, leaving only Allorise, wringing her hands with worry. "Are you all right, Carousel?" she demanded. "I would have come and helped you, but I was scared of slipping and making a fool of myself too. Do you need to sit down?"

"Please!" Caro realised she was shaking, and her knee throbbed.

Allorise clicked her fingers for a servant to fetch a chair from the villa, and pressed her into it as soon as it was set down. "I'll fetch you some nuts. You stay right here!"

Korl nodded at her. "You'll be fine now?" he asked.

"I think so. Thank you."

"Any time!" He grinned. "I'll take you for a spin on the pond later, if you feel up to it."

"I think I might have had enough of the ice today, thanks for the offer."

"Come and find me if you change your mind." A woman hailed him from the far side of the pool and he turned away, sliding across the ice with long strides in his flat-bottomed boots. Carousel felt a twinge of jealousy, but she was grateful to have another ally in this strange new world she had been thrust into.

Allorise stood by the brazier where the nuts were roasting, deep in conversation with a dark-haired man and a girl with broad, sweeping cheekbones stained with too much powder. The powdered girl glanced her way, and a smile flickered across her face, to let Carousel know they were talking about her. Carousel shrugged, licked her palm and rubbed her stinging knee, and concentrated on the skaters, the blades on their boots scraping over the ice. On the far side of the pool was a red-curtained booth, and a few of Allorise's friends gathered around it to watch a lewd puppet show.

"Sketch you for a copper?" A man holding a pad and charcoal sidled up to her. Carousel shook her head.

"I don't have a copper, sorry."

He scowled. "You could just say no. There's no reason to be stupid about it."

"I'm not—" but he had moved on before she could protest. She glared after him, shaking her head, but was distracted as two girls skidded to a halt in front of her, breath steaming, throwing up a powder of ice sheared off by their skates.

"Are you Carousel?" the older one asked, while the younger, so alike she must be her sister, knelt and freed her shoes from the blades strapped to them. "You're here with Allo Carey?"

The younger girl looked up, hazel eyes wide. "Is it true you're a street rat?"

"Harmonie!" Her sister gave her a playful shove, tumbling her into the snow. "Don't call her that, it's rude! I'm sorry," she addressed Caro once more. "My sister has no manners. I like your hair. Do you work for Allorise?"

"Allorise is my friend." Harmonie might be curious, but she was only a kid. About fifteen summers, Caro guessed. Her sister's smile was wide and welcoming.

"Of course she is! We're all friends here. I'm Derata." She extended her gloved hand, Telesian style, and Carousel shook it.

Derata kicked off her own blades and ordered a maid to bring more chairs. Laughter rang across the garden at some obscenity provided by the puppets, and she rolled her eyes. "I don't know why they have to be so crude!" she remarked.

"I like it," Harmonie said. "But it's one I've seen before. Do you like puppets, Carousel?"

Carousel had seen puppet shows on street corners before, but she never had time to linger. Most of the ones she had glimpsed had been for children. She nodded, uncertain, wanting desperately to fit in.

"Where did you see this before?" Derata demanded of her sister.

"Maxie's." She coloured. "You won't tell Mama—?"

"What were you doing at Maxie's, at your age?"

Harmonie stared at the toe of her boot as she dug it into the compacted snow. "Everybody goes," she muttered. "All the fashionable people. I'll wager even Carousel goes!"

"Goes where?" Allorise had returned, holding a bag of warm nuts which she offered around.

"Maxie's," Derata said.

Allorise smiled. "Why wouldn't she? All the best people go to Maxie's. You go there, don't you, Carousel?"

Carousel had never heard of Maxie's, but Allorise was looking at her with wide, inquisitive eyes. She had tried so hard to help Carousel fit in . . .

"Yes," she lied. "I go there a lot."

Derata swallowed a handful of the nuts. "I'm surprised I've never seen you there," she observed.

"Do you mostly stay upstairs?" Allorise asked. "There's the smaller dance floor upstairs. More exclusive."

Like a drowning woman snatching at a straw, Carousel clutched the lifeline Allorise threw to her.

"Yes," she said. "I usually stay upstairs. It's less crowded."

"It is, isn't it," Derata agreed. "Maybe I'll see you there next moon. Do you always go?"

Harmonie jumped to her feet, muttering something about wanting to see the climax of the puppet show. Derata let her go with a shrug, her attention on Carousel, as the couple Allo had been talking to earlier wandered over to join them.

Allorise introduced them as Sharla and Duk. "This is Carousel," she said, waving her hand as if showing off a new gem.

Duk bowed, and his lip curled. "The famous Carousel, at last!"

"She goes to Maxie's, you know," Derata said, as if imparting some vital wisdom.

"But she stays upstairs," Allorise added, "so you might not have seen her there."

"Upstairs?" He arched an eyebrow. "That explains it. I would have remembered running into you."

"I'm sure you would." Sharla tightened her grip on his arm and upturned her wide blue eyes to the sky, where grey clouds gathered. "Do you think it's going to come on to snow?" she asked.

He followed her gaze. "I think we've got a bell or two of skating yet! Do you skate, Carousel?"

"Only in the road," Derata muttered. Allorise stifled a giggle.

"Don't tease so!" she said, before Carousel could protest. "I brought her here for entertainment, after all!"

"Then let me take her skating." Carousel didn't know why Duk was asking Allorise, as if she was a child and couldn't decide for herself.

"I don't know—" she managed.

"Come on, it's easy!" He was already freeing her feet from her horrible, ridiculous shoes. "Sharla, are there spare boots in the house? There must be!"

Sharla hastened into the villa, the heels dangling from her hands, and returned with a stout pair of boots of roughly the same size. Her face darkened at the sight of Duk kneeling in the snow with his gloved hands wrapped around Carousel's numb toes, and she elbowed him out of the way. "Put these on," she insisted.

The warmth of fur against her feet was worth any humiliation she might encounter on the frozen pond. Sharla strapped her own blades to the bottom of the boots, and Duk helped her to her feet. It was no worse than balancing on the high heels. He kept a tight grip on her arm as she shuffled out on to the ice.

"Don't look at your feet, keep your head up, and just slide. Follow my legs."

It was easier than she anticipated, not much different from dancing on the high wire. It was all about balance, and concentration. Carousel didn't know why she hadn't been able to walk in the shoes, but skating was lovely.

"My, you're a natural!" Duk's hands were tight about her waist, hard thumbs digging into her flesh. "Shall I let you go?"

"Go on then." She glided across the ice, passing the puppet show in a multi-coloured blur, breathless and exhilarated. Let them call her a street rat now. She was a better skater at her first attempt than most of these lordlings.

She stumbled as a sharp elbow hit her in the back, tripping off the edge of the pond into the snowy bank, into arms that didn't try to catch her. She managed to remain upright more by willpower than good balance, and glared around to see who had hit her.

Sharla skidded to a halt at her side. "I'm so sorry!" she gasped. "I tripped. I didn't mean to grab hold of you. Are you hurt?"

It hadn't felt like a grab, more like a punch, but Carousel wasn't going to cause an argument. "No harm done," she said, grudgingly.

"Let's go into the house. I'll get you a drink."

Sharla kicked off her blades, and Carousel followed suit. The sky was darkening rapidly, and the puppet master started to dismantle his stand. People drifted towards the villa. Carousel looked around for Allorise, but she couldn't see her. Maybe she was already indoors.

Sharla led her through the kitchen, grabbing two tiny glasses from a tray held by a poised butler and passing one back to Carousel. She took a sip, and winced at the fiery liquid trickling down her throat. "What is this stuff?"

Sharla shrugged. "It's no different to the ones they serve at Maxie's. Just a bit stronger." She knocked back her own drink in one mouthful, and dropped the glass on the floor for the servants to clean up. "What are you waiting for?"

Carousel drained her own glass, trying not to retch. The drink burned her throat and tongue. Sharla nodded, apparently pleased.

"Through here," she said.

The room she showed Carousel into was soft, with thick crimson carpet and red-tapestried walls. There were two fires blazing, one at either end of the room. The fires provided the only light, as the windows were tightly shuttered against the winter evening. There were plenty of comfortable couches, the same rich shade as the carpet, and cushions scattered across the floor to sprawl on. Masked servants moved among them, handing out more glasses of the liquid and jellied sweetments, like the ones little kids liked to eat.

She took a sweetment and chewed it awkwardly, unsure whether she should sit down. Allorise hailed her from close to the nearest fireplace. She lay on her back, her head in the lap of a man Carousel hadn't been introduced to, and she had acquired a whole tray of the fiery drinks. She held one up as Carousel approached. "Drink?"

"No thank you." Only the sweetment had got rid of the taste of the last one.

Allorise scowled. "You have to. What sort of party is it if you don't drink? Just have one for me?"

She sat up, watching closely while Carousel swallowed. "That's better," she declared. "Come and sit with us. This is my friend Einon."

Einon nodded, and Carousel sat. The floor felt unsteady beneath her, like it did when she hadn't eaten for a few days. The second drink had been less unpleasant. Maybe she was developing a taste for it.

Allorise lay back, her arms draped over Einon's legs, which were wrapped around her waist. She gestured for Carousel to help herself to the tray. The fire was hot against her face, drying out her mouth, and the smoke prickled her eyes. Without thinking, she took another drink.

"That's my girl," Allorise murmured.

The light hurt Carousel's eyes. It had been dark a moment ago, but now the shutters stood open. The low winter sun streaming through the windows was dazzling. Where had the night gone?

She screwed up her eyes and tried to think. From somewhere

close by she could hear the animal grunts of people fucking and trying to be quiet about it. She knew the sound from the cavern, lying in her bunk at night trying to block her ears to the noises around her. If she got up, she would disturb them. She lay still, but there was an uncomfortable draft and something wasn't right. She lay on the floor with a cushion under her head, and there was a dead weight across her legs, cutting off the blood to her feet.

It was her legs that were cold. She opened her eyes again, the sun spearing through her fragile skull. She was hungry, but the slightest movement made her feel sick. Holding her breath, she lifted her aching head to survey the red room.

Bodies sprawled all over the room, naked limbs tangled with each other amid the cushions and discarded glasses. The sex noises grew louder, and she saw Duk, pumping into Sharla from behind. She didn't look like she was even awake. He looked up, caught Carousel's eye, winked and mouthed something that could have been "you're next." Sharla's eyelids fluttered, and she whimpered. Carousel hadn't been with many men, but she could tell faking when she heard it.

Duk rolled off his woman and lay still. Carousel sat up straight, and carefully pulled her legs out from beneath the naked woman sprawled face down across them, trying not to disturb her. Her skirt was hiked up around her waist, and as she pulled it down, she noticed her thighs were bruised and sticky. What in all hells had happened last night? She remembered drinking, then there was nothing but a deep, black, blankness. She felt sure, if she had fucked someone, she would have remembered.

She rose to her feet, unsteady, looking around for Allorise. She lounged in the embrace of a dark-haired stranger, fast asleep, and Caro was reluctant to call out to her. Despite her nausea, Carousel had a raging thirst. She needed something to drink.

As she picked her way across the room she was relieved to hear Duk begin to snore.

The kitchen was bright, cold and deserted. The back door stood ajar to let the frosty air in. There were Telesian fruits in a bowl on the counter, but she hesitated before she took one, aware of their cost.

"It's all right," a voice said behind her. "Take what you like. I think you deserve it!"

She managed to swallow a surprised curse. "I didn't think anyone else was awake."

Korl hoiked himself up on to the kitchen table, and grabbed one of the fruits, digging his teeth into it and answering with his mouth full. "I saw you leave the red room. I thought I'd better follow and see if you were all right. Have one, these are good."

He lobbed a fruit at her and she caught it between her palms.

Then his face darkened. " What can you remember about last night?"

She felt herself blush. "I think something happened, but I can't remember. The drink . . ."

"It's savage if you're not used to it. Come on—" someone stumbled and cursed in the passage between the red room and the kitchen, and Korl jumped down and took her arm. "Eat and walk. I'll pay for a carriage to take you home."

He hustled her out of the kitchen into the courtyard, her mouth too full to raise a protest. The ice on the pond was ruffled with new-fallen snow, but the sky was high and clear, and there was no breath of wind. She swallowed hard, feeling the tart juice sting her throat. "What about Allorise? I can't leave her . . ."

"Believe me," he escorted her through the gate, "you don't want her with you. Allorise is not your friend."

"She is! She—"

"What happened last night . . . she did nothing to stop it."

Carousel scowled. "That's not fair. I don't know what happened last night. I've only got your word."

He was silent a moment, thoughtful. "Besides," Caro added, "she stuck up for me when the other girls were talking about Maxie's."

"I heard that," Korl said. "She said you liked to dance upstairs."

She caught his sceptical tone. "So?"

"Maxie's is a villa, like the one we just left. It doesn't have an upstairs. Everyone at the party knows that, and so does Allo Carey. She made you look a fool." He flagged down a passing carriage, and leaned in to give Carousel a brief kiss on the cheek. "Go home," he said. "Make sure you take some kingcopper, after last night. And don't trust Allorise!"

He handed her into the carriage, and went round to pay the driver. Carousel leaned her head against the door as it rumbled into life. She was confused, and exhausted, and sore. All at once she missed Spark fiercely. She wondered how she could find him again.

࿖

At least he wasn't cold any more, Spark reflected. That seemed the only thought he could muster, with a mind that swarmed and buzzed like a beehive. Every inch of his skin burned with fever, and it was a supreme effort to stay upright, to keep moving. He knew if he stopped they would find him, but he wasn't even sure who "they" were any more. He couldn't remember a time when he hadn't been trudging through the frozen city, jumping at shadows, coughing until his bones rattled. He couldn't remember the last time he had eaten, beyond cramming mouthfuls of snow into his mouth to slake his thirst. He passed through the crowds in a fever-dream, until eventually, after an eternity of walking, he came to a dead end.

Spark stared at the wall, blankly. The wall stared back. It

didn't seem inclined to get out of the way.

Move. He didn't know if he spoke aloud, or in his head. It seemed there was a time in the dim past when walls were no obstacle to him, but he couldn't remember it now, and to turn and go back required too much thought. He leaned on the wall, pushing his hands against it. *Move!*

The wall stayed firm, and Spark slowly slithered down it, face dragging against the stone, feeling nothing. He curled up at the base of the wall, knees pressed tight to his chest, too tired to rise. This was it. The end of the long run. He closed his eyes, and it was like falling through clouds. High above, someone called the name that used to be his.

"Liathan! Liathan, can you hear me?"

His eyelids were heavy, but he forced them open to see the eyes of his old master looking down at him in grave concern. "Am I dead?" he croaked, before the darkness swept over him and carried him away.

Seventeen

ELVIENNE SAT AT the boy's bedside, not sleeping, eating only what Nomi brought her. She had sought him for so long, and now Liathan hovered in that dark plane between life and death. When she opened the windows to ward off the taint of sickness, she could see the demons milling in the yard below, drawn by the scent of his power, like dogs after a bitch in season. They quarrelled and snarled like dogs now, as she looked down at them, sniffing around the invisible line of protection she had drawn around the inn, frustrated in their efforts to cross.

"Has he woken up yet?" Elvienne hadn't heard Nomi come into the room. The big woman had a soft tread when she wanted to be quiet.

"No, but he'll live, now the fever's broken."

Nomi cleared her throat. "Can he be moved?"

Elvienne heard the question Nomi did not voice. "You want us gone."

"I'm sorry, Elvienne. If there was any other way . . . But they," she spat out of the window towards the grumbling pack, "they're killing my business. I can't lose the Mouse, Elvienne. I've got nothing else."

"I understand."

Nomi shuffled her feet. "I can call you a carriage, when you're ready. You don't have to leave right now . . ."

Elvienne took pity on her, seeing how bad the White Giantess felt. She stroked her arm. "You're a loyal friend, Nomi. I'll leave the barrier up. No matter what happens, the Mouse will be safe."

"I feel terrible . . ." Her small red eyes brimmed with tears.

"Don't. I shouldn't have brought him here, but there was nowhere else. I brought danger to your house. I'm the one who should feel bad." Elvienne sighed. "I hate the way my duties bring grief to my friends. Have you heard from Kayall?"

"Nothing." Nomi shook her head. "What about you?"

"Not a word." She had called out with her mind, but there was no response. At first she thought Kayall had just picked up a lover and passed out in bed, but now she was getting worried. He wasn't dead. She would have felt the impact if he'd died. But when they worked together he was rarely out of touch for so long. She would go looking for him, but she couldn't leave Liathan alone.

"If he comes . . . ?"

"If he turns up, I'll tell him where to find you." Nomi hesitated a moment. "Where will that be?"

"I'll let you know when I get there. Help me carry Liathan downstairs, and then fetch us a cab." She tried to smile. "We'll be out of your hair before you know it!"

"I'm so sorry . . ." Nomi scooped Liathan, and his blankets, from the bed in one easy movement, his head lolling against her broad shoulder. Elvienne followed her downstairs, her heavy footsteps shaking the walls of the tavern. Nomi propped the boy in a soft chair by the fire, fetched a stout club from under the bar, and smiled at Elvienne.

"Walk me a circle, my dear, and I'll fetch your carriage."

"Are you sure?" Elvienne was stung with guilt. "I could go myself . . ."

"I won't risk you, or the boy. If he's the only one who can stop *that*—" she jerked her head towards the door, "and you're the only one who can protect him with magical flim-flammery –" she wriggled her free hand in a mock-mystic fashion, "then you're not to leave him! I won't hear another word about it."

Elvienne raised a delicate eyebrow. "Flim-flammery?"

"You know what I mean." Nomi thumped the cudgel into her massive palm. "Circle me. I'm ready."

Standing, Elvienne's head reached the bottom of Nomi's breastbone, and her arms wouldn't have reached around the White Giantess's waist. "Stand still," she warned her.

Nomi nodded. Elvienne drew in her breath and closed her eyes, concentrating on drawing up the powers that rippled beneath the earth. She drew the strands into her hands and twisted them to her will, until she felt herself tingling all over, charged with magical energy. When she opened her eyes and looked down at her hands, they shimmered with blue light that left crackling traces in the air when she moved.

Nomi had her eyes screwed shut, and her chalky skin looked paler than usual. Her lips twitched, maybe in silent prayer, as Elvienne began to pace around her. Every footstep left a glowing imprint on the floorboards behind her as she walked the protective circle, stepping between her own footprints, making sure there were no gaps.

The shimmering wall rose higher, enclosing Nomi in a translucent dome of light. Elvienne stepped back, broke the connection, and the light faded, leaving the White Giantess basking in a faint blue glow.

She opened her eyes. "Is that it?"

"That's it," Elvienne confirmed.

Nomi shuddered. "I hate that. It's like the moment before you jump off a roof."

Elvienne forbore asking whether Nomi was in the habit of jumping off roofs. "Go quickly," she said. "It won't last forever. You won't need the club."

"I'd rather take it with me." Nomi swung the club, admiring the faint blue trace it left in the air. "How does it work? Can they see me?"

"No, and they won't be able to touch you either. Which is why you don't need the club."

Nomi shrugged, and tightened her grip on the weapon. "I won't be long," she promised. "Be ready to go!"

Elvienne watched from the safety of the doorway as Nomi strode without hesitation towards the line on the ground that held the demons at bay, and into the horde. There seemed to be twice as many demons as before, more joining them all the time. They parted before Nomi like the sea, as if she was a great white ship. Demons were thrown back, bouncing in the gutters, some turning on each other in their confusion and hurt, howling and clawing at each other.

The horde closed once more behind Nomi, and she was lost to sight.

⸙

Spark was moving, a vibration shaking his skinny frame. He kept his eyes closed, trying to work out where he was. He was warm, but it wasn't the prickly, uncomfortable heat of fever. He felt hungry for the first time in days.

He risked looking around, keeping as still as he could. He was in a carriage. He could see the buildings of the city rumbling past outside, a blur of grey and brown. He was wrapped tightly in a blanket, arms pinned to his sides so tight he wondered for a moment if he was bound. And he wasn't alone.

He couldn't see the old woman's face; she was staring out of the opposite window of the carriage; but he didn't think he recognised her from the Nobility. Her hood was down and her grey hair curled in soft waves. He could see one hand, resting on her arm, skin pale and creased as ancient parchment. She was utterly still.

"I see you're awake. How do you feel?"

There was no chance she could have seen his eyes flicker with her head turned away, but she spoke with complete confidence that unnerved him totally. "How did you—?" Spark blurted out, before he could bite his lip.

"Call it a knack. I've been looking for you a long time, Liathan."

He shook his head, though she couldn't see the gesture. "You've got me mixed up with someone else, Lady."

"Have I?" There was a chuckle in her voice. "I think you underestimate me."

The old woman shifted in her seat to look at him directly for the first time, and Spark's heart stopped. Beneath the grey curls, set deep into her rounded face with its deep lines of age, her gemstone-bright eyes glittered green. The Old Ones had caught up with him.

For a moment he was frozen, pinned by her gaze, and then his senses rushed back and he lunged for the door, groping for the handle, with no heed for how fast the carriage was travelling. Her hand shot out, whip-fast, seizing him by the wrist as the door swung open to reveal the grey road racing past beneath their wheels.

"I wouldn't try it," she advised. "I haven't crossed the kingdom to find you only to lose you under the wheels of a cart." She stretched across him and pulled the door closed with her free hand.

"Now," she said, briskly, "what was that about?"

Her hand was cool, but restraining, against Spark's arm. This old woman was tougher than she looked, but she'd had him in her power for a while and she hadn't tried to kill him yet. If he played along with her, maybe he could slip away when she let her guard down. He tried to make it look as if he had relaxed back against the seat.

"Why were you looking for me?"

"I think you know that, Liathan."

He shook his head. "That's not my name. People call me Spark."

The old lady nodded. "I'd heard that about this city," she said. "No one uses their real name if they have something to hide. What do you have to hide, Spark?"

He set his lips firm and stared at the frayed buttons of the seat opposite. He wasn't going to hang himself for her.

"Please yourself." She shrugged. "My name is Elvienne. I have nothing to hide from you." The carriage slowed, and she groped for her walking stick. "We're nearly there."

"Where are we going?" Spark asked.

"Somewhere safe."

For you maybe, lady. Nowhere in the city was safe for Spark, and now he had blundered into the grip of the mages. Dying by their hand or Noble's, the final result was the same. He bunched his muscles, ready to make a break as soon as the carriage drew up.

They halted with a soft jerk, and Spark sprang from the cart, trying to run on legs that suddenly had all the strength of wet string. They collapsed beneath him, pitching him face-down on the cobbles. From far above, he heard Elvienne's chuckle.

"I thought I'd have to cast a spell to keep you from running, but it looks like the fever's done my job for me!"

Spark rolled on to his back, and wiped the blood from his chin. He sniffed. "If you're going to kill me, just do it. I'm ready."

He closed his eyes, and braced himself. Maybe it would be like a thunderbolt, stripping his flesh from his bones. Or maybe his life would be snuffed out with a snap of Elvienne's fingers, quick and painless. He hoped it would be like that. He was tired of being in pain, tired of running.

The last thing he expected was laughter. Warm and generous, it rolled over him like water. He opened his eyes to see Elvienne's extended hand, and he stared at it dumbly, like a dog unsure if the hand held a treat or a club.

"Why in the world," the old woman asked, "would I want to kill you?"

"Because of what I did." It seemed impossible that she didn't know. Her face darkened at his words.

"I know what you did," she said. "We don't condemn without seeking to understand. Get up and come with me now. It's not safe here. We can talk indoors."

Spark let her help him to his feet, the contact between their hands sparking blue with magic, making him jump. "Was that your magic?" he asked, scared being with her would trigger his own power.

"Indoors," Elvienne repeated, gesturing towards a tapering, three-storey town house, one of a long street of similar buildings. "Quickly!"

"Why—?" There was a flurry of sound, like a pack of hounds in full cry. A creature rounded the corner, headed directly for them. It ran on four legs, like a huge dog, with great bounding strides, and Spark caught the barest glimpse of fangs and foam-flecked jowls as Elvienne grabbed him, kicked the door open and hurled him through it. He saw a flash, heard a howl of pain, and the door slammed, cutting off the noise.

"What was that?" He sat up, winded. His arm was bruised where he had struck the wall. He massaged it, glowering at Elvienne.

"Demon." She held up her hand to forestall him before he could ask any more questions. She was pacing in front of the door, building a shield from her footprints. Spark had seen his old master do that, long ago, when the Atrathenes swept out of the mountains. The memory brought a lump to his throat. He swallowed hard.

He heard footsteps on the stairs, and a man's voice. "Elvienne? What are you doing here?"

"Can't talk." She vanished into the adjoining room as the man came down the stairs. He regarded Spark with a wry expression.

"Are you with her, kid?"

Spark nodded.

"What's she doing?"

"Walking a shield."

The man shrugged. "Good for her. You want a bite to eat? You look raddled."

"Please."

The man helped him to his feet and led the way to the back of the house, to a warm kitchen with a red-tiled floor and cupboards of cherry-hued wood. Spark sat at the table and watched the man scratch through the cupboards for bread and cheese.

"I don't keep much in, as it's just me," he apologised, pouring a small glass of wine. "And the bread's a few days old, sorry."

"You don't need to be sorry," Spark mumbled, mouth full of the chewy roll, struggling not to devour it like a wolf with a lamb. He wiped his mouth with the back of his hand, and remembered his good manners. "Thanks!"

"Any time." The man took a dainty bite of his own meal. "What's your name, kid?"

"Spark." He thought, too late, that he should have given another name, but the stranger didn't seem to recognise it.

"I'm Brynmar. Good to meet you, Spark."

"Likewise."

"Any of that wine left for me?" Elvienne joined them at the table with a sigh. The hollows under her eyes were dark.

Brynmar handed it over. "You look tired, sweet. Anything I can do?"

"All this shielding is taking it out of me." She smiled. "Thank you for letting me use your house."

"You didn't give me any option!" He laughed, but Spark noticed his smile didn't reach his eyes. "Listen, kid, don't get involved with mages, or you might find your front door kicked in and hellish explosions in your kitchen!"

"Once!" Elvienne was indignant. "Once, I did that, and it was a very small explosion. Almost trivial!"

Brynmar sighed. "I like that you're here, Elvienne, but why *are* you here?"

"Nomi asked me to leave the Mouse. The demons were scaring off her customers."

"Demons? Elvienne, you didn't—?"

"Not me!" But Brynmar had leapt up from the table and marched to the front door, throwing it open.

Elvienne hurried after him into the hall, and Spark trailed behind. "Don't cross the shield!" she warned.

"I'm not a fool, Elvienne!" Brynmar halted on the threshold, raising his voice over the howls and snarling in the street beyond. Looking past him, Spark saw the pack straining against the invisible barrier, raking at it with their claws as if the air was made of iron-hard glass. Some of them were hideous, twisted creatures, with huge, blinking eyes and hunched backs. Others, the ones that stood on two legs, could almost pass for human, if they hadn't worked themselves up into a lashing, spitting frenzy.

Brynmar turned on Elvienne. "Did you do this?"

She pointed at Spark. "He did."

"Me?"

"And I'm trying to fix it. Shut the door, Brynmar. Let's talk in the kitchen."

He slammed the door with a curse. "I need more wine to deal with this."

☙

The last of the wine was drunk, and none of the trio had spoken. Spark wanted to break the silence, to ask Elvienne why she thought he was to blame for the demons surrounding Brynmar's house, but her face was so dour he bit his tongue and stared at his plate. He wondered if she'd changed her mind about killing him.

Maybe she read his thoughts. "Let's start at the beginning," she said. "Liathan—Spark—why do you think I want to kill you? I already know what you did, why you ran from Lydyce, and I know why . . ."

"He asked me to do it!" The protest tumbled from his lips. "He was old and sick, and he begged me to help him . . . He said it was mercy!" His cheeks were wet, and he dashed away the tears.

Elvienne nodded. "Mercy. It's a powerful word. A powerful plea. I can't say, if I'd been you, that I wouldn't have done the same thing. But why run? You must have known we'd come and find you. Didn't Carlon tell you about our order?"

"He was," Spark wiped his eyes again, "his mind was gone. He didn't know who I was, or who he was. He thought he was on a boat half the time. And when he could think clearly, he *knew*. He knew he talked nonsense, he knew he pissed the bed, and he couldn't bear the thought of living like that. Knowing one day that would be all there was, that he would never be able to find his way back. And I couldn't bear it either!"

"No one is blaming you, Spark," Elvienne said softly.

"I blame me! I should have done more, got help. I didn't want to kill him! He begged me . . ." He sniffed hard. "And then he was gone. I was on my own, and I'd killed my master. A *mage*. I—I panicked. I didn't know what else to do, so I ran."

"You led us a dance trying to catch up with you!" Elvienne said. "And the demons?"

"I don't know anything about the bloody demons! Why do you think they've got anything to do with me?"

"Because you let them out!" Elvienne slapped the flat of her hand down on the table.

"I didn't! I don't know how to do that!"

Elvienne's face was strained. "You let them out," she repeated, quieter now. "You cracked the world, and they broke through. It's a powerful magic, too strong for an untrained boy. Only you can send them back."

"How did I—?"

"At the Gilded Lily. Whatever you did—and I don't know what you did—you tore the fabric that separates our world from the hells beneath. It's not just layers of rock that keep the creatures of the underworld where they should be, but magical wards, woven into the earth. You ripped them apart, and the beasts of hell spilled through."

"Magical wards?" Brynmar asked. "Like your shields?"

Elvienne nodded. "The same principle, yes."

"So could your wards—the wards on this house—tear open in the same way?"

She squeezed his wrist. "No. Not unless I take them down, or Spark loses his temper! You're not going to do that, are you, Spark?"

He squirmed under her emerald gaze, feeling sick. "Is it because of the people I killed? Is that what let the demons out?"

Brynmar stiffened. "People? More than one?"

Spark gripped the edge of the table. It felt like the only solid thing in a room that was spinning around him. "There was a man," he said, "in the alley behind the Lily. I only meant to lift his purse, but it went wrong. He wasn't meant to die! And . . ."

"And?" Elvienne prompted.

"And Dweller. He worked for Noble. He made me so angry, I couldn't hold the fire back. And Ram and Arabie—I didn't kill them, but they died, and so did the barkeep at the Woodsman's . . . ."

"Oh, it just goes on and on!" Brynmar sprang to his feet and began clearing the plates away, clashing the metal platters together. He wouldn't look Spark in the eye. "You've trapped us here with the kid," he said to Elvienne. "Fix it."

"That's what I'm trying to do," she told him. "Spark, only you can send the demons back to where they came from. To do that you need to learn to accept and control your power. Can you do that?"

He shook his head. "No. I don't want it. You can make it go away."

"I can't." Her voice was gentler than ever. "It's part of you. It will always be part of you. You don't have to take the green, but magic as powerful as yours needs to be controlled. You've seen what happens when it isn't."

He nodded, mute, frightened by her serious tone.

"My companion and I can bind you, if I can track him down. All this wild magic flying round in the air has made our communication impossible. But we can't do that until you seal up the cracks you made in the world. Do we have a deal, young Spark? Is there anything else you want?"

"There is one thing," he admitted. "Carousel . . ."

"The fairground ride?" Brynmar asked. His temper seemed to have eased.

"She's a girl. She's my friend. She went to work for Lady Carey . . ." He trailed off at the darkness in Elvienne's expression. "You know about Lady Carey? Something's wrong at that house, I felt it . . ."

"I felt it too," she said. "A darkness, an unnatural evil that has nothing to do with demons. I wouldn't want a friend of mine anywhere near that mansion."

"Can you help me get her out? Then I'll do whatever I must to get rid of the demons and you can bind my power and all this will be over, and I can be normal again." The words spilled out in a rush. Had he pushed his bargaining too far?

Elvienne nodded. "Let's deal with the demons first. I'm sure Carousel will be safe for a few days. Brynmar, can we use Etty's bedroom to train?"

He frowned. "No explosions? I saw what happened to the Lily . . ."

"No explosions. I'll keep the boy under control."

He nodded. "And those things outside," he waved his arm vaguely towards the front of the house, "they can't get in?"

Elvienne shook her head.

"But at the same time they're pressed up against my front door, so we can't get out?"

"Not until I train Spark to deal with them, no."

He sighed. "In that case you'd better get on with it, hadn't you?"

The spare room had a narrow bed, child-sized, covered with a rug embroidered with bold flowers. The motif was repeated in stencil on the walls. There was a dusty shelf lined with moth-nibbled rag dolls and a spinning top, tipped over on its side. In the wardrobe that stood against the wall he found a line of dresses, mainly brown and white, though some were bright under their thin veneer of dust, and none would have fitted a grown woman. He shut the door quickly, feeling as if he was intruding. "Will I stay in here?" he asked. "What about when Brynmar's little girl comes home?"

"Brynmar hasn't got a little girl," Elvienne told him.

"But the dresses, and the toys—?"

"Brynmar hasn't got a little girl." The firm set of her lips warned him to drop the subject.

"Did she die?"

"Yes, she died. He doesn't like to talk about it."

Spark nodded, and sat down on the bed, raising a faint cloud of dust around him. He had heard dust was the skin of the long dead. He hoped he wasn't disturbing the spirit of Brynmar's lost daughter.

Elvienne stood in front of him, hands on hips. "Show me what you can do."

"It doesn't work like that," Spark told her miserably. "It happens when it happens. I can't make it work. Dweller tried. That was when he—when I killed him—I mean, I don't want—"

"Nothing is going to happen to me as a result of your magic," Elvienne said firmly.

"Are you sure? How can you be certain?"

"Because I'm far more skilled than this Dweller, and I won't let it."

Spark shook his head. "You didn't know Dweller—"

"Exactly. If he had the power you have, my order would have been aware of him long ago. It's our duty to know about people like that. People," she smiled, "like you. So you don't need to be scared, or angry, and I'm not going to provoke you. Let's try a different approach."

Elvienne's approach was less hostile than Dweller's but it was exhausting, both mentally and physically. The concentration required to build up, and then rein in, the energy fizzing through his body left Spark feeling weak and dizzy, until in the end he begged her to let him stop. She nodded at this, with a sly smile.

"Learn to accept your limitations is a hard lesson, Spark. You've done well today. We'll carry on tomorrow."

Spark sank down onto the bed, the strength ebbing from limbs that felt like water, and a feverish quiver in the pit of his stomach. "Do I sleep here?" he asked. "Brynmar won't mind?"

"He won't mind. Goodnight, Liathan."

He was too tired to correct her, but as she placed her hand on the door he called her back, and she hesitated.

"Elvienne? Where will you sleep?"

"Don't worry about me." She winked. "I'll be just fine. See you in the morning, Spark."

The door clicked shut behind her, and he slipped under the dusty blanket, trying not to sneeze. His body craved sleep, but his mind was racing with all he had learned and seen since he woke up in the carriage. The bed was cold, and he felt awkward sleeping beneath the blankets of a dead girl. Had she died in this room? Maybe he couldn't sleep because her spirit resented his presence. Or maybe it was the shuffling horde of demons outside . . .

Elvienne had kept him away from the window while they worked on his control. They were attracted by his magic, she explained. If they saw him it would only inflame their desire. But they were quiet now, only the faint scrape of claws on stone and soft snarls to interrupt the still of the winter night.

Spark got up, pulling the blanket around his narrow shoulders, and padded over to the window on bare feet. He lifted the latch on the shutters and opened them a crack, letting the cold night breezes swirl around him. The moons were fat and yellow, barely obscured by scudding cloud, and they spilled their light across the horde below. It had grown since he last looked, the ranks of demons swollen until they filled the street. Hot red eyes stared, hungry mouths gaped open, and there was a scuffle, a surge as he moved. The creatures pressed against the shimmering blue shield Elvienne had built, claws straining for, but not touching, the besieged house. In other parts of the city the demons might run riot, but not here. Here they sat, and softly snarled, and waited. Waited for him.

He shuddered, closing the latch quickly, before the surge could spread. There was menace in that coal-ember gaze, menace worse than violence, and he sensed they wanted him for some terrible purpose. He hurried back to bed and pulled the blankets over his head, as if wool and dust could protect him from what lay in wait on the street below.

The growling rumbled into silence, to be replaced with another faint sound. Not from outside, but from the room next door. He heard it through the wall, soft, rhythmic squeaks and a woman—Elvienne—moaning softly.

Spark felt the flush travel up his face. He would have taken demons growling over the noise of Brynmar and Elvienne in bed together any day of the moon. How could he bear it? She was so old, at least thirty summers older than him, but he had taken her to bed and was doing things to her she was clearly enjoying. If it had been him, Spark doubted he would have been able to rise to the occasion. The sounds made him think of Carousel, and Noble, and when he finally slept, their faces, their naked limbs twisted together, haunted his dreams.

After lunch, to Brynmar's consternation, Elvienne pinned targets printed on parchment to Spark's bedroom wall. "You promised no explosions!" he complained, hauling up a bucket of water from the pump in the walled-in back yard that he shared with the neighbouring houses.

"Nothing is going to explode," she reassured him. "Have I ever lied to you?"

"I'm not going to dignify that with an answer." He glared out of the window. "You know there's no food left in the house? Whatever you're up to, you'd better get on and do it."

"Trust me." Her smile faded as he left the room, and she turned to Spark. "This is more serious than I thought. You're going to have to work bloody hard. Can you handle it?"

"I think so." He wasn't sure he could, and Elvienne didn't look convinced by his tone. His arms were already heavy and aching from the morning's work, and he didn't feel an inch closer to taking command of the power that burned inside him.

"Let's try it then. Like we practised this morning. Focus . . ."

He felt the ache in his head, pressure building on his skull, the moments before a breaking storm. His arms tingled, his hands burned.

"Steady," Elvienne warned. She stood behind him, one arm around his waist, the other steadying his wrist. He flushed scarlet at the contact, remembering the sounds she had made in the night. She had become a sexual being, and it unnerved him to his core.

"Concentrate!" She pinched his elbow, a sharp little nip to bring back his focus. The heat surged down his arm, building into a blast that erupted from his fingertips, struck the nearest parchment and seared it to ash, leaving a sooty stain on the wall. Spark staggered back under the force of it and collapsed on the bed.

Elvienne shook her head. "Your aim is better, but it's still too much." She scowled at the wall. "You'll have to scrub that before Brynmar sees it. He can't abide changes, not in this room."

"Is there some way I can practice without making a mess?" Spark asked. "What else can I use as a target?"

Elvienne's eyes flicked to the window. "I have an idea," she said.

The shoving, irritable throng pushed forward as she threw open the shutters, straining against the barrier. Spark took an involuntary step back, steadied by Elvienne's hand on his shoulder. "Don't be scared of them," she said. "You brought them here, you control them. But if you lose control, they'll rip you apart the same as they would anyone. Choose one."

"Choose?"

She flexed her hands. "Like you practised on the targets."

"I'm not doing that! They're living creatures!"

"Listen to me." She spun him around to face her. "They have no respect for life. Not human life, not their own. The only reason they haven't destroyed the city is because they're fascinated with you. But your control of them is a thread that can snap in a heartbeat, and if it does," she took a deep breath, "*when* it does—because it will—no one will be able to stop them from destroying the city. Thousands will die if you don't master them and send them back! I can't do it. Only you have that power." Elvienne let go of him, and stepped back. "I suggest you use it."

She retreated to the far side of the room, giving him space. Spark leaned his elbows on the window ledge and looked down into the street, trying to push down the fluttery, sick feeling in his gut, and focus his feelings as Elvienne had told him.

He settled on a demon just below the window, a soft, white creature. It looked like a huge lizard, but one fashioned from unbaked dough, oozing at the edges. The side of its long jaw was pressed up against the barrier, upper incisors overhanging its rubbery lower lip. Its teeth looked anything but soft.

And it was far from human. He couldn't bring himself to target the human-looking beasts.

He looked down at the teeth, the flattened jaw, the baleful, slitted eye, and he thought about the kindly landlord of the Woodsman's Rest, how he had let Spark and Carousel share his fire, at his own risk. He thought about the shrouded bodies lined up in the street, dirty with ash, and the blackened shell of the building. Demons had done that. He might have brought them here, but they acted of their own free will. Slaughtered innocent people for no reason. The hot anger welled within him.

He lashed out, a sizzling bolt of white light. He expected it to splash against Elvienne's barrier, but it passed through, sending a ripple through the wall. It struck the doughy lizard full on the side of the head. It howled, a high pitched shriek, smashing its flaming skull against the invisible wall, clawed feet scrabbling on the cobbles.

It might have fallen, if the press of bodies around it hadn't held it up. Sensing weakness, the pack turned. They finished Spark's work for him. He could not tear his eyes away, but stood and watched, fighting the bile rising in his throat, as the demons ripped apart and devoured the doughy lizard. It was over before he had time to draw more than a few quick breaths.

"Again!" Elvienne urged.

"I don't want to—" But his hands lifted of their own accord, seeking out a target. This time the bolt caught a squat demon full on the chest, throwing it back into the hungry arms of the pack, squealing and thrashing in agony.

Spark slammed his hands down on the window sill. "Enough!" He turned on Elvienne. "I'm not doing this! I don't mind sending them back, but I'm not going to kill without reason. I'm sick of killing! I want," he felt his face burning, and shameful tears spilled down his cheeks, "I want to see Carousel. I want to get out of the city. I want to go home."

"Back to Lydyce?" Elvienne's voice was soft. "They'll follow you there, don't doubt it. There's powerful magic, good and ill, around Lydyce. Here, they could just destroy the city. If they tap into the magic at Lydyce, they could destroy the world." She sighed. "I know how you feel. I used to live there, a long time ago. Before the lake turned dark."

Her eyes were so full of pain he had to turn away, and he noticed a movement at the fringes of the horde in the street below. The crowd was breaking up, drifting away.

"Elvienne? Come and look at this . . ."

She was beside him in an instant.

"Are they leaving because of me?" Spark asked. "Do you think we've fought them off?" He felt a glimmer of hope. "Have we won?"

"Don't count on it." Elvienne pointed. Every head in the pack had turned in the same direction. The demons with ears had them pricked. Nostrils flared and a rumble spread through the horde, of anticipation, of hunger. "Something else is calling to them. Something more powerful than you."

"What? Who?"

"I don't know." The street was emptying rapidly, every demon headed in the same direction, moving as one. "I think we should follow them."

The front door slammed. Brynmar, making a run for some food. He waved towards the window with a distracted gesture. Elvienne gripped Spark's shoulder. "Quick!" she said. "Before we lose them!"

Losing several hundred demons in the city streets seemed unlikely to Spark, but the pack moved fast, and they didn't stick to the lanes and alleys. They barrelled through Cape Carey like an arrow loosed from a bow, through houses and shops, over—sometimes through—walls, leaving a broad swathe of destruction in their wake. Spark saw bodies in the rubble, the overturned wreckage of a carriage that hadn't got out of the way quick enough, the statues by the bridge neatly decapitated by swinging demon hands. His steps faltered as he realised, too late, where they were leading him. He broke into a run, determined to overtake the demonic horde, to throw himself into their path if he had to. But he wasn't fast enough.

The wrought-metal gates of the Carey mansion lay on the ground, ripped from their hinges and trampled flat, and the mansion was besieged on all sides by an army that flung itself at the walls and howled for blood.

Eighteen

CAROUSEL STUMBLED FROM the carriage that drew up before the front door of the mansion, and fumbled in her empty purse for coin, muttering an excuse. "I thought I had a silver in here, hang on a moment . . . ." She patted herself down, while the carriage driver glared down at her from his high seat.

"Can't find your coin?" he said, archly.

"I'll just nip inside and get you some." She waved towards the house. "My maid will bring it out."

"You're not fooling anyone with that act, Miss Carousel. Especially not me."

Her heart skipped. The driver was a stranger. He might not be one of the Nobility, but Noble could still be paying him. "I'll give you extra if you say you haven't seen me."

"You think you can afford more than Noble?" His whip cracked out, catching her around the forearm, dragging her against the side of the carriage. "Get in. He only wants to talk to you."

"I don't want to talk to him!" She dug her heels in and strained against the leather. "Let me go, you bastard!"

"Get in, or be dragged along behind!" He flicked the reins

with his free hand, urging the horses forward, and Carousel stumbled. Her hand was turning blue.

"What in hells is going on out here? You there, stop!"

Carousel had never been so grateful to hear Bastian's voice. She twisted to see him standing before the front door of the mansion, lips pursed in irritation.

"Where are you going with my maid?" he demanded.

The carriage driver touched his hat, respectful to the power of money. "Sir, she didn't have the coin to pay her cab fare—"

"So you thought you'd drag her through the streets? For shame!"

The driver had the sense to look embarrassed. "I only meant to frighten her a bit."

"How much does she owe?" Bastian dug in his pocket and threw a handful of coins onto the gravel beneath the horses' hooves. "Will that do?"

While the driver scrabbled for his coin, Bastian gently disentangled Carousel's arm from the whip, frowning at the red bands left on her skin. "Are you hurt?" he asked.

She massaged life back into her wrist. "Not badly," she said. "Thank you. I owe you."

"I won't take it out of your wage." He looked around, as if something was missing. "Where's Allo?"

When Carousel left the red room, her lady had been sprawled on her back before the fire, naked to the waist, one arm behind her head and the other tangled in the dark hair of a man Caro didn't recognise. But she couldn't tell Bastian that. "She was still asleep," she said. "After the party. We stayed up late. I thought I should come home . . ." She limped across the gravel beside him.

"You should have stayed with her." He looked down at her bare feet. "Where are your shoes?"

Carousel felt the sting of tears welling up in her eyes. "I—I lost them. It was . . ."

"Not what you were expecting?" He offered her a wry grin. "Come inside. I'll find you something to eat."

245

The kitchen was always the warmest room in the Carey house. There was no sign of the cook, but Bastian clattered around in cupboards and pantries until he tracked down some eggs and a loaf of bread, and fried them together in a copper pan over the fire.

"Sorry it's not much," he apologised, bringing his efforts to the table on two metal plates. "I don't know where everything is. I don't cook very often. Never, before the staff left. I've had to learn quickly."

Carousel nodded, not really listening as she scoffed the meal. The bread was greasy, the eggs blackened around the edges, but it filled the hole in her guts. It made her feel like a lady, to have the youngest son of the Carey family waiting on a street rat like her. Bastian watched her as he ate. He took small, dainty bites, and she made an effort to slow down.

"Did Allorise have fun at the party?" he asked.

Carousel nodded. "I think so. There were puppets, and ice-skating . . ."

"But you didn't."

She shook her head. "It felt like people were laughing at me." *Because Allorise made me look a fool, made me wear those stupid shoes, made sure everyone caught me out in a lie . . .*

"Who else was there?" Bastian asked. "Who did my sister talk to?"

"Why don't you ask me yourself, little brother?" Allorise stood in the doorway of the kitchen. Her shoes dangled from her hand, and her bare feet made no sound on the tiles. "I'm glad you got back safely, Carousel. I missed you when I woke up."

Her eyes were bright, with no hint of shadow to show how late she had stayed up or how much she had drunk. She slipped into the chair and speared some bread from Bastian's plate. "This is all very cosy!"

"Carousel was hungry," Bastian muttered.

"You thought you'd wait on the maid? How sweet!" She nudged Caro hard in the ribs. "I think he likes you!"

Carousel stared at her plate, blushing.

"Are you done eating?" Restless, Allorise sprang to her feet once more. "I need you to help me change. I can't ask my brother to do it, can I? Or maybe I can . . . Would you like to help me out of my clothes, Bastian? While I tell you what I got up to at the party?"

He scowled. "Don't be ridiculous, Allo. That's what we have maids for."

"We have maids for cooking, but here you are in the kitchen," she retorted. "Come on, Carousel. We can talk amongst ourselves." She caught her wrist, the one with the whip marks, and jerked her to her feet. "Have fun playing maid, Bastian!"

Allorise hustled Carousel out of the kitchen before Bastian could reply. "Listen," she hissed in her ear as they crossed the hall to the stairs. "I wanted to say sorry."

Carousel stumbled in her tracks. "Sorry?"

"For the little joke about Maxie's. It got completely out of control. I didn't mean to make you look a fool." Allorise beamed, her face free of guile. "It was a silly thing to say. Everyone liked you, you know?"

"They did?"

"They thought you were funny." Allorise winked. "The heart of the party." She threw her shoes in the corner of the room and turned her back so Carousel could release the lacing on her dress.

"Who said that?" Caro asked.

"Everyone. All the boys."

The boys . . . When she moved, Carousel was still sore between her legs, and she remembered Korl's warning that she should take kingcopper. Kingcopper stopped babies growing in your belly. She swallowed. She had to ask.

"Allorise? Last night—did I—?"

"Did you fuck someone?" Carousel had been groping for a polite word, but the obscenity fell easily from Allo's lips, as if she cursed all the time. "Don't you remember?"

Carousel shook her head. "The drink—?"

"Was it too strong for you?" Allorise stepped out of her dress as it slumped around her ankles. There were scratches down her back, across her bare buttocks. "Fetch me something loose and flowing. In green, I think."

Carousel hurried to oblige. "I forget," Allo's voice was muffled as the cloth slipped down over her head, "your tastes aren't very sophisticated. It's easier to stay sober when you get used to it. But," she spun around and gripped Carousel's wrists, "you must be more careful, my dear. I won't tell my brother, but you really lived up to your name last night!"

"My—name?"

"Every man got a ride! Some of the girls too, the ones that incline that way. But don't worry," at Carousel's whimper of dismay, "I've got some kingcopper in my drawer, so you'll be fine. And only poor people get scrad. You're more likely to have given them the crotch-rot than the other way about!"

Carousel found her voice. "Why didn't you stop them?"

Allorise sighed. "I tried to talk you out of it, but you said you were having a good time. And having a good time is what it's all about!"

"I don't remember . . ." Carousel muttered. She felt the sting of bile in her throat. How many people had been in the red room? And every one had seen her splayed out on the floor, offering up her body like an Atrathene sacrifice.

"They'll be disappointed to hear that! You should drink less next time, maybe? Gently with my lacings, this is a new dress. It came all the way from Austover."

Carousel realised she had been jerking the laces too hard, and tried to regain control of her movements. Her hands didn't feel like they belonged to her.

"You won't tell anyone—?"

"That you don't remember? Not if you don't want me to. But everyone saw you on your back with your legs open, and they all want to see it again. I won't tell Bastian, I suppose . . . . He'd be so disappointed in you. He likes his women virginal, for some reason. He wouldn't like it if he knew you'd been laying yourself out like a common whore. Brush my hair, it's all tangled. It looks like yours!"

Carousel picked up the brush, battling the urge to slap Allorise around the face with it. The older woman must have sensed her simmering anger.

"I'm trying to protect you, Caro. You might have done something foolish, but everyone likes you, and Bastian need never know. He doesn't go to parties, and he doesn't know my friends. Once you're married and he thinks he's taken your maidenhead, it won't matter how many men you've fucked!"

"Married?" Carousel's hand tightened around the handle of the brush, bristles still deep in Allorise's long blonde tresses.

Allorise shrugged. "Maybe not married. Although Mama isn't here to prod him into a better alliance! But you could be his mistress, that's nearly as good. Better, in some ways. An adored mistress has more power than an unwanted wife. Queen Lydia started out as the King's mistress, you know?"

Carousel had no idea who Queen Lydia was. She felt herself grow calmer as she brushed Allorise's hair. The repetitive action was therapeutic. "Why do you think Lord Bastian would want me for his mistress?" she asked.

"I keep telling you, he likes you! You must have seen the way he watches you when we walk together in the gardens."

True, Carousel had felt the weight of Bastian's stare as she and Allo walked arm in arm across the faded winter lawns, on days when the house became so stuffy and oppressive that Allorise declared she could no longer bear it. But the idea that she could become mistress to a lord, even the youngest son of a fading House, was a new thrill. "Do you think he would?" she asked. "Take me as his mistress, I mean?"

Allorise patted her hand. "I can't see any reason why not. Would you like me to put in a good word for you? My brother is so shy; you could dance in front of him naked and he still wouldn't realise you were interested!" She turned back to the mirror. "Finish brushing my hair, and then I'm going to see Dada. Oh, it's going to be such fun having you as my sister!"

⚶

Bastian looked up from his book, startled, as Allorise slipped into his reception chamber. She wore a high-necked dress of striking green silk, which clung to her breasts and hips and swept the floor around her feet. Her arms were bare, and silver bangles on her wrists jingled as she closed the door behind her. She stole the breath from his lungs every time he looked at her, so he tried not to look, but the tiny print in the book blurred before his eyes. She laid one finger on the novel and gently pressed it into his lap.

He stared down at her hand resting on the book, resting on his groin. Could she feel the tremor that ran through him?

"What do you want, Allorise?"

"I want to give you a gift. A Winterfest gift."

She stood over him, her calves on either side of his knees. He felt the warmth of her flesh through the silk.

"We agreed, no gifts this year. I'm trying to read, Allo."

"Your boring, stuffy book?" She knelt on the sofa, a knee on each side of his legs, pressing him back until the book was crushed between them. "What I'm suggesting is *much* more fun than reading, dear brother!"

He could smell her perfume. The dress covered her from chin to toe, but it was so thin he saw the hard outline of her nipples, barely an inch from his mouth. He uttered a low groan. "Get off, Allo! You've made me lose my place!"

"Like you care about that." She shifted her weight against

him, and he was horrified to feel his cock respond, stretching with lust for his beautiful, impossible, sister. The knitting needles, worn on her hip like a dagger, dug into his thigh. He held her off with a hand against her breastbone, just above the tantalizing softness of her chest.

"What's the gift, Allo?"

She grinned, and kissed him lightly on the cheek, sister to brother once more. "Carousel," she said.

"Carousel?"

"Why not? You haven't had a fuck in ages. You need one." She groped under the crumpled book, and he squirmed away. "See? You're ready to spill any moment, just at the thought of it!"

"Get off!" He slapped her lightly on the forearm. "What does Carousel say about being offered as a gift?"

"She's my maid. She'll do as I tell her."

Bastian shook his head. "Not interested in whores, Allo. You know that."

"She's hardly a whore." Allorise rolled off to snuggle beside him, and draped his arm over her shoulder. "You wouldn't be paying her, for a start. And she likes you. What harm would it to do take a tumble with the maid?"

"Why are you so keen for me to bed her?" The idea wasn't unappealing. Carousel was pretty, in her rough-hewn way. If he closed his eyes, he could pretend it was Allorise moving beneath him. And it had been a long time . . .

She slapped him lightly on the chest. "Because you need to have some fun, brother! I thought with Mama gone you'd be off to the red houses every night, but all you do is curl up in here and read! What sort of life is that?"

"I like reading."

"More than women?"

"More than some women, yes."

She shrugged. "You're very strange. Do you want my gift or not?" Her lower lip curled into a pout. "I'll be terribly hurt if you reject it."

He picked up his book, shook out the crumpled pages, diving back behind the words so he didn't have to look at her. "I'll think about it," he said.

§

The evening air forced its way through the cracks in the shutters, trailed like chill fingers across Carousel's bare skin. She shivered. She wished she could pull the bedfurs around her torso, but Allorise had been adamant. "Wear these," she insisted, "and sit and wait. You're supposed to be a gift parcel, so you'd better act like one!"

Carousel looked down at her flat stomach, and at the ribbons that wound around her breasts and hips, pink wisps of concealment that only made her feel more exposed. Trussed up like a Winterfest parcel, a gift for Bastian. Allorise insisted he would be delighted with her, but Caro wasn't sure. She felt a fool, sitting here shivering, decked out in ribbons for a man who might not want her. But it was better than being a whore.

She heard his tread on the stair, Allorise's giggle, and a fist clenched around her stomach, a tight, hot grip that made her feel sick. Maybe she should lie down, but she was frozen in place, fingers tangled in the bedfurs. The door rattled and she heard Bastian call goodnight to his sister.

He pushed open the door. The breath snagged in her throat and she stared down at her lap, cheeks flaming, not daring to meet his eye. There was a long moment of silence.

Then Bastian laughed, and the tension broke, like a wire stretched too far. "She said she'd give me a gift, but I didn't expect it to be wrapped so prettily! Were the ribbons Allo's idea?"

Carousel nodded.

"Cute." She expected him to come across to the bed, but instead he headed for the drinks cabinet and poured a large measure of wine for himself, and a smaller one for her. She drank it standing by the cabinet, feeling exposed, while he toyed with the trailing ends of the ribbons that bound her breasts. "Are you going to say anything, or did my sister cut out your tongue when she decorated you?"

Carousel found her voice. "I can talk. I wasn't sure what to say, my Lord."

"For this one night, you may call me Bastian."

She thanked him for the honour, and he waved it away with a flick of his fingers. "Do you like the wine? It's a decent vintage . . . ."

It didn't make Caro's head shake too much, so she nodded. She watched Bastian down another bowl-sized goblet while she sipped her own drink. She wouldn't make the mistake she had with Noble, or at the party. She wanted her wits about her.

The wine-flush crept up Bastian's face. "Right," he muttered, appearing to talk to himself more than to her. "Let's get this done, then."

He pulled the loose end of the ribbon around her chest and it fell away, brushing her hips as it tumbled to the floor. Bastian's thumbs ran over her nipples, more in appraisal than caress. He nodded. "They say more than a handful is a waste. Do you agree with that?"

Carousel shrugged, not sure what he wanted to hear. Bastian slipped a hand into the ribbon than encircled her hips, and drew her towards the bed, pulling her down into his arms. His skin was cold. It put her in mind of those tiny snails she had seen in the cemetery, withdrawing into their shells at the slightest touch. She moved to kiss him, and he forestalled her with a hand against her lips.

"Why are you doing this? Because Allorise told you to?"

Caro stiffened. "I thought you liked me. She said—is this not what you want?"

"I do like you, Carousel. You're pretty enough, now you've scrubbed up and sorted out your hair. And I haven't bedded a girl for a while. But I don't want you to feel under any obliga-tion. I know you used to be a whore . . ."

"For one afternoon!" She giggled at his raised eyebrow. "It's a long story. A friend decided to rescue me. I wasn't sure I wanted to be rescued." At the thought of Spark she felt a pang. She hoped he was safe. If she could find him, she would apologise for their quarrel, try and bring him into the house. She was sure Allorise would have a use for him.

"Go on then." Bastian rolled onto his back and closed his eyes, wearing the expression of a man faced with a chore that had to be endured. "Try out your whore's tricks. Let's see if you can bring me off."

Carousel tried everything she knew, everything she had heard, working every inch of Bastian's body with hands and mouth, sucking, licking, massaging. His body was as stiff as a plank of wood, hands clenched on the bedfurs, eyes closed. The only part of him that wasn't stiff was his manhood. No matter what she did it lay soft in her palm, as limp and unresponsive as a newly-dead mouse. Even when she took it in her mouth, it barely stirred with desire.

Frustrated, she swallowed a curse. "Am I doing something wrong?"

Bastian raised his head and looked down at her impassive-ly, kneeling between his pale thighs. "It's not you," he said. "It's me. I don't get hard easily. Only . . ." He rolled onto his side and drew his knee up to hide his cock. "There might be something you can do. But it's never to leave this room, do you understand me? If you breathe a word to anyone, I'll slit your throat."

She withdrew from him, alarmed. He had spoken in such a mild tone, she wasn't sure if he was serious. "What do you want me to do?"

"There's a chest at the foot on the bed. Open it."

She lifted the lid with reluctance, not sure what she would find. Some men, she had heard, the men who visited the

Drover's Wheel, enjoyed whips and shackles and other imple-
ments the older women wouldn't talk about when she was near.
Some men liked to be chained, and whipped. Some liked to do
the whipping. If that was what lay in the box at the foot of the
bed, she hoped Bastian was of the first sort.

There were clothes in the box. Women's clothes, musty
and scented sickly sweet. They had obviously been worn and
packed away without washing. Were they Bastian's? She lifted
a corset, shimmering with silver stitching, a delicate filigree
across the white cloth and bone stays.

Bastian nodded. "Put it on," he said. "I'll lace it for you."

Carousel wrapped the corset around her torso, trying not to
breathe in too deeply. She stood at the side of the bed, allowing
Bastian to pull the laces tight up her back. His fingers lingered
on the fabric, and he pressed his face to her shoulder and
inhaled deeply, one hand creeping between her legs. "You smell
like her now," he muttered. "I could take you from behind,
but your hair's all wrong. Your shape is wrong. Even with the
wig . . . ."

She had seen the blonde mass of hair lying under the corset,
and she liked the way his fingers slipped inside her. It had been
too long since she had been touched like that by Noble. "I
could –" she swallowed a little gasp, "I could put the wig on,
if you like?"

"Damn it, Carousel, it's not enough!" He wrenched his
hand away, nails scratching inside her, and she winced. "You
don't have her curves, her softness. It's not you I need!"

"Do you want me to go?" She wasn't sure if she was disappointed, or relieved.

"Don't move." He pulled his shirt back over his head. It
came down to the middle of his thighs, hiding his nakedness.
Caro wished she could do the same. She felt stupid standing
there in just a corset, small breasts spilling over the top, the
tangle between her legs on display. Bastian had his wardrobe
open and she watched him rummage around inside it. She

wondered if he was going to produce more sweaty clothes for her to parade in.

Whatever brings him off, I suppose.

There was a loud click, and a scraping sound, like stones sliding over each other. Bastian swung the wardrobe away from the wall. It pivoted easily and silently, to reveal a dark opening as tall and wide as a man. If it was a cupboard in the wall, she couldn't see the back of it.

"You first." Bastian steered her into the opening, one hand on her shoulder, the other cupping her exposed right buttock, urging her forward as she hesitated.

"I'm not going in there." Carousel dug her heels in. "There might be spiders, or all kinds of crawlybugs. Besides, I can't see where I'm going."

"For fuck's sake!" Bastian snatched up a stub of candle from the shelf at the back of the wardrobe, and lit it with a *scritch* of candlestones. "Is that better, my lady?"

The passage stretched before her, wood panelled, dusty but free of cobwebs. Bastian pushed her on, and behind them the wardrobe slid into place again, cutting off any prospect of ducking out of his grip and running.

Bastian's mouth was close to her ear. "Just keep walking," he said. "I'll tell you when to stop."

Carousel flinched as the hot wax dripped on her bare shoulder, but she did as he bid, walking forward slowly, hands out in front of her in case she encountered any obstacles.

"You can go faster. There's nothing to fall over."

"I didn't know this was here," she said, as Bastian steered her sharply to the right, and down three shallow steps.

"Of course you didn't." His tone was scornful. "It's a family secret. You're lucky I'm unwilling to kill you afterwards."

She shuddered, still not sure if he was mocking her.

"My great-great grandfather built this house," Bastian went on. "His mistress was delicate, and the castle was too cold and damp for her lungs. He was a man who saw enemies everywhere, and he wanted the ability to spy on them in his own halls. These passages run all over the house. They've proved very . . . useful. There's a step up here, watch your feet."

Carousel quickly gave up trying to work out where in the house he was guiding her, but she thought it was probably on the same floor, despite the seemingly random steps up and down, and the twists and turns the corridor took. She saw glimpses of light shining through the walls as she passed, and she guessed they were spy holes, where the long-dead Lord Carey had kept an eye on his guests, and perhaps on his delicate mistress.

"Stop here." Bastian spoke in a loud whisper, and his hand clamped down hard on her upper arm. They were in a wide section of the passage, and a single thin beam of yellow light sliced the air between them, making the surrounding corridor even darker as Bastian blew out the candle. His teeth flashed white. "We don't want her to see or hear, do we?" He put his eye to the spy hole, blocking out the light. In the darkness Carousel heard him groan softly.

She fidgeted. It was cold in the corridor, and despite Bastian's assertion that there were no spiders, she was sure something had just scuttled across her bare toes. She hoped whatever they were doing here would be over quickly so they could return to the warmth of his bed chamber. "Am I allowed to see?" She knew she sounded petulant, a child, but she couldn't help her curiosity.

"I suppose so." Bastian took a reluctant step back and allowed the light to pierce the corridor once more. Until now, Carousel had only been aware of her own breathing, but now she was conscious of faint, human sounds coming from the far side of the wall. She stepped up and pressed her eye to the opening.

At first it was hard to make out the room beyond, the candlelight on the far side of the wall glaring after the blackness of the corridor. She had to blink to make out the shifting shapes on the bed, but the room was familiar. She had helped Allorise dress in there many times, helped her bathe and brush her hair. And now she was watching her fuck.

Shadow lay on his back on the bed, arms spread wide. She could only see his right hand, but a stout length of chain fastened his wrist to the bedpost. He still wore his mask, long beak pointed towards the ceiling in a grotesque parody of a swollen cock. His chest heaved. He must be suffocating under the leather and glass, but as he raised his free left hand to lift the mask, Allorise slapped it back down again.

"I told you, no! Not until you bring me the boy."

"I'm doing my best, Lady." Shadow's voice was muffled by the mask and the thickness of the wall. Carousel had to strain to hear it. "I got you the girl, didn't I? I hoped she'd bring the wizard kid with her . . ."

Spark, Carousel thought. *They're talking about Spark. And me.*

"Leave her to me," Allorise said, pinning his free arm down and grinding her hips against him in a way that made him arch his back and gasp. "She trusts me. I'll persuade her to bring him in. There's no hurry. I want to find out more about these demons first." She patted the teetering pile of leather-bound books on the bedside table. "Only not tonight."

Allorise hitched her skirts up to reveal her milk-white thighs and straddled Shadow on the bed, lowering herself onto the plague doctor, hips shifting as she took her pleasure with him. Her full breasts spilled from her unlaced dress as she glanced directly towards where Carousel stood concealed in the passage.

She winked.

Caro backed away, treading on Bastian's feet as he crowded in close behind her. "She *saw* me!" she hissed. "She looked right at me!"

"That's nonsense." Bastian elbowed her aside and took her place at the spy hole, one hand twisting the bottom of his shirt. "She can't see us, keep quiet!"

"Bastian, she *winked*—" but he wasn't listening, and as

he snatched her hand and guided it towards his crotch, the horrible certainty dawned on her. "This thing I'm wearing—it's hers, isn't it? You can only get hard by watching your sister screw, is that it?"

Behind the wall, Allo's voice rose, spurring Shadow to greater efforts.

"She's your *sister!* You sick bastard!"

"Don't you speak to me like that!" The slap caught her by surprise. It sent her reeling against the opposite wall, face stinging. "You're a whore, and a maid in this house. You'll do as I say. Get on your knees!"

He wrestled her down in front of him, her head thumping against the wall hard enough to drive her teeth into her tongue. His eye was still pressed to the spy hole, and his swollen cock bobbed an inch from her face. There was nothing of the dead mouse about it now, as he forced it against her lips.

At that moment, Carousel hated Bastian more than she had ever hated anyone. If he thought she was going to take him in her mouth while he watched his sister screw, he was deluded as well as sick. And Caro was a street rat. She knew how to fight dirty.

She screwed her hand up into a fist and drove it upwards into his naked, unprotected balls as hard as she could.

Bastian went down like a sack of oats, his howl of pain echoing around the narrow corridor. If Allorise hadn't known he was there before, she certainly did now.

Caro gave him no chance to regain his feet. She leapt up and raced away down the corridor in the darkness, back the way they had come, loose corset stays slapping at her legs, lungs tight under compressed ribs. She stumbled over hidden steps and stubbed her toes, but she couldn't slow, knowing Bastian would be after her as soon as he'd recovered, and then she'd find out how earnest his threat to slit her throat was.

She couldn't find the back of the wardrobe. The corridor seemed to go on and on, and she wondered, with a moment of horror, whether it led in a circle. Would she suddenly find herself back outside Allorise's bedroom? If that happened all Bastian had to do was stand and wait. She groped for her knife, fingers brushing bare skin, and remembered too late that it lay in Allo's dressing chamber along with the rest of her clothes. She panted curses as she ran. Spark had warned her to stay out of the Carey mansion, but she had known better, and now she was running for her life in Allo's sweaty corset, and she was lost.

By the time she reached the foot of a sheer flight of stairs, she could hear faint, limping footfalls in the corridors behind her. With the echoes it was hard to tell how far away Bastian was, but she had no chance to turn back and try a different route. She took the stairs two at a time, stumbling out on to a short landing that led to a dead end. Two spy holes on either side of the passage cast narrow searchlights across her body, but they didn't reveal any way out.

She beat against the walls, kicked at them, scratched the stone with broken fingernails as she heard the first tread on the stair below. As she backed against the dead end wall, fists poised to fight, something scraped beneath her elbow. She felt the wall behind her move. Just a fraction, but enough to spill a thread of light into the corridor.

She turned and pushed, frantic now, and the wall before her slid aside. Her weight carried her forward into the room, and she grabbed at the furniture to keep from falling. She gasped, and the stink of corpses filled her nose and lungs, making her eyes water. Blinking furiously, Carousel looked for a way out, but the sight of the old man in the bed froze her to the spot.

At first she thought he was dead. He looked decayed, empty yellowed flesh hanging off his bones. His chest sagged down between his ribs, and his withered hands clutched the bedfurs like a hawk's talons gripping his prey. She retreated, banging her elbow on the dresser, and broke the silence of the tomb with a curse.

One eye, huge in the sunken face, flickered open and

swivelled in her direction. His clawed hands twitched, and his mouth drooped open, a black, toothless cavern. He gurgled deep in his chest, and blinked.

Sickened, Carousel pressed her hand to her mouth and stepped back, too scared to turn her back on the figure in the bed that should not, could not, be moving. It had taken only a moment; Bastian's feet were still hard on the stairs behind her. She heard the whisper of his blade, but she couldn't tear her eyes from the old man, even when she felt the cold bite of steel against her throat.

"Tell me," Bastian hissed in her ear, his voice high and strained, "why I shouldn't slit you open right now, you little bitch?"

She managed to raise a trembling hand to point. "Who *is* he?"

The knife clattered to the floor at her feet. If she'd been able to think straight she would have pounced on it, but she could hardly move through terror. She could feel Bastian shaking. "Bastian?"

"He's my father. No!" as she overcame her revulsion and took a step forward. "Don't go near him! He's got some kind of plague."

"Is that what's wrong with his mouth? Poor old man . . ." Lord Carey blinked, and Carousel's eyes watered in sympathy as she stroked the limp hair back from his forehead.

"Carousel, be careful . . ."

She threw Bastian a withering glance. "It doesn't look like any plague I've ever seen."

"You're a whore, Caro, not a healer. You'd be smart to remember that."

"I'm a street rat. I've seen every kind of pox." She bent over the old man, holding her breath against the smell, trying to work out what was so unnerving, so familiar, about his decayed mouth.

Bastian scoffed. "A few cases of scrad and an unwanted

pregnancy are hardly—"

"Shut up." She took hold of Bastian's father's jaw gently, fearing the bones would crumble under the pressure. She eased his mouth open. The severed root of his tongue twitched like the stumpy tail of a fighting dog. "I don't know any plague that cuts a man's tongue out so neatly, do you?"

"What are you talking about?" He shouldered her aside to get a better look at his father's gaping mouth, his impotently twitching tongue. "Dada? What happened?"

Lord Carey thrashed his head back and forth. Little bubbles of spit gathered at the corners of his mouth as he garbled incomprehensible sounds.

Carousel snorted. "Like he's going to answer you. Someone doesn't want him talking, that's pretty clear."

"Maybe the plague got into his tongue, and Shadow had to cut it out?" Bastian sounded less than certain.

"How convenient," Carousel said. She leaned over the old man once more. She was getting used to the stink now. "Can you understand me, sir? Blink twice if you can."

Lord Carey's slow-moving eyelids closed, and opened, then closed once more. Carousel bit her lip. However decayed and ruined his body might be, his mind still functioned. She couldn't imagine a darker hell than the one that embraced Bastian's father.

"Blink once for yes, twice for no. Are you in pain?"

Two slow blinks.

"Do you have the plague?"

No. Clicks and gurgles. Carousel thought they sounded indignant. A horrible suspicion lodged at the pit of her stomach, and she forced the next question from her dry throat.

"Did someone *do* this to you? On purpose?"

A single blink. Lord Carey held his eyes wide and staring, until they watered. There could be no mistake. Someone had turned him into this helpless creature, and they had done it deliberately.

Bastian leaned over her, his hand on his father's shoulder. "Who did this?" he asked. "Was it Shadow?"

Two determined blinks, and a deep rumble in the old man's sunken chest.

"Was it—" Carousel's voice dropped to a whisper, knowing she could be overheard, that the walls of the Carey mansion had eyes and ears and never slept, "was it *Allorise*?"

"No!" Bastian uttered a little cry, but his father's eyes argued the denial. "She couldn't have. You're lying! Allorise would never—"

"What would I never do, little brother?" A sudden burst of lantern light washed over the tableau by the bed. Allorise was a blurred shape behind it, Shadow hulking at her shoulder, blocking the doorway. "I see you've decided to visit Dada. How sweet!"

Bastian stepped in front of Carousel. "Allo, you didn't . . . Tell me you're not responsible for this?"

"My dear, sweet brother." Allorise set the lantern down on a shelf. Shadow followed, and Carousel saw him bar the door behind them. "I'm hurt by the suggestion," Allo went on, snaking her hands round Bastian's neck, drawing his lips down to hers. "You love me," she said, in a soft voice. "How could you doubt me?"

"I love you . . ." His voice was distant. Carousel saw his knees tremble, his arms tighten about her waist as he pulled his sister closer to him. She saw the knife gleam in Allo's hand.

"Bastian, no!" Carousel started forward, but too late. The blade slid into his back as easily as a lover, and his shirt bloomed red. He staggered, slumping in his sisters arms, and she let him slide to the floor, clutching hands raking at her dress. She straightened, and stepped over him as if he was no more than a mound of refuse lying in the gutter. She flashed her teeth at Carousel.

"I'm sorry you had to witness that sordid display, my dear. My brother's feelings towards me were never quite appropriate.

I see you've met my father?"

Carousel backed up, crouching, pressed into the corner between the bed and the wall. She grabbed a candlestick from the night stand and brandished it uselessly. "You stay away from me!"

"As if I had any intention of going near a stinking street rat like you!" Allorise nodded at Shadow. "Guard the exit," she said, "in case our rodent decides to make a break for it. As for you, Dada," she shook her head sorrowfully, "fancy telling tales on me! It's a good job you've almost," she giggled, raising her hand to her mouth, "I was about to say *outlived*, but I'm not sure that's the right word for it. Outlasted, maybe? It's a good job you've almost outlasted your usefulness. I won't feel so bad about ending your life."

Allorise took a seat on the end of the bed and patted her father's withered hand. Carousel tried to back away from her smile, but there was nowhere to go. "What did you do to him?" she asked.

"Would you like to see? He's just a puppet now, poor Dada. Still, it's better than ending up like Bastian, I suppose." She shrugged, and took the knitting needles from her belt, blue wool looping and falling from them. "Do you like it? It's a baby blanket for my latest niece. Might as well make something useful . . ."

The needles flashed in the lantern light, twisting around each other in a delicate, hypnotic dance, manipulated with the skill of a puppet master. A tremor ran through Lord Carey. He lurched upright, flakes of skin drifting from his patched torso. A hand lashed out, caught Carousel across the face. It was a feeble blow, but his other hand caught her around the throat. Bony fingers dug into the flesh around her windpipe.

Carousel tried to scream, but she couldn't drag any air into her lungs. Her vision was filled with Lord Carey's huge, sad eyes, swimming with tears as he pushed her up against the wall and squeezed relentlessly. She was sure she heard the tiny bones in her neck splinter under the pressure, and as if from a great distance she heard Allo's laugh. "What fun! Shadow, do you think I should make him fuck her? I wonder if I can do that . . . ."

Desperation and terror lent strength to Carousel's arm. She swung up her fist, weighted by the candlestick she had forgotten she was holding, and smashed it into the base of Lord Carey's jaw.

With a cracking sound, the resistance his bones offered collapsed. The old man's lower jaw ripped away from his face, flying across the room to shatter in a cloud of dust against the far wall. His grip on her throat relaxed for an instant.

"The little street rat made me drop a stitch! Shadow, this might be too much for Dada to handle on his own. Could you help him out?"

"With pleasure, my Lady." As Shadow stepped towards her, Carousel gave Lord Carey a mighty shove. He toppled towards the plague doctor, the remains of his tongue flopping down onto his neck. She lunged for Allorise, grappling with her for the needles, biting and scratching, struggling to snatch Allo's knife from her belt.

There was a snap. A hot, painful line scored Caro's face, narrowly missing her eye. Lord Carey crumpled to the floor, a puppet whose strings had been severed, and the stench of decay magnified around him, his flesh sloughing from his bones. Carousel tried to reach out to him, but her right arm wouldn't move. Warm, wet liquid dribbled towards her elbow and dripped onto the floor.

She staggered, sick and dizzy, all thoughts of Allo forgotten. There was a broken knitting needle in her left hand, trailing light blue wool that was unravelling and drooping into the dark pool of blood on the floor at her feet. Not Bastian's blood, he lay on the far side of the room. And why couldn't she move her arm?

She looked down at the blunted end of the knitting needle

sticking out of the flesh just below her right collarbone, and she felt Shadow catch her as she collapsed. From far away, Allorise was laughing. It sounded like music.

Nineteen

CAROUSEL'S RIGHT ARM was numb, as if she had slept in the wrong position. When she tried to shake life back into it, it hurt so much it made her heave.

The sun scalded her eyes, long fingers of light pushing through the cracked shutters. How long had she been unconscious? And where was Allorise? Caro tried to rise, and realised with slow, creeping fear, that she couldn't move. She was tied to a high-backed chair by her wrists and ankles, and a thicker rope bound her waist. Her right shoulder was on fire, throbbing with every beat of her heart. Her blood crusted around the knitting needle embedded in her swollen, tender flesh.

This time she was actually sick, twisting her head so most of the watery vomit splashed on the floor, a little falling on her bare thigh. Throwing up made her feel better, as if she had vomited up a lump in her stomach. Trying to avoid looking at her shoulder, she scanned the room, relieved that Allorise and Shadow had left her alone for a while.

Bastian sprawled on the floor, one hand flung out before him as if stretching for something eternally beyond his grasp. His eyes were wide with the shock of his betrayal. She wished she could close them, or at least nudge his face with her foot so he would stop staring at her, but she couldn't break the bonds around her ankles. Beyond him, Lord Carey's bare bones were yellowed and ancient, a muddy stain on the floor around them the only mark of flesh that had decayed too fast.

She had to get out of here before Allorise killed her too. She twisted her ankles, but the ropes around them held firm. Her left wrist was bound so tightly her fingers were numb, and she couldn't move her right arm without fresh explosions of pain bursting in her shoulder. She whimpered.

There had to be another way. Maybe she could use the ragged wood edge of the shutters as a knife, if she could shuffle over to them. Pushing against the floor with her toes, she edged the chair back across the bare wood, one leg at a time, twisting it around until she could no longer see Bastian and the rotten bones of his father. The wood squealed and she held her breath, convinced the sound would summon Allorise and Shadow. Nobody came, and she resumed her slow progress until the chair leg snagged against the fringes of the thick bedroom rug. It teetered on two legs, and for a wild moment she thought it was going to right itself, before it crashed over onto its back. The jarring pain in her shoulder made her pass out once more.

The sun had hardly moved. She must have been unconscious only a short time, but Caro opened her eyes to find Allorise looming over her, a smile playing across her lips. If she'd had a blade, Carousel would have sliced the grin from her face.

"Look, Shadow!" Allorise spoke over her shoulder. Of course Shadow was there, the man had earned his name well. "She's on her back with her legs open. She must be waiting for you!"

He lunged forward eagerly, and Allo grabbed his arm. "I was joking, you great brute! Besides," she sniffed, "she'd probably give you scrad. I don't want you passing it on to me."

"Go fuck yourself, Allorise," Caro snarled. She may be down, she may be humiliated, but she wasn't going out without a fight. "If you set your trained bear on me, I'll rip his cock off."

"Bold words, sweet Carousel. May I remind you," Allorise bent so close Caro could smell the honey on her breath, "you're the puppet now, my dear. There's nothing you can do about it."

Carousel drew in a long breath and spat in her eye.

Allorise's face didn't flicker as she stood up, spittle running down her cheek. "If I didn't need you alive," she said, "I'd kill you for that. When I'm done with you, your death will be delicious." Her tongue flashed across her lips. "I might let Shadow have you first, if he behaves himself."

"Why do you need me alive?" Carousel demanded. "To get Spark? Whatever you want me to do, I won't do it. You can go to hell."

"Spark?" Allorise giggled. "Your little friend who thinks he's a mage? He's another one Shadow wants to spend some time with. It turns out I don't need him after all. Just you." She reached down, seized the needle in Carousel's shoulder, and twisted it savagely. Caro whimpered, digging her nails into her palms and biting her lip in a bid to stay conscious. She would *not* faint in front of Allorise, nor scream or beg for mercy. She would deny her that satisfaction, if nothing else.

Allorise laughed. "You're a strong one! You're just perfect, Caro my dear!" She pushed against Carousel's chest with her palm and slowly, smoothly, drew the long needle free of her flesh. Carousel hadn't thought it possible, but the withdrawal hurt more than the twisting, as the blood bubbled free and pooled on the floor beneath her. Allorise threw the needle with a clatter into the far corner of the room.

The older woman drew her blade, the one she'd stabbed Bastian with. Carousel tried to focus on it as it swept past, a whisker from her eyes. The handle was black, polished stone clasped in Allorise's pale fingers. The blade was a jagged, lethal shard of glass, shining brighter than any glass should. Brilliant red sparks swirled in the depths, and Carousel's eyes were dragged along with them, following the movement of Allo's hand.

"You like my pretty knife?"

Carousel was aware of Shadow moving behind her head, but the room was black and silver and dancing drops of crimson.

"I had it made for me by a Telesian mage. Blade magic, blood magic. Our green-eyed friends are too scared to use it, but the Telesians don't share their fear." The knife darted before Caro's eyes, leaving a glowing trail of sparks. "The most powerful magic there is. I can control demons with it. I have the blade. I just need the blood . . ."

Shadow pushed his mask up to reveal his grinning, scarred face. Carousel assumed he was grinning; his teeth were bared in his lipless mouth, drawn up on the left hand side by shiny, puckered skin in a raw, wide scar that swept past his narrowed eye and up under his hairline. She scowled.

"You ugly bastard. Did Spark do that to you? You wait 'til he next sees you, you filthy, pox-ridden—ah!"

The ball of his thumb fitted perfectly into the gaping hole on her shoulder, and he withdrew it with a dull wet pop as she squealed. He seized her shoulders and held them down, a meaty hand on either side of her head. Allo cut her free of the chair and kicked it away, so Caro's back thumped flat against the floor. "There!" She beamed. "Aren't you more comfortable lying down? Shadow, don't let her sit up."

"Yes, my Silver Lady." The humble tone didn't match the hard gleam in his eyes.

"I told you not to call me that in front of people! Especially not Noble's people! Not," she snickered, "that she'll to be in any state to report back to him when we're done with her. But it pays to be cautious."

Carousel held her breath. *Allorise* was the Silver Lady. She ran Startide. No wonder the City Watch was in Startide's pockets. Beside the wealth of the Carey's, Noble's resources looked poor.

But not that poor. If she survived, that little piece of information would be worth a great deal. Maybe even her freedom, and Spark's life. *If* she survived . . .

Allorise kicked Bastian's body to one side and prowled the room. Lighting candles, muttering rhythmically under her breath. An incantation, in a language Carousel had never heard before.

The room darkened around the points of light, laid out around Carousel in the shape of a star. Seven candles, one for each of the hells. Their glow turned Shadow's twisted, leering face into a new mask, of red and black, and the pattern of flames licked across Allorise's skin as she toyed with her blade. She dropped to her knees at Carousel's side, warm breath sweeping her face. "This might tickle," she said. "Try not to squirm too much, or stars know what might happen! Shadow, hold her firmly. If you fuck this up, you're demon–bait."

He nodded, eyes serious above his rictus grin, shifting so he held her down by shoulder and thigh, his knee squashing the breath out of her stomach. Allorise had her left hand tight on Caro's throat, her right holding the blade.

"Right." She sounded brisk, as though this was an everyday occurrence. "Let's get started."

The tip of the blade bit into Carousel's skin, just below her breastbone. She tried to jerk away, but she was held firm. Allorise glared at her. "If you wriggle about," she said, "I might accidentally gut you, and then I'd have to find someone to take your place. Your little friend Spark, for instance. Hold still and you might just live through this."

Shadow tightened his grip as Allorise carved relentlessly, scoring a white line across Carousel's torso. As the blood welled up, so did the pain. Caro's resolve broke. She screamed, she begged for mercy, she drummed her heels against the floor and bit her lip until her mouth filled with coppery blood. She wished she could faint, but her rebellious body would not succumb to her will. And the agony, the glass knife tearing through her flesh, went on and on.

"There!" Allorise sat up straight, and dragged her bloody

hand across her brow. "That wasn't so bad, was it?" Her teeth flashed cold in the candlelight. "Lift her head, Shadow. Let her look."

Carousel didn't want to see. Her torso, from the base of her breasts to her hips, looked like minced meat. She swallowed the stinging, bloody bile in her throat.

"You don't see it, do you? You dim-witted child, here!" Allorise sluiced cold water from the ewer over the wounds, and Carousel gasped. At the chill, the shock, the revelation. Allorise had not carved at random. Seared into Carousel's flesh was an arcane, elaborate symbol, twisting spirals and concentric circles that seemed to writhe and spin before her watering eyes.

She blinked. "What does it mean?"

"It's the Sealing Charm, branded onto the first door of the first Hell. The last defence between our world and the world of demons. Or at least," her nose wrinkled, "it was the last defence until some fool, maybe your friend Spark, let them out to roam the streets of *my* city. Every demon knows this symbol, and every demon is attracted to it. Blood calls to blood. They'll scent you from all over the city, every street, every gutter, and they'll be heading this way. Do you know how to control them?"

"Do you?" Carousel demanded. The blood, washed away, coursed from her open wounds again. Scarred for life, with a sign that made her irresistible to demons. What had Allorise done to her?

"Fortunately for you, I do. As I said, blood calls to blood. Shadow, give me the cup."

The vessel he handed her was silver, delicate, and smaller than a wine goblet. It had no stem. The embossed metal was cold as Allorise pressed it to Carousel's side to catch the blood pouring from the cuts she had carved. Carousel shied away from it.

"Hold still, street rat. You won't have to suffer much longer," Allorise told her, as the cup filled. She straightened, and carried it over to the window, throwing the shutters wide. "Here they come. Your demon army. What a pity you won't have them for long! Can you even see them from down there on the floor?"

Carousel couldn't see the demons, but she heard them, a grumbling roar, coming closer. She didn't *want* to see anything that made a noise like that, but Allorise leaned right out of the window. Her breathless voice was enchanted.

"Did you hear that?" The clang of metal falling hard on stone. "They ripped through the gate like it was made of parchment. Such power! And it's going to be mine to control."

Shadow cleared his throat. "Ours."

She shrugged. "If you like. Would you like demon tongues to lick your face better, Shadow?"

He glared, but he let go of Carousel to join Allorise by the window. She was no threat to them now. She tried to roll over, to drag herself away, but her limbs wouldn't obey her. Her hands slipped in the blood that pooled around her.

Allorise held up the silver cup in a toast. "To power," she said. Tipping her head back, she drained the vessel in one swift movement.

She shivered, a long ripple running through her body, and moaned softly. "I can feel it." Her voice was hoarse. "It's better than I ever imagined!" She let the cup fall to the floor, and Shadow pounced on it, scrabbling after anything his mistress might have left behind. Allorise ignored him as she advanced on Carousel once more. She stood over her with her hands on her hips.

"Oh dear. Poor little Caro. What *have* you been doing to yourself?"

"Fuck off!"

"That's not very ladylike. I expect better from my maids." She reached down, as if to help Carousel to her feet. Caro ignored the gesture.

"You couldn't have carved up your own fucking skin?"

Her words were defiant, but she knew her voice was

wavering. Allorise's smile drifted in and out of focus.

Allorise laughed. "I probably could, but magic this powerful demands sacrifice, and I'm not giving up my lovely Shadow. Not when I had you, so pliant and well-behaved, to stand in for me. It would be a crime," she ran her hand over her own plump, flawless stomach, "to ruin this perfection, but your skin isn't worth spit, Carousel. No one cares. No one's coming to rescue you, and no one will mourn your death."

"Silver Lady—"

"Not now, Shadow." Allorise held up a hand to silence him. "You see," she went on, "as soon as you knew I ran Startide, you must have realised you were never going to leave this room alive." The knife was back in her hand, glass blade gleaming.

"Lady, I really think you should see this . . ."

"What?" she snapped. "What could be so urgent?"

"Your new pets are doing something weird . . ."

With a curse, Allorise turned her back on Carousel and strode over to the window. "What are they doing? Show me!"

There was no possible chance Caro could get away from the house. She knew that as she rolled over, whimpering in agony. But now it was plain that Allorise meant to kill her, there was equally no chance that she was going to lie here and let it happen. Dragging herself by her fingertips, every movement torture to her mutilated skin, dizzy from blood loss, Carousel inched towards the door.

She could hear Allorise behind her, distracted, annoyed. "Why are they doing that? It's like they're letting something through . . ."

"Or being pushed aside," Shadow said. "Why don't you ask them?"

Another inch, another two, and Carousel's outstretched fingers brushed the wood panels at the bottom of the door. If she could sit up, she could reach the latch . . .

"I command them, Shadow. I'm not in the habit of casually chatting with demons. It seems to have stopped now . . ."

The floor lurched like the surface of a river as Carousel sat up. She retched at the motion, but her fingertips brushed the steel of the latch, lifted it . . .

"Oh no you don't!" Allorise marched over and wrenched her away from the door, flinging her to the ground. "There's no point trying to go for help. You wouldn't get to the foot of the stairs." She sniffed. "I can't fault your courage, though. It's a pity our friendship has to end this way."

All the smart retorts shrivelled and died in Carousel's mind as Allorise raised the knife high, a winning smile on her blood-stained lips. "What, no clever last words? Or are you just going to tell me to fuck myself again? I expected better from you, Caro. I—"

She broke off, flinging up her arm as the door splintered into a thousand fragments, bursting inwards with the force of a gale. "What in all hells—?"

"Drop the knife, Lady Allorise." The voice was a woman's, and it demanded complete obedience. The blade thudded to the floor, point first. It lodged in the woodwork an inch from Carousel's ear.

"Who are you, and what the hell are you doing in my house?" For the first time, Allorise sounded afraid. Carousel strained to see what was going on, but everything above her was a blur, voices fading in and out as if she was on the edge of sleep.

"I've come to stop you. This ends here, Allorise."

"For you, maybe. I know what you are, old woman. Your time has passed. Is that the magical brat lurking at your shoulder? He's taller than I expected."

Spark! Carousel tried to turn her head, but it felt like it was nailed to the floor. She could see Allorise's feet, backing away. Towards Shadow, towards the window.

"Spark, look after your friend," the old woman said. "I'll handle this."

Allorise laughed. "You think *you* can handle me? You don't

understand what I've done here today, do you? With all your powers, you have no idea . . ."

Carousel was dimly aware of a gentle hand on her shoulder, but all her attention was on Allorise. She was framed in the light from the window, her back to the sky, hands gripping the painted frame. The old woman had an empty hand out towards her, and her voice was calm.

"Come on, Allorise. Don't do anything foolish . . ."

"Foolish? Ha!" Her laugh was abrupt. "As I said, you have no idea. But you'll learn, old witch, and you'll learn fast." She scrambled up onto the window ledge. "Is this the exit you used last time, when you came prying into my affairs?"

"Allorise, stop!" The old lady darted forward, but she was too late. Allorise let herself fall backwards, into the arms of the horde that waited below. Into the embrace of her demon army.

Twenty

S PARK WATCHED ALLORISE fall, saw Elvienne's grasping fingers miss hers by an inch. Below, the demons waited, hungry maws lolling open, claws spread wide to rip her limb from limb and reduce her to a bloody smear on the gravel. They howled as she fell into their midst, vanishing into the tangled crowd.

Elvienne stepped back from the window with a heavy sigh. "Well," she said. "That's over, then." She turned her back and took a stride towards Carousel when a peal of glorious, triumphant laughter, *human* laughter, rose up from below.

Allorise lay on her back, lifted by the hands of her new army, letting them carry her. Savage claws stroked her naked form, as tender as a lover's touch. She pointed up at the window, and laughed. "It's not over, green-eyes! Follow me if you dare! You too, Shadow!"

"Shadow, don't—" but he already had one leg out of the window, ignoring Elvienne's warning. He brushed off her hand as she tried to catch his shoulder. "It won't work, you're not—"

"Get away from me, witch!"

Shadow jumped, and as if with one mind, the demons moved. Not forward to catch him, but back from the window, exposing a wide circle of hard gravel. There was a dull thump, and a snort of derision from Allorise. She uttered a command in a tongue alien to Spark's ears, and the whole mob swept forward, carrying her with them over the trampled remains of the gate and out into the streets, leaving Shadow's broken body behind.

Elvienne gave a long shudder. "Let's deal with her later," she said, "when I've had time to think. Your friend needs us now."

Carousel lay on the floor, naked, covered in blood. She looked as if she was sleeping. Spark swallowed. "Is she dead?"

"Not yet." Briskly, Elvienne rolled up her sleeves. "Pass me my herb bag, and then you can get rid of that." She nodded towards the body of a man, bundled against the far wall. Spark hadn't noticed him before.

"Who is he?"

"Bastian Carey. It seems there's no one Allorise wouldn't stab in the back to get what she wanted, even her own brother. Get him out of here. There's nothing I can do for him."

A hand under each armpit, Spark dragged Bastian's body from the room and bundled him onto the couch in the neighbouring reception chamber. It seemed disrespectful to leave him like that, so he closed his staring eyes and covered him with a blanket, as if Bastian was a child to be tucked into bed. He wondered if he should say something.

"Spark! I need your help in here!"

"Sorry, sir," Spark muttered to the unheeding corpse. He hoped that would suffice.

"Spark?"

"Coming!"

He backed out of the room and returned to Elvienne, who was struggling to lift Carousel on to the bed. Her cheeks were red, and she panted. "Give me a hand here? I can treat her better if I don't have to kneel down."

The sheets were stained yellow with sweat, dusty with flaky skin, but there was no alternative. Carousel was as limp as a rag doll in his arms as he lifted her. Abused as it was, the closeness of her naked body made him dizzy and hot, and he almost dropped her on the bed.

"Careful now!" Elvienne darted forward to steady his arm. "Well done. Now let's see what we can do for her." A flash of doubt crossed her face. "This is Carousel, isn't it? Not some other hapless child Allorise managed to snare . . ."

"No, this is her." His fingers brushed the long cut on her cheek, snarled on the blood clotted in her hair. "Is she going to die?"

"Not if I can help it," Elvienne said grimly. "I'll need hot water, and sheets to make bandages. Clean ones! And any thread you can find; ordinary sewing thread will do." She bent over Carousel, brushing light fingers over her wounds, muttering to herself. "And some ale if you can find it!"

Spark hastened to obey, returning with a pile of sheets, a spool of thread, and an earthenware flagon he found in the kitchen. "What's the ale for?" he asked, ripping the sheets into long, thin strips.

"For me." Elvienne took a hefty swig. "To wash the taste of evil out of my mouth. Let's start with that shoulder, before it turns bad. In my satchel there's a packet of flat leaves, pale green. They need to be steeped in hot water until they turn to mush. Think you can manage that?"

He did as he was bid. "I used to treat my master. When he was sick, or when he fell. I know a bit about healing . . ."

"Come back to me when you've been doing it five centuries. See if you can impress me then," Elvienne snapped.

"I was just saying . . ." The pungent scent of the herbs made his eyes water.

"I know." She softened. "It's good you want to embrace the healing arts. A lot of men regard it as women's work. The world will always need healers, sadly. And," she smiled, "it's good to have someone on hand who can thread a needle! My eyes aren't what they were . . ."

While the herbs stewed, Elvienne stitched the wound on Carousel's face. Her stitches were small and neat, but it would leave a scar, and there was no work for a scarred whore in any of Cape Carey's more reputable red houses. As for the marks on her torso . . .

Elvienne blew out her cheeks. "Best I could do, I'm afraid," she admitted. "She's going to have a pretty scar there. At least Allorise was aiming to hurt, not to kill. Even I can't put a man's guts back together when they've been hacked to bits! How's that poultice doing?"

Spark inhaled the fumes from the leaves. They were cold, and they made him light-headed and stung his eyes. The leaves had settled into a dull green mulch at the bottom of the pot. "I think it's done," he said.

Elvienne soaked the bandages in the water and wrapped them around Carousel's shoulder, packing between the layers with the leafy mush. Carousel's nose twitched and her eyelids flickered as she took in a deep breath, and sat up with a gasp.

"Allorise!" she cried, her voice raw and hoarse. "Allorise is the Silver Lady! Tell Noble—" She slumped back down again, and blinked slowly a few times. "Was I shouting?"

"A little," Elvienne told her. "It's good you have the strength to shout. Your friend is here."

"My friend?"

Spark took her hand and squeezed it. "We came to rescue you. Allorise tried—"

"Not now, Spark," Elvienne warned. "Wait until she's stronger—" but Caro struggled to sit up again.

"Allorise—she—Startide—she stabbed him in the back!" Her voice, a bare whisper, cracked on the last word. "Got to tell Noble . . ."

"You're not telling anyone anything until you've rested for a bell or two," Elvienne told her. "You've lost a lot of blood. Whatever Lady Carey is up to, I doubt she'll do it this afternoon. So relax."

Carousel slumped back against the pillows. "Am I going to die?"

"Eventually. Everyone dies eventually. But not today, not under my healing." Elvienne smiled at her. "Are you hungry?"

Carousel shook her head. "My throat hurts. How did you know I was in trouble?"

"We didn't. We followed the demons to see where they were going. They led us here. Spark guessed you might need help. He did very well."

Spark blushed at the rare praise from the old woman.

"You're one of the green-eyes, aren't you?" Elvienne nodded. "How do you know Spark?"

"I've been looking for him for a while. My turn with the questions." Her face was grave. "What happened here? Tell me as much as you can, even if it seems insignificant. The slightest thing might be a crack in Allorise Carey's armour."

Carousel told, about the old man who had seemed dead and alive at the same time, Bastian's death, Allorise cutting sigils into her skin and drinking her blood. "She talked about Telesian magic," she said. "Blood and blade magic. She said," she coloured, "you green mages were too scared to use it."

Elvienne shook her head. "Not scared," she said, "but cautious, and with good reason. These magics have a habit of turning on the user and destroying them, in the end."

"Then can't we just wait for Allorise to be defeated by her own spells?" Spark asked.

"I wish it were as simple as that," Elvienne said. "She could destroy half the city before then. We need to bring her down."

"Noble will fight her," Carousel said confidently. "If he knows she's the Silver Lady, he'll go all out to ruin her, and bring Startide down with her."

"That's the second time you've mentioned Startide," Elvienne said. "What is it?"

Carousel's brow furrowed. "Don't you know? I thought mages knew everything!"

"The private squabbles of the Cape Carey underworld seem to have passed me by," Elvienne snapped. "What's Startide, and what does Allorise have to do with it?"

Spark answered on Carousel's behalf. "Startide run most of the red houses in the city. The gambling dens, the dogfight pits, starstone trading, some of the taverns—"

"A lot of the taverns," Carousel interrupted.

"If there's money to be made, they want a slice of it. They've pushed the Nobility—Noble's gang—right back to the north-east quarter, and they've swallowed up most of the smaller gangs. Nightwing and the Market Street Hounds are keeping their heads up, but that's about it. Startide have all the money, and most of the power. They can squeeze the ordinary folk as much as they like."

"And Noble doesn't?" Elvienne asked.

"No!" Spark and Carousel spoke at the same time.

"He's a good man," Carousel went on. "If the people under his protection get sick, he pays for healers. He looks out for us. All he asks in return is loyalty. If he calls in a favour, you have to do it. In return you get all the protection you need, from Startide, from the Watch . . ."

"The Watch is corrupt?" Elvienne frowned.

"Bent as an old nail," Spark said.

Elvienne shook her head. "Sounds like Cape Carey has become a festering nest of vipers since I was last here! Spark," she turned to him, "get me every bit of paperwork you can find, even if it doesn't look important. Spread it all out on the kitchen table. We'll get to the bottom of Startide's affairs, and then we'll go to your friend Noble with evidence to strengthen Carousel's word. Hopefully he'll listen to us."

"What should I do?" Carousel asked.

"Stay here and go to sleep. I'm not taking you anywhere until you've rested."

There was a lot of paper in the house, armfuls of it, and most of it was useless. Spark sat at the kitchen table, chewing a stale heel of bread and watching Elvienne cast sheet after sheet into the fire with muttered curses. He wanted to ask how it was going, but the grim look in her gemstone eyes told him it wouldn't be smart.

After a long spell of searching, Elvienne straightened with an audible crack, and massaged the knots out of her shoulders. "Here's something," she said. "Lord Carey—the late Lord Carey, signed most of his assets over to Allorise because, it says here, he was too sick to manage his estate. It seems unlikely any man would sign over anything to a daughter, particularly a young unmarried daughter."

"Why not?" Spark asked.

"Because as soon as she married, her husband would control all those assets. Noble women can't hold land or property in their own right, except in very limited circumstances. The Queen does, because her father died without a male issue. At least, he had no legitimate surviving sons that we know of . . ." Her voice trailed off, a pained look in her eyes. "That poor child . . . ." She shook her head, and seemed to snap out of her gloom. "Ancient history, Spark, and it does no good to dwell on it. I think Lord Carey's hand might have been forced, or driven, by his beloved daughter."

"You think she turned him into her puppet-creature to get land and money out of him?" Spark shuddered.

"Not land and money, Spark. Power. The youngest daughter of a noble house, with many brothers and sisters, has little enough of that. She lives by the whim of her father until she marries, and then by the whim of her husband. Who could blame Allorise for trying to escape her fate? Even if the way she went about it was . . . inappropriate."

"Sick, if you ask me," Spark muttered.

"You killed an old man you loved," Elvienne reminded him, pointedly.

"That was different!"

"You lived by Carlon's whim, or by the whim of his decaying mind. Was it really all that different?"

"Yes." It had to be, or Spark was no better than Allorise. "He was in pain. He begged me to help him!"

"Don't you think Allorise used the same excuse? 'He's sick, let me lighten his load'?"

Spark scowled. "The difference is," he said, "that I didn't make him sick in the first place, and I got nothing from it, except grief!"

Elvienne stretched, leaning back in her chair. "I know that." Her voice was gentle again. "But these are the questions you're going to have to face throughout your life. I want you to be able to answer them with confidence. If you take the green, you'll have to live a long time with your conscience."

She lowered her gaze and shuffled through a few more papers. When Spark opened his mouth to speak, she held up a hand for silence. He glared at her, kicking his heels against the legs of his chair. If taking the green meant an eternity stuck with Elvienne, he wasn't sure he wanted it.

They were frozen in this ill-tempered tableau when Carousel arrived in the kitchen, draped in a trailing blanket. She moved with slow, shuffling steps, arms hugging her belly. "I'm hungry now," she declared.

"Spark will get you something." Elvienne waved her hand airily, not bothering to look up. Spark made a face at her behind her back, and Caro giggled, then winced.

"It hurts when I laugh," she admitted, taking a careful seat. "My skin feels like it's too small for me."

"It's going to sting like fire in a bell or two," Elvienne warned her. "Make sure you tell me when it does, and I'll give you something for the pain." She shuffled a neat pile of paper, all that was left now everything else had been discarded. "I think I've got what I need. Eat up, and then we'll pay a call on your friend Noble."

Spark and Carousel exchanged a loaded glance. "All of us?" he asked.

"Any reason why not?"

He shuffled his feet as he pressed a slice of bread and butter into Carousel's hand. "Noble might not be very happy to see us. Last I heard he wanted to kill me and send Caro to the Drover's Wheel."

"What's the Drover's Wheel?"

"A brothel," Caro said. "Not a very nice one."

Elvienne rose, folding the papers precisely in half and stashing them in her satchel. "Nobody's being sent anywhere disreputable, and nobody's being killed," she told them. "Noble will listen to me."

"But—?" Spark protested.

"Noble will listen to me. Everyone does. At least, everyone who isn't a fool." Elvienne grinned. "He doesn't sound like a fool to me. Carousel, can you walk to the carriage rank?"

Carousel nodded. "I think so," she said. "There won't be demons lying in wait for us, will there?"

"I doubt it. I think Allorise must have taken most of her horde somewhere safe while she works out her next move." She flexed her fingers. "Spark and I can handle one or two demons, don't worry!"

Carousel's eyes were wide, trusting. Spark hoped her faith in him wouldn't be betrayed. At the moment, he didn't feel capable of handling anything larger than a rat. He linked his arm through hers and she leaned on him as they followed Elvienne across the tiled hallway to the front door of the Carey mansion. Carousel hesitated on the threshold, looking back up the stairs. "We should do something about Bastian," she said.

"Bastian? Why?"

"He was decent to me, before today. He had no reason to be but he was, and I liked him. I don't want to leave him to rot. And there's Lord Carey. Even Shadow . . ."

Elvienne stopped to listen, her face dark and sombre. "I

agree," she said. "What Allorise did to her father, to deny him even a decent burning, was obscene. We can at least offer that to Bastian. And Shadow, however much of a thug he was. Spark, go and fetch his body."

Spark shot the old woman a sour look, but he knew better than to argue. He sloped off round the side of the house with a show of reluctance, dragging his feet in the gravel, sending tiny stones bouncing away from the toes of his boots. There were deep claw marks scratched in the surface of the drive, stinking piles of demon-shit and bloody stains where the creatures had fought. With a bit of luck, they would turn on Allorise and devour her.

He was three quarters of the way round the house when he realised he had missed Shadow's body. He swore, and retraced his steps. How had he walked past it without noticing? He had fallen right in front of the window.

He paced the back of the house, poking in the low bushes that separated the formal gardens from the gravel drive that encircled the mansion, trying to work out which of the many windows Shadow had jumped from. Here were some spots of blood, a disturbance in the gravel as if some large animal had dragged itself across the drive using only its forelegs, but there was no sign of the man he had burned. Spark shrugged. If Shadow had crawled off to die, it was no concern of his.

"Shadow's gone," he announced as he returned to Elvienne and Carousel, waiting outside the front door. "I can't find him anywhere."

"Maybe he wasn't as badly hurt as he looked," Elvienne said. "No matter. He's not the one you have to watch out for any more." She nodded towards the house. "Spark? I think your skills are appropriate here . . ."

Spark stared at the front door of the house, at the wooden frame, picturing tiny flames licking up the sides, converging and expanding, the tiled floor beyond cracking with the heat. It was a different sensation to the anger he had felt at the Lily, or towards the demonic hoard besieging Brynmar's house. He felt sad, but more for Carousel than for Bastian and his father. She had lost a friend, and her hurts went deeper than the marks on her skin. He wished he could heal her, but all he could do was destroy.

He closed his eyes, feeling the heat travel along his limbs, spreading out from his heart. It was calmer this time, more controlled. He found he could direct the power at the cracked door frame with its flaking paint. Behind him, Caro gave a little squeal. Elvienne hushed her as his concentration wavered.

He felt the heat pull the skin tight across the bones of his face, and he stepped back as the flames took hold, smoke pouring from the damp wood and making him cough. They retreated to the trampled remains of the gate, watching in grim silence as the fire spread, until the flames glowed through the windows on either side of the door. Sparks sputtered and died on the gravel. Elvienne touched Carousel's arm lightly.

"We should leave," she said. "People will be coming."

Caro nodded, and her lips moved in a silent goodbye to Bastian. She turned her back on the burning house and walked away, head held high, exposing the marks on her throat, arms cradling her belly. Spark lingered, watching the mansion burn. The waves of evil he had felt emanating from it were gone, and the house felt empty and abandoned. An emotional shell, soon to be a burned-out husk. He felt he should care, for Carousel's sake, but it was hard to feel anything but loathing.

Elvienne nudged him. "Come on," she said. "You can brood later. First you have to face Noble, and try and come to a reconciliation."

Even with the shutters thrown wide to let the winds of winter play through the halls, the ancestral castle of the Carey family felt musty and damp. Mould clustered around the windows, and it was hard to get a fire going in the massive hearth that dominated the great hall, where Allorise's great-grandfather had once entertained kings and traitors alike. Lighting fires was a servant's work; she would have to get some maids in. Humans, or some of the more human-like of her horde. Not the shambling, slavish creatures that were more deformed animal than anything else, which looked as if they should have been left out to die. The more human-like creatures were capable of speech, of logical thought. Capable of obeying orders. Some of them could almost pass for human, and one or two had caught her eye as potential bedmates.

Bedmates! She laughed out loud at the thought, and some of the more simple creatures fawning around her ankles fled at the sound. Yes, she could take one or two of them to her bed, the smarter ones. She could breed a demon child, bring it up as human. Why not? All the men she knew were useless and weak. Her pathetic brother, Shadow with his pawing and grunting, her father the twisted puppet. A demon son would be stronger, and he would be under her control.

She spun around in the middle of the hall, her ancestor's moth-nibbled robes flying out around her. Barely able to contain her glee, she ran towards the dais at the far end of the hall. The table and chairs were draped with mouldering, dusty sheets, and as she swept them aside a grey cloud burst up, making her cough and wipe her watering eyes. As the dust settled, she felt a thrill. Of recognition, of desire.

In the middle of the dais, in the place of honour and command, was her great-grandfather's seat. The dust had crept into the carvings that adorned the high back and the arms, and mice had nibbled the cushions, but it still looked like what it was. A throne. *Her* throne, and now she had an army to defend it from anyone who claimed otherwise. Just let her mother and her brothers try! Her fingers trailed across the worn, frayed cloth of the seat.

Why not?

It wasn't comfortable. The high wooden back meant she couldn't lounge as she preferred, but she could look down the length of the room from her high seat of power. This was her fortress; this was where she belonged. From this seat she could rule Cape Carey. And after that, why not the kingdom? The new Queen was little more than a girl, pushed and pulled by her advisers. And young, naive girls were easy meat. Just look at the street-rat Carousel.

She put thumb and forefinger in her mouth and whistled to attract the attention of a passing demon, an unladylike gesture her mother would have hated. There were some things her mother would just have to get used to about her daughter.

The demon cringed up to the throne. It was semi-human, walking upright but hunched, a long tail sweeping between its legs. Its forked tongue flickered over split lips.

"You! Do you speak?"

It shook its head. "But you understand me? Then get me one of you who can speak, and some food. *Human* food. Steal it if you have to, I don't care."

The demon nodded slowly, long face bobbing up and down on its springy neck. Less than a day had passed and Allorise was already sick of dealing with them. Let the stupid ones become arrow-fodder, weed them out. What she needed was a demon with half a brain.

"Lady . . . ?"

At first she thought the crippled, broken thing dragging itself down the hall towards her, one leg trailing uselessly, was another one of the horde. It didn't look human, with its twisted, battered face and hunched shoulders. She hoped it was one of the smarter ones.

"What do you want?"

"Lady, I followed you . . ." The creature shuffled closer. "I followed you out of the window. Don't leave me behind . . ."

"Shadow?" She could see it was him now, scarred face even more distorted with pain. "You followed me? Why?"

"To serve you, Silver Lady. I only want to serve . . . I came straight here, from the house." He dragged himself up the steps of the dais, breath laboured, gnawing his lip to bloody rags. It was only a mile from the mansion to Carey Castle, but it had taken him all afternoon, and every step must have been agony. Stupid, blind loyalty. It was exactly what she needed.

"Come here." Allorise patted her knee. Shadow was crawling now, the strength gone from his limbs. He pressed his head into her lap, and she felt him trembling with exhaustion. She smoothed his greasy hair. "Rest now, my Shadow. You've done well, and you can still serve me. I'll have need of you, before we're finished with Cape Carey."

Twenty-One

LIVING UNDERGROUND, LIVING *with* the underground, wasn't as uncomfortable as Kayall had expected. Not as comfortable as he preferred, but things rarely were. It beat seven hells out of living on the road with Elvienne, that was for sure. Noble had given him his own chamber, as befitted a mage, and it was warm and dry, with narrow glazed windows at ground level. When he stood on a chair and looked out, his eyes were level with the waving tops of the cemetery grasses. It was simply decorated, with a chair, a small desk, and a narrow bed, which he had already shared with a few of the Nobility who had expressed an interest in bedding someone with green eyes. He didn't feel like a prisoner, and Noble let him come and go freely. But there was no shaking the feeling that he was under constant surveillance, watched from the shadows by the demon-halfbreed Dweller. The patterned creature made his skin crawl. However open and friendly he appeared, his ability to merge with the shadows left Kayall looking over his shoulder, startling at every movement.

He had joined search parties for Spark, but there was no hint of the boy, or of Elvienne. It was as if they had vanished from the face of the world. He would have felt it if Elvienne had died, he was sure. If the boy had died, maybe she was sulking somewhere, sulking over her failure. He had known her to brood for years over such things. But she couldn't ignore him forever.

He sat in Noble's office, stretching to reach her and encountering nothing but blankness and silence, while the dark man watched him with a deepening frown.

"Any luck?" he asked.

Kayall shook his head. "If you ask me, you're chasing phantoms. The boy is dead. Or long gone from the city, and my companion . . . Either she's with him, in which case he's safe, or she's not."

Noble scowled. "He won't be safe for long. What do you know about the fire at the Carey house this morning?"

"I didn't know there was one."

Noble arched an eyebrow. "Really?"

"How would I? I don't have the networks you do. I don't even know where the bloody Carey house is."

Nobel made a non-committal sound. "One of my girls ended up there. She was close to Spark. I'd wager good coin he's got something to do with it. He specialises in fire and destruction, it seems." He sighed. "I'm pulling my men back. Sending them to the boarding houses."

"What do boarding houses have to do with anything?" Kayall asked.

"I have rooms all over the city. Some in boarding houses, in warehouses, family homes. Just a bedroll, a stash of food and a cache of weapons, but a man can hold out there until he's needed for battle . . ."

"You're expecting a battle?"

Noble cradled his head in his hands. "I don't know what I'm expecting, mage! You don't know anything useful, about the demons, or your friend, or our missing boy! Street fighting I can understand. It's almost a game between the gangs. People get killed, territories change, but there are rules. We all know what we're dealing with. Demons . . ." He shuddered. "That's a new enemy. I don't know how to fight them, except in the way we've always fought."

"Can't Dweller help you out?" Kayall scanned the room. "Is he here?"

"I'm here." The voice came from his left, and there was a flicker in his peripheral vision.

"Then show yourself. Stop creeping about spying on me!"

"I do not *creep.*" Scowling, Dweller flowed from the shadows to hover protectively beside Noble, arms folded across his chest.

"Enough, you two," Noble told them. "You're as bad as kids. You should be working together to solve this crisis, not sniping at each other. You're both . . ." he waved his hand vaguely, "magical. Magic up a solution."

"It doesn't work like that—" Kayall began.

"Demons aren't subject to the same physical laws as humans," Dweller interrupted. "You can't just snap your fingers and send them back to where they came from."

"You can't do that with people either. Be nice if you could!" Kayall sneered at Dweller. "Only the one who released them, or the one who controls them, can send them back."

"Aren't they the same person?" Noble asked.

"Not necessarily," Dweller told him. "The trouble is—"

"The trouble is, we think Spark released them using magic that was too powerful for him, lashing out without training," Kayall explained. "He's the only one who can seal the cracks he made, and I don't think he knows how. I'm not sure *I* do. Elvienne does, but I can't find her . . ."

"Seven fucking hells!" Noble pushed away from his desk and sprang to his feet. "What do I feed you people for? Any of you! I'll tell you what I want. These demons roam in packs, and someone in this city knows how to control them. I want that person found and brought to me, in chains if necessary. I want you –" he snapped his fingers at Dweller, "to try to communicate with them. Find out what they know, what they're doing. You -" he rounded on Kayall, "find your woman, find the kid, and get them here. I'm going to make him undo the harm he's done before I wring his bloody neck . . ."

"No need to find me." The voice from the doorway was amused. "I've brought you what you want. Nobody needs their neck wrung."

"Listen, grandmamma, I don't know how you got in here, but this is no concern of yours—"

"Elvienne!" Kayall pushed past Noble and flung his arms round his friend, crushing her small frame against his chest. "Where the hell have you been?" *Watch yourself with Noble, he's dangerous.*

I've missed you chatting in my head. Stupid demon interference. She smiled. Out loud, she said, "I just walked in. Tried on a different face and the guards let me through."

"Which face?" *Demon interference? Is that what it was? Did you catch the boy?*

"This one." She pushed back from him, the lines on her face blurring and smoothing, hair darkening to a rich shade of honey. She straightened, taller now, the neck of her blouse tugging downwards to reveal an expansive cleavage. Kayall backed off hastily.

"You don't have to use your charms on me, Elvienne. I've seen it all before."

"But he hasn't." Her gesture took in Noble, who had sunk back into his seat and was staring at her open mouthed, and Dweller, up against the wall. "Don't fade into the shadows, my friend. I'll only drag you out again. We all need to talk, and I have someone here with information to impart."

She hiked herself up on the desk, skirt riding up above her knees as she crossed her long, toned legs. "Now," she rested her hand on Noble's, "you're not going to do anything stupid, are you?"

He gulped. "I'm sorry, I mistook you for—"

"I am who I am. No mistake. But you might listen to me if you don't dismiss me as an old woman. Different faces for different circumstances." She raised her voice to carry to the corridor outside. "You can come in now! The patchcat has sheathed his claws."

The girl came in first, holding herself very straight. She was pale beneath a mask of dirt, and she'd be pretty if not for the fresh, livid slash across her face. She clutched Elvienne's cloak tight around her, and it was too short, exposing her bony knees. She swayed, and at Elvienne's sharp kick to his elbow Kayall remembered his manners and offered her a seat.

The boy followed, resting a possessive hand on her shoulder as she sank into the chair. It took a long moment of staring before Kayall realised who he must be. He was thinner than he'd expected, and taller, as if he had been stretched like wire. His eyes darted nervously from side to side, to Noble, to Elvienne. He didn't look capable of killing a mouse, let alone a mage as powerful as Carlon.

Kayall groped for his pocket blade. Let the boy say anything, make a move, and it would be the last thing he ever did. The air in the room crackled with menace and magic, and time slowed to a crawl. The boy's lips moved, but he wasn't looking at Kayall. All his attention was on Noble.

"Noble, I'm so sorry . . ."

The knife was in his hand and he lunged forward, striking for Liathan's heart.

⚜

The man with the make-up and the turquoise eyes had been staring at him from the moment he stepped into the room. Spark felt the hostility rolling off him in waves. He tightened his grip on Carousel's shoulder as he helped her sit down. If anything happened to her the stranger would burn, mage or no mage. His gaze made Sparks's skin crawl.

He tried to focus on Elvienne, who had changed her face again, but the brooding presence of Noble in the seat behind the desk pulled at him. He was looking at Spark too, nothing but disappointment in his expression. The man who had saved him from the streets, given him food and coin, taught him to steal and cheat at dice, looked at him with the eyes of a sorrowing stranger, and Spark couldn't stand it.

"Noble, I'm so sorry . . ."

The movement was a flash in the corner of his eye. He threw a hand up to defend himself, but Elvienne got there first. The air around him swirled with magic, stealing the breath from his lips before he could cry a warning.

The knife struck down towards his chest. Spark saw it coming, felt the heat rush to his hands too late, but it bounced off the air in front of him as if the mage had stabbed a stone wall, striking sparks from the steel. The mage staggered back, clutching his elbow, blade tumbling from limp fingers. It was snatched out of the air by the force of Elvienne's will before it could hit the floor.

"What the hells . . . ?" The mage shook his head. He seemed confused. "Elvienne?"

"I thought you might try something, Kayall." The mage tried to lurch towards Spark again, but his feet were mired in the floor. It seemed to have turned to mud around his boots, creeping up over his ankles and hardening to stone once more before he could take a step. He wobbled, waving his arms to regain his balance and cursing, but he was trapped.

Elvienne set the knife down on the table, out of reach of anyone but her. "Anyone else want to come through me to tangle with Spark?"

Noble drummed his fingers on the desk. "Did you do that, lady?"

"Of course she bloody did!" Kayall twisted as far as he could, but the stone held him firm. "Come on, Elvienne. You're ruining my boots."

She smiled sweetly. "Screw your boots. Are you going to calm down and listen to me?"

"He deserves to die for what he did. You said so yourself." His voice was blunt.

She frowned. "I don't remember saying that."

"I agree." There was a flutter in the shadows behind Spark. A long unheard voice seethed in his ear as decorated fingers reached for his forearm. "If we didn't need him alive . . ."

"Dweller?" He was real. He looked as solid as he ever did. Unchanged. But Spark had left him burning. "I thought you were dead. I thought I killed you! How—?"

"Hands off, demon creature!" Elvienne barked. "No one is dead, and no one is killing anyone, not while I'm here. I've seen too much of death, and so have the children."

"Too much . . ." Carousel mumbled, hand fumbling for Spark's. When he looked into her eyes they were all pupil, like two black coals in the snow. She slipped sideways on the chair, a dead weight in her arms as he sprang to hold her up.

"Elvienne, she fainted! What can I do?"

"Don't let her fall. Noble, do you have anywhere she can lie down?"

He frowned, lines of concern creasing his forehead. "What's wrong with her?"

"She's wounded. I've patched her up, but she's been through a lot today. She needs to rest."

Carousel's eyelids fluttered and she clutched Spark's arm. "Tell them," she whispered. "About Allorise, Startide, all of it. Everything I told you . . . . Promise me?" She slumped again before he could utter the promise.

"She can have my room," Dweller said. "Do you want me to take her?"

"I'll take her." Noble stood up. "You stay here. Be my eyes and ears. Spark," he advanced around the desk, "will you let me have her? I won't hurt her; I think Mistress Elvienne would have my guts if I did!" His smile was forced, and Spark tightened his arms around Caro's limp frame.

"Let him have her, Spark," Elvienne said. "She won't come to any harm."

Reluctantly, Spark let Noble lift the girl out of his embrace and carry her from the room, arms and legs dangling, head lolling against his shoulder. He carried her like a child, a precious doll. It was his care, more than any words of Elvienne's, that left Spark reassured.

An awkward silence settled over the room. Spark had so many questions; for Dweller, for the mage with his feet embedded in the floor; but he didn't know how to start asking them. The mage, Kayall, thrashed about a bit, then sighed.

"Could someone at least pass me a seat, as I'm not going anywhere? Kid?"

"My name is Spark." Spark pushed a chair towards him.

"If that's what you call yourself. This is murdering my knees, and I'm sure our mutual friend," he nodded at Elvienne, "won't let me go any time soon."

"Not until I can trust you not to stab my apprentice in the back," Elvienne told him.

"He's your apprentice now, is he?" Kayall scowled. "Watch yourself, Elvienne. Sleep with one eye open."

"I always do," she said. "Don't you think it's time you heard his side of it?"

"I don't need to hear his side. He killed Carlon. He can't justify—"

"Maybe he can." Spark startled. Dweller was the last man he expected to come to his defence. "What he did to me could be justified. He's a child, and I pushed him until he snapped."

Spark sank down into Noble's chair, feeling as if he was on trial before a lord. "I thought I'd killed you," he said. "It was the same thing, all over again. Ram and Arabie . . . But my master . . . He begged me for mercy! What was I supposed to do?"

Elvienne's face darkened. "It's difficult to refuse a plea for mercy. The boys in the army are trained for it, and they find it hard enough." She squeezed Spark's hand. "I can't say I wouldn't have done the same. I have, in the past."

Spark's eyes were wet. He sniffed. "I didn't mean to hurt Dweller. He was saying things, things about Carousel, and I just . . . I was so angry! It all spilled out, and then he was burning and I didn't know what to do, so I ran." He sniffed again. "I honestly thought you were dead."

"Dweller's tougher than he looks." Noble lounged against the door frame. He waved his hand as Spark moved to scramble from his seat. "No, stay there. We all thought he was dead for a while, but demon blood runs strong. And talking of demon blood, Carousel was saying something along those lines. You," he piniced Spark with a sharp look, "what's all this about the demons, and Allorise Carey?"

"Allorise Carey is the Silver Lady. Carousel found out. Allorise was going to kill her." Spark winced at the memory, Carousel wallowing in her own blood, the strident marks on her skin. "She carved marks into her skin . . ."

"A sigil," Elvienne supplied as he floundered. "Allorise controls the demons now."

Noble sagged. All at once, he looked old, older than Elvienne even when she wore her usual face. "We're finished." He groped for his hip flask, and loosened the stopper with trembling hands. "She'll take the city. I should have known she was Silver . . ."

"What makes you think she'll stop at the city?" Elvienne demanded. "She's got a thirst for power. She's got money and influence, and now she's got an army of demons at her beck and call. She won't stop at Cape Carey, unless we stop her ourselves."

Noble drank deeply. It seemed to ease the shaking in his hands. "How are we supposed to do that?"

Elvienne shrugged. "I'm no strategist. But if everything I've heard since I've been in the city is true, she'll be coming for the

Nobility first."

"What will you do?" Dweller asked. "She might let you live, if you surrender to her." This time Noble gestured for Spark to get out of his chair, and he sank into it, corking and uncorking the flask as if he needed to keep his hands occupied.

"Noble?" Dweller pressed. "What are you going to do?"

"I'd run," Kayall said. "Get down to the sea, find a boat, leave the Kingdom. I *won't!*" as Elvienne caught his eye. "I know, duty, blah blah blah. But if I had the option . . ."

"You gave up that option when you took the green. I warned you it wasn't all magic and women and beer!" She rolled her eyes. Spark guessed it was an old argument.

"We'll stand," she said. "Spark needs guidance, and we have to provide it. It would help to have fighters at our backs, but if you can't do that, at least get your people out."

"Me?" Spark suddenly realised everyone was looking at him. "What can I do? I haven't even taken the green . . ."

"That doesn't mean you're not the most powerful of all of us. You're swirling with magic. You can't see it, and you can't tap into it yet, but it's there. Carlon's magic, star magic from your birthplace, your own innate talent. We need to," she rubbed her hands, "bring those together and use you as a weapon."

"A weapon?" A horrible thought occurred to Spark. "What if I don't survive?"

"Then you'll be dead, like most of the people throughout the history of the world." Elvienne's bluntness was shocking. "If we don't stop Allorise, thousands could die. Don't you feel guilty enough already?"

"Can I think about it?"

"No." She turned back to Noble. "You still haven't said—"

"Hold on a bloody minute!" Spark slammed his hands down on the desk. "This is my *life* you're talking about! You can't throw it away like a scrap of cloth!"

"She's not asking you to throw away your life, kid," Kayall interjected.

"That's what it sounds like to me! Turning me into a weapon, using me against the demons—I'm not having it!"

Elvienne tried to catch his arm, but he shook her off and slammed out of the room, into the corridor. He could walk out, of the Nobility, of the city, strike out on his own . . . He leaned against the wall and closed his eyes, and saw the carvings on Carousel's skin, leaking blood. How could he leave her? How could he let Allorise walk away from what she had done?

"Hey kid." Kayall tapped him on the elbow. He was standing awkwardly, on one foot then the other, trying to shake the life back into his feet. Spark stared down at his crumpled suede boots.

"I thought she trapped you in the floor."

"I offered to talk to you, in the hope that she'd let me go before my boots were ruined." He regarded them ruefully. "I don't think I can afford another new pair, and it's hard to get the colour . . ."

"You didn't follow me to talk about boots. Are you going to kill me?"

"Sit down." One hand on his shoulder, Kayall pressed him to the floor. The mage sank down beside him, back against the stone wall. "I wanted to, obviously," he confessed. "I'd known Carlon for three centuries, give or take a few years. You can't even imagine knowing someone for that long, I'll wager."

Spark shook his head.

"We're not supposed to die. Not really. I mean, we can get killed in battle, or murdered, but getting old and sick and dying—no. But Carlon was older than all of us. He came from Avenhelm, did he tell you—?"

"Over and over." Spark managed a thin smile. "I think part of him was still there."

Kayall snorted. "Wouldn't surprise me! It scared me shitless, the idea of him getting old and losing his wits, and it scared me more that you killed him. I mean, you were his bloody apprentice, kid! You were supposed to look after each other, protect each other . . ."

"I couldn't protect him from what was going on in his head. But I didn't want to do it, and I only did it because he kept pleading with me." Spark stared at his feet, the floor of the corridor blurring before his eyes. "He was scared. He knew what was happening to him, and he didn't want it."

"Would you do the same thing again?" Kayall asked.

Spark thought about it for a moment. "Yes," he said. "Yes I would. But I wouldn't run next time. I think I did the right thing, and I'll defend myself if anyone says otherwise."

Kayall nodded, slowly. "You're a decent kid, Spark. Maybe I was too hasty."

"It doesn't matter though, does it?" The heat was rising again, and he pushed it down. "It doesn't matter how decent I am. Elvienne's going to put me in a catapult and fire me at Allorise Carey's demon army, and I can't do a bloody thing about it!"

"She's not going to fire you in a catapult!" Kayall laughed out loud at this.

"She might as well. I'm going to end up dead either way."

"The trouble with Elvienne is she only sees the big picture," Kayall said. "While you still cling to your small human life, you're just a dot to her. She's thinking about the whole of history, not about the tiny fragment that concerns you."

"My life isn't a tiny fragment to me!"

"She sometimes forgets what it's like to be mortal," Kayall told him. "Carlon's death shook her up too. But I'm a lot younger than Elvienne, and I spend more time in cities, surrounded by mortal people. I won't let her throw your life away over some grand cause, I swear. You're too magically interesting, for a start!"

Spark wasn't sure he wanted to be magically interesting. He sighed. "I never had a choice to be anything else, did I?"

"What are you talking about? You always have a choice!"

"Carlon brought me up. I'm meant to take the green. He

spoke a lot about destiny . . ."

Kayall lowered his voice and spoke directly in his ear. "He never told you, did he? You don't have to accept it. You can always say no and walk away, live a mortal life. Marry, have kids, grow old with Carousel or whoever you chose as your mate. No one is forced to take the green."

"He never told me that! He made it sound—"

"The sneaky old bastard!" Kayall roared with laughter. "I know what that was about!"

"What?"

"He's lost people before, good people. People we needed for our order, people he was desperate to bring over. There was one man, the kind you only meet once in a generation, but he wouldn't leave his woman. Mind you," he nudged Spark hard in the ribs, "I saw his woman. I wouldn't have left her either! He did well for himself, but he would have done better for us. I guess he didn't want to lose you the same way. It's flattering, if you think about it."

Spark didn't feel flattered, but he did feel relieved. "All my life," he said, "I was told what I was supposed to be. Now you're saying I don't have to be that at all?" All at once, the future unrolled before him like a Telesian carpet, bright with possibility. He hadn't realised how hemmed-in he felt until he could take a free breath.

"You can be what you want," Kayall said.

"Provided Elvienne doesn't offer me up like a sacrifice first." The gloomy prospect of his death settled over the carpet like a blanket of dust, obscuring the patterns once more.

"She won't. I'll fight her for you." Kayall shrugged. "Who knows? I might even win, for once!"

Twenty-Two

MY LADY, AN emissary to see you. From the Nobility."
Shadow bowed so low his forehead almost brushed
the floor, an excellent example to the demons around
him.

"Have one of the smart ones show him in," she said. "You
stay with me. I want you to get the measure of him."

Shadow gestured to one of the demons lurking in the
shadows, and barked an order in a guttural tongue. He was
mastering the language of the hells much quicker than she was.
She didn't like the people around her knowing more than she
did. He could teach her, and then she would dispose of him. It
would be easy now he was crippled.

The demon sloped away, shoulders hunched around its ears,
breath rattling in its sunken chest like an old man with bloody
lungs. Allorise fidgeted on the throne. It still wasn't as comfortable as she wanted it to be, even with the addition of cushions.
When she was queen, she would hold court from a sofa, and
everyone would kneel on the carpet before her.

The ambassador from the Nobility was short and flat-headed, with wide, bulging eyes. His face was tattooed with leaves
and shifting patterns, and there was something about him that

was both familiar and uncomfortably exotic. He showed no fear of the creatures lining her walls, the biggest and ugliest demons, armed, with bared claws and teeth. Lesser men had twitched and fled, but this stranger looked neither left nor right.

"You're a courageous one," she said, as he stopped at the foot of the dais. "Aren't you going to bow?"

"You're no queen, Lady Allorise. Even if you were, I bow to no human."

"No human?" She beckoned him closer. "You don't think of yourself as human?"

"It depends on who I'm with." He mounted the five steps up to the dais, and inclined his head, the barest show of politeness. "They call me Dweller."

"You won't give me your true name?" Allorise smiled. "You know mine, after all."

"I know they call you the Silver Lady."

"I thought you might. Tell me, is dear little Carousel still alive?"

Dweller nodded. "She's tough. You underestimated her."

Allorise shrugged. "I left her some pretty reminders of our friendship. You should marry her. You'd make a good match. You could breed demon-patterned babies." The narrowing of his eyes told her she was right. "You're not full demon, are you? You seem to have some wit about you."

"You'd call me a halfbreed, I suppose." He said it in a mocking, sneering tone, as if he despised both the term and himself.

"Do you feel at home here, halfbreed? Surrounded by your father's kind?"

"My mother's. It's not your minions who make me feel uncomfortable, Silver Lady."

His broad face was guileless. Allorise wanted to slap the patterns from his skin. "What do you want, halfbreed? Or should I ask what Noble wants, as you're his pet?"

"You have plenty of pets of your own, Silver Lady."

"What does Noble want?" She paced the words, as if talking to an idiot child.

"He wants to treaty with you."

"And he sent you in his stead? Is he too scared to face me himself?"

Dweller shook his head. "Noble's a busy man. He sees no one. I do his talking for him."

Allorise curled her lip. "Tell him from me, he has an ugly mouthpiece." He showed no offence. "What terms?"

"You keep to the south of the river, he has the north. Beyond that, he doesn't care how you rule. Just leave our people alone."

Allorise pretended to consider it. "Noble wants to make himself Lord of the North Bank? Does he really think my ambition extends no further than the city walls?"

"I don't know what Noble thinks." Dweller shrugged. "I only carry his words."

She scanned him up and down. "I think you have words of your own. You're just not saying them. What do you want to say, halfbreed?"

Silence.

"You're a creature who can't be persuaded? Very well. Tell Noble he can have the whole damned city, if he likes. On two conditions."

"What are they?" Dweller asked, as she paused to frame her words.

"He can have the city when I take the Kingdom. If he helps me, he'll get what he wants a lot quicker."

"Tempting," Dweller said, with a nod of acquiescence. "What else?"

"I want the mage child."

"Spark?"

She scoffed. "How many mage children do you have running about? I've been interested in Spark for a long time. If

Noble hands him over, we can forge a deal. Otherwise the dice game is off."

The halfbreed shook his head. "I don't think he'll agree to that. Even if he did, the other mages would be reluctant to let the boy go. They have their own plans for him."

"To the hells with their plans! An old woman, a dandy and a child; what can they do to me?"

"The old woman—"

"Is old. Too old, and far from the pulse." Allorise snorted. "The time for green magic is long gone. A new magic is loose in the world, and I'm the mistress of it. Not them. You tell them," she leaned forward until they were nose-to-nose, until she could smell the underground stink on Dweller's robes, "to deliver the boy to me, in chains, and Noble can have this worthless fucking city and everyone in it to do with as he pleases!"

He didn't flinch. "If he doesn't agree?"

She sat back. "He has three days. If he doesn't deliver, I'm not prepared to offer any quarter. He'll lose the city, and then his head." She flashed a beguiling smile. "I think he'll agree. If he doesn't . . . You don't want to play the losing hand, do you? I could use someone like you at my side. Someone—" she nodded towards Shadow, standing stiff and silent at the far end of the hall, easing the weight on his twisted leg, "— *whole*. Are you whole, halfbreed?"

"I'm whole." He glowered at her from beneath decorated brows. "But I'm not interested in that kind of offer. Doesn't your companion fill that role?"

She giggled. "Dear Shadow is not as whole as he used to be. He struggles now. The injuries from his fall make him quite . . . *incapable,* if you know what I mean."

"I'm not interested in human women." Dweller turned away.

"In demon women, then? Human men?"

He shrugged.

"You should spend some time with your mother's race, Dweller. Form an understanding with them. I could use someone who understands their way of thinking."

Dweller shook his head. "I was brought up in hell. No human could possibly understand . . ."

"But you do, patterned little halfbreed?" She leant forward, eager for information, fascinated by the strangeness that had brought him to her feet. "What's it like?"

He retreated a step, and she saw real fear in his whirling eyes. Just the thought made him panic, but he hid it well. "Dark," he said. "Hot. Foul and stinking. Violent. So many die trying to get out. Most never make it that far."

"But you're strong?"

Dweller nodded. "I get my strength from my mother."

"Yet here you are, doing minion work for a man so soft he takes orders from an old woman!" She beckoned him closer, and patted his cheek. The marks were raised slightly under her fingers, as if Dweller's skin was embossed. "That must be humiliating. They're going to send you back, you know?"

"They won't send me back." But she felt the quiver run through him, fear, and long-suppressed anger.

"The mages want all the demons off the streets of Cape Carey. You think they'd let you stay, you little flat-headed freak? Think about it, my sweet. Think what I could offer you. I'd spare your life. I'd even spare Noble's, if he lets me have the boy."

He backed away, beyond her touch. "I'll tell him," he said. "But don't expect to get what you want, Silver Lady."

Her laugh was full and rich. "Why not? I have so far!" She flicked her fingers in dismissal. "Go on. Run back to your master. Tell him what I want. His three days start now."

"Three days? Fuck!" Noble slammed the tip of his dagger into his desk, and glared at Spark as if he was the cause of everything wrong in the city. "I should give you up. I hope you appreciate that."

"I do, I really do."

"The only reason I won't hand you over is because Caro begged me not to. She's taken a fancy to you!" He winked.

"She has?"

"That, and Elvienne will have my balls." Noble nodded at her. She sat quietly in one corner of the office, wearing her customary face. Any other elderly woman would be knitting, or sewing, Spark reflected grimly. Elvienne was polishing her dagger.

She didn't look up. "You're not wrong," she said. "And it's two and a half days now. I've yet to see any leadership from you, Noble. Are you waiting until she makes a move?"

Kayall leaned against the wall, picking at the dirt under his nails. "Might as well," he said. "You've sent your men to the bedrolls. They're scattered like ash in the wind. Allorise won't be able to grab hold of anyone. Do you want me to take Spark into hiding?"

"Spark stays with me," Elvienne said.

"How about Spark chooses what he wants, for a change?"

Kayall's question was casual, but Elvienne's eyes flashed with irritation. "I think—"

"Spark?" Kayall raised an eyebrow. "There's no shame in scattering, and there's no shame in staying here. What do you want to do?"

"I want to stay with Carousel." Since Spark had seen what Allorise Carey's knife had done to his friend, he felt an overwhelming urge to protect her. She had whored herself to get food for him, she had risked Noble's wrath and her own life to stay with him, and he had let her walk into that house of darkness all alone. Her scars were his fault. He couldn't heal her broken skin, but he could stop anything else happening to her.

"Young love. How touching." Noble rolled his eyes. "Carousel is going to the bedrolls. I have a responsibility to protect her, after the information she brought me. Kayall, why don't you and Auster take the kids and find somewhere to bunk up? If Allorise attacks the cemetery, it would be wise to hold our little weapon in reserve. Don't you agree, Elvienne?"

She shook her head. "I want him where I can keep an eye on him."

"You think I can't keep an eye on him?" Kayall asked. "He'll be safe with me. I haven't tried to stab him for at least a week!"

"If you're worried, Dweller can keep an eye on them," Noble added. "No?"

"I think the fewer people who know where he is, the better," she said.

"So if Allorise thinks he's with you, she won't be looking for him elsewhere? Makes sense, Elvienne."

She shrugged at Kayall's words. "I think you're wrong, but if that's what Spark wants? As you're so keen on giving him the choice . . ."

It didn't feel like much of a choice, but it was the only one Spark was being offered, and he took it.

To the bedrolls. That was literally what it meant. The attic room held a cache of arrows, a few throwing knives, a rack of swords that had seen much use, and a barge crate packed with dried food and a couple of flagons of ale. There were four bedrolls packed in tight together, and unrolled they took up almost the whole of the floor. You had to walk across them to reach the high window under the eaves. In the rafters, birds cooed and crooned. The room smelled musty with old bird shit, but it was clean, and there seemed to be no rats. Spark had slept in worse places, and the nearness of Carousel made it more tolerable.

She sat with her knees pulled up to her chin, under a shaft of sunlight that turned her brown hair to spun gold. She had not spoken since they arrived, watching with wide eyes while

Kayall and Auster checked the weapons, sighted up and down the street, unrolled the beds and beat them until the dust rose. Now they had gone out for final supplies, and Spark and Carousel were alone.

"How long do we have to stay here?" she asked.

Spark shrugged. "Until we beat Allo Carey, I guess."

"She doesn't give up."

"Elvienne will make her give up. She made her run last time, remember?"

Stupid! Why would she want to remember that?

Carousel shuddered, shrinking in on herself.

"Kayall and Elvienne can take care of her. All we have to do is hide out until it's over."

She nodded, a distant look in her eyes. "I like Kayall. He seems decent."

Spark wasn't sure. Sometimes he caught the mage looking at him strangely, one hand brushing his dagger. He wondered how much forgiveness was really in Kayall's heart.

"Are you hungry?" He changed the subject.

"No." She winced as she moved. "My belly stings. Could you pass me my bag? Elvienne made me up a salve . . . ."

He pressed the pot into her hand and she stared down at it, frown deepening.

"What's wrong?"

"How am I going to do this?"

"What—oh!" Her predicament dawned on him. "I won't look . . ."

She giggled. "It's not that. My right arm is stiff. I can't reach all the places I need to salve. Elvienne was doing it for me, but now . . . I don't want to strip off in front of Kayall and Auster."

"I didn't think you minded that? Stripping off, I mean?" His attempt at humour fell harder than Shadow hitting the gravel outside the Carey mansion. Carousel gave him a withering look.

"I'm not a whore any more, Spark. I don't want strangers to see me like this."

"No. Of course not."

"Would you—?" She lifted her baggy shirt a few inches, exposing the red whorls on tan skin, a shade paler than her arms and legs.

"Me?"

"Like I said, I'd do it myself . . ." She winced as she tried to use her right hand to unscrew the pot of ointment.

"Let me." The smell of the salve brought back the day in the Carey house, in sharp and painful focus. It was the herb he had prepared for Elvienne, while Carousel hung between life and death, the living world and the hells. Her skin still carried that tinge. He smelled it when she brushed past him in the corridors and it made his breath catch. He wondered why the scent had been tugging his memory, and now he knew.

Carousel pushed her top up higher, knotting it awkwardly, one handed, beneath her small breasts. The marks seemed to flow from the cloth, pouring over her skin like spilled wine. In the cold of the attic, they had darkened to purple, scabbed in long, angry lines where Allorise's blade had bitten deepest.

"The scabs are the worst bits," she told him.

Spark scooped a ball of salve onto the tips of his fingers, and smoothed it. It felt gritty, and the smell made him light-headed. He hesitated. "Where—?"

"All over, really." She lay back on the bedroll, sending up a faint cloud of dust, exposing her stomach to the rafters. Still Spark hesitated, until she propped herself up on her elbows and regarded him with an air of amused irritation. "Go on. I won't bite."

Spark rubbed the ball of his thumb over his sticky fingers, and smoothed a line along her skin, tracing the sigil. He felt her tense at the contact, then begin to relax. "That's better," she sighed. "It's so itchy and sore. No wonder Shadow was so mad at you!"

"Don't talk about Shadow." He didn't want her to talk about anyone. Certainly not other men. He worked his way across her skin, smallest finger grazing the lower curve of her breast, trying not to think about pushing his hands up under the fabric and seeking unmarked skin to massage. Kneeling was becoming uncomfortable, and she was bound to notice soon.

"Down here." She pushed her hand against the waistband of her skirt, edging it down to reveal the bones of her hips, her navel, the thin line of downy hair that grew below it. Nowhere had escaped Allorise's blade, but here the design began to taper off, lines swooping round to meet each other again, or to part. The wound was less scabbed below her waistband, knitting into a neat pink scar. And it was definitely warmer in the attic than it had been earlier.

He pushed his hand against the fabric, and felt her twitch in response. "Spark?" Her voice was a breath, almost lost under the crooning of the birds. But Spark heard the question, and he understood it.

"Found some!"

For a girl with a wounded arm, Carousel could move with remarkable speed. All at once she was sitting up, shirt pulled over her knees, blushing and dimpling and smiling as if nothing had been happening, as the door banged open to reveal Kayall and Auster, laden with provisions. Spark sprang to his feet, kicking away the pot of lotion in confusion, and darted for the window. If he kept his back to the room, no one would see his lust until it had died down. He could imagine the delight Kayall would take in his embarrassment.

Kayall hesitated on the threshold, looking suspiciously from Spark to Carousel. "Everything all right?" he asked.

"Fine." *How could she sound so relaxed?*

"No demonic incursions? Spark didn't blow anything up?"

"No one blew anything up." If there was a moment's loaded pause before the word *up*, Spark was the only one to hear it. He pressed himself against the window sill and swallowed a groan of longing.

Kayall stamped across the bedrolls, leaving a trail of muddy footprints behind him, and clapped him on the shoulder. "Keeping a look-out? That's smart thinking, kid. I don't think Allorise will make a move until after her deadline, but it's wise to be prepared. Do you know how to use a crossbow?"

Spark came off his watch at midnight. Auster took his place, lifting the bow from his tired hands with a mumble of thanks. The windowsill was wide, but it was uncomfortable to sit on it hour after hour, staring into the street below, waiting for an assault that didn't come. He tried to ease the cramping from his neck and shoulders, and wondered if he could persuade Carousel to spare a drop of the salve. A little went a long way, and it seemed to help her relax, so why wouldn't it work for him?

Beside him, Kayall lay on his back, nostrils fluttering with each breath. The moon was shrouded, and the night was black, but he had insisted they keep watch. The window was a grey shape, Auster a darker shape against it, long and thin. Spark watched his head drop down to his chest, then jerk up as he woke himself with a stifled snort. He wondered if he should offer to take the next watch as well. He was as far from sleep as Tellis was from the sea.

The space next to him was still warm where Auster had abandoned it. Carousel watched him across the gap, the gleam of her eyes the only light in the darkness. She rolled over into the empty space, catching herself with one hand against Spark's chest. Her lips brushed his.

"What are you—"

"Shhh!" Her hands crept round to the small of his back, pressing him close. He felt her breasts through the thin fabric of their shirts.

"Caro, what if Kayall—?"

She silenced him with a kiss, one hand groping to lift his cock free of his breeches. There seemed to be nothing wrong with her arm now.

"Caro—"

"Hush!" She pressed him onto his back, hands slipping up his shirt, over his nipples, which hardened at her touch. "Don't wake them."

She slipped her leg over his, using his hand to push up her skirt around her waist. Her other hand was over his mouth as she guided him inside her, hips pushing against his through a tangle of cloth. He longed to open her shirt, take her breasts in his mouth, but she caught his wrist and shook her head.

"No time. Don't talk."

He lay back, biting his lip, letting her take her pleasure as she would, until she rolled off him with a soft grunt that sounded like a snore, and he realised he was wet and trembling.

"Carousel?"

The snore was faked, he was sure, but it told him he wouldn't get an answer until morning. He lay on his back, sticky under the blanket, waiting with dry, itching eyes for the grey light of dawn to steal across the sky.

◊

"You look like you were on the ale all night, kid!" Kayall's laughter did nothing to help Spark's fatigued headache. "What happened? Trouble sleeping?"

"Fucking birds kept me awake all night." Spark could see himself reflected over Kayall's shoulder, in the little mirror the mage carried to check his make-up. The rings under his eyes were as black as storm clouds.

"Really? I didn't hear a thing. Not. A. Thing." He winked. "Amazing how quiet a room full of four snoring people can be, wouldn't you say? Auster?"

The lanky man yawned. "What about me?"

"Were you kept awake by fucking birds?"

Auster snorted. "Chances of fucking anything for the rest of my life seem pretty slim right now." He tore a stale bread roll in half and handed it to Spark. "Mind you, at least I'm not going to die a virgin like Spark here!"

Kayall flashed a grin. "Don't be so pessimistic," he said. "I'm pretty sure Spark's not going to die a virgin!"

Carousel was on watch, but Spark could see by her shaking shoulders that she was pissing herself with laughter at the conversation. He scrambled up to the wide seat in the rafters to join her, handing over a wrinkled apple and a slice of cheese. "It's not bloody funny!" he hissed.

"It is from up here." She nursed the loaded crossbow on her knees, and the breeze from the open window flapped her skirt around beneath it. He rested a hand on her ankle and she drew her feet away.

"Don't. I don't want them to think . . ." Her voice was low. "I'm not a whore any more, but some people think if you've done that once, you'll put it around for free for the rest of your life. It puts me in a difficult position. Can you see that?"

"I don't think Auster would . . . And I'm pretty sure Kayall likes men. He *looks* like he likes men."

"That doesn't mean anything."

Spark shrugged. He supposed it didn't. He had never heard Kayall express a preference one way or the other.

"So just—don't say anything, will you?"

"Not if you don't want me to," but she wasn't listening to him any more. She stared beyond him, down the street. Her hand clenched around the bow.

"Something's happening down there."

"Are you sure?" There were flickers in the shadows, but it could be the reflections of clouds scudding across the face of the sun.

"*She* did something to me, when she carved this demon

mark on my skin. It burns, Spark. It burns around Dweller. It's burning now."

He looked down, half expecting to see the mark glowing through her shirt. "What should I do?"

"Kayall!"

They poured into the street, a mob, a black tide that roiled and fought. A few demons ran ahead of the pack, shepherding the horde. The few people who had ventured outdoors fled for their homes.

"What do they want?" Carousel asked as Kayall clambered up into the rafters to join them, brushing dust and crumbly pigeon droppings from the velvet patches on his shoulders. "They're not after Spark again, are they?"

"No," Spark said. The pack had a different feel. Before, they had moved with purpose, straight as arrows, besieging Brynmar's house and refusing to be distracted from their desire to be close to him. This, however, was a rabble.

"Where the hells are the City Watch?" Kayall demanded. "I know Allorise has them in her pocket, but I would have thought there were a few—"

Carousel pointed. From the far end of the street, a squadron from the Watch approached. Some mounted, some on foot, forming a living barrier. They pressed forward, looking to drive the demons back. The demons were more interested in looting the bakery at the end of the street, and paid them no attention. There were a pitiful number of Watchmen, and their pikes looked like twigs in their hands.

Kayall ducked his head so Auster could peer out. "The odds don't look good," he remarked.

"Don't you think we should even them up a bit?" Auster grinned.

"I think it's our civic duty. Spark, Caro, you take this window. Auster and I will take the next one. Let's see if we can pick off a few of Allo Carey's little pets before they eat the last good Watch company in the city!"

He swung down from the window. Auster followed, passing up a bow and a bundle of arrows to Spark. They were simple bolts of steel, but they could bring down a grown man. Or, Spark hoped, a small demon.

The horde had ripped open the front of the shop with ferocious speed. Bread and pastries spilled across the road, and four of the creatures hauled out a set of shelves and smashed them against the shutters of the tavern opposite. From the upper window the landlady screamed at them to stop, raining curses and saucepans down on their heads with equal venom.

Carousel sighted down her bow. "Keep coming this way, you scaly bastards," Spark heard her mutter. He wished he had her courage, but his hands were slipping on the bolt as he tried to load it and he felt sick. Maybe he should use magic instead.

No magic. Kayall's voice spoke directly inside his head. *You might as well send up a flare to let them know where you are.*

"What? How did you—?"

Doesn't matter. Watch the girl, kid.

Carousel loosed a shot. It fell short of the mark, bouncing off the cobbles. She cursed and groped for another, but the moment was enough. It attracted the demon's attention, and now they noticed the tentative advance of the watch.

"Caro!"

"Sorry!"

By some miracle Spark had his own bow loaded, and now he knew the range they had, but it was too late to be careful. The howl rose from a hundred throats, as the demon mob abandoned their assault on the tavern and charged the thin white line of the City Watch, and the Watch charged to meet them.

The spearmen on their horses headed the charge, the infantry hard at their heels. They drove into the demons with the force of a hammer blow, scattering them left and right. Spark fired. His bolt caught a fleeing demon in the thigh, sending it crashing face-down on the cobbles. He had no time to celebrate before he was loading again, fumbling fingers making him slow, while Caro fired off shot after shot. He saw her arm rising and falling, firing and loading, a dim flicker in the corner of his eye. He wondered how she had got so good with a bow, and if she was hitting anything. He didn't think he was, and there were so many demons the flights of arrows didn't make a dent in their ranks.

The Watch struck and wheeled away, struck and wheeled away, leaving their dead behind them, men and horses both. The cobbles were slick and stained red at their passing, their numbers diminishing with every pass.

Spark groped for an arrow and found only empty air. He let the bow fall with a curse. There was nothing he could do now but magic. "Kayall? I'm out of arrows . . ."

"Me too." Kayall's bow clattered to the floor. "Auster? Caro?"

"I'm out," Auster sighed. "I guess all we can do is watch."

Carousel loosed her last bolt. It flew high, skimming the heads of the mob. She sighed.

"Don't stop firing!" The call came from the house opposite. Spark hadn't realised it was part of the tavern, but the woman hailing him was the one who had flung saucepans and cooking pots down on the heads of the horde. He shrugged, holding up his empty hands. She nodded, with a thin smile, and ducked back out of sight.

The Watch had reformed, but their line wavered, falling back as the demons hurled chunks of masonry towards them. Some rocks were the size of a man's torso. Spark winced as he saw a horse go down, chest caved in under the force of the blow.

Carousel's arm crept under his, gripping tightly, fingers sticky with sweat. "The Watch are going to lose, aren't they?"

The dying horse thrashed on the cobbles. Spark couldn't tear his eyes from it, until the mob surged forward and swallowed it up. He saw two Watchmen in the thick of the horde, isolated from their allies. They fought back to back, swords swinging, carving out a circle of air and light around them. Missiles rained down around them, and he saw one man struck, sagging to his knees.

"Here, you bastards! Have some of this!"

It was the woman opposite, back at the window. She used her weight to heave a barrel onto the window ledge. It was nearly as tall and broad as she was. It teetered for a moment, before she bunched her muscles and gave it a shove, sending it crashing to the street below. The barrel exploded in a shower of spirits and wooden shards. The horde scattered for a moment, distracted by the unexpected attack, and the staggering Watchman regained his feet.

The woman leaned out further, arms at full stretch, a candle-stone in each hand. She fumbled her grip as she tried to strike them together, and the grey stones tumbled from her hands, lost in the crowd as the demons closed in on the stranded men.

Spark reacted without thinking. He shook his arm free of Carousel's grip and sprang forward, heat rushing to his palms. The flames erupted in a blazing sphere, whirling down to strike the demons in the street. They caught the spilled ale and flared up, a roaring wall of heat and light. They caught the ale-splashed flesh of the demons who were too close when the barrel fell, and they fled and screamed and barged into their neighbours, spreading the flames across the street. Kayall cheered at the chaos, leaping across the room to clap Spark hard on the shoulder.

"Very stylish, kid! Listen to them squeal!"

"I'm sorry, I didn't mean to use magic . . ."

"They're too busy burning to worry where it came from." He grinned. "Will you look at that?"

The woman who had thrown the barrel burst out of her front door. She wielded a stout blade, laying about her left and right with more energy than grace. Spark heard her yelling as she cleaved demon flesh from bone.

"Fuck off out of my street! These are our roads!"

"Yes!" Kayall leaned far out of the window, urging her on. "Our roads!"

"Our roads!" The cry came from the stranded Watchman, standing over his fallen brother, sword held high. His face was stained with soot and blood. "Our fucking roads!" He swung, and a horned demon head flew in a graceful arc, blood spurting from the severed neck.

Spark nudged Carousel. "Our roads!" he yelled, brandishing the empty crossbow out of the window. "Our roads!" Her voice joined with his in the cry. "Our roads!"

"Our roads!" The street filled with people. Not the Watch, but men and women flooding out of their houses, brandishing makeshift weapons and helms made from cooking pots, rallying around the plump woman with the stout sword. Spark had thought most people had fled the city, but there were plenty who must have stayed behind. The demons, those that weren't burning or dead, milled around in confusion, reeling from blows from club or saucepan or folded kitchen chair.

"Whose roads?" Auster hollered. Kayall twisted round to stare at the sky, drawing patterns in the air with his fingers.

"Our roads!" The cry came from a dozen throats, a score, forty and more. The sun gleamed down through a break in the clouds, a shaft of golden light illuminating the tavern-woman. It glanced off her blade with dazzling brightness, following her as she advanced on the horde. It turned the grey in her hair to silver, the weapon in her hand to fire. The people of the street, the survivors of the Watch, fell in behind her as if they were under a spell. The street was washed in sunlight. The demons, seeing the golden army advancing towards them, broke and fled howling, leaving their dead behind.

The sun flicked out like a snuffed candle. Kayall rolled onto his belly and blew out his cheeks, grinning at the sound of cheering that rose from the street. "Well," he said, "that went better than I expected."

Spark looked up at the sky. It was the same dull grey cloud

that had hung over Cape Carey for the last few days. There was no hint of sunshine.

"You did that?" he asked.

"It's a pathetic talent, I grant you, but it has its uses. Being able to pinpoint a man in armour with a lightning strike is a good one."

"Why?"

"If you don't know that—"

"No," Spark shook his head. "I know about lightning and metal. Why sunshine today?"

"If these people are fool enough to believe in gods, or luck, which I suspect they are, now they'll think the gods are on their side. On *our* side, against Allo Carey and her horde from hell. Hope and optimism can turn the tide in a battle. But they're no substitute for weapons, and we're all out." He frowned. "They know where we are now. It won't be long before they come back, in greater numbers. I don't intend to stick around until they do."

Spark stared out of the window, across the serrated rows of rooftops under the glowering sky. The noise from the street had quietened, fallen sombre as Watch and civilians collected their dead and tended the wounded, while the demons were swept to the gutters that brimmed with sluggish blood.

"I wish there was some way to know what's happening in the rest of the city before we make a move," Kayall said. "I don't want to run into another riot."

Auster nodded. "I'm on it." He slipped from the room before the mage could call him back.

"What does he mean, he's on it?" Kayall asked.

"Auster knows everyone," Carousel told him. She flexed her red-raw fingers. "He's got a network. Give him a couple of bells, he'll tell you what everyone in the city had for lunch."

"We used to have hawks to do that, back in the north," Kayall told her. "More efficient, and less dangerous for the man on the ground. Let's hope he hurries back. Our Lady Carey won't linger for long."

Spark watched Auster slip along the street, using the shadows of the houses as cover. No one paid him any attention. The woman with the sword comforted a thin girl who sobbed into her shoulder, and the leader of the Watch was trying to rally his men. The street was ankle-deep in gore.

"Let's do something about that," Kayall said thoughtfully. "A real rain, to wash the streets clean. None of this drizzly nonsense." He drew his hands together, as if compressing an invisible object between his palms. The sky darkened, cloud swelling and building until it was almost black. Spark felt the air pressing down on his skull, the way it did before a thunderstorm. It made his head heavy and his eyes ache.

Kayall made a slashing motion with his hand, and the clouds tore open. Water gushed from the sky, blinding sheets of rain, a downpour that sent the people in the street running for the shelter of their broken houses. It went on and on. Spark didn't know the sky could hold so much water. The bodies of the demons floated and swirled in the eddies, leaving dissolving trails of blood as they were swept away.

"Auster won't thank you for that," Carousel remarked.

"It's likely not raining where Auster is." The sky over the adjoining streets was clear and blue. "I sucked every bit of cloud from the city and loosed it here. The Carey castle is downhill from here, isn't it?"

Spark shrugged. Carousel nodded.

"I've heard Allorise Carey likes gifts. Let's send her a little present."

The water seeped under the doors, even as far as the hall, despite the demons fighting with brooms and sandbags to keep it out. Allorise sat on her throne, feet tucked beneath her, regarding the brown swill that washed over her floors with revulsion. "Shadow? How long has it been raining?"

"It's not raining, my lady."

"Then where is all this water coming from?"

He shrugged, and her hands balled into fists, fighting down the urge to strike him.

"Find out. Now get out."

He returned quicker than she expected. "My lady? You should come and see this."

"Don't presume to tell me what I should and should not do, Shadow."

"Please. It's important."

He looked worried, as far as she could tell from the mangled remains of his face.

"Fine. But I'm not walking through that." She indicated the filthy water with contempt. "Find someone to carry me."

He did better than that. He found a litter, dusty with neglect, and two burly demons to carry it between them. They brought it to the edge of the dais, so Allorise could step from her throne into the covered chair, while her minions wallowed up to their knees in filth. Maybe she wouldn't kill him today.

They sloshed across the hall, Allorise holding up her skirts to avoid the splashes of mud their passage threw up. Shadow led the way, wading down the hall and out of the open front door. He gestured for the demons who were sweeping to fall back before their mistress. The courtyard in front of the keep was awash, the main wooden gates open but the portcullis down. Allorise frowned.

"Why did you open the gates?"

"The water burst them open, Silver Lady. It came all at once. There was nothing we could do."

She glanced up at the cloudless sky. "Something very odd is going on here, Shadow."

Most of the water had drained from the courtyard, although Allorise suspected most of it had drained into her hall. It left behind vast, muddy puddles, and in the hush she could hear the steady drip and trickle as the flood found its own course. "Set me down," she ordered.

"Are you sure, my lady?"

"A bit of wet won't hurt me. Tell these brutes to kneel."

Shadow coughed out an order, and the pair of demons lowered the litter to the ground. Allorise stepped out, hitching her skirt around her knees, as Shadow pointed at the portcullis. "It's over here."

She tiptoed through the puddles towards the gate, wrinkling her nose at the stench. Every gutter in the city had spilled over into her yard. She didn't want to think what she might be treading in, but she wasn't going to squeal like a girl at a bit of shit on her shoes.

The bodies piled up against the portcullis. She had expected them to be bloated, like the drowned kittens in the bag her father had shown her when she was a little girl, but they hadn't died from drowning. A demon's face, heavy-browed and split-lipped, almost human, pressed up against the metal like a fighting dog in a small cage. A steel bolt pierced the ruin of his left eye, driving deep into his brain, and Allorise couldn't take her eyes off it.

"My Lady?"

Shadow sounded as if he had repeated himself several times. Allo hook herself free of that sickening sight. "Get the gate open," she said. "Have them spread out in the courtyard. I want to see what's happened to my pets."

She withdrew to the steps, where the layer of slime was thinner, and watched as Shadow rounded up some demons and set about the grim task of opening the gate and untangling the mass of bodies and debris swept up against it. She forced herself to watch, to look on the faces of the dead creatures. She had no affection for them, but every corpse was a defeat, a blow against her plans. And who had fired on them? Who would dare stand up to the horde? The ordinary folk would shit themselves and run away rather than face a mob of demons coming down their street. That was what she had counted on. Something had gone awry.

There were human men and women tangled with the horde, but fewer, and they looked as if they had drowned. She walked the lines of the dead like a queen viewing her troops. Some of them had names, but she had never bothered to learn them in her own tongue, when "Hey you!" would suffice. Here they had been struck down by arrows, there cleaved by blades or scalded by flame. A real battle had taken place, and her side had come off worst.

She was nearing the end of the third row when she heard scrabbling claws on damp gravel, and a wet cough. One of the creatures was not as dead as first appeared. Well, demonkind were hard to kill.

"Lady . . ." Its voice was thick, distorted, as though it spoke through a mouthful of wet leaves. Allorise had to crouch to hear it, and she gagged on the smell of the creature's leathery hide.

"You speak my tongue?"

The beast coughed, a fine spray of blood that spattered Allorise's clothes. "I speak . . . enough."

"Enough to tell me what happened, creature?"

"Magic . . . flame from above . . . He was our master before you, Lady . . . ." It spluttered again. "I felt it, the human power . . . ."

"The mage-boy? Spark?"

If the creature had shoulders, it might have shrugged. "Human names mean nothing." It coughed again. The spray of blood was thicker this time, gobbets sliding towards Allo's hem. It whimpered. "I die . . ."

"I'm sorry, creature. Do you want mercy?"

The beast stared at her with blank black eyes. Sympathy and mercy were human concepts. She should push them to the back of her mind. This demon was no use to her now.

She straightened. "Shadow?"

"My Lady?"

"Get rid of these things. Burn or bury them, I don't care."

"Bury—?"

She shrugged. "Whatever's easiest. I'm calling my army to me. It's clear Noble won't give me what I want, so I'm going to go to him and take it by force."

Twenty-Three

AUSTER RETURNED TO the attic room with a grim face, shaking the water from his hair and cloak like a dog. "Shitty weather," he remarked. "Came out of nowhere too."

Kayall had the grace to look embarrassed. "What did you find out?"

"The same story all over the city. Attacks by demons. Some streets fared better than others. It's my guess the Silver Lady is testing us."

"And are we found wanting?"

Auster snorted. "*We're* not. But we've been lucky. The Nobility has been hit hard. I suggest we withdraw. We can hold this street, but that's no good if the rest of the city goes to hell, is it?"

To Spark's surprise, Kayall turned to him. "What do you want to do, kid?"

"Me?"

"This Carey bitch wants you. And we magicked up the place. She'll know where you are, or one of her little pets will tell her. Make no mistake about it, she's coming for you. Do

you want to face her here, or in a nice sturdy cave with all the
weapons you'll ever need?"

Spark glanced sidelong at Carousel. Where would she be
safest? If they withdrew to the cemetery, there were passages in
the rock that could take her right out of the city. She caught his
eye and nodded, fingers brushing the cloth over her stomach.

"We go back," he said.

"Now?" Kayall asked.

Caro answered. "They're not coming yet," she said. "I can
tell when they're near. My scar . . ."

"You're a regular little barometer, aren't you?"

Caro shrugged. "I don't know what that is."

"Never mind. Can you tell us which way to go, the places
to avoid? You and Auster know the city best."

She nodded.

"Then let's get going." The bows were useless now, but
Kayall handed each of them a stout spear, in addition to the
blades they usually carried. Spark's scraped against the low
ceiling as he manoeuvred it down the stairs. He took a chip out
of the lintel over the front door, and swore. Kayall chuckled.
"Give me a sword any day. And a torch; it's about to get foggy."

The mist behaved like no mist Spark had ever seen. It
gathered at either end of the street like heavy grey curtains, but
in between the sun shone fiercely. The street was drying, and
tendrils of steam rose from the cobbles, and from the clothes
of people who had been caught in the downpour. The stout
woman leaned on her sword as if she would fall over without
the support. Spark could see the deep streaks of grey in her
hair, the red of her cheeks. She looked older than she had when
she was fighting.

She nodded to him. "You're the kid with the bow."

"I am." What was he supposed to say? You're the lady with
the barrel?

"That was a neat trick. With the flame. Mage, are you?"

He shrugged. "Not really."

"You should be."

"Why didn't you leave the city?" he asked, to fill the awkward silence between them.

"Didn't want to leave my home," she said. "I've lived there all my life. My ma died in that upstairs room. I wasn't going to give it up for no demon. Mind you," she looked rueful, "That was some good spirit wasted on those creatures. Don't know when I'll have time to brew up another batch!"

"Spark! Are you going to stand around and chat all day?" Kayall rattled the butt of his spear against the cobbles.

The woman gripped his arm. "Come to my inn if you ever need a drink," she said. "Ask for Mari. I'll see you right."

He looked past her, at the inn. The windows were shattered, the door kicked in, and there were scorch marks up the walls. It would take a pot of gold to make it inhabitable again, and Mari must know that. He wondered what would happen to her.

"I will." It seemed a hollow promise.

"Spark! Come on!"

"Coming!" Carousel had vanished into the mist, and he hastened to catch up with her. The cold took his breath, and wet droplets clung to his hair and clothes. He could barely see Kayall moving down the street ahead of him. "Are you doing this?" he asked. "Do we need it?"

"Would you rather walk around exposed to every one of Startide's spies?"

"Well, no, but won't they sense the magic?" He winced as he barked his toes against a hidden paving slab.

"Different sort of magic," Kayall told him. "There's nothing unnatural about fog. And a very little magic might pass unnoticed. Enough to stop you stubbing your toes, for example. Hold out your hand. Keep walking or you'll lose everyone."

Spark did as he was bid.

"Slow breaths. Let the heat out slowly. Not like when you're angry. This is basic magic Carlon should have taught you.

Focus on your palm."

A tiny flame flickered in his hand, and died. Kayall swore.

"Hell's sake, Spark! You can charm up mass destruction, but you can't make a flame?"

"I'm trying!"

"Well stop trying, before you burn down half the street!" Kayall ducked as a jet of fire burst from Spark's palm, lighting up the mist around them, then fading like a firework. "Elvienne's got a lot of work ahead of her to train you!"

"I don't see why she has to train me," Spark grumbled, trailing in his wake, damp and cold. "Why can't you do it?"

"Trust me kid, I'm a terrible teacher. You don't want to learn from me."

"Hush!" Carousel's voice came out of the mist ahead. Spark could see her, a long, slender shape, holding up a hand for quiet. "Not this way. There are demons there, getting closer."

"Take us another way then," Kayall said, in a low voice. "I trust you to lead us, Carousel."

There were many diversions across the city, side roads and double backs until Spark was completely lost. The mist blotted out every landmark. It felt like it was just the four of them, moving on soft feet, spears held ready. There was no one else in Cape Carey, and time had stopped. They could have been travelling this way forever. It was so different from the first time he had trusted Caro to lead him across town. He had been a different person then, but the sudden sharp smell of spice in his nostrils brought it all back. He jerked his head up, alert with recognition.

"I know where we are."

"I hope you're going to tell me we're nearly there," Kayall said. "I'm soaked to the skin, and I need to change, and bathe. Caro, do you think Noble would let me use his bath?"

"Depends what you do for him in return!" she flashed back.

"Why?" Auster asked. "What did *you* do for him, Caro?"

"Nothing you haven't done yourself, I'll wager!" Her feet

clattered on the bridge, and the smell of muddy river-water replaced the spice in Spark's nostrils. He felt the tension easing out of his shoulders and back, and he sniggered at the ribald turn Caro and Auster's conversation was taking. They must have been feeling the same anxiety.

His feet slurped in the mud between the tombs, and the mist thinned. The shapes of grave-houses loomed up out of the fog, and he had never been so glad to see them, or the paths that ran between them. It felt like coming home.

Kayall's voice was low in his ear. "She'll come here. Don't doubt it. She doesn't care about sacred ground."

"Then we'll fight her here, between the tombs." Spark trailed his fingers along the nearest wall, reassured by the solidity of the stone. "If she comes to the cemetery, she comes to die."

Kayall looked at him with surprise, and a touch of admiration. "You sound like a warrior, young Spark! Remind me never to hurt your woman."

"I'm not his woman," Carousel flung over her shoulder as she slipped between the bramble bushes.

"It's not that." Up until now, Spark had thought that was what it was, that he wanted revenge on Allorise for her abuse of Carousel. The mages might have bigger concerns, but he had no part in them. "It was, but she hurt . . . She hurt the city. She's the one who's meant to look after it, to take care of ordinary people. If she won't do that, if she sends her demons against the people she's pledged to protect . . . Well, someone has to stand up for them," he finished, limply. "Aren't mages supposed to protect people?"

"Mages aren't *supposed* to do anything. What we do is interfere. Elvienne excels at that."

"Ram said that. He said something about meddling in the war . . . ."

Kayall laughed. "Oh, we all did that! There are some people who shouldn't be in charge of a barrel of hops, let alone a Kingdom. Valery Northpoint was one of those people. Allorise

Carey is another." He stumbled off the path, and withdrew his boot from the mud with a long slurp. "Anyone who drags me away from my city and makes me slop around in the muck ruining my clothes doesn't deserve the power she craves!"

"But how do you decide? I mean, Ram said his side lost the war because of you, and that wasn't anything to do with muddy boots, was it? Everyone thinks his side is right . . ."

Kayall grinned as he turned sideways and slipped between the stones. "Then you're lucky you and I are on the same side, kid!"

⚷

The caverns beneath the cemetery were heaving. Spark had never seen so many people, all arming themselves for battle. It was hard to locate Noble amongst the press of bodies. He had to follow Kayall to find Elvienne, in a side room that had been made into a healing station with beds, and stacks of bandages. She hunched over a bubbling pot, and he assumed at first that she was brewing salves for the wounded, until he saw her use tongs to lift up a small, gleaming saw. She handed it to the girl who was helping her, who swathed it in silk.

Kayall frowned. "Bone saws? You think it's going to be that bad?"

"Better than giving mercy . . ." Her lips snapped shut as her eyes met Spark's, and her face clouded.

"Have you seen Noble?" Kayall asked. "I wanted to use his bath."

"You'll be lucky." She waved her hand vaguely. "He's out there somewhere. Looking after his people, calling in favours. I don't like what he does, but he's bloody good at it. Is the boy safe?"

"I'm fine, and I can answer for myself," Spark told her.

Elvienne looked from his face to Carousel's, but all she said was, "Good."

Kayall sat on one of the neatly-made beds, muddying the blankets. "So," he flicked open the mirror he carried in his top pocket and checked his face with a frown, "what's the plan of attack?"

"Fight her off, when she comes. Try and regain control of the demons. Turn them on her, if need be. That's Spark's job. The rest of us just need to stay alive, and keep him alive, long enough to do that, and to send them back to the hells. After that," she shrugged, "a couple of pints of ale, find a horse, head out. I thought I might follow the river to Austover. It's been a long time since I saw the sea, and I've a hankering for it."

"How do I turn them on her?" Spark asked. "I'm not carving anyone up to get control!"

"You don't need to," Elvienne told him. "If we can loosen her hold, they'll flock to you. You're the reason they're here, after all." She smiled, but it was a brittle smile. "It's a simple fight. Take out Allorise, and we win."

Kayall snorted. "You know she's going to be more heavily defended than a Telesian princess's cunt? We won't get within a mile of her."

Elvienne's smile widened, but her eyes were hard. "You might not," she said, "but I can. Trust me."

"Elvienne—"

"Trust me," she repeated.

&

"I never trust anyone who says 'trust me' like that."

Carousel was lying with her back pressed against the stone wall of her bunk. It was too narrow for two, and Spark's foot hung over the drop to the cavern floor below, where the muted preparations for battle were still going on. It seemed people were making ready because there was nothing else to do but wait, and the waiting was worse than the activity. He wished Allorise would come and fight, for good or ill. At least then it would be over. He wanted to fight, but he wanted to fuck more, with Caro's length pressed against him and her arm around his back, tracing sigils on his spine.

It seemed she wanted to talk. She evaded his mouth. "My da said 'trust me'. It was the last thing he said to me."

"What happened to him?" It had never occurred to Spark that Carousel had any family outside the Nobility.

"He went to buy bread, and he never came back. I stopped looking, after a few years. I had to keep my brothers and sisters alive. He could be dead, or anywhere." He felt her shrug. "That's when I learned to shoot."

"Where are your brothers and sisters now?"

"Around." She waved her hand vaguely at the cavern. "I was too busy keeping them alive to pay them the attention they needed, and one by one they drifted off. Now it's just me."

"And me."

She dodged the kiss again. "Until tomorrow."

"As long as you need me." He bit his lip. He had nearly said 'trust me'.

She pulled him on top of her, moving beneath him, one arm hanging out in space. His elbow scraped the rough wall, and he felt the snags in the roof of the bunk catch and pull his hair, but this time he could lay his hands on her naked skin, hear her moan and not press his lips to silence him. Beneath their shared blanket she was his world, for a short span of time. He would not die, he swore. He would not let Allorise Carey take this away from him.

The alarm jerked him from his sleep, the taste of sweat and metal on his tongue. Caro sat up, bare to the waist, dragging her shirt over her shoulders. Her knee hit him in the chin and he bit his tongue.

"Sorry!"

She swung down lightly, hand over hand, to the floor, bouncing on the balls of her feet. Spark followed, treading on blankets, and on people's hands and feet. He didn't have her skill, her grace. He was almost barged over by a woman hurrying past with an armful of crossbows. There was no panic. Noble's followers moved purposefully, but with haste, and there was no time for him to stand and gape.

"Come on!" Carousel grabbed his arm and hustled him across the cavern, ducking and weaving through the crowds, heading for Elvienne's room. His feet dragged on the rock. It felt like every muscle in his body was cramping. He didn't think he was capable of doing whatever it was Elvienne had in mind for him, when he felt so sick he could barely breathe.

Elvienne didn't respond to Carousel's knock, and when she pushed open the door, the room beyond was empty. Spark let out a breath. "She's not here. Maybe she doesn't need us after all. We should go and—"

"What are you two doing here?" Kayall strolled down the passage towards them. He wore a breastplate of Telesian design, inlaid with mother-of-pearl. It was far too ornate to be practical, but he had switched his dangling earrings for neat studs, and his hair was drawn back into a short horsetail at the nape of his neck. Perhaps in compensation, his make-up was heavier than usual, his eyes darkly ringed with flicks of kohl at the corners. "Aren't you meant to be with Elvienne?"

"We came looking for her," Caro explained.

"Isn't she here?" Kayall stuck his head around the door, as if to reassure himself that Elvienne was in fact absent, and not hiding or invisible. "I'll call her." His face took on an unfocussed expression, and he shook his head.

"She's not answering," he said. "Either she's too far away, or she's up to something . . . ."

"Shall we wait for her?" Spark scanned the room. "She can't have gone too far. She's left her cane behind."

Kayall stared at the cane, smooth wood with a simple curved handle. Spark knew there was nothing magic about it. Elvienne was an old woman; she used it for getting about. Except for those times when she wasn't an old woman at all . . .

He must have come to the conclusion the same time Kayall did, but it was the mage who voiced it. "She's up to something, and she's changed her face. Where the hell has she gone?"

֎

Elvienne was having trouble with her breasts. They were larger than she was accustomed to, larger than she liked. They spilled over the top of the crumpled dress, the one she kept in the bottom of her bag for such occasions. She hoped it would pass muster.

With a murmur of irritation, she shrunk the offending articles down until they were safely concealed. Droplets of morning mist clung to the fabric and to her skin, gathering in the fine fair hairs on her arms. The cemetery was quiet, the morning holding its breath in anticipation. The only sound was the rhythmic chanting from a nearby funeral. The crypt yawned open, and the elderly woman lay on a wooden bier, waiting to be interred. Her family ringed around her with gifts, and the priest led their chant.

"You should hurry up," she muttered in Telesian as she passed. "Unless you want to join your mother in the next world."

The priest gave her a startled glance, but he heeded the warning and picked up the pace as Elvienne hurried on, hood up and head down. She didn't want Noble's spies to recognise her, but when she reached them she hoped Allorise's would. In fact, she was counting on it.

There was a hiss from behind a nearby tomb, a scrape of claws on stone, and a faint splash. She was spotted. She raised her hand to her hood and pushed it back, shaking loose her long blonde hair. "Creature! Come here!"

She beckoned imperiously. The demon, a plump little beast, shuffled a few hesitant steps towards her.

"Do you know who I am? Come *here.*" She injected her

command with the force of her will. If she couldn't control this low, simple creature, she might as well give up and return to the ranks of the Nobility.

It couldn't speak, but she read its measure by its actions. She looked right, she knew, but the sense that clung to her was wrong.

"Come here before I gut you, you little worm!"

That won the beast over. It simpered around the foot of her cloak, projecting gratitude for its life, seeking scraps of attention, the true child of a dictator.

"Take me to Shadow. Can you do that? Do you understand me?"

It whimpered, tugging her cloak to draw her onward, flitting from shadow to shadow in the gaps between the tombs. It led her to a crumbling gap in the cemetery wall, adjoining the back garden of a sprawling, single-storey Telesian villa. The gap was guarded by two more demons, identical and burly. One flared its cavernous nostrils as she passed, but the other bowed its head and grovelled, and the one that had sniffed her followed suit. She twitched her skirt aside, treating them with all the disdain of a noble lady for her underlings.

The path led straight to the back of the house, criss-crossed by more straight paths that chopped the garden into neat squares. In summer the bushes would be trained into the shapes of birds and foxes, but now their shapes were overgrown and ragged, and the needles formed a carpet around her feet. She saw few demons; some small ones lurking under the bushes, but the bulk of Allorise's army must be elsewhere.

The demon led her to a long avenue of glass, crowned with a curved roof that swept almost to the ground, giving the effect of being in a glazed tunnel. A few panes were missing or cracked, but Elvienne marvelled at the expense of such a structure. It was considerably warmer under the dome, the winter sunlight magnified by the glass, and small fruit bushes bloomed in earthenware pots. It reminded her of the great pomegranate houses of Tellis.

The door to the house was guarded, and she struggled not to let her step falter. These were no demons protecting the entrance, but human men. Perhaps not the smartest of men, and they wouldn't have the instinct demons had, but she must be careful. She pulled her hood up to cast a shadow across her eyes. Even a mage couldn't alter the nature of her eyes.

The guards snapped to attention. "My Lady!"

"I'm looking for Shadow." Had she got the voice right? Sometimes it wandered when she was nervous.

"He's out front, my Lady." A frown crossed the guard's face. "I thought you were with him?"

Shit, she wasn't ready for this . . .

"I decided to talk a walk. Are you questioning me?"

"No, my Lady . . ."

"Do I have to justify myself to you now? You're dismissed, both of you. I'd rather trust demons to guard my doors! Get out!"

The demon at her heels snarled, and the guards dropped their spears and fled back the way she had come. Elvienne kicked the weapons aside. Two fewer men for her friends to fight. She had the feeling it wouldn't make a jot of difference.

The fat little demon fawned around her ankles, and, forgetting her persona, she scratched it between eyebrows and horns. The creature squirmed in abject delight and fear. It was probably the first affection it had ever known, but it was still demon, and deadly.

"Leave me," she ordered. It cringed, as if expecting a blow. She pointed. "Leave me, I said!"

It scampered away, stumbling over its own feet in its desperation to obey. Elvienne pushed open the door leading to the house. The floor was wood, painted to look like marble, and bright sweeping drapes hung from the ceiling. It made her homesick for Tellis. She guessed this was the house of an exile, trying to bring a little Telesian grandeur to a wooden house in a cold, damp northern city. She wondered where he was now.

The rear of the house was like the garden, straight passages dividing the rooms, but as she approached the front she heard noises, a grumbling roar, the stamp of feet against stone, and a woman's voice raised in challenge, in triumph. The voice Elvienne had used to speak to the guard.

She hadn't realised the house was built into the side of a hill, that while the back of the building made it look like a single storey, the front dropped to a second floor. Light streamed in from the first-floor balcony, and Elvienne saw shadowed figures moving there, demons and men. And she could hear Allorise. She drew the dagger at her belt, fingers tightening around it, and stepped towards the light.

She was too late.

At Allorise's command, the horde streamed away from the front of the house, round the sides of the building towards the cemetery wall. A bristling rabble of men and demons, weapons out, claws unsheathed, teeth gnashing. They would hit the Nobility like a hammer on an anvil, unless Elvienne could take control of them and call them back. There was only one way to do that.

She tested her blade with the edge of her thumb, and backed off a pace into the shadows, as Allorise's voice came closer.

"Shadow, have my chair brought round. I want to view the field of my victory. I want it decorated with Noble's head. As for the boy—"

"You'll leave the boy alone." Elvienne stepped forward, knife held at chest-level. It was like stepping in front of a mirror. Allorise gasped, hand flying to her mouth.

"Who the hell—?"

"I think you know." She hefted the blade. "Come with me, Allorise. We can stop this."

"Stop this? Why would I want to, mage?"

Shadow stood dumbstruck, looking from one identical

woman to the other as if his eyes were playing a trick on him. "Lady?"

"Get her!" Allorise shoved him towards Elvienne and raced back towards the balcony. Shadow stumbled as Elvienne's dagger sheared up to meet his throat. He spun away from her, gushing crimson, and she hurdled him as he fell and lay twitching. Her feet tangled in her dress and she lurched, regaining her balance and pounding out onto the balcony in pursuit of Allorise. The biting wind carried drops of rain before it, stinging here eyes. A slow moving demon lunged at her and she ducked its outstretched arm, feeling claws rake her shoulder as her elbow slammed into its throat.

The balcony ran the length of the house. Allorise was at the far end, held at bay with her back against the balustrade. She held the glass knife out in front of her, clutched in both hands. Her skin was grey, and her hair fluttered in the wind. "Take off my face, witch!"

"Don't you like to look at yourself, Allorise?" Elvienne advanced warily, watching the knife. She could do magic, but there was nothing to stop Allorise stabbing her while she was distracted. "Drop the blade. Give up, and I'll make sure you go free."

"Give up?" Allo lunged forward and Elvienne sprang away, the tip of the knife snagging on her dress. "Why would I want to do that? You're losing, witch. You should be the one to surrender."

They circled each other warily, Allo's mouth working as if in a silent spell. There was no spell, no change in the air to indicate magic was being used. All a bluff, Elvienne decided, to distract her from the knife. "You can't get away, Allorise. I don't want to kill you . . ."

"I'd like to see you try, old woman!" Allorise glanced at the sky as a shadow fell over the balcony. Elvienne darted in, slashing at her face. Their blades clashed, and Elvienne gritted her teeth against the jarring in her arm.

Allorise panted. Her sleeve was laid open, and there was a thin red line across her bicep. She held up her arms in mocking challenge. "Come for me then, witch!"

The sky darkened. Elvienne turned her face away from the downrush of buffeting wings as the creature descended. Its leathery wings unfurled, and its long, sharp muzzle, crammed with savage serrated teeth, swung from side to side, snapping at empty air. She expected it to rip Allorise's head off, but long claws closed tenderly around the Silver Lady's shoulders and lifted her from the balcony. Allo laughed, and pointed to the cemetery. "Why don't you chase me, mage?"

Elvienne rushed to the edge of the balcony to watch their flight. The beast laboured, burdened by the extra weight. It hopped like a chicken to the high cemetery wall, and from there to the top of a nearby crypt. It could only fly low, and in short bursts. Allorise had not escaped her yet.

Elvienne rested her hands on the stone balustrade, sending her thoughts into it, bending it to her will. The stone twisted below her in response, scraping and creaking as the end of the balcony ripped away from the wall. It swung out, and she clung on as the motion buffeted her as if she was on the pitching deck of a ship. One end of the balcony was still attached to the house, but the other hung in space, low over the cemetery, forming a bridge. Straggler demons fled in fear before her as she raced along it in pursuit of Allorise. The winged beast perched on top of a nearby tomb, and Allo was still clasped loosely in its claws. It was only a short leap, but by the time Elvienne landed the demon had fluttered away.

"Come back and face me, if you dare!" Another jump, another awkward scramble. Elvienne ripped the tattered remains of her dress free above her knees, and cast the rag behind her. That made it easier to run.

Below, demons raced across the cemetery, swarming like rats around the tombs. They had no interest in the battle above. They headed like a snarling tide towards Noble's fighters, and they would tear them limb from limb, unless Allorise could be stopped. Unless Elvienne could stop her.

She hit the top of the next tomb, jarring her knees. Allo's glass blade lashed out before she could duck. It ripped her cheek open, and her mouth filled with blood. She dropped back, slipped, nearly fell before her reflexes saved her. By the time she recovered Allorise had evaded her again.

The blood streamed down her face, staining her neck and shoulder. Elvienne felt the loose skin flapping as she ran. Her face was on fire. She was lucky she still had her left eye.

"You're going to be scarred, witch!" Allorise was three tombs away, but Elvienne could see the sweat and mud on her dress. She wasn't as strong as she pretended to be. If she weakened and lost control, the winged beast would snap her in half.

"Allorise—" There was a hum in the air, a crackle of static as the sky darkened. Nice of Kayall to join the fight, at last. She flung the sarcastic thought his way, knowing it probably wouldn't reach him. There was too much magic flying about. She wiped her cheek, panting. It was still pouring blood. "Allorise, listen - "

Lighting flashed. A demon screamed as the rain lashed down. The sudden downpour chilled the burning in her face, plastered her clothes to her skin. Rain dripped from her hair, her eyelashes. She dashed the water away and tried to focus.

Allorise stood on the roof of a tomb, arms flung high in challenge, a black shape against the strobing sky. "It that the best you've got? Rain? I control the powers of hell! Do you think a storm will stop me?"

Above her head, the winged demon flapped and yowled, throwing its head from side to side on its sinuous neck. The pressure increased in Elvienne's skull. She saw a flare at the very edge of her vision, sparking into life like a bone-fire on the shore. She ducked.

The fireball caught the demon under the right wing, sending it tumbling away across the cemetery, a smoking hole blasted in its side. It crashed into the side of a tomb and slithered to the ground, and the horde, sensing weakness, tore it to pieces.

Allorise watched it fall, lips tight with frustration. She glared at Elvienne, spat, and fled.

But she was plump, and slow. It took only a moment for Elvienne to change her form, make her legs longer, her body leaner. Stars knew she would pay for this in the morning, but if she didn't stop Allorise, she wouldn't live to see dawn. None of them would.

She didn't bother with her face. It took too much time.

She raced after Allorise, leaping the narrow gaps between the tombs, slipping on wet stone. To fall was to die. Ahead, Allorise scrambled onto the roof of a tomb that was higher than those surrounding it. Elvienne leapt after her, taking a kick to the face. Her nose crunched under the blow, but she kept going. She had to.

Allorise dropped into a fighting crouch, blade lashing in front of her. "I told you, stay away from me!"

There was nowhere she could run to. They had reached the end of the row of tombs. Unless she dropped to the ground and ran with the pack, she couldn't get away. And the walls were too high to jump from.

"What's the matter, Allorise? Don't you trust your little pets to catch you this time?"

She shook her head. "The bloodlust is on them. I can't hold that back. I can feel it welling up through me. I want . . . to kill . . ."

In the lightning, her eyes flashed red.

"Allorise, you can stop this. Break the connection. I'll help you."

"I don't need your help!" She lunged with the knife. Elvienne leapt back, one foot slipping off the edge. The roof of the tomb was square and flat, slick with rain. Allorise lunged, trying to grapple her while she was off balance.

Elvienne ducked under Allo's arm, snatched at it, and

twisted it behind her. Her knee pressed hard against the small of Allo's back. Allorise's knife scored her collar, a burning line, but the younger woman couldn't see what she was doing.

Elvienne prised her fingers apart. The glass knife clattered to the floor. Elvienne kicked it away. "Give up!" she urged.

"Never!" Allo's elbow took her in the gut and she lost her grip. Only a fraction, but enough for the younger woman to wrench free and kick her smartly on the kneecap. Her knee exploded in pain. Elvienne sagged, grabbing Allo's arm. She pulled her down with her, smashing her forehead on the rock. Allo howled, and sank her teeth into the flesh of Elvienne's upper arm.

They grappled on the roof of the crypt, while the rain lashed down and the lightning flashed around them, making their movements jerky, slicing them into a series of individual pictures. Allo tore free, her mouth a bloody, gaping hole. Elvienne tried to rise, but her leg wouldn't support her and Allo was running, running across the roof with her hair trailing in long wet strings behind her. For a moment Elvienne thought she was going to jump, but Allorise crouched, twisted and turned back. It was hard to see anything with the rain in her eyes.

"Come on then!" Allorise screamed, more demon than human, blood-splattered and raging. "Get up and kill me, if you can!"

Biting her lip, Elvienne forced herself to her feet. She launched herself at Allorise, trying to knock her off the side, to the marshy ground below. Allo sidestepped, slapping her hard on the back, sending her stumbling.

Elvienne knew something was wrong. She couldn't suck in a breath, and suddenly her legs wouldn't hold her up. It felt like they were dissolving beneath her. And where had all this blood come from?

She pitched forward. She needed to lie down. Just lie down, for a little while, and everything would be all right. All she needed was to ease the pain in her lungs, get her breath back, and she would finish Allo, save the boy. She just needed to rest . . .

Twenty-Four

I CAN'T SEE! WHAT'S going on? Let me look!" Spark struggled against Kayall's arm, but the mage held him firm. The rain in his eyes made it hard to see, but he could make out the shapes of the two women battling on top of the tomb. Kayall had taken him to hole up on high ground, behind a breastwork of plundered stone, responding to repeated demon assaults with spears, crossbows and magic. It was exhausting. It seemed to have been going on for days, wave after wave, until each attack blurred into the one before. The slope below was a quagmire, and each wave left a fresh layer of dead to be trampled underfoot. Some of the demons had simple weapons, spears or hurled stones, but most relied on claws and teeth. That was the only reason so many of Noble's men were still alive. If the demons ripped down the defensive wall, it would be over. If they worked together, it would be over. But no one was co-ordinating their attacks, while Allorise battled Elvienne for Spark's life.

As the lightning flashed, he saw Elvienne fall forward, slowly, limbs jerking under the white light. A picture captured for an instant, and then everything was in darkness and he was left blinking away the afterimages. Kayall released his grip with a strangled cry, and everything changed.

Allorise clutched at her head as if she was in searing pain. The demons retreated, but not towards their mistress. Dimly, across the noise of battle, he heard her screamed commands going ignored. The black tide had turned.

"Where are they going?" Carousel fired a last, speculative shot over the heads of the retreating horde, and wiped the sweat from her forehead with her sleeve. She offered Spark a smile, but he could see she was shaky, her shirt scorched from her burning scars. He gestured for a water carrier as she sank to her haunches in the mud.

"Hopefully back to whatever hell they came from. What do you think, Kayall?" But Kayall was no longer standing beside him. He had scrambled over the barricade and jogged though the mire of mud and gore towards the spot where Elvienne had fallen.

"Follow him, Spark," Caro urged.

"He doesn't need me. Nothing's going to happen to Elvienne . . ." But doubts gathered like rainclouds in the back of his mind. Mages could die. He knew that as well as anyone.

"Wait here." He scrambled over the wall, down the long drop on the far side, landing with a splash that showered him with mud up to his armpits. It was like dropping into a hell.

The ground was soupy with rain and spilled blood, and the bodies lay three deep at the foot of the wall. Demons and men twisted by death into contorted shapes, limbs missing, eyes gouged out and skulls caved in. He tried not to look, but the corpses were everywhere. Sometimes it was impossible to tell whether the dead had once been human, or creature.

He trotted after Kayall, mired to the knees, calling for him to slow down. The mage didn't respond, but as he reached the foot of the tomb where Elvienne and Allorise fought, he looked back. His eyeliner had been sweated away, making his eyes look smaller than usual, and his brow was furrowed.

"Give me a boost, kid."

Spark formed a step with his hands and helped Kayall scramble up, catching his manicured fingers to heave himself up on to the roof. The stone was slick, though the rain was easing.

It was hard to see Elvienne at first, grey against grey stone. Kayall saw her an instant before Spark. He flung himself down on his knees by her side, lifting her head in his hands.

"Elvienne? Elvienne, talk to me!"

Spark hung back. Something was wrong with the way Elvienne's head flopped against Kayall's arm.

"Come on, you stupid old bag. Wake up and talk to me!"

"Kayall—" Hadn't he seen the knife, sticking out of her back just below his arm? "Kayall, she's hurt. She's hurt badly . . . ."

"No she's not. We don't . . ." Kayall choked as he held her against his chest. Her grey hair was unravelled from its bun. It streamed over his arm like a waterfall of silver, tarnished by the rain that washed the blood from her face. "Someone fetch me a healer!"

Spark reached out. "Let me take her."

"No!" Kayall tightened his grip. "I'll look after her. You're not taking her away from me!"

"Spark?" Carousel's call came from ground level. The top of a ladder appeared over the side of the tomb. "How is she? I brought bandages."

"I don't think we need them." Kayall rocked back and forth, cradling Elvienne. He stroked her hair, telling her she would heal, that the battle was over. That everything would be fine.

Spark didn't feel that anything could be fine. Not now, not ever. There was a roaring in his ears, and all he could think of was the way Carlon had twitched as he had taken his life. Elvienne wasn't even twitching, but he knew . . .

Carousel's head appeared over the side of the tomb. She pressed her hand to her mouth. "Is she—oh no! No!"

"I don't know." Spark knew, but his lips worked soundless around the words. "He won't let me touch her."

"Let me try." She touched Kayall gently on the shoulder. "Kayall? Can I see Elvienne?"

"Did you bring a healer? She needs healing."

"I'm going to heal her. Let me hold her a moment."

He released his fierce grip, entrusting Elvienne into Carousel's embrace. Spark watched her face cloud, her eyes fill with tears. He wished he could say, do, something. His body felt numb and his mind sluggish. All he could feel was the cold, sinking through his limbs.

"Kayall, she's gone. I'm sorry . . ."

"No." He shook his head, rubbed his eyes. "That's not true. I was talking to her yesterday. Make her wake up."

"I can't make her wake up, Kayall. I wish I could." Carousel reached for his hand, but he snatched it away.

"She can't be gone, she's not even old! We're supposed to live for centuries, we're meant to be immortal. That's what she told me . . ."

The stretcher bearers waited at the foot of the tomb, passing up ropes to lower Elvienne down. A couple of them scrambled up the ladder, and Spark waved them to stand back, to give Kayall space.

"Is the witch hurt badly?" one of them asked, in an undertone. Spark could only nod. "Then she needs to be brought down."

"Leave me the ropes." His voice sounded like it belonged to a stranger. "We'll take care of it. There are other people who need your help. Let the mages look after their own."

The man nodded and withdrew, leaving Spark holding the ropes in his limp hands. He crept towards Kayall and Carousel, and cleared his throat.

"We need to move her. Can you help?"

Caro nodded. Between them they tied the rope beneath Elvienne's armpits. Carousel used Spark's body to shield what she was doing from Kayall's gaze, as she slid the glass knife free and crammed it in her belt. "I don't know what else to do with it," she whispered. "It might be magic. What if Allorise comes looking for it?"

Spark had barely spared a thought for Allorise since the demons had fled. He had not seen her run off, but she must have gone to ground, licking her wounds and planning her next move. If the blade was ensorcelled, he had no doubt she would try to retrieve it. He would be ready for her if she did.

Carousel headed back towards the ladder, dragging Elvienne so that her boots scuffed across the stone roof of the tomb. Kayall caught her arm. "Where are you taking her?" he demanded.

"Back to the caverns. It's the right thing to do."

"Let me carry her."

"Are you sure?"

Kayall nodded. "She needs me. She's my friend."

Caro stepped back, allowing him access to the ladder. "If you're sure . . ."

"I don't want anyone else to touch her. I can heal her myself."

"Kayall—" Carousel looked as if she wanted to say more, but she merely shook her head and let him slide down the ladder to the ground. She looked at Spark, standing with her fists clenched tight against her skirt. "Do you think he realises—?"

"Let him deal with it in his own way." Spark pinched the bridge of his nose, wiped his eyes. It didn't help. Nothing helped "I feel sick."

"I know." She slipped an arm around his waist and he kissed the crown of her head. "Let's get it over with. Then we can mourn her."

Between them, they lowered Elvienne's body over the side of the tomb, back into Kayall's arms, and let the rope slither down the side of the stonework. He held her close, arms and legs hanging down, like a child sleeping in her father's arms.

Spark scrambled down the ladder, and waited for Caro to

join him so he could squeeze her hand. She rested her head against his shoulder, drawing deep breaths before she looked up. Her eyes were angry-bright, but her voice was steady. "I don't think we should leave him on his own," she said.

"You're right." But as they rounded the tomb, Kayall backed away. He tightened his grip on his burden as if he feared they would snatch it away from him.

"I told you, you can't take her from me!" There was an ominous rumble of thunder overhead.

"We're not going to take her from you—" Spark took a step forward. The sky darkened.

"You leave us alone! She only came here because of you. This is your fault!"

"Kayall—" Spark ducked as the lightning flashed down, blinking the sudden darkness from his eyes. When his vision cleared, Kayall was gone. The air was hazy with smoke and reeked of scorched stone.

"Shit! Where did he go?"

"Over there." Caro pointed. The mage fled into the maze of tombs, carrying Elvienne with him. Spark started after him, and she caught his arm. "Give him time. He'll come back when he's ready."

"And if he doesn't?"

She had no answer to that.

"What if we lose both mages? What if Allorise comes back?" He stared in the direction Kayall had retreated, and voiced his darkest thought.

"What the hell are we going to do without her?"

※

The rain was Kayall's constant companion, following him across the graveyard. Dark weather for dark thoughts. Elvienne was heavy in his arms but he couldn't put her down, not yet. She deserved somewhere quiet, somewhere safe. There was nowhere in this stinking city good enough for her.

He waded waist high through the undergrowth in the oldest part of the cemetery, ignoring the nettles that stung through the thickness of his linen, the brambles snagging his ankles. He would know the right place when he found it. A secluded spot where he could heal her, bring her back. Allorise had done the same with her father. It couldn't be that hard . . .

He stumbled across the perfect place before he realised it. The crumbling tomb had lost one wall and half the roof, but there was shelter from the rain and a dry patch of floor on the far side of the rubble. He climbed over, Elvienne's boots knocking against the stone, jarring his arms. They ached from carrying her, but he would not let her go until the time was right.

Shrugging off his cloak, he spread it out with his foot, a blanket for his friend to lie on. She had never been uncomfortable on stone, but this floor looked cold, and bare.

He set her down. She looked smaller than yesterday, and older. Face up, he couldn't see the wound in her back. Battered and bruised, but he had seen her after worse fights. She had always walked away with no more than swellings and cuts. It seemed impossible she wasn't going to get up this time.

He sat next to her, ignoring the discomfort of the cold stone beneath him, and brushed her face with the back of his hand.

"Come on, Elvienne. Sit up. Talk to me."

There was nothing, nobody there. He sat for a long time, head on his knees, holding her hand and waiting for her to stir. All the while she grew colder, as the night closed in around them. Under cover of darkness, Kayall began to talk. They had been friends for three centuries, since she'd caught him cheating at dice in a back-alley Lambury tavern, and spotted his potential. There were a lot of memories.

"I know I couldn't stop you coming here, looking for Spark," he said eventually. All the memories were cleared and there was nothing else to say. "I'm glad we did. He's a good kid. But you should have let me take on Allorise, instead of you. You always think you know best. You just plunge ahead and do things without thinking that anyone else might be able to help you!" He tightened his grip on her hand. "You're so stupid, Elvienne! I hope you know how stupid you are, and how pissed off I am that you left me here, and how much I still need you . . ." He inhaled a long breath, pushing back the sob. "You're going to tell me to look after Spark, to sort this whole mess out. I'll do it, because you'd only bitch at me if I ran back to Lambury and left things unfinished. But that's the only reason! After that I'm . . ." He trailed off. What would he do, when he couldn't turn to Elvienne?

"Shit, I'm going to miss you." Fighting back the tears, he rose. It was pitch black in the cemetery. There could be demons behind every tomb, but that didn't matter. Nothing mattered now but commemorating Elvienne in a way she would approve of. First he would burn her, then he would raise a glass in her memory. Maybe three or four glasses.

Spark was on watch when he saw the fire. He heard the consternation below as he reported it. "It's not a torch," he assured Noble, who climbed up to have a look. "It's not getting any closer. I don't think it's a threat. Maybe you could send Dweller to have a look?"

Noble frowned. "I haven't seen Dweller since sunset. No one has."

Spark shrugged. That was nothing unusual. "I expect he'll pop up. Do you want me to go?"

"Hells no, kid! If it is a trap, you'll be the one they most want to blunder into it. As long as it doesn't get any closer or bigger, it's no danger. Just keep an eye on it. It's probably beggars trying to keep warm, but best not take any risks."

Carousel stuck her head over the parapet, emerging from

the hastily-dug tunnel that led to the caverns below. "I know what it is," she said.

Noble moved aside to let her join them in the cramped space behind the rough barricade. "What is it, then?"

"I'll wager it's Elvienne's death pyre."

The three of them stared across the empty, shadowed cemetery towards the distant flickering light of flames. Spark sighed, remembering how the lakeside cottage had burned and freed the spirit of his master. He rubbed his eyes with the heel of his hand, and Carousel slipped her arm though his, pressing close against his side.

"They used to call them bone-fires, in the Estmarch," he said. "That was a long time ago. My master told me about it. He said they burned the dead on the shores of the lake, so the fire could be seen across the water. I think Elvienne might have been from the Estmarch, from some of the things she said."

Noble shrugged. "I think it can be seen well enough. Too well. If the mage brings demons around him, I'm not risking my men to save his neck." He rubbed his face. "The smoke's getting in my eyes. I'm going below. Stay safe, you two."

The wind blew the smoke away from them, into the city, but Spark's eyes prickled too. He held Caro close, taking comfort in her warmth, as the grey light of false dawn crept over the cemetery and the rats and foxes fled from the night's feast. By the time true sunrise arrived, weak light streaming through the clouds, the fire had faded to glowing embers. No demons howled, no blades clashed. Silence hung like the mist between the tombs, and through the mist, a tall, slender figure emerged.

Carousel spotted him first. She jumped down from the rampart before Spark could catch her, running through the brambles on lithe legs. He followed, as usual feeling lumpen in comparison, as she jogged to a halt in front of Kayall. She looked as if she wasn't sure whether to hug him, settling for an awkward, brief clutch of his upper arms. His face was darkened with soot, and the tracks of his tears drew startling white lines in the grime. It made him look like Dweller, until Spark's gaze reached his glittering turquoise eyes.

"Are you all right?" Caro asked. "We saw the fire . . ."

He nodded. "She's really gone. I never thought she would. She was in my life for so long . . ." He shook his head, as if yesterday's events had left him utterly bewildered.

"Is there anything we can do?" Spark asked. He felt so useless. Action would help fill the void.

Kayall smiled. It looked forced, as if he was trying it out, but it was a long time since Spark had seen him smile. "You can do one thing for me, in her memory."

Spark nodded. "Anything."

"You can buy me a pint."

$\clubsuit$

There were taverns open at every bell in Cape Carey, if you knew where to look. The one they found was no more than the back room of a house in the Telesian Quarter. The window, looking out onto an alley, was hung with a vibrant patterned cloth that let light in but kept the curious eyes of the Watch out. The plastered walls were painted with amateurish frescoes of animals and temples, and there was a skylight in the roof, so grimy with dirt and bird shit it was virtually useless. There were only three tables, wrought of rusty metal with a fine lattice of holes in the top, pushed together to make one long counter. Although there were no other drinkers this early in the morning, Kayall pulled their table away from the others to provide some privacy.

"Telesians all like to drink together," he explained. "I've never seen the point. You can't cheat at cards, and you're more likely to get knifed—" He broke off and hammered on the table, shouting in Telesian for beer and food.

The beer came, watered-down ale provided by a small man with a moustache that hung so long he had plaited it and flung it over his shoulder. He haggled with Kayall over the price, a swift conversation Spark couldn't follow, and bared his teeth in a half-smile. "I bring food. Is early. You get what you given."

Kayall took a mouthful of ale, and made a face. "Piss-weak, but he wants three coppers for it! Thieving Telesian bastard. The food had better be good." He raised his leather flagon high. "To Elvienne!"

"To Elvienne!" The three flagons bumped, spilling beer through the lattice of the table top.

"She had such a way with stone and earth." Kayall sighed, and drank deeply. "We won't see her like again."

"She saved my life," Carousel added simply, following him in drinking. She looked enquiringly at Spark.

He rolled the weak ale around in his mouth while he gathered his thoughts, and swallowed.

"Before I met her, I was scared of Elvienne," he confessed. "But she picked me up out of the gutter. She didn't judge me. She encouraged me to be better than I was. I'll miss that in my life."

The flagons thumped together again in toast, as the little Telesian dumped a covered dish on the table and said something rapidly to Kayall. "He says he'll bring us better ale," the mage translated. "He didn't realise we were paying tribute to a friend. I don't know what the hell he thought we were doing in this rat-hole so early in the morning . . ."

Carousel interrupted him by lifting the lid of the dish. The breakfast was a mixture of Telesian and Kingdom food, thrown together at random. There were breaded cod cheeks and small porcelain bowls of sweet porridge, a dish of scrambled eggs topped with cheese and bacon, and, more exotically, slices of citrus fruit, red and gold in their peel, and tiny red Telesian sausages laced with fiery peppers. It wasn't until the smell hit his nostrils that Spark realised how hungry he was. He had eaten nothing the previous day beyond a few slices of bread and honey to keep him going.

Kayall grinned. "I'll say this for the beardies. They might keep their wallets tight, but they put on a good spread!"

Spark nodded, eyes watering at the spicy kick of the sausage, and groped for his ale. His next mouthful was more cautious. Carousel avoided the sausages altogether, helping herself to porridge and scrambled eggs, but Kayall tucked in with gusto. "She always said to me," he said, "that life was too long to avoid trying new things. Sooner or later you should try everything, just to prevent yourself from getting bored." He sighed. "She's left a gap. I don't think I'm good enough to fill it."

Who could fill the hole Elvienne's death had left? Not Spark, he was sure. What had he ever done, besides run away?

They lingered over the meal, the skinny Telesian bringing fresh, strong ale as Kayall demanded it, with many toasts to Elvienne. When the plates were finally cleared, Kayall leant back with a contented belch.

"We should go back to the cemetery," he said. "Find out what Noble wants us to do next. The demons might be routed for now, but we're not rid of them yet. You've still got work to do, young Spark!"

It was as if a cloud darkened the table at his words. Spark shivered. "I don't know what I *can* do, without Elvienne."

"We'll figure something out." Kayall shrugged as he rose. "We may have to improvise."

"Against demons?"

"Fuck, kid, I don't know! I'm floundering as much as you are. Probably more. I need a leader, and I'm lost, so I'm going to cling to Noble and let him tell me what to do. It's either that or piss off out of town and she—" he drew in a deep breath to steady himself, "she'd never forgive me if I ratted out on you. Caro, does your belly tell you it's safe outside?"

Carousel wiped the last few crumbs from her lips, and nodded. "No burning at all. It's a relief, after yesterday . . ."

"Then let's head back, see what we can salvage. Noble's bound to have some ideas."

Carousel led the short distance back to the cemetery. The streets were quiet, but Spark felt no sense of peace. It was an impatient, tense kind of silence, as if the city held its breath, waiting to see what would happen next. Too bloody quiet for his liking. He had the same sensation he always had when Dweller was lurking unseen in the shadows behind him; that of being constantly watched.

There were Nobility guards on the cemetery gate, who allowed them to pass with a nod of recognition. Small work teams toiled to separate dead humans from dead demons, to pile the men up for burning and tumble the demonkind into a swiftly-dug pit for burial. The air smelt of shit, smoke and death, and Spark tried not to gag as he breathed in. It stank worse than the city usually did, worse than the slums. He hankered for the fresh air and open hills of the Estmarch. He wished he could take Carousel there. She had never been outside the city walls, except to the slums. He was sick of Cape Carey, sick of death.

The tomb entrance was twice as heavily guarded, and the main living cavern was quiet; sombre bustle restricted to the side-cave that was set aside as an infirmary. He wouldn't look in there. That was the last place he had seen Elvienne before the battle. It was where she should be right now.

Past more guards, to the closed door of Noble's office. Kayall shook his shoulders out, raised his hand, then let it fall.

"Elvienne would have barged right in," he said.

"You don't have to *be* her," Carousel told him.

He chuckled. "I know, but sometimes it's fun to let a little Elvienne escape, don't you think?" He lifted the latch and pushed the door.

Noble stood in front of his desk, back to the door, talking to someone. He spun around as they entered, hand flying to his dagger, then relaxed. "Oh," he said, "it's you. Where have you been?"

"Drinking in Elvienne's memory over breakfast." Kayall craned to see around Noble, but the dark man blocked his view. Spark could see that his chair was turned round so the high back faced the room. Whoever he had been talking to sat in that chair. A growing feeling of unease gripped his lower gut. He reached for Carousel's hand.

Noble clapped Kayall on the upper arm. "We're all sorry for her loss. She'll be missed. But we have to move on."

"Not sure I'm ready to move on just yet, Noble."

"You might have to adjust your thinking pretty quickly. Things are changing faster than you know."

"What things?" Spark asked.

"Everything. New information has come to light. Perhaps you could tell them?"

He addressed the unseen figure in the chair, who rose to face the room.

Carousel hissed savagely. She would have started forward without Spark's fierce grip on her hand holding her back. Standing before the chair, one hand resting lightly on Noble's desk as if she owned it, was Allorise Carey.

Twenty-Five

KAYALL STARTED FORWARD at the same time as Carousel. Noble caught his arm, digging his fingers into the mage's flesh. Kayall strained against him from an instant, but Noble was a rock.

"What the fuck is *she* doing here?" Kayall spat.

Allorise's lips twitched at his venom. Beside Spark, Carousel bit her lip.

"I don't think I can be in the same room as her without stabbing her," she muttered. She kept her voice low, but Allorise's ears were sharp. Her smile broadened to take in the girl.

"Carousel, sweet. It's been a while. Scars giving you any trouble?"

"Screw you, Allorise."

Allo's eyes narrowed. "You should muzzle your bitch, Noble. She bites." Her eyes flicked past the furious girl to land on Spark. It felt as if she was unpeeling his clothes, then his skin, discarding both in a bedraggled heap on the floor. "I should have taken you with me the day I killed my brother. Spark, isn't it? Or Leyon?"

"Spark." His voice squeaked as if her plump fingers closed

around his throat.

"We don't use true names here, Silver Lady," Noble reminded her.

"Of course not! You all have your adorable little nicknames. Even you, styling yourself a nobleman. But you'd be a fool to think the boy came to town wearing his true name. Who are you really, Spark?"

"That's none of your concern." Kayall butted in before she could drag Spark's secrets from his lips. "As our prisoner, you should be answering our questions."

"Prisoner?" Allorise held out her hands. "Do you see me wearing chains, mage? I have information you want, that's true. Perhaps you could say I came here to trade."

"We want nothing from you," Carousel snarled. Spark felt the tension in her body, drawn taut, ready to fight or flee.

"I'll be the judge of that, Caro," Noble told her. "Silver came to me, offering aid and asking for it. I think we should listen to her."

"Silver? She's one of us now, is she? Elvienne's embers are still warm and you welcome this witch into the Nobility?" Caro's face was white with fury, the red slash scored bright across her cheek. "If she stays, I'm going."

Noble shrugged. "Go then. Silver is of more value to me now than a scarred whore."

His words fell into a long moment of shocked silence. Carousel let go of Spark's hand. "Fuck you, Noble." Her tone was bitter with betrayal. She turned away, but not before Spark saw furious tears flash in her eyes. The slam of the door behind her reverberated through the room.

Allorise sniffed in disdain. "What use is she to any of us? She has no particular talent, beyond one for causing trouble."

Wire walking, crossbow shooting, demon-finding . . . Spark held his tongue. Allorise had underestimated Caro before, to her cost. It seemed she had not learned from her mistake.

Kayall shook his head. "I'm with Caro," he said. "I want

nothing from your Silver Lady. Whatever scheme she's hatching, I want no part in it. The smell of her makes me sick."

Allorise ignored him. All her attention was on Spark. "What about you, Leyon? Do you want me to help you undo what you did? All those deaths on your conscience . . . How do you sleep? Does the scarred whore keep you warm at night?"

"That's enough, Silver!" At Noble's sharp retort Allorise stepped back, but she was still smiling. *Think it over,* she mouthed.

"I'd like to hear what she has to say," Spark confessed. Allorise beamed, and Kayall cursed.

"You're a fucking idiot, Spark. Every word that slithers from her lips is poison. I won't listen to it. I'll be in my room if you need me." He closed the door with less venom than Carousel, but with a soft, decisive click that was somehow more unsettling.

That left Noble, Allorise and Spark, facing each other in a circle of mutual mistrust. Noble shook his head. "You came here to trade, Silver," he said. "What do you have to trade?"

Allorise ran her tongue over her teeth. "Information."

"What do you want in return?"

"My freedom. My life. The south of the city." Her eyes flashed to Spark. "Not the boy any more. Mages are too much trouble."

"I'll give you the south," Noble said, "if you agree to let people pass freely to my side if they don't like living under your rule. And if you stay out of the north, out of my businesses. Leave my people unmolested."

"I won't touch your people if you don't touch mine."

Noble nodded. "What's the information, then?"

Allorise stretched out her arms, catlike and casual. "I should probably let you know you've been betrayed."

"Betrayed? By who?" Noble shot a sharp look at Spark.

"Not by me!" he insisted.

Allorise giggled. "No, the mage-boy is loyal to the point of stupidity, it seems. But your shadow-creature has been showing the wrong side of his cloak . . . ."

"Shadow creature?" Noble frowned. Spark was a step ahead of him.

"She means Dweller," he said. "Am I right, Allorise?"

Noble shook his head, but his hands trembled over his dagger. "Not Dweller. He wouldn't . . ."

"Then where is he?" Allorise asked sweetly. "If he's innocent, why isn't he here? Don't pretend he's lurking in the shadows. I've been around demons long enough. I can see through their little guises."

"He wouldn't . . ." Noble repeated, his voice trailing off.

"Why not? He's half-demon, after all. There's no reason he wouldn't side with his mother's kind."

"He has reason enough to hate humans." Noble's voice was distant. "But I never thought he'd turn on us."

"Can't trust anyone, can you?" Allorise said brightly.

Spark glared at her. "How do you know?"

"I felt the demons leave me. In the cemetery, after I killed the old woman." Her face darkened, and her restless fingers drummed on the desk. "My moment of triumph, and he snatched it away from me! They left me as they left you, Spark. I saw him leading them away. I ran, I'm ashamed to say I hid, while I gathered my thoughts." She shuddered. "Who knows what Dweller plans to do with them?"

"Nothing worse than you planned."

Allorise looked surprised. "Me, Spark? You compare me to a demon? I only wanted the city. I'm sure Dweller wants more. Revenge on humankind, maybe."

"It doesn't matter what he wants," Noble said. "What matters is regaining control. Without Elvienne . . . I don't see how we can."

"Let me help," Allorise said. "I want to make up for what I did. I would never have killed the witch if I'd realised how much we were going to need her. She came at me, and I had to defend myself. I was fighting for my life, after all!" Her eyes flashed, defying Spark to argue with her. "We need to work together, Noble. You, me, the mage and the boy here . . . If we pool our talents we can win this battle. If we try to work separately, we'll fail. You know it makes sense."

"What do you think, Spark?" Noble asked, his face grave.

"Me?"

"Why not you? If you can't work with Allorise—and I wouldn't blame you if you can't—say the word."

"What will you do then?" Spark asked.

Noble had walked around behind Allorise as he spoke, kicking the chair aside. He drew his dagger with a soft scrape, metal sliding over leather. Allorise started forward, but before she could escape he whipped the blade around and pressed it to her pale throat, forcing her back against his chest. Her hands tightened on the edge of the table until her knuckles whitened.

"Say the word, Spark, and I'll open her throat and end her games right now. She works with you, or she dies."

The colour drained from Allo's face, all but one bright red bead of blood, trickling from the point of the blade. She pressed her lips tight, but her eyes were wide and pleading. "You wouldn't—"

"Let him answer!" Noble pulled the blade tighter, scoring a thin red line across her skin. "Spark? What do you say?"

He could let Noble spill Allo's blood, the way she had spilled Carousel's, and Elvienne's. It was tempting. A quick, clean death was too good for her, but at least she would be dead, along with her foul magic and her scheming.

Her eyes filled with tears, and her lips quivered as if she longed to speak. The blood reached the neck of her shirt, soaking into the cream fabric. Spark couldn't tear his eyes from that spreading crimson stain, from the breast beneath it that rose and fell with her quick breaths. The Philosopher's breast had risen and fallen with his dying breaths, and since then there had been nothing but killing in Spark's life. She might be a scheming bitch, but she was still alive, and a word from him could end her life. He had seen enough killing.

He shook his head, and Noble let the knife fall.

"You work for me," Spark told Allorise, who was still trembling. "You do as I say, or I'll kill you myself, and it won't be cleanly, with a dagger. Remember Shadow? I burned his face. I can burn you too."

Allorise massaged the bloody line on her throat, and regarded her fingertips with rueful curiosity. Her eyes were dry. "I'd rather you didn't mar this perfection—"

"I'm serious, Allorise!" He wasn't a child, to be mocked and deceived. "Noble, bind her hands. I want her to understand she's a prisoner, whether she likes it or not."

There was fresh respect on Noble's face as he did Spark's bidding. Allorise held up her hands obediently, like a child receiving sweets.

"Now what, Spark?" Noble seemed relieved he had handed over control of the situation, and his confidence made Spark feel better.

"Now," he said, "the three of us work out a plan."

Carousel had not gone far when she'd barged out of the room. Kayall almost stumbled over her, sitting in the corridor with her back to the wall and her chin resting on her knees, toying with the dry end of one of her long, thin braids. Her eyes were rimmed with red, and she scowled up at him. "If you've come to lecture me—"

"Far from it." He extended a hand and helped her to her feet. "It makes my sword hand twitch to be in the same room as Allorise Carey. If I'd been Noble, I would have gutted her the moment I saw her."

Carousel shuddered. "I don't want to think about her. I could use a drink."

Kayall's hip flask was almost dry, but he let her swallow the last drops. "I think there's more in my room," he said.

"Sounds good." She handed back the flask. "I could use the company. If you don't mind?"

"Why would I mind, sweetheart?"

She shrugged. "Thanks. I need a place to hide away."

"Who from?"

Another shrug. "Everyone, really."

Kayall nodded. He knew that feeling. "Come on."

His room was never warm, not well-ventilated enough for a fire. He piled a blanket from the bed around Carousel's shoulders as she began to shiver, and lit a candle. He had a small earthenware jar of ale stashed under the bed, and he re-filled his hip flask and offered her a swig. She accepted it with a grateful smile.

"Think he'll work with her?" she asked.

"Spark? With the Carey woman? I hope not . . ." Spark's trouble, Kayall reflected, was that he was essentially good-hearted. He would be too soft on Allorise, and she would chew him up and spit him out. "Elvienne would never have let her get this far. She would have walked into that room and killed her where she sat. None of this nonsense about negotiating."

"Would she really?" Carousel asked.

Kayall sighed. "Probably not. She had a soft core, though she hid it well. But she wouldn't stand for people hurting her friends."

"You knew her a long time?" She pulled the blanket tighter around her.

"Three centuries, give or take a decade or two. I can barely remember my life before I met her . . ." His eyes were suspiciously prickly, and he took a quick drink to mask his emotion.

Caro picked at a loose thread on the blanket. "I barely knew her, but she had such an impact on my life . . ."

He laughed. "That was Elvienne! Blazing in like a storm, changing everyone she touched, then leaving all at once. I thought she'd always come back . . . ."

"I miss her." Her voice was so forlorn he couldn't help wrapping his arms around her and pulling her close. She looked up at him, sleepy-eyed, lips slightly parted, and he had to kiss her. He felt her tense in surprise, then relax, mouth open, kissing back as his hands slid round her waist. He pulled back.

"What about—?"

"Hush!" She kissed him again, fiercely, and Spark's name fell away between them. He traced the contours of her body, the red whorls on her torso, and she shuddered.

"She turned you into a regular work of art, Caro!"

"Really?" She squirmed as he traced his tongue along the patterns. "Do that again."

"You know in Telesia men pay handfuls of gold to have markings like these made on their skin? It's a symbol of strength . . ."

She was strong, the strength of a dancer, a wire-walker, and she had the flexibility to go with it. Her thighs embraced his waist, legs carelessly crossed at the ankle, and she crooned as he slid inside her. Her breath came in short, tight gasps, and when she arched her back beneath him and groaned, the sound was muted, the climax of a girl who had grown up with no privacy and had learned to keep quiet.

He held her close until she fell asleep, no more words exchanged between them. Nothing about Allorise, and certainly nothing about Spark. Carousel had come to Kayall for comfort, and he had offered it in the surest way he knew. If he was honest with himself, he needed comfort as much as she did. It didn't fill the gaping hole Elvienne had left, but it made him feel a little less hollow.

&

"Kayall! Kayall, I need you! Are you there?"

Spark hammered on the door once more. This time he was rewarded with a grumble, and a muted exchange of voices. Kayall had a girl in his room. That must be why it was so difficult to rouse him.

"I'm coming in!" He called the warning before he pushed up the latch. Only Noble's private rooms had bolts on the inside, and even they were rarely locked.

"Just a moment!" There was a flurry of movement from inside the room as he pushed the door open, and Kayall stepped up to the gap, breathless, earrings askew. "What do you want, kid?"

"Dweller took the demons. We're going after him. Allorise has agreed to help us, but I need you too. Are you coming?"

"I—" Kayall bit back what was obviously a sarcastic retort. "You're working with Allo Carey?"

"Please. I need your help . . ."

Kayall relented, stepping back from the door to let him into the room. "I suppose I'm not allowed to stab her until we're done?" he said.

Spark didn't reply. He was staring at the girl. At Carousel.

"What are you doing here?"

She sat on the edge of the bed, fastening the lacings on her blouse. She winked at him. "What do you think?"

"I—" He didn't know what he thought, and he didn't have time to assess his feelings. He didn't feel as bad as he had when Dweller had taunted him over Caro's night with Noble. Something had changed between them. He wasn't sure what it was, but if she ended up with Kayall, he couldn't hate her for it. Couldn't hate either of them.

She rose, smooth and supple, and slid her boots on. "Where are you going?" he asked.

"I'm coming with you. If Kayall stabs Allorise, I want to see it."

"It's not safe—"

She strode across the room and kissed him lightly on the

cheek. "Nothing in my life has been safe since I plucked you out of the gutter, Spark! I'm not going to miss this."

"Where are you going?"

"To get a weapon. Meet you in the armoury!"

She closed the door behind her, deliberately. Spark wondered if it was to disguise the fact that she was standing behind it listening to what passed between them. He glared at Kayall. "Well?"

A hint of scarlet in the mage's cheeks. "I probably owe you an apology."

"Why? I don't own Caro. She sleeps where she chooses. There was a time that would have driven me insane, but not now."

Kayall shook his head and blew out his cheeks. "Shit, kid! At your age I would have killed me!"

Spark grinned. "I still might. I need you to come and fight demons first. If we survive, I'll kill you later."

Twenty-Six

THEY CAME TOGETHER by the cemetery gate, a pitiful army to be faced with such a huge task. Kayall and Spark, Carousel with her crossbow and a quiver of steels, and Noble, leading Allorise on a chain that bound her wrists. He handed her over to Spark. "Here you go. Good luck!"

"You're not coming with us?" Spark asked.

"Hells no! If you fail, I need to be here to defend my people. But you won't fail." He clapped Spark on the shoulder. "We're all relying on you, Spark!"

Not *kid* any more, Spark noticed, as he wrapped the chain tight about his wrist. He couldn't look Allorise in the face.

"Well!" She beamed insincerely as she looked around at the party. "A dandy, a whore and a murdering mage-brat! This will be a fun trip!"

"Don't talk!" Kayall caught Carousel's wrist as she started forward. "Just . . . don't, or I'll get Spark to bind your mouth. We don't need you with us as much as you think we do."

"You do. I can track down the demons for you. I still sense where they are. I can feel them in my blood." She looked smug.

"Oh really?" Kayall's teeth flashed. "Show her, Caro."

Carousel lifted her top to expose the livid red whorls on her skin.

"Why would I want to see your disgusting scarred gut, whore?"

"It burns, Allorise. It burns when demons are close. You turned me into a guide. So tell me—" she dropped her shirt and drew a spike from her quiver, "why do we need you?"

"For bait." Spark jerked the chain, but Allorise had frozen to the spot.

"Bait?"

"I'd throw you into the jaws of a demon to save any one of my friends. Now get walking!"

They followed Carousel through the empty streets, swords drawn. Allorise sulked at the end of her leash and dragged her feet in the gutters, but Spark would not let her rest. He realised they were heading, inevitably, towards the wreckage of the Gilded Lily. Of course. It was there things had started to go so badly wrong, and it was there he would fix them. If only he could work out how.

Ahead, Caro halted, waving for them to stop. She leaned against the wall of a building, and steam rose from her skin, misting around her like wraiths when she moved her arms. She took the drink Kayall offered and drained the flask dry.

"This is burning me up," she said. "I don't think I can get much closer."

"I'll look." Spark pulled Allorise round in front of him, using her body as a shield, hoping her presence would forestall any demon attack.

Her lips curled. "Coward!" she hissed, as they moved away down the street.

"Bait," he retorted, but without venom. She made a good point.

"Why don't you use Carousel as your bait? She's fucking the mage, after all. It seems right you should have your revenge, on both of them—"

He jerked the chain to shut her up. "Keep walking."

Her nostrils flared. "I can smell them, the beasts of hell. Can't you scent that? It's intoxicating, all that power. Doesn't it make your skin itch?"

Spark could feel it, like ants swarming all over his skin. His palms were hot and itchy, and the air around him tasted of tin. Static raised the hairs on the back of his neck, made Allo's eyes glow luminescent. They reached the corner, and he held her back while he peered round it at the ruins where the Lily once stood.

Half the building was still there, clinging to the flanks of its neighbours. Spark saw empty rooms on the upper floors, their walls ripped away, like the nests of cave-birds in the mountains. Some still had beds standing on broken floors, ragged dirty curtains flapping at windows that had lost their shutters. The bar in the downstairs tavern stood alone and unscarred, like a wooden altar in a Telesian temple, rising from the rubble around it. The cracks spread across the pavement in all direc-tions, radiating from the point of impact, as wide as he was tall. From some, steam issued in whistling jets, arcing into the sky to fall back to earth as scalding rain. But that wasn't the worst thing emerging from underground. From the cracks with no steam, the demons crawled.

Spark watched one haul itself over the edge and take its first tottering steps in the upper world. It walked on its hind legs, like a man, but hunched over so its shoulders were higher that its head. Its horned skull snaked from side to side on a long, supple neck, sucking in the city air with nostrils that flapped open and closed with every breath. It had puckered skin where its eyes should be, and a lower jaw that overlapped its upper one, curved teeth sticking up at all angles. It shook the dirt from its hide and smacked its lips.

"Can you feel the pull?" Allo's voice was low in his ear.

The Philosopher had taught Spark about magnets. That was how he felt now, as if his body was full of iron, drawn towards a magnet. It felt like his ribs would burst out of his chest if he didn't follow the call.

The demon swung its head in the direction of the unseen magnet, snarled, and headed off in that direction. Behind him, another creature emerged, shorter, more animalistic, and prowled after him.

"Something's drawing them in," Spark said. "Us too."

"Want to follow it?" Allorise asked.

"No. I've seen enough from here."

It was a struggle to walk away from the cracks, to turn his back on the magnetic influence that was trying to wrench the bones and organs out through his skin. His tendons strained with every step, and his feet felt as if they were cased in iron.

"Why is this happening?" He tried to talk without opening his mouth, fearing his teeth might be ripped from his head.

"You controlled the demons, for a while. You have a link with them. So do I, and so does Carousel." Allorise did not look to be in discomfort, but beads of sweat formed on her temples.

The next few steps were easier, and the next easier still. The link was still there, but it had less influence as he moved away. Freed of the constriction in his lungs, he could breathe more easily, and he hastened his stride.

They returned to Kayall and Carousel. The girl had found a horse trough filled with rainwater, and splashed herself to cool the heat in her skin. She shook the droplets off her braids, and grinned at him. "Find anything?"

"The demons are coming through outside the Lily. Some force is drawing them to the west. I think it's Dweller."

"Do we follow them?"

"It's not that simple." He explained about the pull, and her face darkened.

"I thought I was feeling queasy," she admitted.

"So what do we do?"

"Let me try something. Which way?"

Spark pointed, and before he could stop her she hurried in that direction, pulling her wet hair into a knot at the nape of her neck. Allorise shrugged. "I'll wager that's the last we see of her! Either the demons will eat her, or she'll just—"

"Be quiet!" Spark jerked the chain with one hand, and stilled Kayall's sword arm with the other. "Caro's not like you. At least she has a shred of morality and loyalty in her bones."

"Loyalty?" Allorise laughed at this. "How loyal did she feel to you, I wonder, when she was on her back with your friend the mage?"

"Spark, we don't need her—" Still Spark stayed Kayall's hand.

"How do you know about that, Allorise?" he asked. "Did Carousel tell you?"

Allo snorted. "I can just tell. Body language. You can cut the tension between the three of you with a blade. Must be hard to be on such an important mission with people you can't trust. You can't even trust them with your real name, can you, Leyon?"

"My *name* is Spark."

She shrugged. "If you like. Has our dear Caro trusted you with her name, I wonder?"

He had no answer to that.

"She hasn't, has she? She fucked a man behind your back, and you don't even know her real name! How can you trust her not to run to Dweller? All that power . . . It must be tempting for a girl like Caro. What else has she got? You?"

"I know what you're trying to do, Allorise."

"Me?" Allo affected a look of innocence. "I'm giving you something to think about while we wait for Carousel to come back. She's been a long time, hasn't she?"

Kayall backed down, shaking his head. "If you weren't a woman, Carey, I'd slap the smile right off your face."

"I'd like to see you try—"

"Shut up, both of you!" Spark had seen movement on the

rooftops above. Something scurrying, moving fast. He drew his sword and pushed Allorise back into the shadows of the wall. Her hands were chained, and he felt obliged to defend her, whether she needed defending or not.

A slate scraped across the tiles. It slid down from the roof, and shattered at his feet. It was followed by a pair of legs. Human legs.

Carousel dropped lightly in front of him, a little breathless. "I followed them," she said. "It's not as bad on the roofs. You were right, Dweller's in the thick of this." She patted the crossbow slung across her back. "Want me to try and bring him down?"

"I want to see what he's up to first." He glanced up, the way she had come. "Over the roofs, you say?"

"There's a bit of climbing, but the houses are close together." Caro glared at Allorise. "What do we do about *her*?"

Spark sighed. "I guess we have to let her go. She can't climb with her hands chained."

Caro muttered something under her breath as Spark fished in his pockets for the key. Something about doubting Allorise could climb at all.

He freed her, and took a step back as she massaged her chafed wrists. She didn't have a weapon, but her arms were beefy. Her weight behind a punch would send him sprawling. He jerked his head. "Go on then. Piss off. You got what you wanted."

She didn't move.

"Piss off, I said!"

"And miss all the fun? I don't think so!" She flashed her teeth at Carousel. "You climb. I'll keep up with you."

"I doubt that." Carousel scrambled on to the edge of the horse trough and jumped to catch the edge of the roof with her hands. A few kicks of her legs propelled her over the edge and she vanished.

Kayall bowed mockingly towards Allorise. "After you, my Lady!"

"The whore would stab me in the eye the moment I put my head over the parapet. Why don't you take that chance? Spark here," she winked, "can assist me from behind. I'm sure he'd like that. Wouldn't you, mage boy?"

"I wouldn't touch you with my enemy's cock, Allo."

For some reason she found Spark's retort hilarious. She was still giggling about it as Kayall assisted her on to the roof to crouch on the slippery, ill-fixed slates. Spark followed, and crouched beside her. "What now, Caro?" he asked.

"Follow me." She set off across the rooftops, sure-footed and confident, skipping loose patches of slate and running along narrow beams without hesitation. They must feel as wide as roads under the feet of a wire-walker. Kayall moved with equal sure-footedness, and he winked at Spark.

"I've had to escape over the roofs a few times, with angry husbands after me! Try not to look down, and you'll be fine."

The moment Kayall told him not to look down, Spark felt the overwhelming temptation to do just that. He tried to keep his eyes focussed on Carousel's feet, swinging one in front of the other across the beams and tiles, but below them the roofs tumbled away in steep slopes on either side. A slip would land him painfully in the gutter, at best. At worst . . . He didn't want to think about at worst. And he didn't trust Allorise, just behind him, not to trip him and send him tumbling. From her nervous gasps, he guessed she was struggling.

"Are you all right?" he asked, through clenched teeth, not daring to reach back to assist her.

"Fine." She sounded equally tense, but he left it at that. It took all his concentration not to fall, and he didn't have any spare to worry about her. Every time his foot slipped, his heart leapt into his mouth, and he was forced to stop and compose himself.

"What in hells are you doing? Don't stop here!" Allorise

grabbed his arm, and for a sickening moment he thought she was going to pitch them both off the roof. The ground lurched beneath him, swinging up to meet them, and Allorise screamed.

"Here!" Kayall's hands gripped his wrists, pulling him onward, dropping him down. For a moment everything was a blur, and then he stumbled into Carousel's embrace, and the roof widened beneath his feet once more. "Rest here," Kayall was saying. "Catch your breath. This is a good place to stop."

The dizziness passed, and Spark could see clearly once more. They were on a flat square of roof, the top of a building squeezed between two taller, steep-roofed houses. Angular shuttered windows looked down on their resting place on either side, and from below came the low grumble of gathered demons, the sound he had heard constantly outside Brynmar's house. It reminded him of the kind man with the dead daughter, and he wondered if he knew what had happened to Elvienne. If he survived, Spark resolved, he would find him and tell him.

Careful to avoid being skylined, he lay on his stomach and squirmed to the edge of the roof to look over the low parapet that ran around it. He looked down on a small, cobbled square, one of the hundreds that cropped up all over the poorer areas of the city. The rich had their parks and gardens, the poor had squares.

This square must have been used for gaming, for stone tables were laid out at regular intervals. Dweller stood on one of them, raised above his audience. His black cloak swirled around him in the breeze, but he was clearly visible. Spark shrank back. He was sure he couldn't be seen, but it felt like Dweller was looking right at him.

"Is he there?" Carousel asked in a hushed voice. Spark nodded. "What do we do now?"

"I assume you're going to fight him?" Allorise slumped to the floor and was massaging the life back into her calves. "Good luck with that. I'll make sure your bodies are burnt, if I can find all the pieces."

Kayall nudged her with his foot. "Play the game, Allo." There was no humour in his voice. "We brought you to act as bait. Time for your performance."

"You couldn't take him out with magic, or a crossbow spike to the guts?"

"It would take something more extreme than that to kill Dweller, I'm sure."

"What if I choose not to go along with your plan?"

There was a soft click. Carousel levelled her loaded crossbow at Allo's throat, and smiled sweetly. She didn't speak. She didn't have to.

"You don't want to rub the numbness out of my legs, sweet Caro? We were like sisters once . . ."

An upward jerk of the quarrel. Allorise clambered slowly to her feet, and glared at Kayall. "Go on then, mage. Tell me what you want me to do."

A curse on mages, mage-brats and whores! Allorise stood in the shadows just shy of the square, the breeze blowing the demon-stink in her face. There was nothing to stop her from running. From here, she doubted Carousel could land an arrow in her back. The girl handled the bow competently enough, but she wouldn't have the guts to pierce living, human flesh. It wasn't Caro that prevented her escape, but if they thought she was going to bow down to Noble after this, they were very wrong.

She had no blade, not even a belt knife. The mage might as well have sent her down to the square naked. Allorise drew in a long breath, then another. Her legs felt better, but her heart thumped against the inside of her ribs. She wet her lips, and stepped out into the square in full view of Dweller, and his minions that had once been hers.

"Halfbreed!" She had to shout twice, the first call died in

her throat. "Halfbreed, give my army back!"

The words were idiotic, but they served their purpose. A hush fell over the grumbling demons and she stepped forward, more confident. She locked eyes with Dweller on his podium, and he bared his teeth.

"Lady Carey. It's my pleasure that you should join us."

"I don't live to please you, halfbreed. You have something of mine."

Her palms were slippery and she felt sick, but she couldn't let him see that. To show weakness would be fatal. She took another step. She smelt the foetid breath of the beasts around her, but she looked neither left nor right.

"Something of yours? Why don't you come and take it from me?"

"I can. I have the mage boy as my hostage. I can do whatever I like . . . ."

His bulbous eyes narrowed. "I think you play a bluff, Allorise Carey."

She clenched her fists. "If you're willing to take that risk . . . You know what Spark can do."

He waved a patterned hand, almost lazily, at his minions. "Kill her."

Allorise was ready. She started running at the first hint of movement, evading the claws of the nearest beast by a whisker. Her feet pounded on the pavement and the unleashed pack bayed at her heels. All she had to do was keep ahead of them, lead them on. Play the role of bait for two hundred yards . . . one hundred . . . .fifty . . .

The pack gained on her with every stride.

Allorise felt sick. The stitch in her side was crippling, and her legs felt weighted by lead. Twenty yards now. She saw open space ahead of her, but she heard nothing but the blood pounding in her ears and the scrape of claws over stone behind her. A coil of rope shimmied down the side of the building in front of her, and she lunged for it, feet jarring against the wall as razor teeth snapped her ankles. She kicked out, heel slamming into flesh, and the leaping demon howled and dropped away.

It felt like her arms were being wrenched out of their sockets, and her palms were on fire. Strong hands seized her and dragged her back on to the roof, sliding painfully over broken slate. She lay gasping on her stomach, staring at Kayall's boots with their tooled leather design, intricate as the scars carved into Caro's flesh. She spat, and tried to sit up. "Did I win?"

No one paid her any attention. The bastards were all peering over the edge of the roof. If she timed it right, she could send one of them flying into the marauding pack with nothing more than a hard push. She just needed a moment to get her breath back . . .

As she tried to stand, her left heel erupted in pain. She hadn't noticed it was bleeding, but the back of her shoe was missing and so, when she looked at it, was a chunk of flesh from the bottom of her foot, neatly bitten off. It hadn't hurt until she saw it, but now it was agony.

She limped over to the parapet and leaned against it, trying not to vomit. The square outside what had once been the Lily thronged with demons, but there was no sign of Dweller, and more beasts crawled up through the cracks all the time. Kayall's hands were clenched on the low wall, knuckles white, fingertips bleeding. "I can't do it," he muttered. "Don't ask me to."

"We need to cut off their reinforcements," Spark insisted. "Dweller will set flying beasts on us, and we'll be dead. You *have* to do it."

Carousel was watching the sky, hands never leaving her bow. It sounded like the mage was having a crisis of conscience. Stupid, to let his conscience trouble him! Allorise never had that trouble. That was the problem with mages. They were too concerned with guilt, with doing the right thing. She would be ruling the world by now, if she were a mage. She was surrounded by weak people, always had been.

"What won't the mage do?" she asked, trying to ease the weight off her injured foot.

Kayall answered for Spark. "I have a power . . . I don't use it . . ."

"If it will help us win, you should! What's the point of power you don't use?"

His face was strained, deep creases on his brow, and his cheeks were hollow. "I swore I'd never use it again. I never thought I'd be in a position where I had to. Even when I was trapped in the cemetery . . . I just couldn't."

Allorise shook her head. The mage was a fool. "Why not?" she demanded. Badgering him distracted her from the throbbing torment in her heel.

"It was during the war. I had to rescue . . . some people, from Lambury, when the city fell to the other side . . ."

"You don't have to be so vague," Allorise goaded him. "No one gives a shit about the war. I was only a little girl when it ended. Everyone knows the mages fought for the Crown."

He managed a wry grin. "Interfered on the side of the Crown, I think. I was courting a girl at the time. Perfect girl she was, smart, rich, pretty . . . I was as in love with her as I ever have been with anyone. Of course, I was a damned fool and I never told her that—"

The demons howled below. Allorise threw a pointed glance at the sun.

Kayall got the hint. "I used this power, and it scared her so much, everything changed between us. I lost her, and I swore I'd never use it again. I haven't, until now."

"Is this power actually going to be useful?" Allorise was losing patience. The throbbing in her foot sent agonising spikes up her leg. She felt sick, and she dug her nails into her palms to prevent herself from passing out. She wished the mage would just get on with it so she could lie down somewhere and recover.

"I think it is. I can't see any other way. But I feel sick about it, and I can't remember how . . ."

"Kayall!" Carousel fired off a shot, and there was a scream from below. "Kayall, get over it! The demons are climbing the walls. Do it, whatever it is, or we'll die here!" Her hands moved too quickly for Allorise to see them. She edged away from the wall, from the stink of the beast that clambered towards them, dragging its scales over stone and wood. Carousel's arrow protruded from its forehead. It hadn't slowed it down for an instant. Behind it, two more beasts crawled. Stinking, twisted, and coming ever closer.

The creature's head emerged over the parapet, and Spark lashed out with his sword, as a second bolt took the beast in the eye. It howled, mouth a gurgling bloody mess. Claws scrabbled on the wall for purchase, and the demon fell, but there were two more to take its place, and more behind that. The wall was swarming with demons, and Allo didn't even have a pocket knife.

"Kayall, we're going to die here!"

She wasn't sure if the mage heard Spark's shout as he thrust forward with the blade to skewer another demon through the throat. She caught a blast of the beast's breath as they grappled, and she snatched up a loose slate and brought it crashing down on the creature's skull as Spark struggled to throw it from the roof.

"Kayall!"

"All right! I'll do it!" The mage thrust Allo aside and stabbed the demon between the eyes, sending it shrieking to the square below. "Hang on to something!"

Kayall sprang back from the wall, shook out his hands, and closed his eyes. Dark clouds swept in overhead, turning the sky to inky purple. In the strange light, his face was ghostly, and the howls of the demons took on a more urgent pitch.

The wind picked up, flapping their cloaks around them. Spark and Carousel clung together, but Allorise was left alone. She preferred it that way. She would not cling to a man and simper, when the storm hit.

The first jolt nearly threw her off the roof. She snatched at the parapet, clinging on with both hands, a branch tossed by the wind. The rumble reverberated through the building, and the ground it stood on. The demons howled over the crash of falling masonry, and the cracks in the road widened.

The rumbling went on and on. It felt like the teeth were being shaken loose from Allo's head. All she could do was hang on. Carousel screamed, but the sound was lost amid a barrage of noise, of chaos. Through the rising dust she saw demons tumbling back into the cracks they had climbed from, grabbing others to try and prevent their fall, dragging their cohorts down with them. Hundreds of demons, tumbling into the bottomless cracks, back to the hell they climbed up from.

The shaking died away, but Allorise did not stop trembling. It was as if the earthquake lived on in her body. Her hands were clenched so tightly to the wall it hurt to wrench them open. Hells, what stupid girl had rejected Kayall for that display of power? She could use a man like that at her side, now Shadow was dead. It was a bloody shame. Now she had killed Elvienne she doubted Kayall would be as amenable, or as easily manipulated, as she'd like him to be.

The dust settled. There were still demons prowling the wreckage of the Lily, but far fewer than there had been before the earth tremor. Those that remained milled about in confusion. The back of Dweller's army was broken, but they could rise again, too easily, while the gateway to the world below still yawned open.

Kayall pointed. His face was pale, his lips thin and bloodless. "There's Dweller," he said.

The patterned halfbreed ran into the square, not troubling to conceal himself in the shadows. He tried to rally his broken troops around him, but they were slow to obey. He didn't look up.

"Carousel?" Kayall spoke softly, not looking at her.

"Just a moment." Carousel's hands shook. She dropped the

quarrel as she tried to load it. Allorise bit back a curse. Useless frightened girl!

She somehow fumbled a second shot on to the bow, resting it on the wall and winding it tight. Dweller scrambled over the rubble, and the remaining demons flocked towards him. Allorise felt the tug in her own body, and she glanced at Spark to see if he felt it too, but his gaze was fixed on Carousel. On her finger on the trigger.

Allorise heard the click, a soft echo over her racing heart. Dweller stumbled, looking down in surprise at the bolt piercing his abdomen. Carousel muttered a quiet exclamation, already reloading for a second shot.

"You've got his attention now," Kayall said. "Steady, sweet."

Dweller gripped the bolt with both hands. "Spark?" His shout echoed around the square, bouncing off the rubble. "Did you think that would kill me? You know better than that!" He drew the blot free with a slurping sound and cast it behind him. "Show yourself! I'll make you regret –"

The dull thunk of metal hitting flesh. Dweller lurched, the second bolt through his thigh, snarled with his cloak, dragging it into the wound. Spark, green-faced, turned his head away. He looked like he was about to throw up.

Caro's third shot was quicker, striking Dweller under the left armpit as he tried to free the bolt from his leg. He roared with pain, his demons lending their cacophonous voices to his as he stumbled across the square. His right leg dragged uselessly behind him.

"Finish him, Caro!" Kayall urged, but her hands hesitated on the winding mechanism.

"I can't kill him," she said. "He was always good to me. He betrayed Noble, but—"

Allorise had heard enough. "Give it to me!" She snatched the bow from Caro's hands, sighted, and fired. The shot flew high, too high. It skimmed Dweller's head and he ducked, stumbled, lurched forward . . . The crack in the road opened before his feet. His arms flailed like the blades of a windmill, and he screamed, a high sound that went beyond noise. It sliced through Allo's skull like a blade through cheese. The bow slipped from her hands as she clutched her ears to block it out.

And then there was another sensation, blotting out the pain. A glow that crept through her core, setting her skin tingling, sparks flying from her fingertips. She snatched at it, embraced it. She would not let it go this time, no matter what happened, no matter who she had to kill to keep it.

It was the glow of power.

❦

Spark staggered as Dweller fell into the pit. The slam of sudden fierce energy through his body sent him reeling. Carousel doubled up, clutching at her stomach, but he couldn't help her, couldn't think over the lightning crackle in his head.

Allorise began to laugh.

It started as a throaty chuckle, exploding into a roar, of triumph, of delight. She threw up her arms in glee, heedless of the blood pooling around her feet. "Come back to me, my pretty creatures!"

"Allorise, what in hells are you doing?" Kayall caught her arm, and she shook him off.

"You can't feel it, can you? You mages think you're so powerful, so smart . . . I have the demons now, Kayall! Serve me and I'll spare your life."

Spark forced himself upright. His lips felt swollen. It was hard to push the words out through them. "You don't have all of them, Allorise."

"What are you talking about, mage-brat?" She scowled, her pretty face turning ugly and sour. "I can feel them, their energy. They're mine!"

"I can feel them too." They squirmed in the lower levels of his conscious, hungry and confused, growing more angry by the moment. He hoped he could keep them reined in.

"The beasts can't serve two masters, Spark." Her voice was low, threatening.

"I don't want them to serve me! I want to send them back where they came from!" He saw by the thrust of her jaw she was unwilling to help him, but he had to try and reach her. "Please, Allorise! Help me send them back. If we work together, we can save the city. I can't do it without you . . ."

"Save the city?" She laughed. "Fuck the city! I want the world!" Her hand closed on a crossbow bolt, abandoned on the parapet by Carousel after Dweller fell.

"Allorise, please, be reasonable—" Kayall lunged for her, too far away as she darted forward.

"I could have it all, if you were out of the way!" She raised the quarrel in her fist. Spark ducked as it plunged towards his eye, felt it tear the skin of his temple. The blast of fire from his hands ripped past Allo's shoulder, scorching the chimney behind her, singeing her hair. And then she was on him, too close to use magic. He rolled away as the bolt stabbed down, cracking the slate beside his ear.

Spark kicked out blindly, feeling the slates beneath him slip as his feet caught them. They scraped across the roof, leaving a gaping hole beneath his ankles as Allo grabbed his throat and slammed his head against the tiles.

They crunched and splintered beneath his skull. Her face pressed close to his, grinning madly. The quarrel dug in just below his ribs. She spat. "Time to die, mage brat!"

Shattered slate rained down around him, falling in his eyes and mouth. Allorise grunted, her eyes unfocussed, as Carousel's arm wrapped around her throat and jerked her away from him. Caro gave her a shove. She stumbled, landing on her wounded foot with a piercing scream. Her arms stretched out, gripped empty air, and she tumbled screaming from the roof.

The energy rushing into his head knocked Spark flat. All the demons were his to control, all at once. This was worse, so much worse, than at Brynmar's house. They were fired up, craving blood. They longed to tear the city apart. All they needed was his command. Their desire left him paralysed, helpless. His lips twitched.

"Don't say it!" Kayall clapped a hand over his mouth. "Don't say *anything!* Are you alright in there, in your head?"

Spark managed to nod. Kayall helped him sit up, keeping his mouth covered. "Take a deep breath," he urged. "Think about what you're doing. Think carefully."

Spark saw Carousel, hovering behind Kayall's shoulder. Her face swam in and out of focus. It would be so easy, the soft voice in his mind suggested, to have his demons kill Kayall, to take Caro and get out of the city . . .

The hungry roar from below echoed the noise in his head. He shook the thought away. He had to get rid of them. They were infesting his mind, pushing their own thoughts in and his out. Was this what it was like in Allo's head?

"If I let you talk, will you be careful?" At his nod, Kayall let go.

"She thought she controlled them," he managed to whisper. "But all the time they were driving her. Bending her to their will, and she didn't even realise!"

"But you do?" Kayall asked.

"I—I think so . . ."

"You're stronger than her. You were born to this magic." The mage spoke in a low, urgent voice, his face close to Spark's. "You can end this, right now! Do you want to?"

Spark leaned back against the chimney stack. He was tired to the bones, tired of running, of hiding, of fighting the insidious voices in his head. It would be so easy to let the demons have their way, to lie down and let destruction wash over the city. He felt his eyes closing, and he jerked his head back, smacking his bruised skull against the breastwork on the chimney, unleashing a burst of pain like a firework in his skull.

"Yes! I want to end it!"

Kayall clutched both his wrists. "Draw them in, Spark. Undo what you did."

Spark felt the mage's own power flowing through him as Kayall lent him his strength. The demons howled. The crack in the ground was a sucking void, pulling them in. Their claws screeched across the cobbles, and they howled and thrashed in the grip of this new assault, but Spark would not be defied. He pushed them back, further and further, and they screamed and fought him for every inch of ground.

The chasm yawned wide, and the first of the demons tipped headlong into it with a bloody, gurgling scream. Kayall's grip on Spark's hands grew tighter, but Spark could barely see him over the chaos in his head. More screams, desperate pleas from the minions to their master.

Don't reject us, don't push us away. Look what we can give you . . . .

"I don't *want* it!" He gave a mighty shove with his will. Carousel cheered. "That's it!" she cried. "That's the last of them! Now close the gap!"

"Kayall?" Spark's mind was reeling with effort. "I don't think I can do it . . . . Elvienne would be able to—"

"Elvienne's not here. I wish to my gut she was." Kayall closed his eyes in momentary pain. "I've never seen anyone work rock and stone like she could. You could learn that."

"I don't think—"

"You *could*," Kayall insisted. "If you can control this magic, you have the makings of a great mage."

"And if I can't?" The gap was so wide, the stones slippery under his mental touch. His mind skidded over the surface and below, in the depths, broken creatures stretched once more towards the light.

"Then you're dead. We're all dead, and the world will have no more use for mages." The sweat steamed on Kayall's brow, veins standing out with effort. "I'll help you as much as I can, but the will has to come from you. If you can't do this . . ." The sentence fell away into the dark.

It was as if the two sides of Spark's mind were fusing together, becoming whole where once they had been split apart. He screamed and clutched his skull as stone scraped together, and the chasm slowly knit into one long scar, like the lacings on a shirt drawing the fabric in.

The last stone clicked into place. Silence hung over the city like a shroud. Spark leaned back and blinked as if he was emerging into daylight after a long time underground. The sun split his temples open, and he felt bruised from head to foot, but there was a lightness in his spirit he hadn't felt for moons. Since Carlon fell ill, if he was honest. He found himself grinning as he caught Carousel's eye, and she responded with a smile of her own.

"You did it, you little bastard!" She hauled him to his feet and into her arms, while Kayall clapped him on the back and hugged them both and slapped him on the shoulder again. The thin sun gleamed over the wet rooftops of Cape Carey tumbling away around him. The city was at his feet. Not one square foot of it belonged to him, but he had never felt more at home.

Epilogue

SPARK JUMPED TO one side as a carriage swished past, spattering his legs with mud. The driver leaned back and yelled something offensive at him, and Spark responded with a wave, and a grin. Some things didn't change, while others twisted out of all recognition. He felt like he had twisted most of all.

He arrived at the tavern and slipped around the back, trying not to draw attention to himself. Maybe she wouldn't want to see him. Maybe she would be busy. Maybe she would rather he –

He didn't realise he had knocked, but the door swung open while his hand lingered in the air. Long legs, bells in her braided hair, a long pink scar across her cheek, and a smile that faded as she looked at him.

"Your eyes are green," Carousel said.

"I know." It had taken a lot of staring in the glass to get used to it. They weren't the glittering emerald that Elvienne's eyes had been, or the turquoise of Kayall's, but a deep, dark green, the colour of a pine forest after the rain.

Carousel shuffled her feet. "Will you stay the age you are?"

"Kayall says I might. He says if I do age, it will be really slow, and I could stop ageing any time. He says it varies from person—from mage to mage." It was still so hard to think of himself as a mage. He felt like a little kid compared to Kayall.

There was a definite pout to her lips. "I suppose you're leaving with him then. Why would you stick around here?"

This wasn't going at all the way he expected. Carousel seemed offended by his new role. He tried a different tack.

"Look, you're settled here—"

"Who's that?" The call came from behind Carousel, and the White Giantess barrelled into view, filling the doorway with her bulk. "Young Spark? You took the green? Well done!"

It didn't feel well done at all. Spark shrugged.

Nomi beamed. "I'll leave you two alone. You can take the rest of the day off, Caro. Make sure you're awake for work tomorrow!" She winked, and whisked away to bellow at the girl sweeping the bar. "Chalice! Put some effort into it, will you?"

"She seems nice." It was pathetic. Why couldn't he think of anything to say to Caro, when they had been so close before?

"I've only been here a moon and she's taken to telling me I'm the daughter she never had." Carousel smiled. For the first time there was genuine warmth in her face. "It's not anyone who would take on a scarred whore."

Spark snorted. "Half the tavern girls in Cape Carey used to be whores, I'm sure!"

Carousel changed the subject abruptly. "When are you leaving?"

"Tomorrow. Kayall tells me we have to go up North, track down some soldier who's claiming the throne. I don't know much about it. I guess I'll learn as we go along."

"This will be goodbye then." She stretched out her hand, Telesian style.

"There's one more thing . . ."

"What?" she demanded as he hesitated. He indicated the covered basket on his arm, neat white linen splashed with muddy droplets. "What's in there?"

"Fruitrolls, cheese, bread, cold meats, apples, a jar of ale . . ."

Carousel's eyes darkened. "What for?"

"For you. You always said you'd like to go out of the city. Out to the meadows south of the river, like the rich ladies do. Take a blanket and something to eat, and spend the day there. I'd like to take you there now, if you don't mind. Of course, if you're too busy . . ." He made to leave.

"You're inviting me on a picnic?"

"Why not? It's not raining, and it won't be. I made an arrangement with Kayall."

She looked from his eyes, to the basket, then back to his face again. "Just you and me? No magic? I'm bloody sick of magic."

"No magic if you don't want it."

She grinned, and darted forward to kiss him on the cheek. "I'll get my cloak," she said.

It was a short carriage ride out to the meadows. It was still early in the year, and there weren't many people about. Spark found a spot, a rise of ground where they could look over the city. He spread the blanket out and uncorked the ale. He raised the flagon in a silent toast to Elvienne, who had given her life for the city, and hoped he could live up to her legacy.

Carousel stretched out on her elbows, watching the clouds scud above the city. She looked like she had something on her mind. "Spark?"

"What?"

"Are you going to keep your name, now you're leaving the city?"

He hadn't even considered that. There was no need to hide any more, no need to hang on to his street name now he was no longer a street rat. He could be Liathan again. He could be whoever he wanted to be.

"I think I might go back to my real name," he said.

She rolled on to her back and propped herself up, regarding him with narrowed, anxious eyes. She nodded.

"Ylaine."

"What?" He felt he should know what she was talking about, but she had caught him off guard.

"Ylaine. That's my name. My real name, the one I was born with. It sounds strange, I haven't used it in so long, but there it is." She shrugged.

"Ylaine . . ." Spark smiled, and extended his hand. "Pleased to meet you, Ylaine. My name is Liathan."

Carousel giggled, and the sun shone a little brighter over the city.

To the south of the river were the meadows, and, a few miles beyond them the border, with its checkpoints and walls and bored sentinels on eternal guard. Further south, and still further, the landscape gave way to hot, sandy lands where the men wore curled beards and every conversation in their tongue sounded like an argument. A woman could travel a long way in a moon, with money and the right connections. Unfortunately, money and connections had only carried Allorise so far before she ran out of both.

Now she was looking at a camel's arse.

She limped along, hands tied in front of her, kicking up dust with every step. Her skin blistered in the heat. She dreaded looking in a glass, sure her face had reddened to the point where she looked as scarred and hideous as Shadow. She silently cursed all mages, demons, Telesians and camels. Especially camels.

It wasn't all bad, she had to remind herself. She might be a slave, but she hadn't been beaten or raped, and she had been allowed to keep her own clothes. The camel might have eaten better, but she had been fed and given water, and from the little Telesian she knew, she gathered the nearest city was only a few days march across the desert. There were always opportunities in a city for a smart woman. There were opportunities everywhere.

At the front of the meandering column, a man shouted. The camel stopped dead, and Allorise almost walked into its swishing, shit-stained tail. She took a hasty step back, as far as her bonds would allow, and looked around for the water-carrier.

He was a stout man, middle aged, with grey in his beard, and he spoke more softly than the other slavers on the chain. He had three wives, but they were far away in his home city, and she had caught him looking at her more than once on the journey.

She licked her dry lips as he approached, and leaned forward, just enough for him to catch a hint of her form beneath her dress. He smiled, and as he tipped the water into her mouth his thick fingers brushed her chin. He stank of camel, but he was her best route out of here. If she became his junior wife, she could manipulate herself into a better position in no time. Women were so easy, always ready to stab one another in the back given the smallest of pushes. Allorise knew exactly the right spots to push . . .

The water carrier laid a sweaty hand on her bare arm and said something in his garbled tongue, and Allorise smiled sweetly, and flirted, and plotted her way back to where she belonged.

About the Author

Joanne Hall lives in Bristol with her partner, and they are owned by the World's Laziest Dog ™ She is a full time writer, part time editor and occasional procrastinator and is happiest when she's making things up and writing them down. She enjoys movies and music, and owns too many books she hasn't got around to reading yet.

Her short stories have featured in a number of anthologies, and she is the co-editor (with Roz Clarke) of *Colinthology* and *Airship Shape and Bristol Fashion*. When she's not writing or editing, Joanne can be found chairing BristolCon, Bristol's annual SF and Fantasy convention, and hanging about on Twitter. Her blog can be found at www.hierath.co.uk and she always likes to hear from readers.

Acknowledgements

It takes one person to write a book, but it takes a team to see it safely into the world while simultaneously preserving the sanity of the author. I could not have a better team of people at my back, and I'm grateful every day for their support, their nurturing, and their near-constant provision of tea.

In no particular order, and with apologies to the people I will inevitably forget, I'd like to thank the following:

Everyone at Kristell Ink and Grimbold Books including all the authors, with special thanks to Sammy Smith and Zoë Harris for dedication that goes above and beyond, and to Evelinn Enoksen and Ken Dawson for making the book look so damned stunning.

Roz Clarke, my superb editor, writing buddy, partner in crime, provider of surprise cake and shoulder to cry on. It is always an absolute delight to work with you on any project.

Kate Flint (this is the book I always promised Jasmine I'd write for her, and now she's actually old enough to read it), Heather Ashley, Desiree Fischer, Chocolate Jon, John Baverstock, Alan Lonsdale, Scott Lewis, Clare Neilson, Claire Hutt, Myfanwy

Rodman, Gareth L Powell, Richard Bendall, Cheryl Morgan, Mark Robinson, Pete Sutton, Dolly Garland, the BristolCon Committee and the Bristol Fantasy and SF Soc for both driving me nuts and keeping me sane.

Also thanks to Lor Graham, Laura Evans, Andy Fairchild, Richard Webb, Ruth Booth, Danie Ware, Mhairi Simpson, Fran Jacobs, Marc Aplin, Martha Hubbard, Sarah Higbee, and about a million other people who have chatted on Twitter or visited my blog. You're all brilliant.

Thanks to Mum, Saira, Nicky and Mark, Jack and Jenny, Molly, and Will and Jane.

Thanks to Chris, who lifted me from a dark place and has given me sixteen years of occasionally grudging love and support. I love you.

And to Lyra, who is a constant source of joy.

As always, this book is dedicated to the memory of Colin Harvey, and to Nathalie Cassiers, who never got to hold it in her hands. I miss you both very much.

And finally, thanks to you, for reading it. I couldn't do it without you.

Other Titles from Kristell Ink

Cruelty by Ellen Croshain

Once a year, in the caves deep below the house, the Family gathers to perform a ritual to appease their god. But Faroust only accepts payment in blood. Eliza MacTir, youngest daughter of a powerful Irish family, was born into fae gentry without the magical gifts that have coursed through the Family's veins for millennia; she was an outcast from her first breath. Desperate for freedom, Eliza's flight from rural Ireland is thwarted by the Family's head of security. The only weapon she has to fight her captor is her own awakening sexuality. Drawn into the world of magic and gods, Eliza must find a way to break free, even if it means breaking the hearts of those she loves, and letting her own turn to stone. Cruelty, it runs in the Family.

In Search of Gods and Heroes by Sammy H.K Smith

Buried in the scriptures of Ibea lies a story of rivalry, betrayal, stolen love, and the bitter division of the gods into two factions. This rift forced the lesser deities to pledge their divine loyalty either to the shining Eternal Kingdom or the darkness of the Underworld.

When a demon sneaks into the mortal world and murders an innocent girl to get to her sister Chaeli, all pretence of peace between the gods is shattered. For Chaeli is no ordinary mortal, she is a demi-goddess, in hiding for centuries, even from herself. But there are two divine brothers who may have fathered her, and the fate of Ibea rests on the source of her blood.

Chaeli embarks on a journey that tests her heart, her courage, and her humanity. Her only guides are a man who died a thousand years ago in the Dragon Wars, a former assassin for the Underworld, and a changeling who prefers the form of a cat.

The lives of many others – the hideously scarred Anya and her gaoler; the enigmatic and cruel Captain Kerne; the dissolute Prince Dal; and gentle seer Hana – all become entwined. The gods will once more walk the mortal plane spreading love, luck, disease, and despair as they prepare for the final, inevitable battle.

In Search of Gods and Heroes, Book One of Children of Nalowyn, is a true epic of sweeping proportions which becomes progressively darker as the baser side of human nature is explored, the failings and ambitions of the gods is revealed, and lines between sensuality and sadism, love and lust are blurred.

Fear the Reaper by Tom Lloyd

All Shell has ever wanted was a home, a place to belong. But now an angel of the God has tracked her down, intent on using her to hunt the demon that once saved her. The journey will take her into the dead place beyond the borders of the world, there to face her past and witness the coming of a new age.

A stand-alone novella from the author of *The Twilight Reign* series and *Moon's Artifice*.

kristell-ink.com

Lightning Source UK Ltd.
Milton Keynes UK
UKOW04f0616150915

258655UK00002B/10/P